The Secrets of
LIZZIE
BORDEN

Books by Brandy Purdy

THE BOLEYN WIFE

THE TUDOR THRONE

THE QUEEN'S PLEASURE

THE QUEEN'S RIVALS

THE BOLEYN BRIDE

THE RIPPER'S WIFE

THE SECRETS OF LIZZIE BORDEN

Published by Kensington Publishing Corporation

The Secrets of
LIZZIE
BORDEN

BRANDY PURDY

KENSINGTON BOOKS
www.kensingtonbooks.com

KENSINGTON BOOKS are published by

Kensington Publishing Corp.
119 West 40th Street
New York, NY 10018

All Kensington titles, imprints, and distributed lines are available at special quantity discounts for bulk purchases for sales promotion, premiums, fund-raising, and educational or institutional use.

Special book excerpts or customized printings can also be created to fit specific needs. For details, write or phone the office of the Kensington Sales Manager: Kensington Publishing Corp., 119 West 40th Street, New York, NY 10018. Attn. Sales Department. Phone: 1-800-221-2647.

Kensington and the K logo Reg. U.S. Pat. & TM Off.

eISBN-13: 978-0-7582-8892-9
eISBN-10: 0-7582-8892-1
First Kensington Electronic Edition: February 2016

ISBN-13: 978-0-7582-8891-2
ISBN-10: 0-7582-8891-3
First Kensington Trade Paperback Printing: February 2016

10 9 8 7 6 5 4 3 2 1

Printed in the United States of America

AUTHOR'S NOTE

This is a work of fiction inspired by the life of Lizzie Borden and the murders forever linked to her name. It should not be read as a factual account. For those interested in the known facts and various theories, I have included some suggestions for further reading at the end of this novel.

In this world there are only two tragedies.
One is not getting what one wants.
The other is getting it.

—Oscar Wilde

More tears are shed over answered prayers
than unanswered ones.

—Saint Teresa of Avila

The truth shall set you free.

—John 8:32

The Secrets of
LIZZIE
BORDEN

Chapter 1

⌒

I awoke from the dream, wishing, as I always did, that it would vanish right away without lingering to torment me, or, better yet, *never* come to visit me again. I *hated* it! And I didn't want *anything* to spoil this special day I had been looking forward to for so many months. But it had already begun to work its evil spell. Curiously, it often came as a herald to announce the coming of my monthly blood, and this time was no exception. It was as though those *terrible* long-ago memories of the smell of fresh-spilt blood, my bare feet slipping and sliding in it, my bottom thudding down to sit in it, and feeling it soaking through my skirts and drawers seemingly into my very skin, enticed the blood to flow from my own body. How I *hated* it. The blood and the memories so intricately bound they could never be divided.

I have always claimed to have no memories of my mother, Sarah Morse Borden, who died when I was only three years old, but that is not true. Sometimes it is easier to tell a lie. To say *No* closes the door on the conversation, whereas saying *Yes* flings it open wide and invites further inquiry and to slam and bar it then is to be branded *rude* and *inhospitable*.

There are actually three things I remember about my mother.

The first is her appearance, her Gypsy-black hair and deep-set dark eyes, brooding and mysterious, the kind of eyes you could imagine intently scrutinizing a spread of tarot cards, shrewdly divining their secrets. Perhaps these recollections owe more to photographs than actual memories; I only know that she had such a stabbing deep stare that to even look at pictures of her makes me uncomfortable, as though her eyes could bore right through my skull and read every thought inside my head plain as words printed on the page of a book. Had she lived, I doubt I would have ever been able to keep a secret from Mother. As awful as it sounds, sometimes just the sight of those sharp, piercing eyes makes me feel relieved that she died before I had any secrets worth keeping. It is disconcerting at times just how much my sister, Emma, with her dark hair and prying and intrusive eyes resembles her; only the full, womanly curves are lacking. Emma is as skinny as a starving bird, with shoulder blades like scalpels.

The second thing I remember about Mother is her clothes. Everyone said she had the fashion sense of a color-blind gypsy. She loved to wear bright colors, fussy, bold, and garish prints in which violent wars raged perpetually between the shades, and fancy fringed shawls and flowered hats and bonnets the louder and livelier the better, and a crude string of coral beads she clung to religiously, superstitiously convinced that they would ward away all evil.

Maybe it was simply that she didn't know any better. She was after all just a poor farm girl who had the good fortune to attract a prosperous undertaker, and there was no mother- or sister-in-law to take her hand and gently guide her in the direction of good taste and refinement. My father, Andrew Jackson Borden, was a tenacious, bull-headed Yankee businessman who knew nothing, and cared even less, about fashion, only what it cost him. But Mother knew how to make the most of a cheap dress goods sale, it was *amazing* how far she could stretch a dollar at such events, and Father felt blessed to have such a thrifty wife who could bargain a bolt of mauve and orange flowered calico that no one else seemed to want down from a nickel a yard to three cents. And her Sunday best bonnet—a wide-brimmed red-lacquered straw hat adorned with red and green wax tomatoes and a wild spray of sunny yellow dandelions and white meadow daisies sprouting like weeds, cherry-red and apple-green ribbons, and a lace curtain veil—bought on a rare trip to Boston, Father often recounted with great pride, she regarded as her greatest triumph won at only 75¢. If the tomatoes had been real instead of waxen, he always said, they would have rotted long before she bartered its freedom from the milliner's window where it had been languishing the better part of a year. It was the ugliest and loveliest hat I ever saw.

The third, and last, thing I remember about my mother is her blood. The blood that came every month was a time of terror for us all. Father tore at his carroty-red hair and whiskers with worry yet tried to keep his distance, disdaining anything to do with "female matters," preferring the company of corpses instead during what he privately called "hell week," and busying himself with his never-ending, all-consuming pursuit of the almighty dollar. Money was Father's religion, his muse; it occupied his thoughts all day and his dreams all night. He rarely willingly parted with his hard-earned dollars unless he was sure he could make them breed like green rabbits. And my sister, Emma, ten years older than myself, was at school for most of the day, so I was left alone at home with Mother.

Mother *hated* the monthly blood. No medicine could soothe her. She would throw the bottles at the wall when they failed her, devil-damning the false promises printed on their labels. She would crouch down upon the floor, bracing her back against the wall, and howl like a mad dog at the moon, rocking, crying, and *screaming* as the blood oozed out and the cramps seized her. Demons, she insisted, were trying to crush her skull; she could feel their talons digging in, and making wild displays of colored lights dance before her eyes. She would *rage* against God for unfairly visiting this curse upon *all* womankind to punish *one* woman's sin. How my mother *hated* Eve! If a preacher mentioned her in a sermon, Mother would stand up, slash him with the daggers of her eyes, and stomp out of the church as though she were crushing a detested enemy with every step.

It was not time for the blood when she died. I had no inkling that anything was wrong, and neither, I think, did she. She had just finished braiding my unruly red hair into crooked pigtails tied with sky-blue ribbon at the ends and we were in the kitchen baking gingerbread. She was happy and humming as she bent to pick me up. The cookies were shaped like little men and I was to give them raisins for eyes and red currants for mouths and she was going to make some white icing for us to dress them in. What fun we would have, she said, drawing in bow ties and buttons and stripes and flowers on their suits and vests. She swung me up onto her hip, then suddenly her face went white as the new paint Father had just put on the farmhouse, and she dropped me. . . . She just let go and *dropped me!*

I was more surprised than hurt, though I skinned my elbow on the floorboards. I sat up in surprise, rubbing it, whimpering a little when I saw blood, and staring up at her with trembling lips and tears poised to pour. I knew something *must* be wrong. Mother had *never* dropped me before!

She gasped and hunched forward, hunkering down, hugging her lady parts, and I saw the blood seep, like a slow-blooming red rose, through her white apron. She gave a choking, anguished cry and fell to the floor and lay there, her body jerking and spasming while her hands still clutched tight between her legs as though they could somehow stanch the fatal flow. Then she was still. I had never been so afraid. I shook her, and cried, slapped, and shouted at her, but she just lay there, still, silent, and so very white as her blood seeped out and spread slowly across the floor, inching toward me, as if it were a monster reaching out ravenous red fingers, coming to get me, steadily advancing, to grasp the hem of my sky-blue cotton dress and white pinafore. I backed away until my spine bumped the wall and my bottom thudded down onto the floor.

When Emma came home from school she found me crying, howling like Mother used to do, reaching up to her with blood-gloved hands, sitting in the sticky, cooling dark-red pool of our mother's blood. The backside of the ruffled white pantalets I wore beneath my skirt had turned completely red and was glued to my skin. That day my whole world seemed to have been suddenly dyed red. I thought I would never feel clean again.

Serious and grave even in childhood, Emma calmly knelt down in the blood—I vividly remember the ends of her long black pigtails trailing in the blood, like an artist's sable brush being dipped in crimson paint—and rolled Mother over onto her back to make sure the flame of life had truly gone out. Tenderly, Emma kissed the stone-cold brow and closed the wide staring eyes. Then she took Mother's hand, kissed it, and clasped it to the heart beating fast beneath her flat, childish breast covered by the garish purple, yellow, and magenta plaid silk of the last dress Mother had made for her, and solemnly promised to "always look after Baby Lizzie all the days of my life." Only then did she release Mother's hand and turn to me. She gathered me up in her arms, promising my clinging, wailing self that she would "*never* let go."

It was a promise the child I was then was glad she made but the passage of time would often give me cause to regret. What was comforting to a hysterical three-year-old felt to a woman of thirty like a kraken's *crushing* embrace of the ship or whale it was attacking. Every time I saw paintings or engravings of such scenes I *always* thought of Emma. Once, as a subtly intended hint, when I was well into my teens, I gave her such a painting that I found in a little shop in New Bedford as a birthday present, but Emma never guessed its significance; she just couldn't see that I was the whale and she was the kraken.

I tried valiantly to shake the remnants of the dream off, but it kept clinging to me like that red sticky blood. I didn't want to think about Mother or her blood that morning. I was going away. I was excited and didn't want *anything* or *anyone* to spoil it. For the *first* time in my thirty years of life I was about to spread my wings and fly out of Fall River, Massachusetts, and escape into the great big, wide, wonderful world and put an entire ocean between me and the cramped closeness of the place my sister called "the house of hate" because the anger, resentment, and frustration that lived inside it was far stronger than its flimsy drab gray-tinged olive walls, so powerful and palpable it seemed to be the only thing holding our family together. Without that simmering animosity gluing us together, I sometimes thought, we'd fall to pieces and have nothing to say and never give a single thought to one another.

I rolled over and curled onto my side, drawing my knees up tight against the cramps, frowning at the faintly metallic tang and disgusting dampness of blood on my light flowered cotton summer nightgown. Always erratic, defying the discreetly penciled notations on my calendar trying to predict its arrival, my despised monthly visitor had come early.

I had bathed late last night, the lamplight giving a soft golden glow to the dark, dank cellar, keeping the dusty boxes of old tools and odds and ends, and the cobwebs in the corners, in the shadows where they belonged, while I sat with my knees drawn up to my breasts, my ample hips and thighs squashed uncomfortably into the old dented tin hipbath, soaking in lukewarm water heated on the kitchen stove and carried down the steep dark stairs in heavy pails by our Irish Maggie before she retired for the night. I had stopped my ears as usual to Father's penurious tirade, exclaiming for what must have been the ten thousandth time that we women should all arrange to bathe upon the same day—not the night, mind you!—and be quickly in and out of the tub, none of this slothful sitting and soaking, a swift scrubbing with strong lye soap—none of that expensive lavender and rose or lily-of-the-valley nonsense!— then a rapid rinse and a brisk rubdown with a towel was all that was required. Father would never even think to take a bath any other way, for *his* was the *right* way and his mind was a barred and locked door to the idea that someone else's way might be the right way for them. And we should use the same bathwater, he insisted, to save time and water and cause less trouble to the Maggie. None of us were filthy as coal miners after all. We hardly did anything anyway to raise a sweat or gather grime onto our persons; we were just a lot of lazy females who, between the three of us, could not even keep a decent house and had to waste $4 a week—the stupendous sum of $208 a year—upon a maid. And my stepmother, Abby, was so fat she couldn't fit into the tub at all, and could only stand in it and sluice and scrub as best she could, sometimes using a rag tied to a stick to reach difficult areas, since none of us ungrateful girls were charitable enough to help her, so the water could hardly be considered used at all.

The bar of lavender soap that I had stealthily slipped into my purse while I was perusing the wares on display at Sargent's Dry Goods one day, was the only luxurious thing about me as I sat there shivering and hugging my knees, dreaming of a proper, modern bathroom with a big porcelain tub I could stretch out in, like a reclining mermaid, basking in water that ran hot or cold at the mere twist of a nickel-plated knob, and a *real* toilet, instead of a crude hole covered by a wooden box seat, standing regal as a porcelain throne, shining like a pearl, on a floor of gleaming tile instead of hard-packed earth, with proper paper to wipe with instead of a stack of old magazines to rip pages from as the need required. I remember I used to sit there while voiding my bowels and in the dim lamplight gaze yearningly upon the fashion plates depicting the latest styles from Paris, and pictures of beautiful ladies enjoying a life of luxury and ease, of dining and dancing, opening nights at the opera and plays, boating excursions, sleighing parties, oyster suppers, clambakes, and games of tennis and croquet with their beaus, and imagine I was one of them—the belle of the ball in strawberry-pink taffeta dancing till dawn in the arms of a prince! Or a grand lady in pink satin, pearls, and point lace surrounded by adoring gallants serving her dainty cakes with pastel-colored frosting upon a silver tray. When the time came to wipe, I would always seek a page of print instead of soiling the images that inspired my dreams, though the others in the house were not quite as discriminating.

I had so wanted to feel fresh and clean when I awoke and put on my new midnight-blue bengaline dress figured with a delicate pattern of arctic-blue roses and the matching wide-brimmed hat, its crown wreathed with a ring of dainty ice-blue satin rosebuds, and now my monthly visitor had come and spoiled it all. Even my underthings were new, pure white cotton with white lace threaded with blue silk ribbons, and now I must either don old or risk soiling them if the blood overflowed or leaked through the bulky towel pinned to my homemade blue calico waistband and slung between my thighs, raising blisters and chafing them raw every time I moved.

I had been frivolous and ordered an ice-blue satin corset, matching garters trimmed with lace, and black silk stockings from Boston, and navy-blue kid gloves and button boots with *French heels,* the very height of fashion, instead of the usual sensible and sturdy low-heeled brown or black best suited for everyday wear. How Father had frowned over the bills!

"*Blue* boots and gloves, Lizzie! *Mother-of-pearl* buttons *dyed blue! Shame! French heels!* I doubt they will last a fortnight! And *blue silk ribbons* on your unmentionables! Ribbons and lace where no one but you, and the Maggie when she does the laundry, will ever see them! Even if you had a husband, men don't notice things like that, not even on a painted Parisian whore! *Shame, Lizzie, shame!* Will you *ever* learn the value of a dollar? You cannot possess a penny for even half a day without it burning a hole through your pocket! Your mother could stretch a dollar like molasses taffy. I was always amazed at how far that woman could make her pin money go! She could have outfitted herself three times over for what you've spent on your *under*clothes! Why, all the Sunday dresses she owned during our entire marriage, God rest her frugal soul, cost less than your traveling dress alone! People said she had the dress sense of a gypsy, it's true, but that woman was canny with her coins! But *you*...! I almost died when the dressmaker's bill arrived! Just thinking about it gives me heart palpitations! You'll have us all in the poorhouse yet! *Blue* boots and gloves, *French* heels, mother-of-pearl buttons, *God help us all!* Do not expect *me* to sell fish out of a pushcart like my father did to support this family after *your* excesses have *ruined* us, you greedy, ungrateful thing!"

Of course, "the miserly millionaire" was exaggerating, and I rolled my eyes accordingly. It was nothing I hadn't heard before.

I had imagined feeling something of the thrill a bride must experience on her nuptial morning knowing that a whole new life lies before her, but now ... the blood and bulky towel had spoiled it all. I was so angry I could cry! I grimaced and drew my knees up tighter as another wave of pain washed over me, and tried to recapture some of the joy by thinking of all the money-pinching misery and resentment I was leaving behind me.

* * *

By the time Mother died Father was well on his way to becoming one of the richest men in Fall River. He had worked hard, scrimping and saving, shrewdly investing his earnings, seizing, like a champion wrestler, every opportunity to profit in a stranglehold, and persuading heartbroken and tear-blinded mourners that if they *truly* loved their dearly departed spouses, siblings, and offspring they would *prove it* by laying them to rest in the safe, luxurious, moisture-proof, vermin-impervious padded snow-white satin-lined embrace of a *Crane's Patented Burial Casket,* a bed for eternity finer than any these humble folk had likely ever slept on in life, of which he had the honor of being the exclusive local distributor. There was no finer casket to be had in all Massachusetts, not even in Boston, he would declare, proudly patting the one he kept for show in his office, sometimes even inviting them to climb inside and see for themselves, always describing the proffered experience as "a little taste of Heaven."

When they hemmed and hawed about the expense, protesting their love, but uncertain if they could actually afford to lavish their hard-earned dollars upon the dead, Father would offer a simple and happy solution for all—in lieu of his customary fee he would gladly, and graciously, accept a lien upon their property; thus they would have several months to discharge the debt. More often than not, dazed by their bereavement, they put their trust in Father and nodded blindly, acceding to his every expensive suggestion for giving their loved one a grand send-off, thus accumulating a debt these simple country people could hardly ever even hope to repay.

In six months to a year, depending on the terms they had agreed upon, they would have cause to weep again when the bank—by then Father sat proudly on the Board of Directors of half a dozen—inevitably foreclosed and they found themselves homeless and Father snapped their property up like a lucky penny. In this manner he gradually acquired a number of profitable rental properties and a reputation for being the most hard-hearted landlord in Fall River and its environs. If he heard that one of his tenants was prospering, he immediately raised the rent, and if they fell on hard times, out they went. "Which is harder?" a popular joke went. "Granite, marble, or Andrew Borden's heart?"

What little comfort the dispossessed might have derived from the knowledge that they had beggared themselves for a noble cause would be considerably diminished if they knew how great an advantage Father took of broken hearts and tear-blinded eyes.

Those much-touted *Crane's Patented Burial Caskets* Father was so proud of were just about as sturdy and moisture proof as matchboxes; an earthworm bumping its head against one could have knocked the walls down if the lid didn't cave in after the first shovel full of earth thudded down on top of it.

Whenever Father proudly petted his prized display model, which truly was an object of beauty painstakingly crafted with exquisite care, unlike the shoddy product turned out by the factory, and caressed the "heavenly soft" white satin within he was in reality selling a fantasy.

Father always led the bereaved away before the actual interment, telling them they could best honor their loved one's memory by remembering them in the glorious bloom of health and vigor instead of watching their coffin being lowered six feet into the ground and hearing the thud of earth—such a sad sound with the harsh, inescapable ring of finality!—upon the lid. Nor did they know that most adult men, and a few women too, were consigned to their eternal rest without their feet, and also their jewelry, gold fillings, and teeth, and ladies with particularly handsome tresses habitually entered the Kingdom of Heaven shorn like convicts while Father hastened to sell their hair to a wigmaker in Boston with whom he had a lucrative and congenial arrangement. He had a similar agreement with a dentist who used the teeth of the dead to craft dentures to fill the mouths of the living. To cut costs, Father habitually purchased the shortest adult-sized coffins the Crane Company manufactured and then sawed the feet off corpses to make them fit. I often wondered if centuries after we were all returned to dust an archaeologist came along and excavated the land behind the chicken coop of our Swansea farm what he would make of the mass burial of hundreds of human feet. When the rare mourner exhibited a glint of shrewdness and remarked that their loved one looked uncommonly short in his coffin, Father was quick to retort that without life to fill them people always looked smaller in death.

Two years after our mother died, Father decided to forsake the funerary trade and the farm at Swansea and concentrate on his more lucrative and refined business ventures involving banking, textiles, and real estate in the business district of Fall River, thus necessitating our move to that city.

He put the farm, the only home Emma and I had ever known, up for rent, and moved us all into town and an ugly cracker box house at 92 Second Street, painted the most *hideous* shade of drab I ever saw, sort of a dull, muddy olive green tinged with an even uglier gray or brown depending on how the light struck it, though personally I always felt it would have been far better if *lightning* had struck it. Surrounded by a picket fence and situated on an almost pleasant street lined with elms and poplars, the house itself was a monstrosity. It was a former duplex that had been converted, ineptly and as cheaply as possible, into a single-family dwelling; thus there were no hallways and all of the rooms led directly into one another, so no one could reach the privacy of their bedroom without first passing invasively through another's private sanctum. But Father had "gotten it for cheap" and fully, if *hideously,* furnished by hopelessly outmoded people who hadn't the faintest clue about what was au courant even twenty years ago. I *hated* it on sight, but Father said I was the *most* ungrateful girl he ever knew or heard tell of; I didn't even know the meaning of the word *gratitude,* and I should be thankful to have a roof over my head when so many others didn't even have that much.

The sudden change from country life to city life was jarring. We had known no other life. Emma and I had loved the clean, fresh air, green grass, wildflowers, pure water streams, fishing holes, animals, and wide-open spaces of the farm, and the days spent frolicking with our cousins and nearest neighbors, the Gardners. Leaving Swansea for Fall River was almost like moving from Heaven to Hell. Fall River was a thriving mill town booming with big brick chimneys belching clouds of black smoke and red sparks into the sky day and night to the music of the constant thrum, hum, and roar of machinery from the eighty-seven mills that earned it the proud sobriquet of "Spindle City" and made it the largest producer of cotton in America.

But an even more drastic change lay in store. Father decided to take another wife. When Emma wept and said it was disloyal to Mother's memory, Father countered that life was for the living and Mother was as dead as she was ever going to be. It was the sensible thing to do, he said, far cheaper than hiring a housekeeper to look after the house and a pair of growing girls who needed a woman's guidance. When I suggested a governess—Emma had just finished reading *Jane Eyre* and had told me the story—Father *glared* and leveled a finger at me like a Puritan minister about to denounce a woman as a witch or a whore before his entire congregation and thundered the word *SPENDTHRIFT!* as though it was the worst insult he could think to hurl at me.

The year was 1865. Though I was only five, I remember well the Sunday Father took us to the Central Congregational Church and, after the service, introduced us to the woman he had chosen to be our stepmother.

Her name was Abby Durfee Gray; she was thirty-seven years old and had long since resigned herself to spinsterhood and embraced the consolation of sweets in lieu of a sweetheart. She was shy, short, and round as a full moon. Though she was descended, like us Bordens, from one of the first families of Puritan settlers who had arrived in Fall River in the seventeenth century, the branch she sprang from was a poor one. Like our own grandfather, whose poverty-stricken ghost Father was always running away from, hers had been a pushcart peddler, though he sold gewgaws made of tin to delight children, and little pies and cakes his wife baked instead of stinking fish.

She was wearing a massive crinoline beneath her Sunday best and I could not help but stare; I'd never seen a hoop so enormous. She'd made the dress herself, proof of her talent as a seamstress that, along with her cakes, cookies, and pies that no picnic, women's gathering, or church social was ever complete without, often supplemented her meager income. It was charcoal-gray damask trimmed with ribbons the color of ripe plums, with wide pagoda sleeves billowing over puffed clouds of gauzy white under-sleeves trimmed with frills of lace and silk ribbons at the wrists. Beneath a matching feathered hat, her thick dark hair, actually an impressive false piece artfully braided in to lend volume to her own sparse tresses, was caught up in a net of braided purple silk sewn here and there with seed pearls. A pair of amethyst and pearl earbobs dangled like heavy ripe plums from the fleshy pink lobes of her ears and a mother-of-pearl brooch carved in the shape of a peony that her mother had worn upon her wedding day bloomed in the snowy lace at her throat.

She had such a kind face, round and open, the sort of face that knows no artifice and shows every joy and hurt as it happens. She was not like most adults, who when introduced to children stare down at them with superior eyes and a slight, tolerant smile. When Father introduced us she immediately crouched down to shake my hand and smile at me face-to-face.

She *so* wanted to be liked! That *never* changed in all the time I knew her. In that open, sincere, trusting way she had—she truly did wear her heart upon her sleeve—she told me how much she had always wanted a daughter, a little girl, to play dolls and dress-up with, to sew and bake with; she said we could try out new recipes and have a different cake or pie every Saturday. She complimented my hair—"what lovely hair for curling!"—and said that she hoped we would be *real* friends. Her shy smile and hopeful words touched my heart, but even as I nodded and answered her with a smile of my own, I was aware of fifteen-year-old Emma standing vigilantly, and sullenly, behind me, like a skinny black crow, still wearing mourning for our mother and keeping a steadfast, iron grip upon my shoulder while glowering a warning at Abby. Emma had stepped into our mother's shoes where I was concerned and was not about to vacate them. I was hers and she aimed to keep it that way. And I soon found myself caught between my sister and stepmother like a rag doll two little girls were waging a war over.

In those days, when I was a child and thought like one, I genuinely liked Abby; I might even have loved her. But Emma *hated* her right from the start; "the Cow," "that useless cow," "that greedy fat slug," she always called her.

Emma made me choose between herself and Abby—between my own flesh and blood sister who had been like a mother to me since our own had died and the usurper who had come to take, to *steal,* our mother's place—and with the cruelty unique to children, I broke Abby's heart. I turned my back on the woman who, from the day I started school until I left it, made sure the smell of cookies, moist and hot, straight from the oven, greeted me the moment I walked through the door. The woman who had scoffed at Emma's imperious pronouncement that redheads could not wear pink and made me a dress that color and curled my hair with pink ribbons to satisfy my childish craving for that candy-sweet color. The woman who had laboriously lowered her hefty bulk down to sit on the floor and carefully cut the figures of fashionably dressed ladies from the pages of *Godey's Lady's Book* to make paper dolls and play with me. But Emma was *always* there to goad and remind me, to make me feel guilty, and force me to choose. So, to please Emma, and honor our dear dead mother's memory, I hardened my heart against Abby and slammed the door upon her smiling face and the hands that seemed to always be holding out a special gift for me or reaching out to hug me and soothe away all my childish hurts from cruel words spoken by schoolchildren to skinned knees. I know now that I should not have had to choose.

And when Abby, denied the affection of her stepdaughters, and often even simple human courtesy, began to turn more and more to her half sister Sarah Whitehead, thirty-five years younger than herself and the perfect age to fill a daughter's void, I *hated* her for it. I hated Abby, and I hated Sarah! We—Emma and I—used to call them "the greedy sow and her piglet."

Emma was convinced somehow, someway, if ever it were in Abby's power, little Sarah, who grew up into a pathetic, tired, and sniveling woman, hopeless with housework, and saddled with too many children and a drunken brute of a husband who was unwilling to work and beat her regularly to prove himself a man and her master, would somehow supplant us and lay claim to Father's fortune when he died.

"She only married Father to stake their claim to the inheritance that should rightfully be ours," Emma insisted.

That was the bee in Emma's bonnet and it buzzed incessantly and drove her *mad!* If Father died without a will, or wrote one that favored Abby above us, Emma relentlessly reminded me, then, like orphaned girls in a fairy tale, we would be beholden to our stepmother for our every want and need, having to go to her like beggars with our hands out, while Sarah reigned supreme like a little princess upon whom all good things were showered.

This was Emma's obsession, nursed like a poisonous black viper at her breast year after miserable year, and I shared it, faithfully nurturing and tending it alongside her, fearing that it *might* be true, and letting every act of generosity shown to Sarah fuel our fears and animosity, and goad us on to greater cruelty. We were not very kind to "the greedy sow and her piglet"; no wonder Sarah Whitehead *despised* "those uppity Borden girls" and urged Abby to do the same. But Abby only looked at us with the sad and wary eyes of a dog that has been kicked too many times by someone who used to love it. Her smiles grew tentative and fewer and her figure grew rounder as she found the cookies, cakes, and pies she baked more comforting and sweeter than her stepdaughters' sour and cantankerous company. Could anyone, in all honesty, *really* blame her? We—Emma and I—did.

The house only added to our sorrows; it was a never-ending source of kindling to heap upon the bonfire of our hatred and discontent. Though he could easily have afforded to without any discomfort or sacrifice, Father refused to allow the house to be hooked up to the gas main. While even our poorer neighbors' lives were lit by the warm and welcoming glow of gaslight, ours were illuminated by kerosene lamps and candles, and we often went to bed with the sun to save on both rather than listen to Father preach and prate about the expense.

"Sensible people," he always said whenever the subject was broached, "go to bed with the sun just like chickens; only madmen and fools sit up all night."

When I mentioned that I had read in a magazine that both Mozart and Beethoven kept late hours, burning the midnight oil to create immortal and beloved masterpieces that were with us still, he nodded and murmured "madmen and fools," as though I were affirming, not contradicting, his assertion.

Nor were we afforded the by then rather commonplace luxury of hot and cold running water and a proper bathroom with toilet and tub. Instead, in the privacy of our bedrooms we relieved ourselves into tin slop pails, or made our way, lamp in hand, down the steep, dark stairs to the crude cellar privy where we also bathed in a battered old tin tub filled with water heated on the stove that was already tepid by the time one stepped into the tub. The situation was made even more intolerable by walls so thin everyone knew when anyone was making use of the slop pail. A sputtering fundament, the plop of droppings, the tinkle of urine; no cough, belch, or breaking of wind was a secret in that house. Emma and I could even hear every time Father mounted his fat mare and rode her to a grunting, gasping finish. At times I almost envied our Maggie sleeping alone upstairs in a tiny sliver of a room beneath a sharply slanting ceiling. Emma and I could never entertain; we were too ashamed of our shabby outmoded furnishings, the oil lamps and primitive privy, the threadbare carpets and dingy, faded wallpaper where the flowers had lost all their color. "This house has sucked all the life out of them," I once said to Emma, "just like it is trying to do to us." And any thoughts of gentleman callers when we reached courting age were quickly abandoned; we just couldn't bear for them to see the way we were made to live.

We didn't live rich, but everyone knew the truth—while reasonable thrift was in most eyes accounted a virtue, Father took it to the opposite extreme; he was niggardly to a fault and made sharecroppers look like the nouveau riche. His parsimony made us laughingstocks and kept us from assuming our proper place in society. We were, after all, descendants of one of Fall River's founding families, and deserved to be right in the fast, beating heart of fashionable society, the crème de la crème who lived up on The Hill in opulent, modernized mansions, instead of sulking pitiably on its fringes.

And neither Emma nor I could be considered a beauty even in the most charitable terms, to call us *pretty* was even a stretch of the imagination; we *needed* the promise of a generous dowry to help bait our traps for a suitable husband. But thanks to Father all we had was vinegar, not honey, and that was no way to catch a beau! No worthwhile gentleman of respectable means or prospects would ever bother courting a girl who lived in such deplorable and miserly conditions. Unless she was a rare and raving beauty, like a rose blooming through the cracked and parched sidewalks of a tenement slum, he would instead do the sensible thing and look elsewhere for a bride. And who could blame him?

By then Father oversaw his business empire from a big three-story red granite building downtown bearing his name, the A. J. Borden Building, where he rented out shops to purveyors of luxury goods on the ground floor, while denying his daughters a house up on The Hill, where all the richest and best people lived a life of luxury and ease and even the dogs wore diamond collars. *What good was all that money piling up in the bank if it couldn't make our lives better?* There were no debuts in white dresses and pearls for the Borden girls and we drifted wretchedly, painstakingly, through our marriageable years and became old maids without any gentlemen ever knocking upon our door, hat in hand, asking to go out walking with us or to escort us to a dance, clambake, sing-along, or sleighing party. We sat alone, or with other old maids, at church socials and Sunday band concerts in the park, enviously eying the more fortunate girls and their beaus, and privately wept over the marriage announcements in *The Fall River Globe*. Our dance cards were always empty because we never even made it to the dance. We never had the chance!

Father scoffed at our desires and called us pretentious and silly; to him all men were fortune hunters and his dollars, not his daughters, were the glittering prizes that dazzled their eyes. The idea that any man could ever love us for any other reason was utterly absurd to him. Emma in her perpetual black, gloomily and dutifully mourning Mother and a life that had passed her by, was dried up and old before her time. She would have made the perfect witch flying on her broomstick across the midnight sky of a picture postcard for Halloween. And I was a short, stocky, stout-waisted, ruddy-faced redhead with skin inclined to freckle, and washed-out, almost colorless, blue eyes, and whose jawline was inclined to be jowly. I was beautiful only in my dreams, inspired by the romantic novels I devoured, where I dwelled in splendid castles and danced through life in my lover's arms in sorbet- and candy-colored dresses of the latest Parisian fashion with my fiery red hair piled up in mounds and masses of curls entwined with silk ribbons, diamonds, and pearls. In my sleeping kingdom my complexion was porcelain and pink roses perfection and not the least bit florid or mottled, my profile was as perfect as the one on the cameo at my breast, and my waist formed an exquisite hourglass my beloved could easily span within his two strong, manly hands, and after the dancing was done he carried me away in his arms to make love in a bed of roses or upon a blanket of ermine depending on the season. And sometimes he sang his love to me in a wonderful tenor voice, thrilling my soul with his high notes. (I was always rather fanciful.)

But Father could *never* see it my way—we *had* the money to make our dreams come true if we could only *spend* it! Good solid investments that paid well and regular dividends so the wolf of poverty wasn't even lurking anywhere remotely near our door, why he wasn't even within shooting range! But no, Father *always* shook his head and said it was better that we bide at home and save our money, make it last the whole of our lifetimes, instead of spending it on fripperies to try to attract some worthless fellow; we would only be disappointed otherwise. We really were poor little rich girls, prisoners in a day and age when nice, respectable girls didn't leave their father's house except to go to their husband's. *We* were

Bordens and thus above the poor mill girls and Irish "Maggies," as the denizens of Fall River always called the poor Irish girls who hired out as maidservants and had to earn their bread and butter and even the plate it was put upon. We were too good, and proud, to go out and work for a living, to actually earn the pennies to pay for the lives we longed for, if we even could; no typewriter girl or governess I ever heard of wore diamonds and ermine.

I remember the summer I turned thirteen and my courses came for the first time. We were visiting our farm in Swansea. Emma, in our mother's stead, explained what it meant and showed me how to fashion the thick cloth towels, fold, and attach them to the home-made calico belts women used in those days, and how to soak them in a pail of cold water and borax kept discreetly out of sight be-neath the bed or under the sink in the cellar until the Maggie laun-dered them and tucked them away in the bureau drawer in readiness for the next month. Father took me fishing. As we sat on the bank, holding our poles, waiting for the fish to bite, he spoke to me for the first time of courtship and marriage. I will *never* forget the words he said to me: "When men look at you, Lizzie, they will *never* see anything but my money; *no one* will *ever* love you for any-thing else. It's the way of the world; when people know you've got money they all want a share. You will *never* be anything but a dol-lar sign in men's eyes, Lizzie!"

Father always did have a low opinion of my personal attractions. He had a definite knack for making me feel worthless and was end-lessly "just funning" about my figure, calling me things like "piggy in a blue gown," shaking his head dolefully and clucking his tongue whenever he saw me taking a second helping at table or grazing idly on sweets, and urging me to take a good long look in the mir-ror and see myself the way others saw me. And if I dared lose my temper, or angry tears appeared in my eyes, he would say I was de-void of humor and could not take a joke.

The only bright spot in my existence was Bridget Sullivan, our Maggie. When Father refused to pay her a reasonable wage and Bridget threatened to leave us, Abby, Emma, and I all chipped in to pay her out of our pin money.

Bridget—*I* was the only one who called her by her given name; the others just called her "Maggie"—flitted flirtily through that drab and dreary house brandishing her feather duster like a fairy's wand, a lively twinkle lighting up her green eyes, giving an occasional pert toss to the thick, curly black hair hanging down her back below the frills of her white ruffled cap. Often she would pause when she saw me brooding or frowning to chuck me under the chin and say, "Now, now, *macushla*"—*my darling!* I'd never heard a sweeter word!—"surely it's not as bad as all that?" *Macushla*—my darling, my dear—I had looked it up at the library and discovered it was a Gaelic word that literally translated meant "my blood." Trust my Bridget to make even nauseating, sickening, sticky red blood seem sweet as strawberry jam! Bridget! Her dainty feet seemed to be always dancing, light as air beneath her black skirt and long white apron despite the sturdy black boots weighing them down. She was always humming or singing her favorite song, "Oh, Dem Golden Slippers," until my longing to give her a pair became almost unbearable.

There were days when I would sit for *hours,* glassy-eyed with boredom, chin propped heavily upon my fist, and dream of kneeling worshipfully at her feet, lifting her skirts, unlacing those clunky black boots, and cradling each little foot in my hand, gently as a dove, before I eased it into a dainty, elegant slipper of gleaming gold with a French heel encrusted with diamonds that had come all the way from Paris, France, as my gift to her. If she came upon me and spoke to me when I was lost in this sweet reverie I would blush and grow so flustered I would have to leave her. I couldn't even bear to look at her lest she read the truth in my eyes. The Thursday and Sunday afternoons she had off always seemed the dullest, darkest, and longest of the week, and I was always boorish and ill-tempered in her absence, perplexed and half-ashamed that I was having such outlandish thoughts about our Maggie. I spent countless restless hours pouting, pacing, and worrying about what she was doing, and who she might be walking out with. She was so young, lovely, and lively I lived in perpetual fear that some poor but earnest Irish Paddy would entice her away from us with the promise of a brass wedding band. I tried to curtail my emotions; I was *terrified* someone would remark the coincidence and link my bad moods to Bridget's absence, but fortunately not even eagle-eyed Emma ever did.

No wonder I was so eager to leave, to spread my wings and fly far, far away!

Chapter 2

"My sweet taste of freedom," that is how I always think of the eighteen glorious weeks I spent in Europe that magical summer of 1890. It was my *one,* and I feared *only,* chance to *truly* live, to *fly,* and soar free, before I was shut back inside my cage where the bars were the cheapest base metal and not even gilded. I stayed in fully electrified hotels equipped with every comfort, modern convenience, and luxury. There were telephones on the bedside tables, room service, impeccably mannered servants who seemed to live only to please me, and private baths with hot and cold running water where I could lie back, stretch out my limbs, and soak for *hours* in rose-scented water and dream I was a mermaid sunning myself on a rock waiting for my prince to come along and carry me away to his castle in the clouds. I dined every night on gourmet meals in elegant restaurants, saw the scandalous Can-Can danced at the Moulin Rouge, and had my hair done by a real French coiffeur. I swirled and glided across high-polished ballroom floors in the arms of the most wonderful man in the world and wore my first ball gown, a dress straight out of my dreams, with yards of rustling peach taffeta billowing like a bell about my limbs, and feasted my eyes on great works of art and grand cathedrals so beautiful they made me weep.

And to think I owed it all to the Central Congregational Church. That staid and proper institution that was the bedrock of every respectable maiden lady's life in Fall River had sent me, like Alice, down the rabbit hole to my own Wonderland—*Europe!*

Without the church I would have had *nothing* to do except sit at home reading romance novels and eating Abby's cookies, pies, and cakes and just getting fatter and fatter. Though I *longed* to be one of the happy, carefree girls from up on The Hill being called for by handsome boys in tennis whites, gaily skipping away, racket in hand, in a white pique skirt and starched white shirtwaist with a big sailor collar and wide-brimmed straw hat with long grosgrain streamers to ride to The Hillside Country Club in a smart pony cart for games and refreshments, and maybe a sing-along around the piano and some dancing, Father didn't approve of ladies engaging in social activities unrelated to church or charity.

Every Monday I attended a meeting of the Women's Christian Temperance Union, where we gathered to drink tea or lemonade and heatedly denounce the demon rum between passing around plates of cookies and dainty cakes and painting a placard or sewing a banner or two for us to display once a month when we stood outside a local saloon to protest their peddling of the Devil's elixir, frowning, waggling a disapproving finger, and saying *Shame!* to everyone who went in or out. Wednesdays I acted as treasurer for the Christian Endeavor Society and doled out the dollars and cents to finance our good deeds and sold cookies Abby had baked to raise funds for the Fall River Philanthropic Burial Society, to provide decent burials for the deserving poor. Tuesdays and Saturdays were devoted to my favorite charity, the Fruit and Flower Mission. First we met to discuss our mission; then, every Saturday, without fail, we brought baskets of fruit to those we knew who were convalescing at home or in the hospital and, like angels of mercy bearing bright, happy bouquets, bravely ventured into the part of town known as The Flats that was nearest to the mills, where the workers lived in the most deplorable and squalid conditions, in tumbledown tenements and hovels. It was a horrible fetid and filthy place, made muddy from the mill waste, with stagnant puddles standing deep enough to drown a small child.

Emma always said we had it backward, our charity should have been the other way around; we should have given the flowers to our friends, and taken the fruit to nourish the needy poor instead, citing something she had read about citrus fruits and scurvy sailors. But such "radical thinking" was not in keeping with our mission and she was politely asked to reconsider her membership, though the dues were nonrefundable of course.

I just couldn't understand Emma taking a position like that! More than once I had been moved to tears when I beheld the awed expressions upon the faces of a poor family of mill workers when I bestowed upon them the regal red beauty of roses, and when, instead of a new baby, I laid a bouquet of festive autumn-hued chrysanthemums in the arms of a poor worn-out Irish woman who was already the mother of *nine* children, all bawling and tugging at her tattered skirt while her husband was passed out from the drink. ... . The look on her face was *indescribable!* It was truly a moment to treasure, and I knew that I had made a difference. The recipients of our floral gifts were always so stunned that they were rendered speechless; some of their dear faces actually turned red and quivered and looked ready to burst from the overpowering feelings they didn't know how to express. But *I* understood; I knew *exactly* how they felt. Their eyes were so *starved* for beauty in the decrepit leaky-roofed hovels where they lived it made me happy beyond words to give them something to feast on. That was what the Fruit and Flower Mission was all about.

And then there was my Sunday school class where I stood before the chalkboard like a brave captain at the helm of his storm-tossed ship *determined* to imbue the Oriental heathens who worked in the town's mills and laundries with goodly Christian virtues. I taught them to sing hymns, read Bible stories, and write their names, and every Christmas we staged a pageant in which my pupils sang Christmas carols and hymns and enacted the Nativity story. Everyone looked forward to it all year ... except our organist, Mrs.

Stowe, but that was only because she tripped over a sheep and broke her collarbone during a rehearsal of the manger scene one year, but that was not *my* fault, so she really had no cause to turn against me and the dear Celestials. My pupils *loved* me, and not just because I gave them each candies and a new pencil and a pretty card with a Bible verse printed on it every Sunday, and both the Reverends Buck and Jubb said I was a *wonderful* teacher who was personally responsible for saving countless heathen souls, and that the Sunday school Christmas pageant always sent the congregation home with much to ponder.

The events that would lead to my "sweet taste of freedom" began with just an ordinary meeting of the Fruit and Flower Mission. We were taking a civilized pause to cool our tempers after a rather heated discussion about which blossoms the poor Irish Catholic denizens of our city would find most uplifting. Addie Whip and her best friend, Minnie Macomber, had just astonished us all by saying they thought the gay, brilliant pink hue of azaleas would be more in keeping with "Catholic tastes" than the tired old lily-of-the-valley and lavender bouquets Ella Sheen and her sisters, Evy and Annabelle, always insisted upon. I could well understand the Irish being in the mood for something festive and new and dared to venture that I thought purple satin ribbon to bind the stems of the azaleas would be a most bright and becoming touch— imagine what vivid joy it would bring into their dismal, drab little lives! It was then that my beautiful ash-blond cousin, Anna Borden, who lived in a grand mansion up on The Hill leading the life I longed for, impulsively proposed a trip to Europe as a culturally broadening experience to relieve our ennui, and to shop for dresses, of course. It was getting rather tiresome, she said, gadding about the wrong side of town handing out chrysanthemums to cleaning women. Her sister Carrie and their friend Nellie Shore enthusiastically embraced the idea.

They were all in their twenties and as yet unmarried, but not without hopes like me; whereas I was but a few months shy of thirty with no hope of a savior to end my spinsterhood in sight. All three had rich, doting fathers who could deny them nothing, but I stuck out like an ugly weed in a garden of American Beauty Roses that had stubbornly insinuated itself into their majestic midst. But I didn't care; I wanted to go out into the world *so badly,* to experience and see with my own eyes all the wonderful and exciting things I had only read and dreamed about. I just *had* to go with them; I just *had* to!

The Reverend Buck lent his support to the venture, wistfully recalling his own Grand Tour as a young man and lamenting that he could not join us. But, in all fairness, he stipulated, anyone who wished to come and had the means to pay for the passage must be allowed to join us, and it was essential that we equip ourselves with a suitable chaperone, and for this role he recommended Miss Hannah Mowbry. Once the most popular teacher at the high school, she had in her respectable but impoverished retirement parlayed her love of travel into the lucrative role of professional companion, paid to escort affluent and unmarried young ladies wherever in the civilized portions of the whole wide world they wished to go.

How I pestered and plagued Father night and day to let me go. I started when he came down to breakfast and ended at his bedroom door after supper. I begged; I wept; I took to my bed with a monster of a migraine and shunned all food. I went down on my knees and tried to make him see just how important this was to me. He was afraid that I would desert him in his old age, abandon him in his gray hairs for some worthless European scoundrel, some slick-haired cad I found in a casino or lurking around the halls of a castle somewhere just like a spider waiting to snare naïve and wealthy women in his fiendish web. I vehemently swore *NEVER!,* crossed my heart, and promised faithfully that I would *always* be there to care for him. Even if he lived to 105, my face would be the last he saw upon his dying day, I declared.

"We both know I cannot depend on Emma," Father said, and I was quick to agree. By this point if Father had fallen into the sea and was drowning, Emma would not have thrown him a life preserver; instead she would have shoved Abby in after him and sought a bucket of blood to pour over their heads to attract sharks. But I, I was his little girl born to be a comfort in his old age. He had given me his name, Andrew, as my middle name since he had been denied the consolation of a son to follow in his footsteps that every man deserves.

I told him *exactly* what he wanted to hear, that my *first* duty was to him, and him alone, and *never* would I betray him, turn my back, or relinquish that role, not even for the most loving of husbands. Rashly, I ripped the gold and enamel class ring from my finger and shoved it onto his gnarled and hairy pinkie, the only one it would fit, to seal this eternal pledge of devotion and kissed it as solemnly as if it were a bishop's ring. *Anything* to get my way, to get *away!*

Emma, so taciturn and disagreeable that Father actually welcomed her absence, had her twice-yearly trips to visit her friends, the elderly Mrs. Brownell and her spinster daughter, Helen, in Fairhaven, but this obedient little sheep Lizzie had never strayed from the fold. I was almost thirty and had never left Massachusetts; I wanted a taste of freedom too! I *deserved* it!

Finally, when I was hoarse as a bullfrog and half-blind from weeping, Father reluctantly gave his consent. He came into my room, where I was lying sick and wretched in my bed, my pillow soaked with tears, and gave me the steamship ticket and told me I should see about my passport as soon as I was able. He surprised me the night before my departure with a most extravagant gift. When he came home from his daily round of business meetings, he had a large cardboard box tucked under his arm. He sat it on the sofa and told me to turn my back to him. I heard the lid lift and a tantalizing rustle of tissue paper; then the most beautiful sealskin cape lined with lustrous chocolate satin was draped around my shoulders and a matching muff was thrust over my hand. I had never been so happy in all my life! I felt just like a butterfly coming out of its cocoon.

We sailed aboard the SS *Scythia* on June 21, 1890. Carrie and Nellie were fast friends, so there was no question that they would be rooming together, and Miss Mowbry always made it a proud point, stipulated firmly in her contract, that she prized her solitude and shared accommodations with no one, so I was left by default to bunk with my haughty cousin Anna. Ah Anna! She never deigned to acknowledge our kinship and put me in my place by always treating me like her maid, regally commanding me to brush her hair, do up or undo her buttons and hooks, lace or unlace her stays, or wash her back when she sat in the bath wreathed by clouds of lavender-scented steam, never guessing that just the touch of her exquisite skin, the sight of her bountiful bosom freed from the prison of her mauve satin corset, and the imperious lavender-blue flash of her eyes was like an electric thrill to me. Whenever I was alone with her in our stateroom I felt weak-kneed, like a woman sculpted of pink candle wax melting beneath a hot flame. And given her shabby treatment of me, I found it strangely comforting that I would never be a dollar sign in Cousin Anna's eyes, just dirt beneath her feet.

Carrie, who lived for fashion, made frequent snide remarks about my clothes, observing that I was traveling very light whereas she herself had not one but *five* steamer trunks and planned to return with at least half a dozen more. She would inquire where my dresses had been made, if it were in New York or Boston perhaps, and implore me to give her my dressmaker's name when she knew full well that all my clothes were made in Fall River by local seamstresses or, in the case of simpler calico or cotton housedresses and wrappers, home sewn to while away the endless hours of boredom. And she remarked more than once upon the preponderance of blue in my meager wardrobe, saying I must be *excessively fond* of the color to wear it so often.

In truth, by this point, though I didn't dislike the hue, I was bored to death by blue. But Emma was convinced that blue was my best and *only* color. Browns, light or dark, she insisted, made me look depressingly plain and doused the fire in my hair; white for daily wear was just plain impractical; gray made me look washed out and glum; green was such a cliché on redheads any sensible woman with hair that color would do well to avoid it; yellow made me look jaundiced and stouter; black, despite the slight slimming illusion it worked upon my waist, was far too funereal and made my jaw look heavier in comparison; and the purples, pinks, peaches, oranges, and reds, all those soft sorbet and bright candy colors, my soul *hungered* for heightened the unfortunate tendency of my face to an ugly, mottled floridness; only blue did anything for me, though, granted, that was not saying much.

But Miss Mowbry was very kind; she spoke up for me whenever such remarks penetrated her ear trumpet. She said that I was right to favor blue, as it was clearly my best color and worked wonders with my eyes, chilling or warming them according to the shade I was wearing. Traveling light, she also thought, was very wise; I would have more room in my trunk for new dresses and souvenirs without having to spend my father's money on another trunk to put them in. "Lizzie is a sensible girl who opts for quality, not quantity," she said with a look that implied that Carrie, despite her seemingly endless wealth, most decidedly was not. "That girl buys and discards dresses like a bumblebee drifting from flower to flower," Miss Mowbry whispered to me, and I could not but agree and hope that the vivid raspberry-and-lemon-striped and ruffled confection Carrie was then sporting would soon find a place amongst her discards, as I feared just looking at it would bring on one of my awful migraines.

And Nellie Shore, with her acerbic tongue, thank goodness, was largely indifferent to me. She obviously didn't consider me a worthy subject to waste her wit and quips upon and always looked straight through me as though I were made of glass, and deafness seemed to afflict her whenever I spoke. Sometimes I was sorely tempted to rush into her stateroom in the wee hours and shake her out of a sound sleep and shout, "The ship is sinking!" right in her ear just to see if she would hear me. But, of course, I never did; it would have been behavior ill becoming of a lady and one of the Bordens of Fall River.

We were all laid low with seasickness for most of the voyage even though Miss Mowbry, the only seasoned traveler amongst us, had brought along a goodly supply of *Gully's Tablets for Mal-de-Mer,* which she swore by, and we obediently sucked on them even though they tasted like solidified quicklime.

When we steamed into port at Liverpool the sky was so gray it was very near black and the rain was so dense I had to squint and strain my eyes to make out the rooftops and church steeples in the distance. My companions shrieked in dismay, but they were more concerned about ruined hats and clothes, or, in the case of Miss Mowbry, dying of diphtheria, than this rather bleak introduction to the land of our forefathers. But *I* didn't care. I stood at the rail and drank it all in, letting the rain do whatever it would to my hat and drench me to the skin until my skirts and petticoats were soaked clean through and plastered to my limbs and my hair torn loose from its pins. I'm sure the others thought I was quite mad, but I didn't care; I was *determined* to let *nothing* spoil this. It was a once in a lifetime moment that would never come again. Even if I ever did venture across the Atlantic again, it would never be the same as the first time.

At the hotel, where we were once again sharing accommodations, I was quickly rushed into a hot bath and then bundled into bed in a warm flannel nightgown with a hot-water bottle. Miss Mowbry was certain I would catch my death and even wanted to send for the hotel physician, but my will was stronger than any contagions floating about in the air, and I refused to let even so much as a sneeze or a sniffle rob me of a single moment of my time in England. There was too much to see and do to be sick!

"What a stouthearted girl you are, Lizzie! Strong as a horse!" Miss Mowbry said admiringly. "We'll make a traveler of you yet!" Though the compliment was a trifle spoiled when she leaned in close and whispered in my ear, "You know, Lizzie, I am getting on in years and there are many girls from Fall River's finest families growing up all the time and wanting to broaden their horizons with European travel. If your father would permit it, I should be pleased to take you under my wing. . . ."

The idea of *me* as a paid companion to those girls when I was just as good and rich as they were! Pride blinded me, and in her offer I saw only the shame, not the doorway Freedom was holding open for me, while eagerly beckoning me across the threshold.

The other girls quickly went their own way; they were more interested in seeing the insides of dress shops than anything of cultural or historical significance. Great cathedrals, so beautiful they could make a man weep, paled in comparison beside the couturiers' confections in their eyes, and Michelangelo's sculptures didn't thrill them anywhere near as much as the hats on display in the front window of a milliner's shop. Gems, not Great Masters, made their breath catch in wonder and their eyes sparkle. They whiled away their time batting their eyelashes at eligible Englishmen, dreaming of snaring a duke or a lord and going to live in his ancestral castle, playing lady bountiful to the tenants, and presiding over well-laden tea tables serving petit fours and cucumber sandwiches to the crème de la crème of society, and, of course, the ultimate honor of being presented to Queen Victoria in white satin and plumes.

Romance was something I had long since consigned to the land of dreams. Of course I had had schoolgirl crushes on my teachers, and a classmate or two, daydreamed over the wedding gowns in *Godey's Lady's Book,* and sighed wistfully over poetry and romantic scenes in the novels I read, but I had long since grudgingly accepted spinsterhood as my lot. But in Europe I began to feel like the princess in a fairy tale who slept for a hundred years before she was awakened by Prince Charming's kiss. I was stirring, waking up; it was terrifying yet *so exciting!*

I was only just beginning to realize then what I know all too well now. Every old maid, crabapple virgin, and prim spinster lady has a story, and it is usually a story about love, but it is always a sad one, bittersweet at best, that does not end with a wedding or "happily ever after." We are not all the innocent naïve virgins the world likes to think. We may stay at home, protected by well-meaning relatives, buffered from the *real* world of cads and bounders, but we have hearts and minds and bodies; we *can,* and *do,* hope and dream, and *feel,* often with a burning, hot intensity that, if they knew, would shock our relations to the core and consign us to the care of an overzealous doctor for one of those discreet operations to calm hysterics and free women of these libidinous demons by cutting out the source of these unwholesome and unseemly passions. But they don't know; we're too wise to let them. We all have secrets we keep in the heart-shaped lockbox in our breasts.

From the start my life seemed destined to be one of secrets—a kiss stolen in the shadows of a shady tree, a petty theft from a shop, a glass of absinthe and the loss of all inhibitions behind a locked door—doing what no proper, well-brought-up lady would *ever* do. I have never wagered so much as a penny on a game of chance, but I think I understand what compels the gambler. I saw the roulette wheels spin on the Riviera, and fortunes lost and won, and the high euphoria and plummeting despair that came after depending on the outcome, and I think that I, sheltered old maid that I am, understand *exactly* how it feels to court destruction and risk everything for a momentary thrill. Few gamblers stop once they've won; they *always* go back for more. I understand that too. How many times have I followed the lure of love, the hope of opening my eyes to a dream come true? We shall have to count them all as this story unfolds, the whole sad tally of love lost, denied, thwarted, or rejected, and trust misplaced. Let us begin with the prince who woke the sleeping princess up and aroused all the longings she thought had died in her long stagnant slumber.

I shall not tell you his name. There is no point; nothing would be served by it except prurient curiosity, and I will not let yet another innocent person be tarred and feathered by association with me; that has happened too many times already. People who should have been able to live out their lives in peace now have their names mentioned in books and lurid articles about crime because their path in some way crossed mine. And every woman is entitled to keep *one* secret tied up in the red ribbons of her heart, so let *his* name be the secret I take with me to the grave.

He was an architect, a few years older than myself. His eyes were blue and his hair was blond, like golden wheat kissed by the summer sun, and even when it was subdued by pomade and combed back had an irrepressible tendency to flop boyishly over his brow. I like to think he saw more in me than anyone else ever has before or since. Many Americans believe that the English are singularly lacking in warmth, that they are frigid and imperious as icebergs, and shun emotion as if it were leprosy, but I *know* this is not universally true. As I am a woman who has often unjustly been called "cold" and "undemonstrative" because I don't give vent to impassioned displays in public places to oblige the spectators who think they have the right to know everything about me because of the infamous course my life has taken, you may trust me implicitly upon this point.

We met in a secondhand bookshop on a rainy day in London when we both reached for the same volume. It fell with a thud and a puff of dust that made us both sneeze. We laughed and bent to retrieve it at the same time and bumped heads, knocking each other's hat off. It was not a proper introduction. Some might have mistaken him for a masher and me for a forward American girl setting her cap for an English milord—it is after all a common assumption about all unattached American females of marriageable age traveling abroad—but from the moment our eyes met neither of us cared what anyone else thought; we knew the truth and who we *really* were, and nothing else mattered.

He had an umbrella, a trusty black umbrella—what Englishman does not? I held tight to his arm as we crowded beneath it, being jostled by the crowd on the pavement as they stepped around us.

I asked him if the sun ever shines in England; it had been raining since the day I arrived. He laughed—he had such a merry laugh that made his blue eyes sparkle like sapphire-colored fireworks on the Fourth of July—and assured me that yes, it did upon occasion.

We went to a quiet but respectable little tearoom he favored and had tea and Banbury tarts—the cook's specialty made from an old family recipe—that reminded me of Abby's mincemeat. We talked for *hours,* of *so many* things; it was as if we had known each other all our lives. His world was wider than mine, but we found enough common ground to meet upon. I felt like a tight little rosebud slowly unfurling beneath the sun of his kindness and attention. I wanted only to be with him; when I was with him I *thrived,* I felt *so alive!*

Yes, Dear Reader, I know, when I read back over these words I also have to shake my head and smile. I sound so starry-eyed, like a silly girl just struck for the first time by Cupid's dart, a Juliet ready, willing, and eager to die for love, when in truth I had just passed my thirtieth birthday and was already a confirmed spinster withering on the vine. But that is how it was. I *cannot* lie; that is *exactly* how I felt. It was *marvelous* and *new* and *wonderful* and made everything seem so fresh and beautiful! I had never felt so happy and alive! And *awake!* He made me feel as though I had been sleepwalking through life!

He threw my *Baedeker* into the Thames and took time away from his office to show me the sights in London and beyond. We toured the Tower, where a bold raven snatched at the hem of my skirt, and he told me stories from its bloody past, and how a sentry had not ten years ago almost been court-martialed for sleeping on duty after he encountered the diaphanous white phantom of Queen Anne Boleyn. He had challenged her with his halberd and she countered by lifting off her head and he fainted dead away. Fortunately for him, he was saved at the last moment when another guard, who had witnessed it all from a stairway above, came forward and confirmed his story.

He showed me Hampton Court, the Houses of Parliament, the tombs at Westminster Abbey, and we spent a whole day at the National Gallery, and through it all he told me stories about the places, the craftsmanship and architecture, and the people who had left their mark upon his country's glorious past. One day he took me into Shakespeare land. We stopped at Anne Hathaway's cottage, where the Bard's wife had dwelled. I felt quite at home amongst the red brick chimneys and rustic Tudor gingerbread and imagined our making our home in a place just like this, a little spot of Heaven in the heart of the English countryside. I saw myself sitting on a bench in the garden waiting for him to come home from a busy day in London, reading a book while our children frolicked about, and the housekeeper prepared dinner for us and Banbury tarts for dessert. And on a ridge between Warwickshire and Oxfordshire, where his family had a country home, he showed me a favorite site since his boyhood—the Rollright Stones, a circle of seventy-seven standing stones, centuries old. Legend claims they were once a king and his army who set out to conquer all Britain. But along the way they offended a wizened crone who turned out to be a witch. As punishment, she turned them all to stone, and then transformed herself into an elder tree to stand eternal sentry and make sure the curse was never lifted. If cut while in full flower, local folk said, the tree would bleed human blood. At midnight, on certain sacred nights, my beloved told me, the king and his knights are magically restored to human life, and dance hand in hand, round and round, unceasingly while the witch keeps time to the fairy music, tapping her toe, and clapping her gnarled hands with long yellow nails like talons, until cock's crow turned them back to stone and tree again. Yet any mortal who has the misfortune to stumble upon this spectacle will go stone blind or mad. "When I was a lad," my architect confided, "I used to sneak out at night and watch the witches gather and perform their rituals within the sacred circle of the Rollright Stones." He saw black cocks sacrificed, held upside down as their blood was drained into goblets that were then passed around, and other acts not fit for a lady's ears.

But the day I cherish most of all is the day when the sun *finally* shone, the day he took me to Glastonbury. He showed me where the graves of King Arthur and golden-haired Guinevere had been discovered in the time of Henry II, buried sixteen feet down in the hollowed-out trunk of a mighty oak tree. Arthur was a giant of a man, his great and noble skull bashed in by at least ten mortal blows inflicted in his final battle, and Guinevere, small and delicate boned, lay humbly like a dog at his feet with her long blond hair tangled in her husband's bones, like clinging golden vines twined around his ankles. When an awestruck young monk reached out to touch a lock it crumbled into dust. We rented tin cups from a vendor and drank of the red-tinged iron-rich waters from the Chalice Well that are reputed to possess healing powers. As we sipped he told me the legend. Joseph of Arimathea had brought the Holy Grail—the cup that Jesus Christ drank from at the Last Supper and was afterward used to catch his blood as he died upon the cross—with him to Glastonbury, to lay the foundation for the Christian faith in Britain. To hide it from tenacious pagans and thieves, he had buried it within the hill, and the waters of the spring had ever since passed over the Grail and been dyed red and imbued with miraculous powers by the holy blood. We saw the crutches and canes of former cripples and blind men that hung upon the gates as proof.

"You see, the sun really does shine in England; it is shining for you today," he said, then added, more boldly, reaching out to caress my hair beneath the bluebell-covered brim of my straw hat, "I shall never forget the way it teases out the golden glints in your fiery hair, Lizbeth."

With him I felt reborn, reinvented. He even gave me a new name—Lizbeth. I didn't have the heart to disillusion him by telling him that I was born just plain Lizzie, not even traditional, ordinary Elizabeth; I let him believe it was just a family nickname.

"*Lizzie* sounds like a barmaid, a servant girl," he said a tad disdainfully, scrunching up his nose as though he smelled something bad. "The world is full of Elizabeths, but *Lizbeth* is rarer. It has the spark of drama; in its two syllables are married elegance and grandeur! *Lizzie be gone!*" He snapped his fingers in the air. "To me you shall *always* be *Lizbeth!*"

He made a sketch of Glastonbury Abbey for me. I have it still, along with the book—*our* book—the one that led us to meet. Never believe for an instant that books aren't magic; they have the power to bring people together. But I will not tell you its name either. Let the book have its own life; let it fade quietly into obscurity or be remembered by posterity on its own merits. No connection with me shall ordain its fate.

I remember the way his hand moved over the page of his sketchbook, so confident, so sure, the charcoal pencil leaving a black smudge against his calloused finger. He was an architect after all; he understood the beauty of a line, a curve, an arch. He told me of the Abbey's history and made me appreciate, and see, Glastonbury with new eyes not obscured by the rosy-tinted spectacles of romance and legends of Avalon and Arthur. And we talked of other cathedrals in other countries, and when I saw them later, on my own, and purchased pictures of them to take back home with me, to cover my naked walls, I remembered every word he had told me about their creation and history.

He showed me the thorn tree that supposedly sprang from the staff of Joseph of Arimathea when he first set foot on Glastonbury and had ever since flowered every Christmas. He told me how carolers still came to sing its praises and a flowering branch was presented each year at Christmastime to Queen Victoria. We stood in its verdant shadows and I felt his hand upon my waist, so light, so delicate, almost *reverent*—it *was* a sacred place, so how fitting that his touch should be just so! Through the blue satin sash and my eyelet dress of an even lighter blue and the rigid whalebone of my corset beneath, his fingertips felt like ghosts, so feathery light, so gently elusive, and intangible that I have at times wondered if I only imagined their caress. I wanted them to *burn* through, to *brand* me, so I could actually *feel* his fingers against my flesh just as their faint memory is still seared there. I wanted more and I thought, in time, I would have it. So slowly that time seemed almost to stop, he leaned down and pressed his lips lingeringly to mine in the tenderest kiss I have ever known.

My experience of kisses has been limited but varied. I have had rougher, clumsier, lustier, probing kisses where tongues touched, saliva mingled, and teeth scraped, but none of them has ever matched, or even come close to, the tender kiss of the blond, blue-eyed architect beneath the thorn tree at Glastonbury.

For me, it is my one unsullied moment of breathless wonder that no one can ever spoil or take away from me. I have never told anyone. I have kept it locked close, zealously guarded, within my heart, cherished it, and lived on it every day of my life. By the time you read these words I will be dead, so I will not hear you if you laugh and scoff at this silly old maid and her romantic notions and dreams. Perhaps I am overly sentimental. Men tend to take a different view of such matters; perhaps to him it was just a kiss and he went on to kiss many other American girls beneath that thorn tree. I do not know; nor do I want to. I cherish my illusion, if illusion it was.

Later, after we had our picnic lunch, he lay back on the warm green grass with his head in my lap, his hat shading his eyes from the summer sun, and we talked of our respective countries. He had been to America before, to study and on occasional business trips, but he always pined for England the whole time he was away.

He recited a poem to me, his favorite, by a Scottish poet, Alan

Cunningham, written about the Stuart monarchs, exiled from their native land and longing to return. His mother had embroidered it and had it framed for him and it always hung on his bedroom wall wherever he went in the world to remind him of home.

Hame, hame, hame, O hame fain wad I be,
O hame, hame, hame, to my ain countrie!
When the flower is i' the bud and the leaf is on the tree,
The larks shall sing me hame in my ain countrie;
Hame, hame, hame, O hame fain wad I be,
O hame, hame, hame to my ain countrie!

The green leaf of loyaltie's beginning to fall.
The bonnie White Rose it is withering an' all.
But I'll water it with the blood of usurping tyrannie,
An' green it will grow in my ain countrie!

O, there's nocht now frae ruin my countrie can save,
But the keys o' kind Heaven, to open the grave;
That a' the noble martyrs who died for loyalty
May rise again an' fight for their ain countrie.

The great now are gone, a' wha ventured to save,
The new grass is springing on the top o' their grave;
But the sun through the murk blinks blythe in my e'e,
"I'll shine on ye yet in your ain countrie."

Hame, hame, hame, O hame fain wad I be,
O hame, hame, hame, to my ain countrie!

Despite all the rash promises made as I knelt at my father's feet before I left home, I would have gladly stayed in England with my beloved forever if only he had asked me to. No one will ever know how much I wanted to. I would have, I know, regretted being seen as a traitor, disloyal to my blood, but I wanted a life of my own—a life of color and excitement and wonder and love! I was tired of seeing the world through the window of printed words and pictures frozen in time. I wanted to see it all with my *own* eyes in vibrant, rich, full, blazing color—living, breathing, moving life, not just still black-and-white or sepia images capturing only one motionless moment in time. I wanted to reach out and *touch* life with my *own* hands, and to breathe it all deep into *my* lungs. I wanted to have my *own* experiences; I was tired of making do with the siphoned, secondhand recollections of others who went out into the world and actually *did* things, *wonderful, exciting things,* while I stayed home like a good and obedient daughter and just read about them in memoirs and magazines. And Love . . . I thought Love had forgotten me, and long ago passed me by as unworthy, I never thought, I never expected, that it would remember me, and bring me someone who suited me so splendidly. If I had dreamed him he could not have been more perfect! He was like the hero of a novel stepped out from between the covers of a book—he was the architect of my dreams!

That night in the ballroom of his uncle's London house I wore my first ball gown—a delicate shimmering peach taffeta with yards of trailing skirt and a bustle in back, with ruffles on the sleeves and skirt, and matching satin dancing slippers with roses on the toes and peach silk stockings. Anna, despite her disdain for me, loved to play with hair, and deigned to arrange mine in a mound of glossy, gleaming red curls artfully woven through with peach ribbons and strands of delicate seed pearls, leaving one long ringlet to fall over my bare right shoulder.

I danced all night in the warm circle of his arms. I thought it was the safest and most wonderful place in the world and there was nowhere else I wanted to be. *I am happy here!* my eyes and my heart kept blissfully sighing.

I stood on the terrace at his side with his cloak draped over my shoulders, the white silk lining icily delicious against my bare skin, and, together, we watched the sun rise. And then I went back to the hotel and to bed, though I wasn't the least bit tired and was much too restless to even *think* of sleeping. The waltzes we had danced to still played in my mind, and my legs would not stay still; I twisted and turned in my bed and hugged my pillow close, as if I still danced with him. And while Anna slept obliviously in the bed beside mine, so close I could have reached out and tweaked her proud patrician nose, beneath the covers I boldly lifted my nightgown all the way to my chin and touched myself and pretended that it was *his* hands upon me, boldly and tenderly by turns caressing my passion-inflamed breasts and the hot pink petals of my womanhood.

He never told me that he loved me, that is true, and I was never bold or shameless enough to tell him that I loved him, but even without the words, we both knew. Tentatively, I confided my hopes by letter to Emma; my heart welled to bursting and I *needed* the relief of confession and there was no one else I could trust, but she betrayed me. Just like Judas, my *sister* betrayed me, for *nothing,* not even a pittance of silver. I was dismissed as a fool, a gullible girl who had read too many romance novels, an innocent abroad who knew *nothing* about life, love, the world, and the liars and beasts called "men." She made my wonderful, kind, gentle, courteous, thoroughly respectable architect sound like the worst kind of cad. My cheeks still burn at the memory of her stinging words even after all these years. She—and Father—never let me forget what they called "my foolishness" and how I "lost my head" over "*that Englishman.*" Their words fairly dripped with scathing scorn like venom whenever they spoke of him.

The last time I saw him he was walking away from me, after seeing me and my party safely aboard the train that would take us on the next stage of our journey. He was most solicitous and even brought a selection of newspapers and magazines and a box of chocolates to help us pass the time. And he had thoughtfully written out a list of sights for us to see in France and Italy, but it was of interest only to me; the others could talk of nothing but dresses and hats and the high-society beaus they hoped to catch.

I can see him now, walking away from me, out of my life, his broad shoulders bent against the wind, his right hand holding his derby clamped tight upon his head, and his stormy gray overcoat flapping like wild-goose wings about his legs. I couldn't stay and he couldn't go with me; we had to say good-bye. He promised he would write to me, and there was something in his eyes and the way his lips lingered when he kissed my hand that told me I would one day soon see the words I so longed to hear set down in black and white. That he would say the words that I, as a woman, could not say.

In Paris everyone seemed to be in love, or at least in lustful thrall, and brazenly unafraid of showing it. It seemed everywhere I looked I saw couples strolling arm in arm, women laying their heads upon their escorts' strong shoulders, or sitting opposite them at small tables for two in sidewalk cafés, leaning toward each other, holding hands, or even boldly daring to kiss in broad daylight on the boulevard or a park bench.

Carrie, Anna, and Nellie turned up their noses at the notion of visiting the Louvre and Notre Dame, and instead rushed off to the dress shops. They could not hail a cab or find a post office without imploring help from some English-speaking bystander, but they could say "Where are the dress shops?" in four different languages. And poor Miss Mowbry indignantly took to her bed and refused to leave it for days after an "impertinent waiter" suggested she try the *escargots*. When she accepted his recommendation "with pleasure" he smilingly set a plate of *snails* before her, bidding her, "*Bon apétit,* madame."

"Young man, in America we do not *eat* snails; we *step* on them!" she witheringly reprimanded him. "Take these away and dispose of them properly!" she commanded, then, nose high in the air, retreated grandly to her hotel room and ordered tea and toast sent up.

But we all had a weakness for the sweets. The French pastries—chocolate éclairs, cream puffs, marrons glacés, and chocolate bon-bons stuffed with decadent creams, supple caramel, or rich fruity syrups.

I saw the *Mona Lisa* on my own; I thought she looked like a woman made most unhappy by love and wondered what secrets she had kept in the lockbox of her heart. I saw love—its promises, fulfillment, the lack or loss of it, and the longing for it—in almost every painting and statue my lovesick eyes lighted upon.

I heard the bells of Notre Dame and gazed up in awe at its magnificent Gothic edifice, the first to use flying buttresses, to prevent stress fractures in the walls, my architect had told me. Inside I stood, with my arms spread wide and my head thrown back, and let a rainbow of light wash over me as the sun shone through the stained glass, bathing me in vibrant color.

And I went, alone, to see Monsieur Eiffel's controversial tower, the tallest in the world, just completed the previous year. Some called it "an eyesore," "a pox upon the skyline of Paris"; they thought that it was too modern, that the riveted iron structure lacked the romance and grace of Gothic cathedrals and the palaces of kings. They did not see it the way my architect did—as a triumph of engineering and mathematics—or understand the prime importance of wind resistance in its design. Though I far preferred the palaces and cathedrals myself, I still thought it magnificent. I climbed its many stairs and stood for over an hour, alone with my thoughts, staring out at the view wishing my love were there beside me.

The one place my traveling companions did accompany me was to the Moulin Rouge, the notorious Red Mill; even Miss Mowbry roused herself from her bed of wounded dignity, because she felt a chaperone was an absolute necessity if we were to venture into such a hedonistic atmosphere, though the hotel desk clerk assured us that respectable ladies went there all the time and we simply could not miss the Can-Can; we would reproach ourselves for the rest of our lives if we left Paris without seeing that. Then he kissed his fingers and launched a volley of rhapsodic rapid-fire French so dizzyingly fast that it went right over our heads but set our curiosity on fire. So away we went to the Moulin Rouge to see the Can-Can.

And it *was amazing,* to see the blades of the giant windmill spinning slowly against the night sky, lit up with *thousands* of red, gold, and white electric lights. I never dreamed there could be so many lightbulbs on one structure!

Inside, it was as big, bright, and gaudy as it was out. Amidst the rapid, carefree music and babble of voices we were relieved to see a great many women of seemingly respectable appearance, both escorted and unescorted, seated at the tables, and this eased our fears somewhat. A band in red and gold jackets played and the floor swarmed with dancers. It was the most vibrant and vivid place I had ever seen and I longed to lose myself and become a part of it.

There were bejeweled courtesans, the famed and fabled Grand Horizontals, in extravagant gowns trimmed with feathers and gems, silk flowers, ermine, sable, beads and glittering appliqués, so décolleté that every time they moved their breasts threatened to overflow like cherry-topped blancmanges. Jewels sparkled on their ears, necks, and wrists, the cold, star-bright light of diamonds and whole rainbows of vibrant colors—emeralds, rubies, sapphires, amethysts, and topazes. Their faces were rouged and painted, their lashes blackened, and their eyes lined dramatically with kohl, and they wore their hair, its color often of such a startling shade it could hardly be natural, piled high in mounds of curls, twists, and braids, embellished with feathers, flowers, and jewels. One woman even had a small gilded birdcage with a chirping canary perched on a tiny swing inside woven into her tall pompadour of very blond hair, like a modern-day Marie Antoinette. Her hairdresser must have been something of an architect himself to build such a towering mass of hair!

We were shocked to see a Negro man, his skin as black as tar, seated intimately at a table with a woman with milk-pale skin and the reddest hair I had ever seen in my life. She wore canary-yellow satin, her bare shoulders and overflowing bosom ringed with billowing yellow feathers, and what must have been a fortune in honey-colored topaz and diamonds glittering on her gown and about her neck and wrists and snaking through her scarlet tresses. The Negro boldly opened her purse, as if it were the most natural thing in the world for him to do, and took out a gold cigarette case. He put two in his mouth and lit them, then took one out and put it between his companion's lips. We had never seen such a thing in America nor thought to see it elsewhere. In America just looking at a white woman would have been enough to get the Negro lynched, but in Paris no one seemed to think anything of it at all. *Freedom, glorious freedom!* the whole city seemed to scream. No one was a slave here—except to their own passions!

There was a group of women, a select society, like a club unto themselves, in which all others were unwelcome. They did not paint their faces and seemed to disdain feminine frills and flirtatious manners. Some of them wore men's clothing, complete suits that looked straight out of the shops on Savile Row, dove gray, coffee and toffee colored, dark blue, or black frock coats with carnations in the buttonholes, beautiful brocade or watered-silk or garish checkered waistcoats, striped and flowered neckties, and tight-fitting trousers, or starkly elegant black and white evening clothes with black silk top hats and long, dashing opera cloaks lined in either red or white silk. Many of them wore their hair cropped short just like a man's, slicked back until it shone like patent leather or else erupting in a riot of curls or waves that would have made a seasoned sailor seasick. Some of them even smoked cigarettes, pipes, or cigars and drank strong liquor! There were a few who were a tad more feminine; they dressed in proper women's suits, but severely tailored, with mannish jackets and prominent, padded shoulders, and no feminine frills at all, not a bit of lace anywhere that I could see, or even a silk rose or a flirty feather on their hats, and their hair was plainly coiffed, severely scraped back from their faces and painfully pinned with not even a curl or a frizz to soften the effect. The only softness was in their manner to each other. These women danced *together,* waltzing in each other's arms, lost in their own little word, or else sat close together holding hands, sharing cigarettes, and even daring to kiss, openly, upon the mouth, just like lovers. No men, except the waiters, ever went near them. Yet no one except us bewildered Americans looked askance; to everyone else they seemed to be just part of the scenery.

Men and women behaved toward one another with a shocking degree of familiarity, as if they had completely forgotten that they were in a public place. We saw women sitting on men's laps and allowing themselves to be fondled and kissed. They did not even slap the men's hands away when they dared to slip boldly beneath their skirts. Sometimes coins changed hands before these actions commenced, so I doubted whether love had anything to do with it, but it was shocking to behold just the same.

We were in complete accord that we would leave just as soon as we had seen the famous dance—the Can-Can that everyone talked so much about.

All of a sudden the music stopped and the floor cleared before it struck up again, with an insistent, pulsing, lively, infectious rhythm as six women rushed in, shrieking and shaking their skirts wildly, black plumes billowing on their bonnets. The crowd began to applaud, raucously; some of the men whistled and stomped their feet or screamed out names, presumably those of the dancers they liked best.

The dancers' costumes were the most revealing I had ever seen a woman wear in public. Their ruffled white blouses were so sheer their nipples glowed through like hot pink embers, and their pink skirts were so short they barely grazed their calves. In the center of the floor they paused for one tantalizing, teasing moment to lift their skirts to show row upon row of white ruffles sewn onto their petticoats and gossamer white pantalets trimmed with ruffles and dangling pink silk ribbons that danced along with them; then they began to kick their legs high into the air, higher than I would have ever thought possible, fast and free to the music, while emitting exuberant shrieks.

Miss Mowbry was so mortified that she fainted, and some sailors from the next table tried to revive her by throwing her skirts up over her head and fumbling with her corset. She came to her senses with a cheeky young rogue's hands groping around inside her flannel drawers as though he was looking for buried treasure. She almost slapped his head off and, red-faced and weeping, she forgot all about her duties as chaperone and immediately fled, beating a path for herself through the gay and laughing crowd with her trusty black umbrella.

I had never imagined that the Can-Can would be so risqué! I sat there dumbstruck watching the dancing beauties' black-stockinged legs rise and fall in time to the music, captivated by the coy and joyful smiles that lit up their faces as they swiveled their trim ankles in the air, making the laces on their black ankle boots dance. Their drawers were so sheer I was certain I could see dark triangles of hair beneath, and a blazing hot blush set my face aflame. But I could not look away. I sat there staring, mesmerized. And I felt the strangest sensation in the pit of my stomach, and lower down, a sweet, frightening fluttering, something I knew I should not be feeling, followed by a sudden sharp aching wetness between my thighs. Instantly I knew what it was. The pain that followed and nearly bent me double made it quite clear. In my distraction, I had completely forgotten the calendar, useless as it was with my maddeningly erratic monthly visitor. It might at least have given me some inkling when to expect its arrival so I could have strapped on a towel or at least worn a darker skirt!

The music soared in a dizzying crescendo and the dancers kicked and spun as pain gripped me in a series of stabbing, squeezing, clutching cramps, as if the pain were determined to wring every drop of blood from my womb. I knew the longer I sat there the worse it would be. Soon the blood would seep through my underclothes onto my pale blue satin skirt. *It's not going to get better; it's only going to get worse,* I kept telling myself over and over until the words began to blur and jumble and lose all meaning, yet I was powerless to make myself move, I just sat there staring at the dancers' tantalizingly veiled crotches and feeling shame flood my face as my nipples hardened. *I shouldn't be feeling this,* I told myself. *It isn't right; it isn't normal!* But I could not leave or look away.

I'm sure my anguish must have shown upon my face; it was all I could do not to burst into tears. I was so ashamed and confused I didn't know what to do. And someone *did* notice my distress. One of those mannish women approached me—an older woman, with deep lines etched around her eyes and mouth. Her thick, cropped, curly black hair was liberally peppered with gray and she wore an English tweed suit and a lemon-colored waistcoat and kid gloves and spats of the same vivid shade. She stubbed out her cigarette on Nellie's dessert plate, narrowly missing the remaining half of the chocolate éclair lying there leaking custard filling, and bent down as if to speak to me, but instead her lips lingeringly grazed mine. I was so stunned I could not react. I just sat there, blinking my eyes, surprised that my tears didn't start to boil against my flaming face.

"Surely it cannot be as bad as all that, mademoiselle?" she said kindly in heavily accented English. The same words Bridget used to always say to me!

I heard laughter all around me. Whether they were truly laughing at me, I do not know, but I felt like they were. I could not even turn and meet my companions' eyes; I did not want to see the expressions upon their faces. Oh, the horror! The *shame!*

Life surged back into my limbs and I bolted up and ran, plowing through the crowd as if I were running for my life, certain that everyone was staring at the big red stain blossoming on the back of my skirt.

I don't know how I got back to the hotel; somehow I found a cab. I filled the bathtub and scrubbed my skirts as best I could, then gave up and left them for the laundress. Then I tried to scrub the shame from my skin. I lay on the bathroom floor, huddled in my flower-sprigged nightgown upon the chilly tiles, with a towel pinned to the homemade blue calico waistband clutched tight between my thighs, curled up and bent double with cramps, and cried and cried as if my world were about to end and the sun would never rise and shine for me again. I don't know how long I lay there before I finally dragged myself to bed.

All that night I was troubled by dreams of beautiful Can-Can dancers, taunting me with their raised skirts and veiled crotches and breasts, their diaphanous blouses and drawers suddenly dissolving before my astonished eyes like sugar crystals in the rain, and mannish ladies who were not afraid to put their lips, and hands, on me even though we both knew it was the dancing beauties with their feminine frills and hourglass figures, delicious and decadent as French pastries, that I truly hungered for. But I had to make do. What else could I do when the beauties only tormented and teased? Reminding me with every shake of their pink skirts and glimpse of what lay beneath that they, these *glorious* creatures, were not for me. Beauty wants beauty and only suffers plain or ugly to touch it if the dazzle of dollar signs and diamonds, the promise of opulent rewards, blinds its eyes. Suddenly their ranks parted to reveal one who was all in gold with yellow feathers and diamond-tipped pins in her raven hair. She was wearing black silk stockings and golden slippers with high diamond-encrusted French heels that flashed with every movement of her dainty dancing feet. She teasingly shook her skirts right in my face, the white ruffles and yellow silk ribbons on her petticoats tickling my nose, and I looked up, startled, to see that it was Bridget Sullivan, rouged and painted as I had never seen her before. The gold paint on her eyelids twinkled when she winked at me. Without thinking, I flung myself at her feet and yanked her cobwebby white drawers down right in front of *everyone* at the Moulin Rouge and buried my face between her legs, wallowing and kissing with such a powerful, hungry passion that I had never in real, waking life experienced.

I woke up with a start, feeling so hot and wretched, shaky and weak, that I staggered into the bathroom with blood trickling down my legs and filled the tub with cold water and sat weeping and shivering in it until I turned blue as a penance to mortify my shameful flesh.

Nothing was ever said about the Moulin Rouge or the Can-Can: we were all too proper and polite to mention it. We never went back, and we left Paris soon afterward. On our last afternoon I defiantly went out alone to a dress shop and, flying boldly in the face of every word of fashion advice that had ever been given to me, bought the two gaudiest dresses I had ever owned—an iridescent raspberry silk that gave winks of purple and blue whenever I moved, and a caramel-and-apple-green-striped linen suit that came with a necktie and a straw boater with a matching band to wear with it. Without a comment or word of complaint I paid extra for rushed alterations as though it were the most natural thing in the world for me. I didn't care if Father dropped dead when he saw the bill.

Though Miss Mowbry and I could have done without the Riviera—we heard all sorts of unsavory tales about gamblers and suicides and crimes and affairs of passion—the others insisted. They were keen to see the grand casinos and parade about in their finest jewels and dresses with feathers in their hair pretending to be more sophisticated than they really were. So I let them lead me where they would. A certain ennui had by then stolen over me and I was too tired to protest; it simply wasn't worth it. My heart was no longer in this trip, but I didn't want to go home.

They had great fun—and a great laugh at my expense, I suppose—dressing me up like a life-sized doll. Albert—snootily pronounced *albear* without the *t*—a genuine French coiffeur, with a fussy, fastidious manner, washed and combed out my long red tresses, then coiled and braided and twisted them up into an intricate arrangement entwined with strands of blue-green glass beads and, as the pièce de résistance, a fan of tall peacock plumes at the back of my head, all to match my first—and only—French ball gown, a shimmering peacock satin that looked at once blue and green, with a long train and a daringly décolleté bodice covered in glass beads. A French corset, a *beautiful* Nile-green creation of whalebone sheathed inside satin embroidered with gold and azalea pink roses, that was really more like a medieval implement of torture in disguise cinched my waist so cruelly that it felt like the stem of a champagne glass and my bosom and hips overflowed above and below it. I was almost scared to sit down or breathe! For once, Anna laced *me* and I felt the impersonal, imperious touch of *her* hands flying over my skin like brisk white doves. I almost had to sit on my hands not to grab and kiss them when she used her very own pink puff to powder me. Coughing amidst clouds of rose-scented powder, I wanted to lay those lovely hands on my breasts and whisper "linger awhile!" And Carrie applied shimmering blue-green paint mixed with gold dust to my eyelids and, despite my protests that it wasn't ladylike, Nellie blackened my lashes and rouged my lips a vivid scarlet. When at last they led me to stand before the full-length mirror, I almost didn't know myself; I thought it was a stranger reflected in the glass.

We must have looked like a flock of tropical birds as we entered the casino, all painted and decked out in our bright, showy finery, not at all like the prim New England girls we really were—Carrie in her canary satin garnished with golden laurel leaves with a stuffed yellow bird in a gilded nest with blue crystal eggs perched at the pinnacle of her root-straining pompadour of butter-gold hair; Anna in amethyst and mauve satin garnished with silver-veined diamond-dusted dusky-blue lace with a stole of silver foxes lined in lilac satin about her bare shoulders, silver-gilt hair piled high in a pompadour Marie Antoinette would have envied agleam with blue and purple gems and pale pink and mauve plumes and silk roses; Nellie in sunset orange encrusted with gold and silver embroidery and gold lace swags and flounces; and me, trailing behind, looking like an exotic redheaded peacock. But they said it was all in fun, like going to a masquerade ball, and no one back home need ever know unless we chose to tell them about it.

I found it unexpectedly thrilling, watching the dice roll across the green felt, the cards being shuffled and dealt and played out, to win or lose, the stacks of multicolored chips that grew higher or lower or disappeared altogether, and the little silver ball going clackety-clack-clack as the red and black roulette wheel spun around, making or breaking fortunes.

None of us, except Anna, were brave enough to make a wager, but we all watched, entranced by the games of chance.

And the men! There were a few Americans and Englishmen, many older men, some accompanied by fawning, clinging women young enough to be their granddaughters, but most of them seemed an altogether different breed. Tall and dapper in immaculately tailored evening clothes, with black hair slicked back and shiny as patent leather reflecting the electric lights, they clicked their heels and bowed suavely over our hands. They were very bold in approaching us. Every one of them was a count, a duke, or an exiled prince, all impoverished, alas, each with a tale of woe they were eager to tell about family fortunes lost, castles burned to the ground by invading armies, and so forth.

Some of them hung on the arms of much older women, holding their fluffy little dogs while they played roulette, fetching them glasses of champagne, draping a fur wrap about their shoulders, leaning in close to nuzzle and kiss their ludicrously rouged withered apple cheeks or sagging necks and whisper in their bejeweled ears. Those who were not already attached to someone were very attentive to us all—even Miss Mowbry in her funereal black velvet and snowy needlepoint lace was approached by a "prince" young enough to have been her grandson!—asking us a myriad of questions about ourselves and our lives in America and who our fathers were and what they did for a living. One of them, a duke with hungry eyes, actually proposed to Nellie when he found out her father was the major shareholder in the Crystal Springs Bleach Company! My father sat on the board of directors too, but I didn't deem it worth mentioning; I just stood there gaping with all the rest as the duke dropped to his knees, grasping Nellie's hand like a lifeline, and began serenading her with "My Nelly's Blue Eyes." I supposed it could still be accounted a great compliment even though her eyes were in fact hazel.

I understood then that more games were being played here than cards or roulette. These impoverished "noblemen" were shopping for rich American wives. It was a game of barter—*my title to impress your American relatives and friends in exchange for access to your fortune.* This was a game of titles and bank accounts, not love.

I let the other girls chatter away and play what games they would and wandered out alone onto the terrace.

How eerily white the marbled terrace glowed in the silvery-blue moonlight, lined with Grecian nudes of hard men and soft women, standing there like frozen, vacant-eyed ghosts. I stood between the two, one hand resting upon each heart, and felt myself *desperately, hopelessly* torn, longing for a man's strong arms and hardness tempered by tenderness and chivalry, and a woman's softness, sympathy, and secret places.

I never understood why I should be tormented by such thoughts. My eyes were always open wide to the danger of desiring either sex. I liked men well enough; I always thrilled to the heroes of the romance novels I read and the actors strutting handsomely across the stage to sweep their lady love up in a passionate embrace and smother her with kisses. I would always gasp and sigh along with the other ladies in the audience and pretend it was me in the actors' arms. And tenors with beautiful voices soaring up as though upon divine wings to Heaven always sent me into weak-kneed raptures. Yet I was always a little afraid of them.

Caution *always* tempered my desire. Every day of a woman's life from the cradle to the grave, by word, deed, or example, it is drummed into our heads that men are our masters, that we are born and bred to serve them. A woman belongs first to her father and then to her husband—he rules the roost and controls the purse strings, and she is entirely in his power; any freedom she is given is his gift to her, *not* her God-given right. Most women accepted this without complaint or question, so why did it frighten me so?

I suppose I was afraid that I would end up with someone like Father. People change with the passage of time, and if I married in love I might wake up one morning to discover that my loving, adoring, and indulgent husband had suddenly turned as tight-fisted and begrudging as my father, and I couldn't bear that. I *wanted* love. I wanted romance. I *craved* the ecstatic physical expression of passion, to be held and touched and caressed, to feel like I belonged to someone body and soul, but the coldhearted legalities attached to the formalization of that sweet submission made me quail back in uncertainty and terror.

What was wrong with me? Was it a disease of the body or of the brain? Sometimes I thought of going veiled and giving a false name to consult a doctor in another city where no one knew me; the idea had even crossed my mind once or twice in Europe, but fear always got the better of me. What if the doctor considered my condition so dire that he called the police or summoned strong-armed men from a hospital and had me taken away in chains to wherever they put such troubled and afflicted people and I never saw the light of day again? I'd heard such horrible tales of ice-water douches, of women set in tubs of ice water to *freeze* the desire out of them, or else left lying wrapped like mummies in cold sheets until their skin turned blue. And then there were the stories about surgeries to cut lust from the brain or even where it reposed nestled amidst pink petals of flesh between a woman's legs. That *terrified* me! I'd rather take my secret to the grave than have it exposed and cut out of me.

I first became aware of this strange duality of desires in my nature when I was in school. I would watch my favorite teacher standing in front of the class and dream that I was invited to spend the night at her house, and sleep in her bed with her, and that before we retired she would bathe me, sometimes even sharing the tub with me, brush my hair until it crackled like a comforting fire, and help me into my nightgown; then we would cuddle in the warm bed and hold each other under the quilt and share chaste kisses all night long. As I grew older, the dream kisses lost their chastity to red-hot ardor, and evolved into fantasies in which she took a hand mirror and held it between my legs to patiently instruct me in the secrets of my womanhood, mirroring my own private, secret explorations. But I never revealed my crushes except in hot blushes and flustered stammers whenever I was called upon to read aloud or answer a question in class and in shy gifts of flowers, fruit, and candy I bought with my pocket money, sacrificing my own greed for sweets for the even sweeter thought of the pleasure they would give my secret love.

There was a girl my senior year of high school named Lulie Stillwell who lived up on The Hill in one of the grandest houses, like a princess surrounded by gilt, marble, brocades, satins, silks, velvets, crystal, polished oak, mahogany, and stained glass, with fresh flowers in every room every day. Rumor had it that the house was actually a genuine castle, bought and shipped piece by piece from somewhere in Europe—people used to get into sedately heated arguments about whether it came from England, France, Italy, Spain, or Germany—and the sprawling emerald lawn had been imported from England rolled up and carried aboard a ship and then unfurled like a carpet when it reached Fall River. People had come from all over Fall River to watch them roll that lawn out just like a big green carpet, so I knew that was true, I'd heard so many tell of it.

Lulie looked just like Snow White stepped out of the pages of a storybook—ebony hair, skin white as snow, lips red as blood, eyes like regal sapphires. She was *almost* my friend. She invited me out for ice cream and afternoon strolls a few times, and to sit beside her and listen to the band playing in the park. Sometimes she was so moved by the music that she clutched my hand. It made my heart swell with pride to know that she had chosen me over any of the other girls from The Hill. Addie Whip, Minnie Macomber, Evy, Ella, and Annabelle Sheen, Nellie Shore, Rachel Almay, Carrietta

Wold, Charlotte Grosvenor, Lotta Cork, Fannie Huntington, Alicia May Covell, Cora and Cornelia Stratford, and Sadie, Alma, Fidelia, and Minerva Remington, and my own cousins Anna and Carrie Borden would all have given their eyeteeth to walk out with Lulie Stillwell, but she had chosen *me—Lizzie Borden!*

Once we went to visit the little museum of curiosities housed in the back room of Gay's, the town's only photography studio, and saw a hen with pink feathers that laid colored eggs, a pair of dancing turkeys, a two-headed snake preserved in a glass jar, a trout that had grown a white fur coat to protect itself from the cold that was a specimen of a species found in a singularly chilly lake somewhere in Arkansas, a dead baby with one head but two faces, and, rarest of all, a young mermaid who must have perished in agonizing pain, her features, blackened by the preservatives the taxidermist had used, were so grotesquely contorted, as though frozen in the midst of a bloodcurdling scream.

During our walks we would always stop to listen to Old Black Joe the roving balladeer sing "Down in a Coal Mine" and "Mother in the Cold, Cold Ground," and buy a paper cone filled with gooey pink or vanilla taffy from Taffy Harry, who roamed the sidewalks in his red-and-white-striped apron selling his wares from a tray hung round his neck while his little black and tan dog barked and ran circles around Harry's ankles. Lulie and I would share our taffy, giggling as we tried to see how far we could stretch it between us, always trying, but never quite succeeding, in stretching it across the street.

I used to dream she was lying beside me in bed at night, brow to brow, bosom to bosom, lips barely a breath apart, sharing secrets and kisses sweeter than vanilla and strawberry taffy. I was *wild* to touch her the way I touched myself beneath the covers; just the fantasy left me flushing and feverish. After the circus came to town I dreamed of her in pink tights, dressed in silver spangles, with feathers in her hair, swinging on a trapeze or balanced on the back of a prancing horse. And when I read in the newspaper about a *bal-de-masque* up on The Hill where all the guests had come costumed as characters from Mother Goose Rhymes for weeks afterward Lulie appeared as Little Bo Peep in my dreams.

If anyone had asked me when I was seventeen, I would have said the most wonderful day of my life was when Johnny Hiram, who was sweet on Lulie, walked into Negus' Confectionery and saw Lulie and me sitting at one of the little round white tables draped with pink and white gingham, giggling with our heads close together over a big bowl of vanilla and strawberry ice cream drenched in chocolate sauce. He completely lost his temper because she was spending time with me instead of him and shoved the bowl into the lap of my new powder-blue skirt with the elegant knife pleats—the one I had impetuously ordered without consulting Father; I was that *desperate* to impress Lulie. Johnny's face turned red as the cherries on top of our ice cream and he called me a "*stupid, fat heifer!*"

Lulie leapt up and slapped Johnny so hard I'm surprised his head didn't spin, then *flew* to my side, flung herself down on her knees before me, and, with tears of outrage glistening like a crystal veil over the brilliant sapphires of her eyes, swiped futilely at my skirt. But the flimsy napkin was no match against the melting mound that was already chilling my hot thighs.

Lulie took my hand and said, "Come home with me, Lizzie." And I did. I would have risen from my deathbed and followed her to the ends of the earth if she had asked me to!

Her parents were away, traveling in Europe, so we had the rare privilege of her mother's opulent rose marble bath. It was big enough for four, perhaps even more; had I been more worldly back then my fertile imagination would have surely conjured up images of delightfully decadent Roman orgies with slick and slippery naked beauties filling that rosy tub. While her maid—a *real French maid from Paris, not* a dirt-common, ignorant Irish Maggie!—divested me of my clothes, Lulie nonchalantly stripped off hers, leaving them where they fell for the maid to pick up later, and stepped into the tub to show me "the best part": how the water flowed out of the mouths of golden fishes set at various heights into the wall. It was one of the first shower baths in Fall River.

While I stood there stark naked, trying to cover my flabby breasts with one hand and my coarse frizzy red bush with the other, Lulie, imperious as an alabaster princess, sent my clothes away with her maid. To be laundered "as good as new or Johnny Hiram will pay for new!" she promised with a furious toss of her curls. "I don't know what got into that boy, unless it was the Devil, doing such a thing to you!"

I nodded dumbly. I couldn't summon words to answer; all I could think about was the wonderful and terrifying fact that I was standing there in the midst of that beautiful pink and gold bathroom stark naked in front of Lulie Stillwell and that she was naked too. It was like a dream come true; I was so excited I could hardly breathe. I was sweating profusely, like an overworked plow horse, my armpits were drenched, and I imagined the sweat rushing down my back like a raging rank waterfall, and there was a silky hot slickness between my tightly clenched thighs. I was sure my unfortunate habit of flushing made me look like a fat tomato that had suddenly sprouted a stout body and four thick, sturdy limbs. And I was afraid Lulie would hear my knees knocking.

Lulie looked like a delicate ebony-haired water nymph standing there against the rose marble and gilt fish with water pouring over her shoulder and rushing down, like a waterfall, between her little pink and white breasts. I wanted to suckle those pink tips like a greedy infant; I knew they would taste as sweet as little cakes.

Flaming-faced, I stood and stared, like a person struck dumb or hypnotized, at the beads of water spangling the lush bush of black hair between her white thighs like little crystals.

But Lulie just smiled, seemingly oblivious to my lust. After all, she'd been in her skin her whole life and by seventeen she knew she was beautiful and was accustomed to accepting admiration as her due. But she wasn't blind; she never had any trouble seeing the blackboard even in the back row. Surely she could see how red my face was! She had set me on fire! I couldn't understand it! Was she stone-blind to my embarrassment or merely a model of impeccable breeding? She was in her element, and I was a fish out of water, gasping and dying, in secret ecstasy, on a perilous rocky shore. And then Lulie laughed and reached out for my hand and pulled me into the tub, and into her arms, so close that our bellies brushed and red mingled with black down below. I'll never forget the way Lulie giggled and smiled! There was no music sweeter than her laughter to my ears!

In that instant, I forgot my shame, and everything else, except that we were together, touching, naked as pagans in that sumptuous pink bath, with golden fishes spewing warm water decadently down on us, while our bodies glided slickly against each other and we took turns bathing each other with a cake of pink perfumed soap imported from Paris molded in the shape of a perfect prize-winning rose. Before I went home, I would slip that soap into my pocket, to take home as a memento of the day my dreams came true and I shared a bath with Lulie Stillwell. I used to take it out and bury my nose in the heart of that pink rose with the bath-blunted petals and dream that I was blissfully burying my face between Lulie's legs, nuzzling her own pink petals, making her melt.

Afterward, our bodies still flushed pink from the hot bath we had shared, we waged a playful battle, arming ourselves with fat white powder puffs that we repeatedly plunged into the pretty porcelain bowls on Mrs. Stillwell's dressing table whenever the need arose. They were painted all around with swirls of gilt ribbon and pink roses and lavender blossoms to identify the fragrance of the powder within, nothing at all like the common tins sold at Sargent's. We ran about the room, screeching and whooping like naked savages, climbing like nimble mountain goats over the wide quilted pink satin expanse of the bed, playfully pummeling each other with the fragrant puffs, coughing and giggling in the dense white clouds of scent that swirled around us like the sweetest snow and settled on our heads like the white powdered wigs of eighteenth-century courtiers.

When I paused to cough and sneeze and swipe the powder from my lashes, Lulie lunged and tackled me and we fell as one onto the big bed, screaming with laughter.

Did I only imagine it, or as we writhed in a welter of naked limbs and tickling fingers amidst heavenly clouds of perfumed powder did she playfully rub her pussy against mine as her fingers glided swiftly over my breasts, tickling them like the keys of the piano Lulie played so exquisitely? I like to believe the billowing powder was a Heaven-sent disguise to hide a desire we both secretly harbored but were too ashamed and afraid to admit even to each other.

We created such a ruckus that Mrs. Morner, the Swedish house-keeper, came rushing upstairs to see what all the commotion was about. She staggered in the doorway with her hand pressed against her heart and stared aghast as Lulie, the "darling child" she had known from birth, triumphantly straddled me on the bed in a cloud of perfumed powder, plying her puff like a demented confectioner over my florid breasts while I giggled and writhed beneath her, my tickling fingers groping blindly over her bosom, lingering for a sweet fleeting instant on her nipples, like little hard pink candies, and tried to rub against her in such a way that, if I needed to, I could afterward insist was unintentional. But inside I was secretly fighting with all my might the almost overpowering urge to master-fully grab her wrists and roll on top of her and *grind* my loins against hers.

Mrs. Morner fell back against the door and gave a scandalized screech, then proceeded to deliver a sharp tongue-lashing de-nouncing our "lewd horseplay."

"Shame on the both of you, running about naked as heathens! You're supposed to be decent, God-fearing young *ladies!*" she cried, and ordered us back to Lulie's room to "put some clothes on!"

Sheepishly, daring sly, sideways glances at each other and sput-tering and stifling our giggles as best we could, we wrapped our-selves in Mrs. Stillwell's big plush pink towels—thankfully she was a woman with ample hips and breasts; otherwise they would have been too scanty to cover me—and filed dutifully past Mrs. Morner with our eyes downcast and down the sapphire, amethyst, and gold floral carpeted corridor to Lulie's blue watered-silk bedroom where pink net water lilies, their petals sewn with shimmering tiny pink beads, bloomed upon the bedspread.

I perched nervously on the edge of a quilted blue satin armchair by the pink marble fireplace, the towel clenched tightly over my breasts, frowning at the way the fat under my arms spilled over and feeling suddenly awkwardly self-conscious of my nakedness as I watched Lulie dress.

Lulie was slender and delicate boned even without her corset, and not even her dressing gowns would fit me, so I had no choice but to stay as I was until her maid returned with my clothes. When Lulie stepped into her frilly white lace and ribbon trimmed batiste drawers I noticed the white powder still clinging, like powdered sugar, to her licorice-black bush. When she lifted her leg I caught a glimpse of deep pink and a wave of hot desire threatened to knock me off my seat. I wanted her to stay as she was, naked with me, to frolic and play some more, but I knew instinctively that the moment had passed and it would only be embarrassing and awkward if I tried to bring it back. So I turned my flaming face to the window and made some dull-witted remarks about the weather and how beautiful the garden was and when Lulie asked me to lace her stays my hands trembled like an old woman's.

Then came the disastrous day when we went horseback riding.

I was so excited when she invited me that I told the teacher I had my monthly illness and didn't feel well and rushed home to beg Father to buy me a riding habit; I had been too ashamed to tell Lulie that I didn't have one and barely knew how to ride. I dreamed of something dashing and romantic like Nell Gwyn or some other heroine of history would have worn, gilt-braided burnt-orange, cinnamon, crimson, or bottle-green velvet, and I simply *must* have a wide-brimmed hat with a fluffy cloud-white ostrich plume held in place by a magnificent jeweled brooch as big as a lady's clenched fist. And leather gloves and a riding crop and boots of course! I forgot all about the reality my mirror would show me—a plump, frizzy red-haired, florid and freckle faced and heavy-jawed, broad-shouldered, stout-waisted girl of seventeen—and imagined myself as one of the beautiful, elegant, poised, wasp-waisted ladies pictured in the pages of *Godey's Lady's Book* perched sidesaddle atop high-stepping steeds as they regally waved to one another, the long skirts of their riding habits cascading like waterfalls over the lean, muscled flanks of their mounts.

Father scoffed at my pretensions, my "silly notions" that he blamed on my reading matter: "Velvet riding habits and feathered hats, I never heard such folderol in my life!" Plain black or brown broadcloth, he said, was what respectable women wore when they went riding. "Only those spoiled and silly ninnies up on The Hill who don't know the value of a dollar wear anything else," he continued, and went on to declare that their fathers were all "jackasses who don't have the sense to rein their daughters in. It's their backs that need a riding crop, not the horses they ride!"

Abby—still trying to be my friend—tried to soften the blow by buying a reddish-brown broadcloth that would "work wonderfully" with my hair, and making me a new shirtwaist of white eyelet with thin bands of bright orange satin ribbon and wide white ruffles at the collar and cuffs and trimming my otherwise boring brown hat with a lovely swathe of rust-colored veiling and a dainty spray of colorful silk flowers she had been saving for something special "just like this—my Lizzie's first riding habit," she beamed as she drew me close and kissed my cheek.

We only had three days and Abby stayed up late and worked long hours every day at the sewing machine and doing the more delicate work like finishing the buttonholes by hand so that everything would be ready in time for our Saturday ride. But when Saturday finally came and I stood before the mirror I burst into tears and almost howled the house down. I lashed out at my reflection with my newly purchased riding crop and boots, then flung myself sobbing onto my bed, kicking the mattress and pummeling it with my fists, because I was so ugly. The tailored riding habit made me look even more broad shouldered and mannish and did *nothing* for my stocky figure and florid complexion. I looked *nothing* like the smiling sidesaddle beauties in the ladies' magazines! Lulie was *sure* to think I was ugly and wouldn't want to be my friend anymore, and I couldn't blame her. *I* didn't even want to be seen with me! Not even the loan of Abby's mother-of-pearl peony wedding brooch could ease my torment.

Sidesaddle on an ebony steed from her father's prizewinning pedigreed stable, Lulie looked every inch a princess in deep-blue velvet to match the precious gems of her eyes, with antiqued silver buttons set with sapphires, and there was an ostrich plume, just like the one I had dreamed of, curling back gracefully over the brim of her hat, like a fluffy white cloud. Her jacket, edged in silver braid, cinched tightly in at the smallest point of her perfect hourglass waist, then flowed out gracefully over her hips. Her hair was all in ringlets, and a brooch shaped like a bouquet with flowers formed of pearls and sapphires, adorned her throat, beneath which spilled a jabot of the finest milk-white lace.

I stood there feeling lumpy and miserable, and ugly as a fat brown toad, beside the unimpressive dun-colored mare Father had grudgingly hired from the livery stable for me. I wished the ground would open wide and swallow me before Lulie's sapphire eyes flashed cold blue fire and imperiously banished ugly, unworthy me from her exalted and elegant presence. But to my immense relief, when she saw me Lulie just smiled, and I saw no condescension or pity in her ruby lips or sapphire eyes. I wanted to jump for joy and throw my arms around her and kiss her a hundred times.

As we rode away together I prayed for a sudden downpour that would drench us to the skin, sending us scurrying back to the perfumed bacchanal of the rose marble bath again.

When we stopped to rest, the beautiful dream became a terrible, ugly nightmare in real waking life and broad daylight. We stood together under a big shady tree, leaning against its massive trunk, laughing and hugging each other the way girlfriends do. I dreamed of laying her down on the warm emerald grass and lifting her sapphire skirts, the elegant French heels of her boots tangling in the snow-white ruffles of her drawers as I tugged them off. I impulsively put my hands around that tiny blue velvet waist and pulled her closer, reveling in the feel of her bosom brushing against mine, and then—I couldn't help myself!—I *kissed* her, deep and lingeringly, the way I imagined it was done in all the novels that I had read, only in their pages it was men who always did the kissing.

But Lulie didn't swoon and melt in my arms or cling to me like passionate ivy the way the heroines in romances always did. She shoved me away so hard I fell and barked both my palms against the tree's ugly, gnarled roots. I will *never* forget the *disgust* burning in her blue eyes as she wiped her mouth with the back of her hand

and then her hand on the skirt of her riding habit. She *glared* down at me as though she *hated* me, and I felt loathsome and small, like something ugly and pathetic she wanted to step on.

"You're a wicked, evil creature, Lizzie Borden, and I *hate* you!" she cried. Each word was like a hammer on my heart.

We rode back toward town in silence. I was so afraid Lulie would tell, that I would be ruined and everyone would laugh at me and I would replace that unfortunate boy who ate paste, though at eighteen he was surely old enough to know better, as the butt of all my classmates' jokes. I couldn't bear to see the shame and disgust in Father's, Emma's, and Abby's eyes, and to hear their voices speaking of sin, shame and disgrace. I was afraid doctors would come, maybe even priests, and I would be sent away, to a madhouse or one of those quiet, secluded sanitariums in the country, and given some hellish treatment. Possibly they would cut open my head and try to remove the evil thoughts they would say the Devil had planted there like black roses and I would never be allowed in civilized company again for fear that I would be unable to control my unnatural urges and would disgrace myself again. I would be shunned like a leper. People would say I couldn't be trusted around pretty girls. Maybe I would be locked in the attic the way they did madwomen in novels. I would spend the rest of my life in darkness and shackles, barely kept alive on stale crusts of bread and tepid water.

Terror stole my breath away; I couldn't breathe! Then everything went black and I felt myself falling. My head struck a stone like the clapper of a bell and for an instant I was excruciatingly aware of the most *terrible* pain radiating from the back of my head all the way down to the bottom of my spine and a loud ringing in my ears. I awakened lying on my own bed with Father hovering anxiously over me and Emma fighting Abby to assist Dr. Bowen in undressing me until he finally shoved Emma out the door and sent her downstairs to the kitchen to boil some water just to get her out of the way. I was bruised and bleeding in several places and ached all over and kept drifting in and out of consciousness, yet my anguished brain kept keening, *Lulie doesn't love me!*

I wanted to *die* when, between them, Abby and Dr. Bowen wrestled my corset and chemise off, carelessly baring my pudgy pink breasts with nipples like hard tawny-peach buttons before Father's eyes. No one even thought of asking him to leave the room! I *tried,* but they dismissed me as delirious. Father helped Abby hold my arms down when I tried to cover myself, wincing and weeping in humiliation and the pain that shot through my torso like lightning bolts when Dr. Bowen's prodding revealed two, possibly three, broken ribs. When the doctor pulled off my drawers and rolled me over and exposed my bare bottom, jabbed with his index finger, and, in answer to my pain-filled scream, opined that I had fractured my tailbone I *knew* there was no escaping shame; in one form or another, it would be with me all my life. And I would *always* be afraid. The only consolation was that at least this was a private disgrace, in my bedroom, surrounded by family, away from the bullies and merciless queens of the schoolyard, and the blue blaze of hate emanating from beautiful Lulie's eyes.

I never went back to school. For a few weeks the teachers sent my homework, but I didn't feel like doing it, so after a while they didn't bother anymore. By the time I had fully recovered there were only two months left till graduation. I was smart enough, I could have caught up, but I couldn't bring myself to go back. I just couldn't bear to face Lulie, to see her glance spitefully at me with that blue blaze of hate in her eyes, then lean over, cup her hand to her mouth, and whisper mean-spirited remarks about me into a friend's ear. Word would rapidly spread and soon they would *all* be laughing at me, all those uppity girls from up on The Hill. So I dropped out. Father bought me my class ring anyway; he said I deserved it after what I had been through.

A few weeks after she wore a white chiffon dress to the graduation ceremony, Lulie Stillwell put on another white dress and married Johnny Hiram. He was the rich, tall, dark, and handsome boy in the faux medieval mansion next door, perfectly cast to play Prince Charming to Lulie's Snow White and live happily ever after with her in a house grand as a castle that was a wedding gift from her father furnished floor to ceiling, with Johnny's father's money paying for all the beautiful things they would buy on their six-month European honeymoon.

Everyone said she was the most beautiful bride Fall River had ever seen in white Duchesse satin, priceless pearls, and yards of heirloom lace, lace and pearl and diamond encrusted cathedral-length train and veil, with an exquisite coronet woven of silk orange blossoms, diamonds, and pearls crowning the midnight glory of her hair. I still have a picture of her in that beautiful dress I cut out of *The Fall River Globe;* I never did find the courage to go to Gay's Photography Studio and inquire about purchasing a print. I was afraid they would have to ask Lulie's permission first and, of course, she would say *No.*

There were a full dozen bridesmaids, all girls from The Hill, in shimmering shell-pink satin overlaid with chiffon, and broad-brimmed hats laden with roses, ruffles, and ribbons, each with a single strand of delicate blush-pink pearls around her throat and a pink shell cameo framed in gold and pearls at her breast as a gift from the bride. *It wasn't fair! I* should have been one of them! Lulie should have kissed *me* and pinned a cameo on *my* breast that lovely wedding morning; I *deserved* it more than any of the girls she had chosen. *I* loved her more than any of them did, including the groom!

A few weeks later I would happen across Flossie Grew suffering a nosebleed outside Gifford's Jewelry & Fine Gifts, and when I stopped to assist her I also helped myself to the cameo on the silk-braid-bordered lapel of her fashionable moss-green linen suit. It wasn't *really* stealing; I was only taking back what rightfully belonged to me.

For years to come, I would lie back on my bed, Lulie's wedding picture propped up on the table beside me where I could see Fall River's most beautiful bride, and hold that precious pink cameo cupped tenderly in my palm, while I touched myself and dreamed of Lulie smiling at me, radiant with love, not burning with contempt—*that* was the way it *should* have been! I already knew the ghost of the carefree, bewitching black-haired girl who had straddled me, giggling, rubbing, and tickling, amidst clouds of rose-and-lavender-perfumed powder—like the phantom petals of bridal flowers showering down on us or a wedding veil to cloak our naked lust in the respectable garb of girlish horseplay—would haunt me for the rest of my life.

I sent Lulie a porcelain candy dish with a pattern of blue love-birds as a wedding gift, but she never acknowledged it. Everyone else got a thank-you note, written on the new Mrs. Hiram's gilt-bordered and monogrammed cream stationery, but not me. I was so upset I wanted to jab her eyes out with one of the plethora of sterling silver pickle forks she was rumored to have received from her poorer friends and relations. I wanted to hurt her as much as she had hurt me. How *dare* she ignore me when all I had done was love her? *Was that really such a crime?*

The years passed. I became an old maid. I lost hope and gave up on love. I convinced myself it was only the stuff of stories or a rare and glorious miracle, a gift from God given only to the most beau-tiful and undeserving, pretty girls with vivacious personalities that sparkled like champagne and indulgent, selfless fathers who wanted them to be happy and were willing to let them go instead of keeping them chained and bound to be the comfort of their par-ents' old age. And then, like a miracle, the answer to my prayers, Bridget Sullivan had come dancing into my life with her twinkling green eyes, musical Irish brogue, and ready smile. Even an ocean apart I could still hear her singing:

> *Oh, dem golden slippers,*
> *Oh, dem golden slippers*
> *Golden slippers I'se going to wear*
> *Because they look so neat.*

> *Oh, dem golden slippers,*
> *Oh, dem golden slippers,*
> *Golden slippers I'se going to wear*
> *To walk the golden street.*

The evening breeze blew me out of my reverie, back to the hedonistic Riviera and out of the past, and I snatched my hands away from the statues, startled to see how far they had strayed down the marble bodies. My face flaming, I glanced guiltily around, hoping no one had seen me standing there between those marble nudes with my head thrown back, and my eyes closed, caressing them as I remembered Lulie. Anyone would think me pathetic or mad, perhaps both. I shivered and wished I had brought my sealskin cape. Not only my chilled flesh but also my modesty craved it—my nipples were standing up, unmistakably, achingly prominent, beneath my satin bodice, *begging* for a lover's attention like a dog for a bone.

Suddenly a shoulder brushed brusquely against my own and a tall young man in evening clothes walked past me. He stopped at the railing and took something from his pocket. It was a *pistol!* As he raised it and pressed the barrel to his temple I ran and caught hold of his arm. I was too naïve to realize that this was a common ploy certain men used to prey upon gullible women, to extract funds and favors from them. I honestly thought I was saving a human life.

He had lost all his money at the roulette wheel, he said; he had nothing left to live for. I was startled to suddenly find him in my arms, weeping on my shoulder, and to feel his warm, salty tears dripping down between my breasts. And then he kissed me, bruising hard and urgently upon my mouth at the same time as his hands found my breasts and began squeezing and kneading them. It was *nothing* like the books I had read had led me to believe it would be, and not at all like the tender, treasured kiss from my architect. It was at once *brutal* and *exciting* and for the life of me I couldn't make up my mind whether to order him to stop or sigh breathlessly and whisper, *Darling, never stop!*

Suddenly my back was against a cold white wall, and his lips, hot and hungry, were on mine, and his questing tongue was endeavoring to part them as his hands gathered up my skirts and roved beneath where no one except me had ever dared touch before. His passion frightened me even as it stirred and thrilled me, but Fear was the victor, and I pushed him from me and fled.

My heart was beating like a voodoo drum. My stays were so tight, I felt certain I would faint. But I didn't. The panic passed, but not so quickly the pangs of passion. As soon as I was safe back inside the casino, I castigated myself for being such a coward. I wanted to turn and go back, to give in, surrender and melt beneath those hot lips and ardent hands. But it was too late. By the time I had tiptoed tremulously to the threshold leading out onto the terrace and peeped out he was already gone. And so was my purse, but I didn't notice that until after we were safely back at the hotel. I told Anna that in all the excitement I must have laid it down somewhere and it was likely long gone by now. Fortunately, Anna, giddy from the golden wine, was feeling generous and gave me $100 she had won at roulette and told me to dry my eyes and not worry a moment more about it.

The next night, our last before leaving, we were back at the casino despite my protests that once was enough. I submitted to the coiffeur's finicky attentions one more time and was painted and laced back into the breathless, bone-crushing embrace of the corset and too-tight peacock satin gown. Though Carrie and Anna sniffed derisively about appearing in public two nights in a row in the same gown, I would not wear my peach taffeta, the only other ball gown I owned; I would not have another man's hand touch where my beloved's had rested against my waist when we waltzed. I would not let the slick men lounging like lizards around the casino sully my sweet and tender memories, or my dress, with their selfish, self-interested caresses.

I boldly ventured out onto the terrace again, both hoping and dreading that I would meet that young man and he would take me in his arms again and this time not let me go until *he* was ready to. I shouldn't have, yet I felt drawn, pulled as if I were one half of two magnets facing each other. I wanted to be held and touched again. I wanted to be stirred. There was an indescribable ache within me that I wanted to appease, even though it scared me, because this was my body alone being assailed by these aching yearnings; it had *nothing* at all to do with my head or my heart.

Then there he was—locked in a smoldering embrace with a brassy-haired buxom beauty in gold brocade blazing from the diadem on her head to the hem of her gown with a fortune in diamonds. A pistol lay forgotten at their feet. A diamond bracelet that must have slipped from her wrist dangled from his pocket. Startled by my abrupt intrusion, they broke apart. She at least had the good breeding to blush, but he gave me a scornful look, a lifted eyebrow accompanied by a smirk that seemed to say *you had your chance* as he bent to retrieve his weapon. He put it in his pocket, then took his companion's arm and led her back inside the casino. From the doorway I watched her give him money to place a bet. I turned my back then and wandered, alone, back onto the terrace, burning with a fever that I alone couldn't quench.

It was a loss, and yet it wasn't. His ardent mouth and roving hands had finesse, yes, he knew *exactly* what to do because he had done it so many times before, but there was no magic, no *true* feeling or connection of the soul; it was nothing at all like that day at Glastonbury under the thorn tree. He did not touch my heart, only my body. I was lonely and couldn't be with the one I loved, and that—my wretched longing loneliness—I think had more to do with these sudden wanton spasms of lust than anything else. I wanted love, I just never knew how much until I left Fall River, and I must find a way to quench, or *kill,* these improper passions before I did something to disgrace myself, something unforgivable, with no hope of redemption.

Suddenly there was a rumble of thunder and a zigzag of silver lightning lit up the darkened sky. I nearly jumped out of my skin, then laughed at my own foolishness. The rain started to fall, at first a stray plop and then a steady drip-drip; then the sky ripped open like a piece of cheap midnight-blue calico filled with a million silvery needles. This rain was hard and violent, stabbing into my skin until I thought it would surely bruise me. But I didn't care. I threw back my head and opened my arms to it, flinging them wide, not caring that my corset pinched and my breasts jutted and strained alarmingly against my bodice, like a glass of milk about to overflow. I wantonly, brazenly opened myself to it and let it soak me to the skin and lick the paint from my face. I wanted to be washed clean, to feel fresh and new. I abandoned myself to the rain as if it were my lover, surrendered, and let it cool, wash away, and drown my fevered passion.

As a cold wind blew the rain sideways the strand of blue-green glass beads twined like a sleeping snake in my hair broke and, blown by the wind, went skittering and clattering all over the terrace. The fan of peacock plumes fell from my hair as it came tumbling down and I laughed as I watched it fly away like a tropical bird fleeing a hurricane.

My gown was ruined; it, like my hair, hung down straight, heavy with the weight of water, plastered to my body like a second skin. The skirt slapped and wrapped itself around my limbs so that I staggered like one intoxicated and nearly fell more than once as I made my way back into the bright lights of the casino, dragging my long, sopping-wet train along behind me like a mermaid with a crippled tail. I knew my companions would be *horrified* at the sight and sad, soggy state of me, but it was worth it, and the price of the Paris gown. I had needed this rain in a way that I could never hope to explain.

But I paid another price for "my foolishness," "my wanton frolic in the rain." I came down with a *dreadful* cold that I had great difficulty shaking off despite the plethora of pills and potions Miss Mowbry forced down my throat. But sunny Italy was a balm, a godsend, like a tonic for the soul to me. I sat in the sun, despite the risk of freckles, and let it bake the illness out of me.

The signora at the *pensione* where we stayed in Naples was a great, round, motherly woman and she instantly conceived a great liking for me. She plied me with food—plates heaped high with pasta covered with hearty, robust sauces, which I, at her encouragement, devoured with gusto. I fell in love with the food—the pastas swimming in rich sauces, breads, cakes, and, most of all, *Capezzoli di Venere,* the exquisite bonbons called "Nipples of Venus." Roman chestnuts enrobed in white chocolate and brandied sugar with a daub of dark chocolate sitting atop the dome just like a woman's nipple, they tasted simply *divine,* and I could never get enough of them. I felt so daring and decadent when I cast off my shoes and stockings and all the manifold layers of my increasingly tight, stifling, binding, and confining clothes and lay back on the chaise longue in my room, naked as God made me, and languorously suckled and licked those divine candies. Sometimes I rose and went to stand rebelliously naked, sweaty and pink, with my hair all a-frizz, and my face and fingertips all stained with chocolate, before the looking glass and called myself a "greedy pig" before I threw a shawl over my reflection in disgust, then went right back to my chaise and chocolates, already knowing that as soon as they were gone I would throw on a robe and send the signora's boy out for more.

I was getting fat; there was no pretending otherwise. I cared and yet I didn't. Eating brought me a kind of comfort, and I began to eat more and more, to try to fill up the emptiness inside me. Even when I was no longer hungry I kept on eating, hoping I would eventually be full, even though I knew in my heart that it was not food I was craving. No mere food, no matter how enticing and delicious, could slake the hunger in my soul, but I kept on hoping, and eating.

The signora smilingly helped me let out the seams of all my dresses. She kissed away my tears when she took the measure of my waist and assured me that *real* men liked a woman with meat on her bones who knew how to appreciate good food.

"A woman with a lusty appetite is worth her weight in gold," she said with a bawdy, knowing chuckle, "because a wise man knows she will bring her appetite with her to bed."

I saw the ruins at Pompeii by moonlight alone but for a hired guide who was as annoying as a fly; he just kept buzzing around me talking all the while. I was tempted to dismiss him so I would be free to contemplate all the beauty spread out before me in blessed silence; besides, he only made me feel lonelier, and angry at him for not being the one I wanted most of all. I dreamed of my architect, of having him there, to kiss in the moonlight, and enthrall me with his tales of history. I *yearned* to have him hold my hand and guide me through Italy, explaining everything we saw, like why that tower in Pisa leaned, opening my eyes to all its wonders. I wanted *him,* not a guide or a book, to tell me.

In Rome, while the others were busy buying dresses, I visited churches, cathedrals, palaces, art galleries, and museums and went to the opera almost every night. Even though I could not understand the words, the passion of the singers and the beauty of their voices—lilting, soaring, cascading!—never failed to move me to tears. I'm sure I must have spent $100 throwing roses at the feet of tenors. But I didn't care. I was enraptured by the art, especially Raphael's *Sistine Madonna.* I could have gazed for hours upon the various Madonnas, cherubs, saints, and angels; even the devils fascinated me. I purchased a number of photographs and engravings to take home with me, but they were all in black and white when I longed most for color—*rich, vivid, vibrant, living color!* I loved the Sistine Chapel; I craned my neck and stared up at the ceiling until my neck ached, not daring to do what I really wanted to do and lie down upon the floor and gaze up at it to my lonely heart's content. And I toured St. Peter's twice, again alone; I did not care for the brash, noisy, but well-meaning chatter of the guides, they only made my heart ache worse.

In Venice I drifted for hours, listless and glassy-eyed, lost in daydreams and lusty longings, in a gondola, barely conscious of the Italian songs the gondoliers sang to me in their decadent dark baritone or sensual tenor voices, blind and impervious to the gorgeous scenery going by that I, most likely, would never see again.

Then it was back to Liverpool in bustle and haste with our evergrowing mountain of luggage to catch the next sailing of the SS *Scythia.*

There was a letter waiting for me—a letter that made my heart sing! He could not be there to bid me *bon voyage* on my homeward-bound journey, but he was still thinking of me fondly. *Fondly!* Thinking of *me!* I almost died of delight!

I stood at the railing as the ship pulled out to sea; this time it was not raining, and the sun was shining down on me like a golden blessing straight from God. When England was but a mere speck too small for me to see I went back to the cabin I shared with Anna and lay down on my bed and read his letter again and again until I had committed every precious, wonderful word to memory. And then I wept, but I was smiling through my tears, like sunshine through rain. A woman's heart and hopes are contradictory things; no wonder so many men take such a dim view of feminine constancy and think us fickle and contrary. "La donna è mobile" indeed!

Chapter 3

Returning to Fall River and reentering my father's house felt just like being found guilty of a terrible crime and being sentenced to live out the rest of my life in a dreary prison with no amenities to make life pleasant or even bearable.

The first thing that greeted me when I stepped through the front door of 92 Second Street was the smell of mincemeat. Abby was in the kitchen baking a pie and I could hear her singing as she bustled about the kitchen, her voice mingling with Bridget's rhapsodizing about "the golden slippers I'se goin' to wear to walk the golden street."

There were times when I thought hating Abby was more trouble than it was worth just to keep the peace with Emma, and this was one of them.

Emma was thirteen when our mother died; she had already built up a treasure trove of memories, and was ready to resent *any* woman Father married. And if I forgot, as any child would, and shared a smile or a laugh with Abby, Emma *always* made sure I regretted it; she would call me "a traitor to our mother's memory," punish me with a savage pinch, and refuse to speak to me for *days* afterward. And in the early years of their marriage, she was always quick to remind me that Abby was still young enough to bear children. She was old enough to make it dangerous for herself, that was certainly true, but she still bled every month. Father had always wanted a son; I was supposed to be the boy he always wanted. But if Abby gave him the son our mother never could . . . he—that boy, Abby's greedy, suckling male piglet—would inherit *everything,* what should, by right, be ours, and another male would follow in Father's footsteps and have control of us until the day we died. God we could trust to be merciful, but *NEVER* the son of Abby and Andrew Borden!

Emma made me see all the possibilities; she relentlessly hammered them into my head and made sure I *never* forgot that Father could at *any* time change his will, and even if Abby never gave him a son—and she never did, and within a few years all possibility of that had ceased—he could still leave everything to her and make us beholden to "The Cow" for every blessed little thing all the days of her life, until Abby herself died and left everything to her precious little piglet sister Sarah. So I let Emma, "my little mother," guide and counsel me, I let her fuel my fears, and I erected an ice-cold wall between myself and Abby.

But hearing her in the kitchen still made me smile. How she loved to bake sweet things, all my favorite things—cookies, cakes, and pies! I was five years old when she married Father, and I used to spend my days with her while Emma was at school and Father was away tending to business. Abby told me the secret of her mincemeat pies, exactly what made them so special—she only baked them for people she liked, and *always* sprinkled them with rosewater. And now she was baking one to welcome me home. Tears pricked my eyes and I fought the urge to go into the kitchen and give her a hug, something I hadn't done in years.

One day, in that first year, when we were all still getting used to one another, Abby made me a pretty pink dress with ruffles and a sunshine-yellow sash even though Emma said girls with red hair should *never* wear pink. And Abby curled my hair with hot irons, taking the time to make sure that each ringlet was perfectly shaped and shining. I remember she held my hair up to the light and showed me the multitude of shades, the red, orange, brown and gold, the colors, the ingredients, like the love and rosewater she always put in her mincemeat pies, that made redheads so special. She knew children could be cruel and that I had already been teased many times about my red hair, and she was trying to make me feel better, just like when she told me that each one of the freckles I detested was a kiss from an angel, a blessing on my very own skin. Then she stepped back to look at me, clasped her hands over her ample breasts, and, beaming, declared that I looked "just like a little French doll."

When Emma saw me she flew into a rage. She dragged me upstairs to our room, barking my shins against the steps, and *tore* that beautiful dress off me. She took it outside and pounded it into the pile of horse manure Father kept for fertilizer. She stood there with a shovel, hitting it, again and again and again, until her arms were too tired to continue and she was splattered head to foot with manure and bleeding from where she had bit her lip clean through. Then she came back to deal with me. She ripped the ribbons from my hair and poured water into our basin and plunged my head into it. I began to cry, I thought she was trying to drown me, but she was just wetting my hair. Then she took the comb and raked it viciously from the top of my scalp to the ends of my hair. I *screamed* as the teeth bit into my scalp, brutal enough to draw blood. When the ringlets resisted she yanked the comb harder, pulling the hair out in clumps, until I was afraid she would snatch me bald headed. But that was Emma's way. How very ironic that all the world sees her as the very picture of the meek as a mouse prim and pious brittle and birdlike little maiden lady in eternal mourning too afraid to ever say *Boo!* to a goose. They don't know the *real* Emma; no one does except me.

I was still standing there savoring the scent of Abby's mincemeat pie when Emma appeared, staring me in the face with hard, piercing eyes, pulling me out of the past to confront the present.

"Father is waiting for you in the sitting room," was all she said. It was all she had to say.

Then I was standing before him. I had not even taken off my hat and sealskin cape or removed my muff and gloves.

I saw him rise up from the sofa. He was clenching his jaw and that made his snow-white whiskers quiver. He was looking at me with such utter contempt that I wanted to run away and hide.

And then he began to speak, unleashing a torrent of angry words, coming closer all the while, until he was gripping my shoulders and *shaking* me so hard that my hat fell off and my hairpins rained down onto the carpet.

"I never thought I would have cause to say this, Lizzie, but I am *ashamed* of you! I let you, out of the goodness of my heart, go gadding off to Europe, let you see something of the world, I let you have your heaping dose of culture, and what do you do? Fall in love with some *foreigner!* Some scoundrel who preys on innocent women traveling abroad! Gullible American women are probably his bread and butter! For shame, Lizzie! *Shame!* I thought you had more respect for yourself, for your family, for *me!* I thought you were a decent, respectable girl, a virtuous, God-fearing girl, but I was wrong; you've proven that! What did you just say? Don't you *dare* tell me not to treat you like a child, miss! I treat you like a child because you *act* like a child! A silly, credulous child who would believe the moon is made of green cheese if someone told her so, especially if he was handsome and had an English accent!"

Father released me so suddenly that I stumbled and fell to my knees. I caught frantically at his hands. I tried to reason with him, I tried to tell him that he was wrong, that it had not been like that at all. My architect was not the sort of man he thought. He was not one of those oily faux counts who preyed on American heiresses, or a barefoot peasant selling olives on the street; he was kind, and intelligent, a hard worker, diligent and respectable in *every* way. Father was free to make all the inquiries he wished; I knew my love and was confident that he could withstand even the most painstaking scrutiny. But private detectives cost money—*lots* of money— and Father wasn't about to pay a Pinkerton man to confirm what he already knew; he was that certain that no respectable man of solid and impeccable reputation and means could ever fall in love with me.

"I don't want to hear another word about him!" Father cut me off. "I am *ashamed* of you, Lizzie Borden! *Ashamed,* of *you,* my own flesh and blood! And you a Sunday school teacher!" he shuddered. "God help those poor Celestials with *you* for a teacher!"

Suddenly he reached down and jerked me to my feet. "Did you let him touch you?" he demanded. "Did you let him kiss you?"

The memory of that kiss flashed behind my eyes and Father saw that he had struck a nerve, that there was *something:* No matter how innocent it might have been, there was *something.*

"*You DID! No!* Don't bother to deny it; I can see it in your eyes! Your own face betrays you!"

"Father, *please,* let me explain—"

"Explain what? That you behaved like a *whore?* I already *know* that! For all your churchgoing, you're a hypocrite, Lizzie Borden. You have the soul of a whore; just like a bitch in heat, you want a man between your legs no matter the cost. Someone must have a care for your soul, since you are unfit to govern yourself, and as your father that duty falls to me, and as long as I live you *will* walk the straight and narrow; there'll be no straying onto the primrose path and dillydallying with fortune hunters, worthless men who want to fritter away my hard-earned money!"

"Father, no, it isn't like that—"

He dealt me a stinging slap that knocked me flat upon the floor. "*I am ashamed to call you my daughter!*" he roared.

And he walked away from me. There was no hesitation in his footsteps and he never looked back. I lay on the floor and wept, watering the faded flowers on the carpet with my tears. No one came near me. Not Abby, not Emma, not even Bridget. I cried until I had no tears left.

The next morning, when I came downstairs, Father informed me that he had made an appointment for me to see Dr. Bowen promptly at three o'clock.

"You are looking a little fatter, a little rounder, than you were when you left us, Lizzie, and I want to make certain there are no surprises a few months from now."

I grasped his sleeve as he was walking away from me and tried to tell him about all the rich foods, the pastries in France, the pas-

tas and sauces in Italy, all the cheese and cream, the sinfully soothing chocolates, but he would not listen or believe me.

"Three o'clock, Lizzie, promptly at three," was all he would say
to me.

Dr. Seabury Warren Bowen lived across the street from us. I
had known him almost my entire life; it seemed like he had always
been our family physician, neighbor, and friend. Indeed, I could
not remember a time when he had *not* been there. He was a kind
man with gentle and wise brown eyes. His brown hair was receding
from his brow, and he had a fine mustache which he always kept
waxed in a perfect handlebar.

As three o'clock approached, I sat in his waiting room staring
down at my shoes, my knees shaking bad enough to bruise beneath
my blue flowered skirt. I was so embarrassed, so ashamed, at what
I knew was about to happen. I had never had cause to submit to an
intimate examination; I thought they were only for expectant
ladies. He had to call me twice before I could make my legs obey
and stand up and stagger clumsily through the door he held open
for me.

He pointed to a dressing screen and asked me to strip down to
my chemise and remove my drawers, then lie flat upon his examination table. He draped a white sheet modestly over me and asked
me to spread my legs wide and draw up my knees. I stared up at the
ceiling, my face burning with shame and tears blurring my eyes. He
asked me when I had last had fleas. That was a euphemism unique
to Fall River that we used to refer to a woman's monthly illness, and
any stains resulting from it were known as flea bites. I answered his
question as best I could. He nodded and bent down and lifted the
bottom edge of the sheet.

I tensed at the sudden intrusion of his fingers as he parted the
pink petals of my sex and reached inside to test my purity. He told
me to try to relax, that it would all be over soon. But I was only able
to relax when he finally withdrew, after what seemed like an eternity but was only minutes, I'm sure, and turned away to wash his
hands.

"Intact. I shall assure your father that all is as it should be," he said. Then he turned back to face me. I was sitting up, but my face still burned scarlet with shame, and I could not meet his eyes.

He came to me and gently took my hand.

"I am a doctor, Lizzie; I am *your* doctor, Lizzie, and anything you say to me is just between us. Would you like to tell me why your father insisted on this examination? It might make you feel better."

I hesitated for a moment; then it all came pouring out, and once I started talking I couldn't stop. I told him all about my Englishman, the *wonderful* architect who I was quite certain loved me. When I had finished, Dr. Bowen put his arms around me, drew my head down onto his shoulder, and let me cry.

"Your father is a hard man, Lizzie," he said. And I saw the anger in his eyes. He had been our family doctor for years; he knew what Father was like. Doubtlessly Father would wrangle with him over the bill he presented for this examination too; he always put up a fuss about Dr. Bowen's bills, though everyone else thought he was quite reasonable.

"I want to give you something, Lizzie," Dr. Bowen said. "Just a little morphine to calm your nerves and help you rest. Don't be afraid," he said when I gasped and instinctively drew back at the sight of the fearsome metal and glass syringe.

He took my arm and, as gently as he could, injected the drug. He made soothing noises, as one would for a hurt and frightened child or animal, when I winced and whimpered at the sharp pinch as the needle penetrated my skin and sent liquid rest into my vein.

By the time I had finished dressing, my head felt very strange, like my brain had turned into a great big sopping-wet ball of cotton. I had trouble speaking, I confused and muddled my words, I could not think clearly or say what I meant, and my feet found walking to be a nearly insurmountable quandary.

"It's all right, Lizzie," Dr. Bowen said soothingly as he took my arm, "nothing to be afraid of. Apparently a very small dose of this affects you more strongly than it does most; I shall have to remember that in the future should you have need of it again. Come on now; I'll see you safely home. And your father is waiting for my report."

Dr. Bowen took me home and I never forgot the last thing he said to me before he rang our doorbell. "You have a friend in me, Lizzie; always remember that."

Bridget helped me upstairs to my room, her arm about my waist, holding me close to her, coaxing me to be "careful now, Miss Lizzie," whenever I stumbled like a drunkard.

"Oh, Bridget!" I sighed with the most wanton delight as she undressed me.

I fell onto my bed, clad only in my drawers and chemise, and tried to pull her down on top of me. Smiling good-naturedly, Bridget wriggled out of my embrace, chiding me gently when I untied her apron strings and tried to kiss her with clumsy lips that wouldn't quite obey.

"Now, now, *macushla*"—she smiled and stroked my brow— "you just lie there an' rest quietly now like a good girl. You're not quite yourself, but you'll be better soon, Dr. Bowen said."

Macushla! She had called me *her darling, her dear! Macushla!* I'd never heard a sweeter word! I smiled up at her with love shining in my eyes as she covered me with my quilt. I slept the rest of the day and the whole night through. Morphine and Morpheus, the God of Sleep, stripped away my shame and sent me dreams so sweet, so luxuriantly lascivious, it would tarnish them forever if I dared set them down on paper. *Macushla!* Then as now—I'll live on that word for the rest of my life!

Much to my surprise, pining for my architect as I was day and night, I think I fell a little in love with Dr. Bowen after that. It wasn't that I no longer cared for my architect, but he was a whole world away with a great big ocean between us and Dr. Bowen was here *now* and just across the street. Maybe I was just so hungry for love that *any* love would do as long as it was lasting and true?

The pictures I'd hung on my walls to remind me of my "sweet taste of freedom" only seemed to mock me with bittersweet memories. And I had been too afraid of my family's mockery and laughter to show myself in any of the dresses I had bought in Paris. In the end, when I could no longer bear to look at them, I bundled them up and discreetly, anonymously, left them for the church to distribute to those in need. I was mortified the Saturday I ventured into the worst part of town with my arms full of peonies with the other ladies of the Fruit and Flower Mission and saw a fancy woman with a painted face and black hair glinting bold blue lights wearing my discarded caramel and apple-green stripes. She'd shortened the skirt to show off her shapely calves, trim ankles, and tiny feet, and recut the bodice to reveal as much of her bosom as was permissible on a public street and sheared off the sleeves to bare her fleshy white arms. Despite the indecent alterations, it looked much better on her than it ever had on me. I couldn't believe I had been fool enough to buy it and was glad I had never been foolish enough to wear it in Fall River; I would surely have been laughed off the street if I had. In the months to come I also caught glimpses of some of her "sisters of the pavement" strutting about like flaunting peacocks in my forsaken finery. Every time, I felt the warring tug of admiration and envy. They were so bold, so brave, so beautiful, so *free*—free like I wanted to be! They lived their lives unchained, charting their own course, answering to no man, their hungers and desires unfettered by duty and rules.

That summer, when my family went to the farm in Swansea I stayed behind. I wanted to be alone, I felt stifled and wanted space and time to reflect in; my hungry soul *craved* the illusion of freedom.

Every Sunday Dr. Bowen would call for me in his buggy and drive me to church. We were neighbors, after all, and he was our family doctor, so I never thought anyone would make anything of it. But we soon became the subject of gossip, with people hinting that perhaps I was not entirely alone in the house at 92 Second Street.

Bridget was there, of course, but without the drugs swimming like a school of brave and fearless sharks through my veins I was so ashamed of my drowsily and dreamily remembered morphine-induced attempt at seduction, I held myself aloof and kept my distance. I found it exceedingly difficult to meet her eyes without blushing, and trying to talk to her at all, even about the most innocuous, mundane things like marketing, laundry, and dinner, tied my tongue in knots every time.

Yet most nights when I lay alone in my bed, staring at the ceiling, it was Bridget whom I thought of, so near, yet so far, in the attic above me. I thought of her lying there on her narrow cot. What was she wearing? Did she don a nightgown for bed or did she sleep au naturel or in her chemise? I wondered if she ever touched herself and if she ever thought of me and sighed, "*Lizzie!*" into the sultry night.

At first, I would always stop and scold myself and try to make myself think of my architect, or Dr. Bowen, or the hero of the latest novel that I had read, instead, but dreams of Bridget, and sometimes, like a ghost from the past, vibrant images of Lulie Stillwell, straddling me stark naked in sugary-sweet clouds of perfumed powder, kept intruding no matter how hard I tried, and in the end I just gave up and put out the light, trusting my secrets to the night.

One night, after I had put the candle out, I awakened suddenly at the feel of long hair grazing my face and tickling my naked breasts. I felt a hot breath caress my cheek. "This is just a dream," a husky Irish voice whispered in my ear right before a pair of warm lips descended hungrily over mine. *Wonderful* things happened in the darkness. *Wonderful, wonderful things!*

"This is just a dream," the voice whispered again before love vanished from my arms and I was left alone again.

The next morning in the kitchen I tentatively said to Bridget as she served me my breakfast, "I had the most wonderful dream last night."

"Did you now, Miss Lizzie?" she asked casually as she poured me a cup of coffee.

"Yes." I nodded, then added eagerly, "I hope I will have it again tonight."

"Dreams don't work that way, *macushla,*" Bridget said, then went on with her work. "Oh, dem golden slippers, oh, dem golden slippers, golden slippers I'se going to wear because they look so neat . . ." she sang with gusto as she turned her back to me and began to wash the dishes.

That night I lay tense and hopeful in the darkness, my breath catching at each creak of the old cracker box house, hoping it heralded a footstep outside my door followed by the knob turning. But I was destined to pass that night, and every other after, alone in disappointment. Bridget was right about dreams. I never did have that one again.

On the last Sunday of the summer, before my family returned, Dr. Bowen and I went for a buggy ride after church. I was wearing the blue eyelet dress with the satin sash I had worn that magical day at Glastonbury and a new straw hat with silk ribbon streamers trailing down my back.

We alighted, to stretch our legs and let his team of handsome chestnuts have a rest and graze upon the emerald grass. The sun was blazing bright and we sought a respite under a shady tree and I shamelessly let him kiss me. My mind was an ocean away, and I suppose I was trying to re-create the most magical moment of my life.

Dr. Bowen drew back from me as if I were a snake and had bitten him, though he had initiated our embrace . . . I think? There are moments, I admit, when I am really not quite sure and think perhaps that *I* may have kissed him.

"My word, you are a forward girl; aren't you, Lizzie?" Dr. Bowen said, his voice a disturbing, shaky blend of disapproval and feigned joviality. The smile wavered uncertainly on his lips but never quite reached his eyes.

The sky had begun to darken, portending one of those sudden summer storms, and we sat in tomb-like silence as we drove home under a leaden sky.

A few months later when Dr. Bowen married the beautiful sylph-like brunette Phoebe Southard I was there, florid faced, sweating, and straining to keep my false smile from slipping into an honest scowl, laced to lung-bursting tightness in a fussy bow and ruffle-bedecked lavender chiffon bridesmaid's dress and an enormous ruffled monstrosity of a hat haphazardly dripping swags of seed pearls and sprouting lily of the valley like a garden grown out of control. It was the fussiest, *ugliest* bridesmaid's dress I had ever seen in my life! There were swags of imitation pearls all over it, draped around the shoulders, bodice, and skirt, that snagged on every blessed thing! Phoebe Bowen had the most abominable taste of any female I ever knew! Her parlor looked like it was decorated by circus clowns!

As Dr. Bowen, with his beaming bride clinging to his arm, passed by me, on their way to their ribbon-and-flower-bedecked wedding buggy, the new Mrs. Bowen's veil caught briefly on the bouquet I clutched murderously in my trembling and perspiring pig-pink hands. I wanted to beat her over the head with it! But Phoebe didn't have a clue, she just smiled at me, radiant with a delight we both knew I could never share, and I don't think her eyes actually even saw me, they were so blinded by bliss, as she quickly disentangled her *hideous* veil.

Dr. Bowen didn't even glance at me, not even when the girl standing beside me caught the wedding bouquet. He stared pointedly past me.

Forwardness in a New England girl is not easily forgiven, or forgotten.

As for my Englishman, he kept his promise; he did indeed write to me. But he was a man meant to go out into the world and do great things, and I was a woman, a daughter, meant to bide at home, chained and bound by convention and familial duty. Had I only possessed the courage to break the shackles of tradition and risk the loss of my inheritance . . . But would he have had me with such a stain upon me? Men prize a woman's virtue and respectability, her obedience, and chastity; they make us into ivory statues of domestic goddesses, paragons of the hearth and home, and put us up on pedestals to venerate and admire. Never realizing, or caring, how precarious it is to teeter up so high and to look down and see how far one risks to fall. And if perchance one actually does fall . . . How many fallen women have managed to claw their way back up to that dizzyingly high pinnacle of respectability? A good name once blackened can never be scrubbed virgin white clean again.

As much as I longed for his letters, I also came to dread them. I feared what he might one day tell me: that he had spoken the words I so longed to hear to another. Every time a letter arrived I would sit and hold it in my trembling hands for the longest time while an icy fear gripped my heart and threatened to loosen my bowels. My head would start to ache and a cold sweat would trickle slowly down my spine even though I felt so hot I would have to open my gown and loosen my corset.

For what seemed like hours, I would sit there holding his precious letter, which had traveled all the way across the sea to bring his words to me, until the sun went down and it was too dark to read without lighting a lamp, and by then I was too tired, so I went to bed, always promising myself that I would read it in the morning, right after breakfast, only to postpone it as there was work to be done, an errand I must run, or a meeting I must attend, and then repeat the whole scene again and again and again.

Somehow not knowing was better, but it was also worse. I left them unopened until I had accumulated a small stack. What must he have thought of me? That I was fickle and had lost interest or fallen ill or even died? Fear and longing possessed me; they fought a battle royal within my soul. I wanted to be with him so badly! I could not sleep or eat. My cheeks grew gaunt, fat melted from my frame, and my eyes sank into deep dark circles.

At last, I summoned all my courage and carried the letters downstairs to the kitchen stove one Thursday afternoon when everyone else was out. I added kindling and watched the fire blaze and then, tears running down my face, with a wrenching cry, the howl of a broken heart, bursting from my breast, I threw them in and watched them burn. I regretted it the moment I did it and burned my fingers trying to snatch them back again. But it was too late . . . *too late!*

The letters are long gone now, reduced to ashes, and I can but wonder what he had to say and whether it would have thrilled my heart or wounded it to the core. He will never know how much I loved him or that I never truly stopped, despite whatever I might have felt for others. He remains my one true love, the only one I never let myself, or the reality of my life, ruin; he exists only in my dreams, more god in his perfection than any flesh and blood man could ever hope to be. Perhaps it truly is better that way.

From the moment his letters crumbled into ashes I wanted to turn back the clock and undo what I had done, to find a way to make everything right. Oh, the reams of paper I wasted trying to write and tell him, to explain everything, what I had done and why. But every word I wrote seemed to make even a worse muddle of it and in the end I stopped trying. Maybe silence truly was best? And I was too great a coward to write the truth that was in my heart. I was a *lady*. I could not be so brazen as to speak of love; a lady *always* waits for a gentleman to broach the subject first. I felt the distance that yawned between us so keenly, the miles of land and sea. I felt it grow greater with every day that passed until it was so vast that no mere letter or telegram, not even a steamship, could bridge the gulf between us. And so I let go of the one person I wanted more than anything to draw closer to me, even though Reason said it could never be. Father would never let me go, he would see marriage and a life abroad as abandonment and disinherit me, and I could not ask my architect to exchange bustling exciting, beautiful, cosmopolitan London and the whole wide world for the narrow confines and even smaller minds of Fall River. And I was far too proud to ask him to accept no other dowry but me—the miserly millionaire's now penniless, spinster daughter. I loved him too much to do that to him; it would have been akin to a life prison term, a punishment, and in time his love for me, if it ever really was love, would have soured and turned to resentment and eventually hate. And I could not bear that.

I have not kept up with the details of his life. Though I wish him every happiness, I do not want to know, I cannot bear to know, about the woman who walks and sleeps at his side and has the life, the love, that should have been mine. In the years to come, whenever I visited New York and Boston and mingled with people who regularly traveled abroad I would feel such a sharp sense of dread, of trepidation, that made my head so light and my knees frightfully wobbly and weak, as I both yearned and feared to hear his name spoken, but I never did.

I've often wondered what he must have thought of me when news of my infamy crossed the sea. And yet, somehow, I've always felt a little less lonely knowing that he is out there somewhere, living his life, even if a whole ocean and half the world lie between us. I like to think of him working in his office in London, brow furrowed with concentration as he bends over his plans, meticulously drawing the lines that would give birth to a new building or re-checking his calculations, pencil smudges on his hands and his blond hair flopping down vexingly into his eyes, or walking across the countryside with his sketchbook and charcoal pencils sketching the great wonders of mankind and nature.

Sometimes the sadness still steals over me and I cry for what might have been. How different my life would have been! I would have been lost to history; there would have been no murders at 92 Second Street, no immortal singsong rhyme about forty whacks; no one would have even remembered my name after I died—I would have had a *different* name; he would have changed that, just like he changed my life.

Chapter 4

When Emma came in I was lying on my bed, dreaming over a romance novel about a beautiful geisha girl named Snow Lily dying of love for an American sailor who treated everyone who ever loved him badly. Emma slammed the lid back on the nearly empty box of chocolates beside me and shoved it away in disgust and snatched the book from where it lay open over my breasts and flung it across the room so that its spine cracked against the wall.

"You rot your brain and your insides with such rubbish!" she cried.

"If that's all you came for, Emma..." I endeavored unsuccessfully to stifle a yawn as I reached for the candy box again.

Emma just glared at me, then heaved a heavy sigh and sat down on the bed beside me.

"That treacherous sow is at work again; she and her greedy piglet are conniving against us...."

Emma's eyes burned like coal as she proceeded to tell me that Sarah Whitehead had come that very morning to visit Abby. Over coffee, watered down with Sarah's tears, and mincemeat pie—Sarah ate two slices and Abby four—Sarah had sobbed out her dilemma. Her mother wanted to sell the house and move away, to a warmer clime more hospitable to her rheumatism and asthma, and Sarah and her drunken, good-for-nothing husband could barely make ends meet, so it was simply *impossible* for them to buy the house.

"We shall have to move!" Sarah sobbed and laid her head down, blind in her despair to the slice of pie Abby had just set on her empty plate.

Clucking sympathetically, Abby gathered Sarah in her arms, tenderly wiping the mincemeat and crumbs from her blotchy wet face, and promised everything would be all right, they wouldn't lose the house. "I'll have a word with Mr. Borden as soon as he comes home. . . ."

"Don't you see what's going to happen, Lizzie?" Emma hunched over me like an evil black crow.

I shrugged and yawned disinterestedly, then, since Emma clearly required it, recited tiredly: "Abby will persuade Father to buy the house, which he of course will, since he *never* lets the chance for another rental property pass him by, and the Whiteheads will be *so grateful* to have a roof over their miserable heads, even if it does leak and threaten to fall down on them at every turn, that they will forget that in the bargain they have also acquired a landlord who makes Satan look like Father Christmas and being related to him by marriage doesn't ease their plight any. If they don't already know it, woe to them if they're late with the rent by so much as half a day or short by even one penny. Father only takes goods in exchange for money if he can sell them at a profit. And what have the Whiteheads got to offer him? George is drunk all the time, the garden went to weeds long ago, and even if it hadn't none of them can grow beans; the hens don't lay and wander around eating worms until foxes or thieves carry them all off. No one would pay to eat Sarah's cooking; her baked goods don't win her prizes like Abby's do, only black eyes for her and bellyaches for her husband and children. She can't take in laundry; Heaven knows that woman ruins everything she tries to clean; you'd think bluing and starch were her worst enemies the way they act in her hands! And she can't sew either! Remember the time she ran over here weeping to Abby, begging her to fix George's shirt before he woke up and needed to put it on, and it turned out that in trying to sew the buttons back on she'd actually sewn it shut. If it weren't for Abby, the children would be running around stark naked or else wearing flour sacks with holes cut out for their heads and arms; they go to school barefoot as it is."

I yawned again and got up to retrieve my book. Snow Lily had been about to throw herself in a volcano and I was very anxious about her fate; I was hoping the handsome cannibal chieftain who loved her secretly from afar would come to her rescue in time. "So what's to worry about?" I shrugged again and asked Emma. "The Whiteheads don't have anything *I* want."

"*You stupid girl!*" Emma cuffed my ear. "Look to the future! Or are you too lazy to even *think* about tomorrow?"

"Just a moment, Emma," I said tartly as I cradled my smarting ear. "Let me try and think where I left my crystal ball."

Emma slapped me again. "Don't you even *care* that our inheritance is being stolen right out from under our noses?"

"How so, Emma?" I lay back and frowned as I examined the ugly brownish-red paint stains marring the whole left side of the skirt of my lovely new diamond-patterned sky- and navy-blue housedress. It made me want to cry! I had been careless and brushed up against a wall of wet paint when Father had given in to my complaining and had the painters in last month just to please me, "to spiff the old place up." Then I had gone and ruined my new dress the very first day I had worn it and Mrs. Raymond didn't have any of the fabric left to make me a new one and I didn't like any of the other patterns she offered me. Emma said I was just being obstinate, but I didn't think so; those double blue diamonds arranged so you couldn't quite decide whether they were dark blue on a light blue ground or the other way around were quite unusual and I hadn't seen anything else like them. Abby and Bridget had both tried all the remedies they knew for removing stains, but to no avail; their well-intended ministrations had only left my lovely dress looking woefully tired out and faded. To look at it now, one would think it was ten years old instead of a practically new dress.

"It's just another rental property," I continued. "The money will go into Father's bank account, just like the other rents do."

Emma slapped down my ruffled hem in disgust—"I don't know why you don't tear that thing up for rags or, better yet, *burn* it! *I* wouldn't be caught dead wearing it in the state it's in!"—and caught my chin in her hand, her nails *biting* into my skin as she leaned over me and stared deep into my eyes. "And what if he leaves the house to Abby in his will and she gives it to the Whiteheads? Did you ever bother to think about *that*, Lizzie? Whether she gives it to them in her lifetime, or leaves it to them in her will, the result is the same—*we* will lose all future claim to it!"

"Emma"—I pulled away from her, frowning as I rubbed at the smarting red indentations her nails had left in my skin—"the three little pigs could have built a sturdier and more attractive house out of sticks and mud! As rental properties go, it's a *raging* headache; let someone else have it, even if it is Abby and, eventually, Sarah! It's just *one* little ramshackle falling-to-bits house, and I for one don't care a fig about it and you shouldn't either!"

"But *I* do!" Emma leapt up and began pacing frantically back and forth before my bed, her black skirt sweeping the floor as I kept meaning, and forgetting, to do. "It's the principle of the thing, Lizzie! Father's money—*our inheritance*—will buy the house, and if he gives it to Abby, now or later, he will be cheating us out of money that is rightfully *ours!* That Cow is cheating us right under our very noses and *you're* either too blind to see it or too stupid to care! But I do, *I do!* By Heaven, I won't let them get away with this!" Emma shook her fist in the air like some madwoman in a melodrama, then stormed out of my room, slamming the door behind her.

I rolled my eyes and flopped back onto my pillows and returned to my book. Frankly, I was more interested in the fate of Snow Lily than I was in the Whiteheads and their miserable hovel of a house.

Emma raised such a row over the Whiteheads' house that, just to quiet her, Father ended up deeding our grandfather's old house on Ferry Street jointly to us, so we could draw a monthly rent, divided and deposited into each of our bank accounts, to save or spend as we pleased.

It seemed at first an ideal solution for all. But we resented being bothered by the tenants—we only wanted their money, not their problems. We didn't want to hear hard-luck stories or their wretched whining about problems with the plumbing; they made our heads ache. And I, for one, resented taking money out of *my* bank account to pay for repairs to a house someone else was living in. Why did they have to try to make their leaks and breaks *my* problem? Why didn't they just deal with it themselves and leave me alone? We—Emma and I—were giving them a roof over their heads, keeping them out of the rain, for God's sake; they should have been *grateful!* And I had problems enough of my own without taking on theirs! In the end, just to appease us, and avoid a lawsuit, Father bought the house back from us for $5,000, which was more than it was worth. He said it made his head ache too and this was a perfect example of why women should keep to the home and hearth and leave business matters solely in the hands of men.

Privately, I couldn't help but agree and decided then and there that if I ever had to deal with the like again I would hire a trusty and efficient business manager who would never even *think* to bother me about such trifles, and in addition to that I would purchase the best insurance to cover every eventuality.

But Emma just could not let go. She never did stop simmering about the Whiteheads' house. She took it as a personal slight. Father had in fact deeded the property to Abby, warning her not to be too softhearted and to think of her own future and not just of her kinfolk's comfort and well-being, and to remember that after he was gone the rents on that house would provide her with a regular income. Emma was even more miffed when Father took the rent the Whiteheads paid to Abby and started a savings account; "a nest egg for her widowhood," he called it.

I really couldn't understand why Emma was so upset. I, for one, *hated* being a landlord. I was happy to let Abby have that house; even squinting and looking at it from across the road with one eye covered I could tell that it was nothing but a pile of headaches waiting to happen, and I didn't want to be the one they happened to. I much preferred the dividends from the shares in the Globe Yarn Mill and the Crystal Springs Bleach Company that Father had given me in lieu of a graduation present when I dropped out of high school. As for Abby's little nest egg, I thought it rather sensible; I honestly didn't see it as the "greedy siphoning of our inheritance" like Emma did.

The situation only worsened a few months later when George Whitehead woke up after a long drunk and found a stray goat that had wandered in through the broken back door licking his bare feet and took it into his head that he and his family deserved better and that Abby, being married to Fall River's miserly millionaire, could do *much* better for them if she *really* wanted to. If she loved Sarah as much as she said she did, why didn't she prove it? Mincemeat pies and clothes for the children were all well and good, but a decent house would be much better.

After a lengthy series of drunken rants and beatings Sarah ended up back at our kitchen table in tears again with both her eyes blackened and her lips burst and blood crusted.

I don't know if the idea sprang from George's head into Sarah's or straight from Abby's, but someone suggested our farm in Swansea as the perfect happy and wholesome home for the Whiteheads, somewhere green where they could make a fresh start.

Emma and I were in complete accord—*this* was a betrayal of the *worst* kind. That farm, where we had spent our childhoods, playing with our cousins the Gardners, and even after we had moved to Fall River often returned to spend the summers, was bound to our mother's memory as though with a lovers' knot. It was *special;* it was *sacred;* it was *OURS,* Emma's and mine. Renting it was one thing, but *giving* it away . . . The very idea of the Whiteheads, or anyone else, taking it away from us *made us see red.* It was *unthinkable* that it could *ever* belong to anyone but us!

Father put his foot down and flatly refused to even discuss it with us; sentiment, he said, had no place in business. Whenever we tried to plead our case, he turned a deaf ear. The situation with the house on Ferry Street had shown him that we were not equipped to deal responsibly with real estate, and he had seen nothing since to persuade him that we deserved another chance. And we wouldn't lower ourselves by going begging and beseeching to Abby. Whenever she tried, often with tears in her eyes, to talk to us about it, we turned our backs on her.

It was then that Emma decided that we would steal from Abby the same as she was stealing from us even if it must, by necessity, be on a much smaller scale. So we began a series of, in hindsight, rather childish and obvious burglaries. We ransacked the master bedroom one rare Thursday afternoon when both Father and Abby were out, choosing Bridget's day off so she could not be blamed, since in novels suspicion always falls first upon the servants.

The fruits of our first little foray into crime consisted of $110 in greenbacks and gold, and some streetcar tickets, Abby's meager collection of earbobs and brooches (excluding the mother-of-pearl peony brooch and pearl earbobs she was wearing that day), a red pebbled-leather pocketbook with a gold clasp, a rope of imitation pearls, a gold tassel necklace set with red glass stones, and a lady's gold pocket watch. We hid our mean-spirited little haul in the barn, beneath the straw in the cage where I kept my pet pigeons, until we could safely dispose of it.

The biggest prize was Abby's watch, the one Father had given her on their wedding day, a delicate gold ladies' pocket watch I had helped him pick out at Gifford's with a lovely lavish floral design encircled by a double border of white diamonds and Abby's initials engraved upon the back of the case. Emma later took it and the rest of Abby's jewelry and dropped it in the Taunton River inside the red leather pocketbook weighed down with stones, since it would have been too dangerous to pawn. We burned the streetcar tickets, since they were numbered and could have been traced if we had dared use them, and divided the cash between us and spent it carefully over many months lest we draw suspicion to ourselves.

When the robbery was discovered, and Abby rushed back downstairs, hysterical and spouting tears like a fountain, we were sitting placidly in the parlor. Emma was sewing and I was idly leafing through a magazine. When the police came and found the cellar doors standing open wide I helpfully pointed out an eight-penny nail wedged into the padlock.

While Abby wept and blubbered to the police, "I prize that watch very much, and I wish and hope that you can get it back, but I have a feeling that you never will," Father just frowned and stood there stiff-backed and silent and stared first at Emma, then at me, then back at Emma again, and then at me, back and forth, just like a tennis ball bouncing between two rackets.

Later he had some quiet words with the police outside. I don't know what was said, but they never came back, and no one ever said another word about the burglary; it was as though it had never happened at all. But from that day forward, whenever Father went out he made a point of locking the door of the bedroom he shared with Abby and laying the key prominently, in plain sight, right smack in the middle of the sitting room mantel, as though he was *daring* anyone to touch it. It was as though he *knew* we were the ones responsible but was punishing us with his silence. And that was somehow much worse than dragging it all out into the open and having hot words. Instead, he let the guilt hang, like a sword, over our heads.

About a week later, I was late getting home for supper. I had been helping to revive poor Flossie Grew, who had fainted dead away after a *beastly* drunken *brute* of an Irishman had *seized* her in his arms and *kissed* her—right on the mouth in front of *everyone!*—then *vomited* all over her new shoes when the Women's Christian Temperance Union was protesting outside of McCurdy's Saloon. Naturally we had all gone after him, whacking him over the head with our parasols and purses until the police came along and carried him off to jail, as the wretched coward was sniveling for them to do, where he would be safe from our outrage. *Poor Flossie!* I just hoped she would be recovered in time to go out with the Fruit and Flower Mission on Saturday to hand out bouquets of cherry blossoms as a sweet thank-you to the Celestials who worked so hard in the town's laundries and mills.

I had just put down the handsome placard I had painted, depicting the Devil in all his vile scarlet, horned, hoofed, and forked-tailed satanic glory, swilling from a bottle of rum, too drunk to hold on to his own pitchfork, and taken off my hat and was sliding into my chair at the dining room table and was making my apologies to everyone for my tardiness, though it truly was for a noble cause and thus completely excusable, when Bridget brought in a tray.

"Ah! Eight tender young squabs!" Father beamed with delight and reached out a fork to spear one. "Two for each of us! I hope you're hungry, Lizzie!" He smiled like the Devil as he deposited a pigeon on my plate, stabbing it with the fork, right in the breast, to show me how succulent and juicy it was!

I blanched and bolted from my chair. I ran out into the barn. My pigeons were gone! All that remained were a few gray and white feathers and some blood on the straw and staining the blade of the hatchet that had been left standing propped up against their empty cage. I fell down on my knees and vomited.

Later that night, Bridget crept into my bed and comforted me as best she could.

"I know just how you feel, *macushla,*" she said, hugging me close as she spooned her body around mine.

She told me about a little red hen she'd made a pet of back in Ireland when she was a little girl. Even though she knew the hen was meant for the cooking pot she could not help but love it. She'd clung to her brother and cried as he marched steadfastly across the yard with the hatchet in his hand and watched in horror as he chopped off the chicken's head. To teach Bridget a lesson, her ma had made her sit by the hearth, even though she was crying her eyes out, and pluck the bird naked for the pot.

"I soaked ev'ry feather with my tears, I did, *macushla,*" she sighed. "An' only the hunger gnawin' at my belly made me eat it, but I sicked it all back up afterward."

She lay with me for hours, softly crooning sweet Irish lullabies, stroking my hair, and calling me "*macushla,*" and kissing me until I slept. When she started to creep out I stirred sleepily and reached out a hand and caught hold of her wrist.

"Stay with me!" I whispered urgently, and she did. I passed the entire night in her arms.

Father never said a word about my pigeons. Everyone pretended it hadn't happened. No one ever mentioned that supper or the pets that no longer drew me out to spend hours in the barn. It was as though my pigeons had never existed. The only good to come out of Father's malicious act was that it had brought Bridget to my bed.

Sometimes I wished I could kick the old man down, plant my foot on the back of his head, and *grind* his face into a pile of fresh manure and say, *Thank you for that, at least!* while I remembered the sweet touch of her lips and the way she had passively allowed me to untie the green silk ribbons of her nightdress and slip my hand inside. I had given her those ribbons, casually tossing them down one day while she was ironing, saying I had no use for them and thought she might like to have them. I'd even wrinkled them to make it look like they truly were odds and ends I'd found at the bottom of my sewing box instead of new ones I'd bought just for her. I'd *die* of embarrassment if she ever knew about the fifteen minutes I had spent *agonizing* over the selection at Sargent's to choose the shade of green that was the best match for her beautiful eyes. But those memories were *mine,* and precious, and I was a coward; I didn't have the courage to crow like a rooster and gloatingly proclaim my sweet, sweet secret shame to one who had it within his power to punish me for the intoxicating and doubly sinful combination of unnaturalness and bliss.

Chapter 5

I never meant for it to happen. David Anthony was *not* the man for me. He was too young, too wild, dark and dangerous. Oh, but he was a handsome, sulky, sultry brute, all man and muscle, leather and spice, with his slick black hair and pencil-thin mustache. He reminded me a little of the suave and slightly dangerous men I had seen at the casino on the Riviera, but in a much cruder, rougher way. His hands were calloused, and hard with dirt-caked nails not immaculate, soft, manicured ones with silky finesse instead of brute force in their caresses. While the sophistication might have been lacking, the veneer of danger was not. He drove his father's meat wagon, drawn by a team of four sturdy white steeds. It was painted a glaring white and each side was emblazoned with a big red pig branded ANTHONY & SWIFT MEAT CO. OF FALL RIVER in white letters. David made the daily deliveries to private residences and businesses, and was rumored to entice pretty girls into the back of the meat wagon with the promise that he would give them a nice, fat sausage.

Reason decreed that he was far too young for me; at twenty-two he was a full ten years my junior. But Passion was blind. And when you're starved for love and the sensual glide of a tender, knowing hand, sometimes being wanted is enough. After all, there are worse compromises.

In another couple, ten years might not have made such a difference, but between us it was a yawning chasm. Besides, he was the butcher's son and I was Andrew Borden's daughter and I knew what my father—and other people—would say: that David only wanted an old maid like me for my father's money, that when he looked at me visions of dollar signs danced in his head like a child's sugarplum dreams the night before Christmas. We had *nothing* in common, no shared interests, and our conversations were awkward and stilted at best. But he wanted me, and I wanted to be wanted. And, for a little while, I deluded myself into believing that that was enough. So I kept reality at bay; whenever it threatened to rudely intrude I shoved it away, and let myself go on dreaming. But I let things go further than I should. It only happened once, but once was enough to change my life forever.

I had started teaching a twice-weekly evening reading and writing class for the poor immigrant girls who worked in the mills. Afterward, David would be waiting for me outside, to walk me home—or almost home; we'd always say good night on the corner so Father wouldn't see us together. I was flattered by the attention. Then we started to meet in the barn where I used to keep my pigeons and go and visit the horse, before Father decided I spent too much time out there and that the carrots and apples I snuck sweet Fred as treats rightly belonged in the stews and pies Abby made instead. *You don't feed animals that don't feed you, Lizzie!* Father always said; it was his way of justifying the slaughter of my pets and the selling of Fred. The barn quickly became our favorite trysting spot. Sometimes we sat and fondled and kissed each other in the old sleigh Father had been unable to sell because of its deplorably decrepit state, with the cracks in the red leather seat pinching the bare flesh above my black stocking tops whenever David could coax my skirts up over my hips. Sometimes we sat and snuggled in the straw of Fred's former stall, sharing a sack of penny candy and sugary kisses, or lolled about in the loft eating pears from the tree in our backyard or grapes from our straggling vine. Once David brought decadent dark cherries from his mother's garden and dangled them enticingly by their stems over my mouth as he fed them to me one by one. Another day, when Abby unexpectedly went out, we stole the blueberry pie she had left cooling on the windowsill and left telltale blue stains all over our skin wherever we touched and kissed.

At first, we only talked, but we had little to talk about; there were so many awkward silences and long, uncomfortable pauses. Then he tried to fill the anxious silence with kisses that would make us both forget that we really had nothing to say to each other. Then he groped my breasts and fumbled clumsily with my clothes and told me I was pretty and grabbed my wrist with bruising, hard fingers and pressed my hand against the plump "sausage" in his pants and whispered hot, urgent words into my ear, urging me to take it out and hold and pet it. "It" wanted "to come out and play," he said, but "it" was never satisfied with just play; what "it" wanted most was a kiss from me, David said, assuring me that once I became accustomed I wouldn't gag and feel queasy like I had the one time I gave in and tried, but I could never stomach a second attempt; just the thought was enough to make me roll over in the straw and retch.

Part of me wanted to push him away, but another part of me, the part that wanted *so badly* to be wanted, yearned to draw him nearer, deep inside, to fill me up with all the love I had spent my whole life longing for. I kept telling myself it was a compliment, to be desired by a handsome young man like David Anthony, so dark and dangerous; everyone has to play with fire once in their life in order to discover that it burns. It was my mistake to think that I, being older and richer, had the upper hand and could control the game.

He said he wanted to marry me, but I had only to look at his perpetually pregnant sisters, sisters-in-law, cousins, and aunts, and his mother, wretched and worn out from bearing a child almost every year since she was nineteen, to know what life with him would be like: a life spent in servitude to the Anthony men, marked by black eyes, burst lips, and broken ribs, and other bruises conveniently hidden by high collars and long skirts and sleeves, veils, and discreet applications of powder and paint. A life spent out of sight in the kitchen, or on well-dressed parade at Sunday services and afterward sitting placidly in the parlor or around the dinner table, silent unless spoken to, rising only to cater to the needs of the menfolk. To marry David Anthony would have been to exchange one prison for another, one where generous brutality, not excessive frugality, defined the jailer.

I made excuses; I told him that Father would *never* give his consent. I was too cowardly to tell David the truth—that *I* would *never* give *my* consent. I didn't want to marry him, but I didn't want him to leave me either, not just yet; it felt *so good* to be desired, to lie there in the straw with my shirtwaist and corset open, letting him kiss my breasts, so I kept postponing the inevitable. I wanted to play with fire for just a little while longer. Though I feared the burn, I liked the heat of it very much.

But David Anthony was a dangerous man to play games with; I should have known better than to think I could just stop and dismiss him like a servant whenever I liked. At our last rendezvous in the barn I found that out. That was the day I got burned, but no one ever knew; the pain, the fear, the charring, and the scarring were all beneath the skin. Fires are furious, merciless things, I discovered, and hard to control, and so was David Anthony.

That day we were up in the loft. I was laughing, and had my hands up above my head, holding on to a rafter, swaying and giggling like a silly girl. David had told me a joke; I can't remember what it was now. My white cotton shirtwaist was hanging open and my breasts were bare, my blue satin corset unhooked and the long blue silk ribbons on my chemise dangling free, teasingly tickling his face whenever I leaned down. I was happy and enjoying the unaccustomed sensual freedom and the feel of his admiring eyes on me.

Kneeling at my feet, David twirled a piece of straw between his fingers. He reached up to tickle my nipples with it before he let it fall and then he reached for me. Suddenly his hands were under my navy-blue skirt, gliding over my black stockings, playfully snapping the sky-blue satin garters, then, rising higher and higher, his fingers hooked over the waistband of my white cotton drawers.

For what seemed like a very long moment, Time, and the two of us, seemed to stand still as we gazed deep into each other's eyes. Then, with one quick movement, he yanked my drawers down. I *wanted* him to! I stepped out of them, willingly, savoring this special moment of brazen bare-bottomed delight, of being naked under my skirts. It felt *so* wonderfully wanton, so decadently daring! David smiled up at me. With a swift motion, he ducked his head beneath my petticoat. I felt his mouth on the most secret part of me and I was lost, drowning in the most exquisite pleasure; it was even better than my wicked, wanton dreams. I felt like I was melting into his mouth and I would soon lose all of me and be swallowed up whole and devoured by David. I bore down, pressing into him, and felt his broken front tooth, cracked on a diagonal, against the secret pink pearl of my womanhood. It felt *so* good, I thought I was going to die; surely no one could withstand such pleasure and survive.

The next thing I knew I was flat on my back in the hay and he was on top of me, grinding his loins hard against mine. That was the moment when all the pleasure died. His hand was clamped hard over my mouth, and my legs, kicking futilely, were splayed wide around his hips, the pounding of my heels upon the wooden floor of the loft muffled by the straw we were lying upon. I felt a pain, like a railway spike was being driven between my thighs. I struggled and squirmed and tried to break free, to scratch and bite, *anything* to break free of him. He took his hand away, but before I could scream or wriggle free, his fist struck. I felt my lip split and tasted my own blood, salty and hot, as I lay back in the hay, still and stunned, stars dancing before my eyes. Then David was upon me again and a gushing wet warmth filled me, to mingle with my virgin blood, but it soon grew cold and did nothing to ease the burning pain.

I lay there gasping. I felt like a noose was tightening around my throat; I couldn't seem to get enough air. *What have I done? What have I done?* I kept desperately repeating in my mind. I had just given a woman's most precious gift, the one that can be given only once, the chastity that should be preserved for her wedding night, to this man who did not deserve it. No one must ever know, I decided then and there; this must be my most deeply guarded secret and go to the grave with me. If anyone ever found out, I would be ruined, or worse . . . I would be thrown into the prison of wedlock with David Anthony as my jailer.

David picked up my arm, as stiff and lifeless as a corpse's, and pulled my handkerchief from my sleeve, then let my arm fall back into the straw again. It was one of my best handkerchiefs, snowy white, painstakingly embroidered with my initials in blue silk thread. He reached under my skirt and roughly wiped at me. I winced at his touch, at the rawness, the terrible searing, throbbing pain. I briefly saw the bloodstain before he wadded the handkerchief up, wet and sticky, and thrust it into his pocket; then he retrieved my drawers from where they lay abandoned in the straw and pocketed them too. *Evidence, proof,* my befuddled brain instantly understood.

He stood up and stared down at me with hard, unfeeling eyes. I should have known he had no heart!

"Now you'll *have* to marry me." He smiled fiendishly with a devilish gleam lighting up his eyes. "*You're caught!*"

As he towered over me and did up the row of small black buttons on the front of his trousers, he boasted to me about how fertile the Anthony men were. There was always more than one woman expecting in the family.

"*You're caught, Lizzie Borden; you're caught!*" He bolted from the barn laughing all the way, jubilant and mocking. He had set a trap for the miserly millionaire's daughter and I had walked right into it, blind and trusting. *I was a fool!* Father had been right all along! I was nothing but a dollar sign in men's eyes! No one would ever *really* love *me!*

I do not know how long I lay there in that hay, weeping, with blood seeping from between my legs. At last, I struggled to my feet, blood crusted on my lips and chin and staining the collar of my shirtwaist where it had dripped down—I would tell everyone that I had tripped and fallen in the barn—and slowly made my way down the ladder. Wincing and nearly weeping at the raw stabbing sore-

ness between my thighs, I hobbled into the kitchen. I remember
thinking what an odd feeling it was to be naked underneath my
skirts, to feel David's seed, mingling with my blood, trickling down
my thighs to sop into my stocking tops.

I don't know how I did it without breaking down and weeping,
sobbing the whole sorry story out to someone, anyone, but I managed to keep a calm exterior and tell the lie I had concocted about
a fall as I was coming down the ladder from the loft, as I heated
enough water to fill the tub and went down into the dark privacy of
the cellar to bathe. I wanted to be clean. I wanted to forget. I
wanted to wash away every trace of David Anthony from my life
and skin and forget what he had done to me, even the pleasure that
had come before the pain. But I was afraid of what he had left inside me, and I couldn't get that out of my mind, or, I feared, of my
body.

I knew I should just wait for my courses to come. Worrying
about it, and whether they would come or not, would do no good
and might even delay them, but I couldn't help it; I couldn't stop
thinking about it and what would happen to me if they didn't.
Somehow I remembered the discreetly worded advertisements I
had seen in the backs of women's magazines, the ones that promised a remedy for "delayed courses and feminine obstruction," their
discreet, coded references for unwanted or inconvenient pregnancies.

After I was bathed and dressed in clean clothes, everything fresh
and uncontaminated by David Anthony, I found myself in the sitting room seated on the horsehair sofa where Father liked to nap in
the afternoons, frantically flipping through old magazines searching for those ads.

There were several of them, more than I remembered from the
casual, mildly curious glances I had given them in the past when I
had no need of them. My eye lit upon three nestled right in a row.

But *which* to choose? Dr. Harmony seemed commendably
straightforward, a man who seemed to understand the worries and
woe that went hand in hand with my predicament, and even sugar-
coated his pills to make them more palatable, but Swami Fecundi
had *centuries* of success on his side and *thousands* of testimonials

from satisfied customers all over the world. He was a holy man with exotic wisdom and herbs and his spiel had me swaying like a charmed cobra in his direction.

But then I thought that surely, in a situation like this, a *woman,* and a worldly, sophisticated *French* woman at that, *must* know best? And with *Saint* as part of her name, well, *surely* that was a good sign. A saint wouldn't lie!

And wasn't Saint Genevieve some sort of patron saint to troubled girls, or had she saved a village from a horde of raping and pillaging barbarian invaders? It seemed like I had seen a shrine to her somewhere during my travels or read an informative tidbit somewhere. Perhaps upon a bronze plaque mounted on a church wall or in a magazine or *Baedeker?* Or it might have been a romance novel wherein a troubled heroine had knelt veiled and in tears and lit candles before the saint's benevolent statue. But it seemed a most fortuitous memory, perhaps even a gift from that very saint to *this* troubled girl besieged by the barbarian David Anthony.

I made up my mind then and there to put my trust in Madame Saint-Genevieve. Praying that the address was still good—the magazine was after all several months old—I ran upstairs to address the envelope and enclose the requisite dollar.

I *had* to take action. I couldn't wait for Mother Nature to tell me if I was in trouble. My courses weren't due for over two weeks and that seemed an eternity, and I didn't want to wait for them, I knew all too well their leisurely, laggardly ways. I wanted the blood to come *now* and set me free from this prison of uncertainty and panic! I wanted to bleed and be done with it, and David Anthony, forever! I prayed that Madame Saint-Genevieve's promises were real and that she would be my salvation and the answer to my prayers.

Even though my hair was still wet, I put up my braid and pinned on my hat and set out for the post office. I *needed* my dollar to start its journey today; I *needed* to know that my remedy was on its way, and if my courses came before it did . . . it was only *one* dollar wasted in the quest for peace of mind, so it was worth it. As I strode boldly down the sidewalk, I felt my confidence returning now that I was actually *doing* something to save myself from a fate worse than death instead of sitting around waiting, worrying, and wallowing in misery.

Madame Saint-Genevieve was prompt, not fashionably late like I feared a Frenchwoman would be. The remedy arrived on Tuesday, August 2, 1892. She kept her promise of assured discretion, sending the preparation in a plain white wrapper bearing the elegant fleur-de-lis-embossed label of *Madame Saint-Genevive de Paris, Parfumier to Royalty,* but I can't really say whether it contained a miracle or not.

Father brought the mail home with him after his daily business rounds. An immense sense of relief filled me as I held the small discreet packet that contained my salvation in my trembling hands. I took it into the kitchen. Bridget was occupied elsewhere, and the stew made from the leftover mutton was simmering on the stove and didn't require her attention. I stood beside the stove and threw the wrapper in to feed the fire. I held the little amber glass vial of hope in my hand and pulled out the cork that sealed it and shook two little brown pills out onto my palm, which was quivering like a leaf. At that most inconvenient moment, Father called me. I heard footsteps and thought he was about to come in. I nearly leapt out of my skin. The vial and pills fell from my hand and, with a splash that sent a spray of scalding droplets onto my face, plummeted into the mutton stew. I burned my hand trying to fish them out before I thought to use a spoon, but it was too late. All I was able to retrieve was the empty vial; the pills had already melted and mingled with the mutton broth.

Hopelessness overwhelmed me. I stared despairingly down into the nauseating muddy brown depths of the mutton stew after my lost hope and wondered what to do. I could not take it upon myself to throw it out, or even feign an accident by knocking the pot off the stove, though it would have brought joy to every soul in the house except Father; we'd been having it for days on end for every meal and could not wait to see the last of it. But Father would have been *furious* at such wastefulness. That was why we were having mutton in the hottest summer Fall River had ever known; he had been given the meat by the tenant of our Swansea farm, and we had to make use of it quickly before it spoiled.

Abby had already tentatively voiced her concern that it might have gone bad already; she'd been feeling a trifle poorly since the mutton sandwich she'd brought up to bed with her last night. But Father scoffed at her concerns. There were few things he deplored more than the wasting of food, and as long as there was a morsel of meat left or a drop of juice that mutton would be on our table and there was no getting round it. Nor would he sanction anyone in the household eating anything else than what was laid before them on the table; he even balked at special food for invalids. "You will eat what is set before you or go without," he always said. "There will be no special meals in *this* house!" To think, I actually feared Father's anger more than I did accidentally poisoning us all!

So, foolishly, I did nothing. I just let the pot sit and simmer until supper. Perhaps it was naïve of me, but with all the advertisement's promises of safety and gentleness, I didn't think it would hurt anyone. It was an herbal preparation after all, not poison. Since no one else was in the same predicament I feared that I was in, I thought it would just pass through their bodies harmlessly as water. Madame Saint-Genevieve had promised that it did its work without pain or nausea or detrimental effects of any kind and she, this acclaimed Parisian specialist with *Saint* in her name, certainly didn't strike me as a charlatan who would presume to peddle a dishonest product in the pages of a popular and highly respected women's magazine. The publishers most assuredly would not stand for it; they had a reputation to uphold, and there *must* be laws about that kind of thing. And they must think very highly of her indeed to put her on the same page, in the *same column,* as the compassionate and renowned Dr. Harmony and a holy man like Swami Fecundi! Why the latter must practically be upon a par with the Pope!

Father, as a man, should have been immune, and Abby was well past childbearing years. Emma's courses had also stopped; she was, regrettably, in all ways withered and dried up, and she was away visiting the Brownells in Fairhaven, so she would not be affected by my blunder at all. Bridget and I were the only women in the household of childbearing age, and she did not even have a fellow as far as I knew, and thus no cause for concern, so surely it would not hurt her. Madame Saint-Genevieve promised prominently in all capital letters that her product posed no detriment to future health and domestic happiness.

And it was a big stewpot, and there were only six, or maybe eight, or ten at most, tiny pills. So *surely* there was *nothing* to worry about. I only hoped, whatever little bit I ingested, might be enough to do me some good and save me from the bleak future I feared and foresaw for myself trapped in wedded misery with David Anthony. If I were found out to be with child by him, he would be compelled to make an honest woman of me, and that was what he had intended all along. That I did not want him was both insignificant and immaterial. We must save face and do what was morally and socially proper; Father was certain to insist upon it, and the Anthonys doubtlessly would also.

We had all gone to bed by nine o'clock because of Father's maddeningly incessant nightly reminders that kerosene and candles cost money, money that should be saved and invested to make *more* money, not squandered on creature comforts.

I lay in my bed, in stifling hot misery listening to the crickets chirp and a dog barking in the distance. I *hated* August! Everyone said that this was the hottest summer they could remember. In my thirty-two years I certainly could not recall a hotter one. Even the night brought little relief; though I left my windows open wide in eager invitation, no breeze crept through the mesh of the screen to stir the lace curtains. It was too hot to sleep. And I was too restless, too worried. Already my sheets were damp with sweat; my lightweight summer nightgown stuck to my body and, with the sodden sheets, tangled my limbs. I hated the way my thighs rubbed together whenever I moved. I lifted my arms above my head but instantly put them down again, sickened by the smell emanating from my armpits. Sweat pooled beneath my breasts, irritating the skin, and when I sat up, freed from the daytime prison of my corset, they felt uncomfortably heavy and pendulous. Despite the delight it can give, a bountiful bosom can be a bane at times. I never felt clean in summer, oil seeped from the pores of my face and no matter how often I washed it, it didn't seem to help. I *longed* for a proper bath-tub, to immerse myself in the blissful chill of cold running water and to lie back and dream that I was a mermaid, a sensual, bare-breasted red-haired siren, trying to beguile a ship full of handsome sailors trapped by the ice of an Arctic expedition. My hair frizzed damply about my face. Though I had braided it tight, already my braid was a fuzzy, bedraggled mess. I felt so restless, I wanted to get up and walk, pace, and move about, but I knew that with the paper-thin walls and the way all the rooms opened into one another I could not do so without disturbing Father and Abby, sleeping, or trying to, on the other side of the locked door blocked, and half-concealed, by my bureau. And I was too distracted to read. I could get up, pour water in the basin, and wet a cloth and wash, I thought, but the water would be warm from the heat and provide little re-lief; my discomfort would be restored to the full degree within mo-ments, so it was hardly worth the bother.

Impulsively I sat up and yanked my nightgown over my head and flung it aside. I turned around and lay down again with my head at the foot of the bed and propped my legs high against the wall. Feet braced flat against the faded wallpaper, I spread them wide, and felt a wanton thrill as my hand dipped greedily between my thighs. The door leading into my bedroom did not have a lock; Emma's room was a dead end, she could not gain entrance to it any other way except by passing through mine, but Emma was away . . . and the other two doors posed no threat. The one leading into the master bedroom was locked and blocked by my bureau, and the guest room was empty, and the door was half blocked by my desk, so I was really quite safe. But still . . . If I were caught in such a po-sition . . . the shame, the humiliation. Father might even part with some of his cherished dollars to consult one of those doctors who specialized in madwomen whose symptoms often took the form of unabashed wantonness. I had to put a hand over my mouth to stifle a giggle, though it really was no laughing matter.

But the truth was my shocking behavior was born more out of boredom than any real desire; it was just something to do, and I was trying not to think about what was happening inside me. Even though I was not hungry, I had forced myself to eat more of the mutton stew than I had any appetite for. I knew the medicine would be greatly diluted and I wanted to ingest enough to do me some good. But, so far, I felt nothing, no signs or clues to tell me it was working. Sometimes I thought I felt a slight heaviness, a sluggishness, and a bloated feeling in my stomach and a faint ache below, as I normally did each month, but a part of me was afraid I was only imagining it, that it was wishful thinking, because I wanted it *so much. Please, God, please, Madame Saint-Genevieve,* I prayed as my hand moved rapidly, slick and sweaty between my thighs, *bring my courses on NOW!*

A moan on the other side of the wall startled me and I started up guiltily and grabbed my nightgown. I sometimes think this style of house is called "cracker box" because the walls are as thin as cheap crackers. In Father and Abby's room someone moaned again and made a desperate scramble for their slop pail and began to vomit. These sounds were repeated as the room's other occupant did likewise. Then came the sputtering of watery bowels. This continued throughout the night.

But I still felt fine and eventually drifted off to sleep. Around six o'clock, however, an urgent loosening in my bowels caused me to start awake. My skin was hot and clammy and my throat was burning as though it were on fire. I barely managed to squat over my slop pail in time before the vile torrent was unleashed. But it was an upset of the stomach, not what I had been hoping for; there was still no sign of that.

At half past nine when I went downstairs, Abby was as white as Death, shivering, despite the sheen of sweat on her brow, sitting at the table in abject misery, complaining that since last night her throat had felt as if she had swallowed a lit match, and such cramps assailed her stomach she felt as if she were being stabbed by a hundred knives. She shivered and complained of clammy skin, then was interrupted by the sudden need to vomit again.

A little while later, though she knew Father would disapprove, she stole across the street to see Dr. Bowen. He was most sympathetic. He blamed her illness on the mutton; he suspected it had gone putrid in the hot weather. After she had vomited again right there in his office he prescribed a dose of castor oil to be washed down with a small glass of port wine, and even escorted her back across the street so he could see for himself how the rest of us fared. I was simply *mortified* when Father, despite feeling poorly himself, ordered him out and told him in no uncertain terms that his services were not required and, furthermore, not to even think of sending him a bill for a house call he had not requested.

Bridget was sick as well; she complained of nausea, of being sick several times during the night. A few times she had to stop what she was doing about the house and rush out into the backyard and vomit again. Each time she came back, moving slowly, cradling her sides tenderly as if they ached, ashen faced, with a heavy sweat shimmering on her skin. But I . . . beyond the early-morning stomach upset, I didn't feel ill at all.

The more I brooded over it, the more desperate I became. I couldn't bear the waiting. Even if I dispatched another dollar right away it would be *days* before another dose of Madame Saint-Genevieve's Miracle could reach me. Finally, I could endure no more; I changed out of my housedress and into a deep-blue bengaline suitable for town, put on my hat and gloves, and went out.

I remembered reading something, in a detective story or a book of household hints—I really wasn't sure which—about Prussic Acid being used to get rid of pests. The name had stuck in my mind because at the time I had just finished reading the most *thrilling* romance, in which the heroine was carried off on a white horse by a dashing Prussian cavalry officer who was nothing but a trifler and a real cad where women were concerned. He had stolen her peerless, priceless necklace of pearls to settle a debt of honor and then her heart and, by discreetly worded implication, her virtue, but a wedding quickly followed and the final page contained the comforting assurance that they lived happily ever after in the rustic magnificence of an English country estate with their eleven children. I thought perhaps . . . just a *small* dose . . . and if perchance in the unlikely event that it killed me too despite my carefulness . . . well, that would still be better than living out the rest of my life as David Anthony's unhappy and maltreated wife and the mother of his equally wretched offspring.

I was obviously *desperate* and not thinking clearly. Only later would I discover just how dangerous Prussic Acid really was, that a *single* grain brought *instantaneous* death—and to think I had been on the verge of slapping that idiot druggist after I imperiously informed him that *he* was mistaken! My face flames at the memory and I feel an utter fool! If I had been thinking more clearly, I would not have gone at all, or, if I had, I would have asked for something safer like arsenic instead, where a minuscule dose stood a greater chance of bringing about the desired result—abortion—and entailed a much slighter risk of immediate and agonizing death.

Indeed, time *would* tell me that I *really* should *not* have gone to that drugstore at all; that little foray into the wrong part of town would come back to haunt me. All I can say in my defense is that it was an act of the most desperate impulse. I didn't really think it out; I just turned my steps toward the south side of town, the one where the shops were of a decidedly inferior class, so none of the shopkeepers would know me and I was unlikely to meet anyone of my milieu, and went into the first drugstore I saw—Smith's.

The clerk, Eli Bence, was a supercilious little man, and I disliked him at first glance. But I squared my shoulders, lifted my chin, and haughtily demanded ten cents' worth of Prussic Acid. I had my excuse at the ready; I wanted it to kill moths infesting my sealskin cape.

But Mr. Bence refused to sell me any, saying that in all his years as a pharmacist he had never before heard of Prussic Acid being used for such a purpose. I held my ground and insisted I had purchased it for this purpose many times before. He then had the *gall* to tell me that sealskins are impervious to moths, which I later found out was actually true. But that doesn't matter in the least—a *gentleman never* contradicts a lady, so he really shouldn't have said it; the fact that he did shows a decided lack of breeding. No wonder he was working in a drugstore on the *wrong* side of town!

I tried to sway him, smiling and saying surely just a teeny-tiny bit couldn't possibly do any harm, except to the moths, of course, but that impertinent nincompoop Mr. Bence was adamant: "My good lady, it is something we don't sell unless by a prescription from a doctor, as it is a *very* dangerous thing to handle."

There was no point in arguing with such an ignorant and inso-
lent person, and I left the store in an empty-handed huff. As I was
walking down the sidewalk, I felt an ache, a clenching cramp in my
nether parts, and . . . Could it be? *Yes!* It was! The ache grew more
insistent, more pronounced, clutching, stabbing, *wringing* my
womb. But this time I didn't deplore the pain; instead I *welcomed*
it and thanked God for it. My prayers had been answered. My
courses had come; if I had just been patient and waited . . . I could
have saved all that time and worry, and Father's dollar, and not had
to contend with such a rude, ignorant, uninformed fool as Eli
Bence. I hadn't been pregnant after all! I almost laughed at myself
for my foolishness! I was so relieved I wanted to dance a jig and at
the same time fall down on my knees right there in the middle of
the sidewalk and thank God. Instead, I quickened my steps and
hurried home before the telltale red stains began to seep through
my skirts. I was so happy I was practically skipping along the sidewalk.

As I neared the house, I saw David Anthony lurking outside the
gate, a contented look on his face like a cat that has just swallowed
a fat yellow canary and still has the telltale feathers stuck in his
whiskers. He had a little brown sack of lemon drops in his hand, a
silent reminder of the happy days when we had shared candies and
kisses in the barn.

"*What are you doing here?*" I demanded.

"Just biding my time," he answered with a menacing smile.

"*Go away!*" I hissed like an angry cat.

He shrugged and tipped his straw boater at me. "I'll go away,
Lizzie, but I'll be back. You *will* be mine; it's only a matter of time.
And when I do you'll welcome me. Think about it. . . ." He forced
a lemon drop into my mouth, which I promptly spat out, but he just
laughed at me. "You don't want to be a sour old maid, do you?"

I stood and watched him walk away; then I ran into the house
and flew up the stairs to my room.

My former jubilation was gone. I couldn't calm down. Relentlessly, I paced the floor. My nerves just wouldn't settle. I felt a
tense, taut pounding behind my eyes, and around my skull a tightening, like a vise, as though my skull were shrinking, putting in-

tense pressure on my brain, trying to squeeze it down to the size of a walnut and then *crack* it. Suddenly I bent double. I felt the wringing pain in my womb and the blood oozing out between my legs. I felt sick and scrambled for my slop pail, but vomited all over the floor before I found it, but I didn't care. At least now I knew for certain that I wasn't pregnant, but my lost virtue, and the proof of it in David's possession, could still condemn me. Now *that* worry consumed me. But I hadn't the faintest idea what to do about it.

I lay flat on the floor sweating profusely through my clothes and gasping like a fish out of water, dying for want of breath. Behind my tightly clenched lids it was like watching a fireworks show—a dizzying explosion of vivid colors, mostly a *furious* red. Migraines often came hand in hand with my monthly courses, and in the summer heat they were always much worse. The bleeding always played havoc with my emotions, making the slightest upset seem as monumental as the end of the world. I slowly pulled myself up and lay down on my bed and drew up my knees, trying to ease the cramping, and recalled again David Anthony's ominous words: "I'll go away, Lizzie, but I'll be back. You *will* be mine; it's only a matter of time."

His words froze my heart with fear. His dark eyes, black as the Devil's soul, told me every word was true. He would be back and try to claim me as his own, body and soul; David *would* damn me.

With every hour that passed the feeling of fear intensified, turning up the flame of pain inside my head and womb. I kept wondering *what* David would do and *when* he would do it. How much time did I have? Could I get my wits together enough to outmaneuver him? Was that even possible? I needed to talk to *someone, anyone* who would be patient, kind, and listen. I needed to unburden myself. In that moment I almost wished I were Catholic so I could go to confession. Who could I turn to? I could not disclose the full extent of my shame; my lost virtue would have to remain my burden alone to carry. I could not trust anyone not to betray me, but I *had* to get out; I needed the consolation, the balm, of human sympathy. Suddenly I thought of Alice—Alice Russell. Emma and I had known her for years. A kindly but fussy, fidgety bird-boned spinster subsisting in genteel poverty in rented rooms above a bakery.

It was already late to go calling, but I got up off my bed, tidied my hair and clothes, put on my hat, and rushed around the corner to knock on Alice's door.

When I saw her smiling, expectant face and the welcome shining in her blue eyes behind the glass lenses of her gold-rimmed spectacles, I was so relieved I flung myself into her arms.

I told Alice that I was *so* afraid that *someone* would do *something,* something *terrible!* I clung to her and confided in an ominous whisper that I had seen, several times, a dark man loitering outside the house and that I slept every night with one eye open for fear that this dark man of mystery would burn the house down over our heads. I told her about the recent illness that had afflicted our household, but I blamed it on the milk, suggesting that perhaps this mysterious man had poisoned it in the dark hours before dawn when the milkman left the cans sitting outside the back door for Bridget to bring in when she awoke. I told Alice how mortified I had been by Father's treatment of Dr. Bowen when he called round to check on us after Abby's visit. I think I said something about Father having an enemy, a fearsome, burly red-haired Scotsman, "with arms like Thor, who had spent eternity hammering at his anvil," I added colorfully. He had come to the house and quarreled loudly with Father because he refused to rent him a store in his pride and joy the A. J. Borden Building, saying he would not let a shop for such a purpose, so surely the Scot must be a man of evil intentions, or, at the very least, a purveyor of immoral goods.

I told Alice "all" about the broad daylight burglary, and the theft of money, jewelry, and streetcar tickets from Abby's desk in the master bedroom, the eight-penny nail I had found stuck in the cellar door padlock, and that the barn had been broken into and my precious pigeons most cruelly *murdered—decapitated; poor creatures!* Though, of course, I neglected to disclose the fact that this was done by Father and that their plump roasted bodies had come to grace our dinner table afterward, or that Emma and I had been responsible for the crime that had precipitated it. I simply *couldn't* tell Alice something like *that!* What would she think of us if she knew? *Nice* girls—*Borden* girls, *Fall River* girls—didn't stage burglaries; it simply wasn't done.

Alice was *very* kind and consoling. I could not have found a better shoulder to cry on. She held me close and patted my back and suggested I go away for a little while, take "a lovely little holiday," somewhere by the sea like Buzzards Bay perhaps. Undisturbed rest and a change of scenery would surely do me good, she said, and I might try my hand at some worthwhile handicraft like basket weaving, and it might also be a good idea, she added, to restrict my reading to the Bible and abstain entirely from the more lurid and melodramatic forms of literature, as they tended to stir the imagination like a witches' brew.

What she really meant but was too kind to say was: *You are letting your imagination run away with you, Lizzie.* It was clear she did not take me seriously, but I didn't care. *Confession really is good for the soul,* I marveled. *No wonder the Catholics think so highly of it!* Talking to Alice actually *had* made me feel better, though admittedly it didn't help resolve the dilemma of David one jot.

"I don't know but what *somebody* will do *something,*" I said, digging in my heels and clinging to Alice as she bid me good night and gently, but firmly, and none too subtly, pushed me out the door. "I am afraid *somebody* will do *something—something terrible*. . . ."

When the door shut behind me I felt as though I had been relieved of a great and terrible burden. I had blurted out my fears into a kind and caring ear; even though I had lied, twisted, and concealed the true source of them somewhat, I still felt better for it. I smiled, and I had to stop myself from skipping as I hurried home. It was nearly nine o'clock.

As I fastened all three locks on the front door behind me I heard voices coming from the sitting room, but I didn't go in. Father's voice, and Abby's, I recognized, and it took me only a moment to identify the third: Uncle John Vinnicum Morse, our late mother's brother, or "that ol' fanny pincher," as Bridget called him in unconcealed disgust.

Damn, damn, damn! I wanted to stamp my feet, pull my hair, and *scream.*

Though to all the women in the house he was a thankfully infrequent guest, in Father's eyes Uncle John was always a welcome one. He was one of the few people Father trusted, especially when it came to financial matters, and when Uncle John darkened our doorstep it was certain money was the magnet that drew him. Until recently he had been living in Hastings, Iowa, as a farmer and horse trader, but he had since moved nearer, to New Bedford, where he shared a house with a blind butcher. Though Uncle John professed to have our—Emma's and my—best interests at heart, always referring to us as "dear Sarah's girls," neither of us really liked him and we often went out of our way to avoid him, as I understand many other women did also. To put it delicately, Uncle John was a real bottom pincher, and all of us, even the unsightly mountain of flesh that was Abby, had the bruises to show for it every time he came to visit us.

He also liked to chew raw garlic, being thoroughly convinced that it was of great benefit to his health—"a cure-all in one clove," he called it and "a damn sight cheaper than seein' the doctor"— and to walk around in his red flannel union suit as a sacrifice upon the altar of the God of Thrift, to save his good and only suit, the same shiny, rusty black one he had been wearing since our mother's funeral, despite the fact that he was rich enough to buy out Savile Row and still be rich as Midas. His only extravagance was consulting fortune-tellers. He had sworn by them ever since as a barefoot boy he had been warned by an old gypsy woman whom he had allowed to read his palm upon a dare that he would step upon a piece of broken glass and cut his foot open one summer's day, bad enough to bleed almost a bucket full and leave a lifelong scar, and lo and behold, he did, and ever since that prophecy was fulfilled he *never* made a decision without consulting some gypsy seer hovering over her crystal ball, tarot cards, tea leaves, or the palm he held out crossed with silver. Otherwise, he made Father's parsimony seem like largesse on the grandest scale.

I shuddered with loathing and bent to unlace my boots before tiptoeing upstairs in my stockinged feet. I would rather go to bed without supper than sit down with Uncle John. The next morning, I decided, I would lie abed late and come down only when I was certain that Uncle John had gone out. My courses provided the perfect excuse to cloak my incivility. And, with any luck, I could avoid Uncle John altogether; he rarely stayed more than a day or two. And even if he ventured into my bedroom to say hello, if I kept my bottom in the bed he couldn't very well pinch it.

Chapter 6

Squeezing my eyelids tight against the blazing bright intrusion of another blistering August day that seemed to scorch right through my lace curtains, I awoke, greatly annoyed, to the sound of voices—Uncle John and Father talking as they descended the stairs together to partake of Uncle John's favorite breakfast of johnny-cakes with maple syrup and sliced bananas that Abby always prepared when he visited us. Just the thought of food made me nauseous. I thought I smelled fish. Of course, never one to squander a morsel, Father would have ordered the fried swordfish from last night's supper reheated along with what was left of that ghastly mutton stew. Even Abby's pleas to dispose of it, that it was surely heat spoiled and had made us all sick, could not induce him to let Bridget throw it out. I moaned as pain wrung more blood from my womb, and rolled over in bed and pulled the covers up over my head despite the heat. I knew I should rise and change the blood-soaked towel chafing a blister between my tightly clenched thighs before it seeped through my nightgown onto the sheets, if it hadn't already, but I was just too tired and wretched. David still had my drawers and handkerchief, proof that I was no longer a virgin. I could of course claim a nosebleed, but that would only explain the bloodstains on my handkerchief, not how he happened to be in possession of it. Then there was the even more embarrassing matter of my underpants. Somehow I very much doubted anyone would believe he had stolen them off the clothesline in our back-yard when Bridget hung the laundry up to dry just to blackmail me into becoming his bride.

I had hardly slept at all the night before. I had awakened around midnight to what sounded like someone banging on the back fence. I rose and peered through the lace curtains and in the moonlight saw the silhouette of a man jumping the fence. He crept stealthily across the yard, light-footed as a cat, to stand beneath the pear tree, and bent to gather up an armful of the fallen fruit. I watched him steal into the barn. A few minutes later he emerged and stood boldly in the yard, fully illuminated by the moonlight, staring up at my window. It was David Anthony. Our eyes met. He smiled and tipped his hat to me and then sprang back over the fence like a sat-isfied tomcat. Maybe I only imagined it, but I thought I heard him whistling "The Wedding March."

I returned to my bed, but I could not rest. I kept wondering what David had been doing in our barn. I tossed and turned until dawn. Finally, in the first gray light of morning, after the milkman had come and gone, I could stand it no longer. I rose from my bed and, in my nightgown and bare feet, crept downstairs and out the back door. As soon as I opened the barn door I saw it—the yellow-green pears lying on the dirt floor arranged in the shape of a heart. With a stick, driven deep into the hard-packed earthen floor, David had drawn an arrow piercing it and above and below its shaft had crudely inscribed our initials—*D.A. & L.B.*—and scrawled the ominous, emphatic word *FOREVER!*

I fell to my knees and furiously rubbed out the inscription. Then I gathered the pears up in the now badly soiled skirt of my night-gown and carried them back outside and dumped them on the ground at the foot of the pear tree, scattering them with my bare foot, before I tiptoed back inside.

When I heard Father and Uncle John bidding each other good

day as they parted ways, I gave up on trying to fall back asleep and dragged myself out of bed. There was dirt on my hands and feet and all over the front of my nightgown, so I knew the heart of pears David had left for me had not been just a bad dream. I washed in the lukewarm water that had been standing overnight in my washstand and fastened on a fresh towel and daubed some greasy ointment on the sore, chafed skin and the blisters the bulky towels always raised on my inner thighs, though I knew I was only wasting my time, and the ointment; as soon as I started walking it would rub off. I tossed the soiled towel into the pail half-filled with water and borax that I kept under my bed for this purpose and then with my toes shoved it back out of sight. I barely bothered with my hair, braiding it and twisting it up and pinning it on top of my head in a sloppy, frizzy bun. The pins made my head ache, but I couldn't bear to have my hair down sticking to my neck in this abominable heat. I didn't feel like bothering with stays or stockings, it was just too hot, so I stepped into my drawers and yanked on my thinnest summer chemise, a single petticoat, and my old, by now badly faded, paint-stained blue diamond housedress and thrust my feet back into my comfortable old black house slippers and, with them slapping against my sweaty heels, sulkily descended the stairs with my slop pail to empty it in the cellar privy. I would tend to the pail of soiled napkins later. There would be plenty of time for Bridget to launder them before my bothersome and detested visitor arrived again next month to torment me.

It was so hot I didn't feel like doing anything. I sat in the kitchen, nursing the red-hot, hammering ache behind my blood-shot sleep-gummed eyes with a cup of steaming coffee, listlessly crumbling one of the oatmeal cookies Abby had baked to welcome Uncle John. I heard Abby lumbering about upstairs, like an elephant, tidying up the guest room where Uncle John had slept last night, and groaned and laid my head upon the table.

"Are you all right, Miss Lizzie?" Bridget asked, pausing on her way outside to wash the windows. Abby had been patient, letting Bridget put off this most detested of chores for weeks, but had woken up this morning adamant that today was the day it *must* be done despite the hellish heat and food poisoning, as "Mr. Borden had had some words to say about it." Knowing Father, he was probably upset that a visitor, even one like Uncle John who wouldn't give a fig about it, had arrived to find the house with dirty windows.

I just groaned and banged my brow against the table. It was then that I spied the banana lying on the table just inches from my head. It made me think of David Anthony's organ of masculinity, and all the times I had touched it and held it in my hand, and the one time I had, with misgivings, taken it into my mouth. And the last time, when I had felt it thrust forcefully, powerfully, and painfully into my body, to trap me into a marriage I didn't want. With an angry cry, I shot up from my chair, wrenched off the peel, and smashed the banana into a pulp before I burst into tears and fled back upstairs with the mushy mess still clinging to my fingers and palm, ignoring the odd, pitying look Bridget gave me. I half-hoped she would follow me, take me in her arms, and call me "*macushla*," but she didn't. She was already out the back door jostling her soap, pail, and mop against the beautiful, bountiful curve of her hip. I knew she must still be feeling poorly, since she was not singing about those golden slippers like she always did when she was about her chores.

As the morning wore on, I felt caged and restless in my room, tormented by my fears about David Anthony and the damning linens in his possession. I tried to read and took up countless books and magazines only to toss them aside; my mind was like a sieve and wouldn't hold any of the words. I felt like I was a pot simmering with secrets and fears that were about to boil over and scald and scar me and change my life forever. Somehow I think I knew it was all about to end. Finally, I could stand it no more. I gathered up the handkerchiefs I had been meaning to iron for a fortnight and trudged back downstairs to the kitchen.

I was sitting at the kitchen table idly leafing through an old magazine, trying to interest myself in a very entertaining and revealing article about a year in the life of a corset salesman, and nibbling oatmeal cookies and sipping coffee while I waited for the iron to heat, when I suddenly became aware of muffled voices. Though

I could not distinguish actual words, there was a sense of urgency about them. I instinctively knew that *something* was wrong and, with my heart pounding, followed the sound into the sitting room. I knew the woman's voice was Abby's, but who did the other voice, the masculine one, belong to? Father and Uncle John had both gone out and I doubted either of them had returned so soon. And Bridget was outside, balancing precariously on the top rung of the ladder to reach the upper windows. She was so intent on her work, and not falling down and breaking her neck, she probably wasn't even aware that company had come calling, much less clambered down to let them in like a proper maidservant should.

I was curious, and I had a right to be, this was after all my home too, so I went to see who was in the sitting room. I froze on the threshold while in my mind, like a magic lantern show, I saw a series of vivid and horrifying pictures, a terrifying *tableau vivant* of bloodied lips, broken ribs, bruises, blackened eyes, and grotesquely bulging pregnant bellies, red-faced squalling infants, and toddlers clinging to my skirts with jam-sticky fingers, illustrating what my life would be like as David Anthony's wife. I couldn't move or speak; I don't think I even breathed. I just stood and stared at them.

Hat in hands, like a humble man, David stood before Abby. She was seated on the horsehair sofa in her old mint-sprigged white cotton tent of a housedress, with a deep frown furrowing her brow, and her hands, folded in her lap, were clenched tight and shaking. When she turned and looked at me I *knew* she was wishing that those furious fat fingers were curled tight around my neck; she was mad enough to want to murder me. It was then I noticed what lay draped over the sofa arm beside her—my drawers and the handkerchief David had used to wipe me. It was no use denying that they were mine; the hanky was embroidered with my initials *L.B.* in blue silk thread and the bloomers were trimmed with matching blue ribbons and lace, a "senseless extravagance" much deplored by Father. Now he would know that someone besides me and the Maggie had seen them.

David and Abby abruptly stopped speaking when I walked into the room. He gave a quick nod to Abby and swiftly took his leave.

As he passed me, I saw triumph in his eyes and caught a snippet of "The Wedding March" wafting back at me from his puckered lips. I reeled backward as though he had just slapped me.

Like a crucified figure, I braced myself in the doorway, before turning slowly back around to face Abby. My fate was in her hands and both of us knew it. I knew before a single word was spoken that I was doomed.

I am sorry to disappoint those who have been salivating all these years for a blow-by-blow account of what happened that blistering August morning, but I cannot provide one. There were moments when I felt as though I were living under deep murky water like a lazy catfish, when everything seemed to happen *sooooooo ssssss-llllllloooooooowwwwwwwwwwllllllllyyyyyy,* and others when everything seemed to speed up so fast and pass in a dizzying blur. In spite of what some might think, my vagueness about that day has never been intentional or feigned.

I remember Abby sharply expressing her disappointment in me, her shame and disgust at me and my wanton, whorish ways. Her kindness was a thing of the past; a gift I had disdained once too often, now it was gone forever. I stood there, lost for words, blundering and blubbering, desperately wringing my hands, feeling the blood oozing out from between my thighs, in a silent mockery, proving that I was not carrying David Anthony's child. But that didn't matter now; my dirty linen was lying on the sofa, proving that my chastity and good name were both things of the past.

At one point, I fell on my knees and caught desperately at Abby's hands, groveling and weeping, begging and pleading, but to no avail. Abby pulled her hands away from me as though my touch might give her leprosy. *Unclean thing!* her eyes screamed, telling me that I was not a smidgen better than the painted whores who walked the streets on the wrong side of town. I called her "Mother"— "*MOTHER, PLEASE!*"—I sobbed, but this time it was Abby who coldly reminded *me* that she was not my mother, only my *stepmother.* Now it was she, not Emma and me, who had no mercy, no pity, no kindness in her heart. When I told her I did not want to be David Anthony's wife, she told me I should have thought of that before I opened my legs to him.

Abby said I was "cheap" and "lucky" that David was "willing" to marry me. "Most men won't bother to buy the cow if they can get the milk for free. That's the trouble with you; you've never realized just how *lucky* you are, Lizzie. So much has simply been handed to you, but you've never shown a mite of gratitude for anything."

"*You're* a *COW* and I *HATE* you!" I blurted out before I could stop myself, then clamped a hand tight over my mouth after it was too late to take the words back.

"Well then, there's nothing more to be said, is there? Until your father comes home," she added pointedly.

And then Abby turned her back on *me*. That was the end. She no longer wanted me to be her little girl. She no longer wanted to be my mother. Talking with David Anthony had transformed her into the wicked stepmother Emma and I had imagined she was all along. The doughy-soft sugary-sweet Abby was gone; now she was like a gigantic granite boulder glazed with ice that was determined to *crush* me. I heard her going up the stairs, her heavy, lumbering tread just like an elephant's, leaving me alone to contemplate my dishonor and disgrace and the unhappy future that lay before me as Mrs. Anthony. I snatched up those damning linens, furiously wadding them into a bundle, as tight and small as I could make them, wishing I could just make them disappear. But what good would that do now? Abby had already seen them. Father would believe her . . . and David. I didn't stand a chance against them. I was trapped. *Trapped!* Just like David had said.

I had to get out. I was suffocating. I couldn't breathe in that house! I felt the walls closing in on me. I needed air; I needed to think, to clear my head. Hazy red stars danced maddeningly before my eyes and I felt so hot I thought surely I was going to die if I didn't get out. As I rushed through the kitchen I shoved my shameful bundle into the fire. Let it burn! Devil take the damning evidence against me straight to Hell! I didn't want to see it, touch it, or think about it! I just wanted it to disappear! Abby could tell Father whatever she liked, but at least now he couldn't see the evidence with his own eyes. I ran outside, gasping frantically for air, gulping it in hungrily by the mouthful, but I couldn't stand the open space of the backyard either. Suddenly I felt so exposed and vulnerable, like a woman about to face a firing squad.

I darted desperately into the barn, seeking some sort of haven there, though I knew it would be hotter than an oven inside, and dreadfully dusty, and I hated it now for all the memories it held of David. As I slumped light-headed against the wall, willing myself not to faint, to stay alert and think—*Think, Lizzie, think! Find a way to save yourself!*—a silver gilt glimmer caught the corner of my eye.

The hatchet! It was practically new. It had been used only once as far as I knew, when Father had killed my pigeons. I took it up. I felt its weight in my hands. In a peculiar, perplexing way I can't truly explain, it was almost *comforting.* It gave the illusion of power back to me; it made me feel that *I* was in *control* of my own destiny, that it was my own sense of powerlessness that was truly the illusion. The power was in *my* hands, *not* theirs; no one else had mastery over me unless I was meek and allowed it!

The funny pattern in the wood grain of the hickory handle almost coaxed a smile and a chuckle from me. Bridget and I thought it resembled the late President Lincoln's profile, and she had called it "the Great Emancipator" in jest because in the right, or wrong, hands, given the circumstances, it could set souls free. It occurred to me then that it could, like Lincoln freeing the slaves, also set *me* free.

Save me; save me; set me free! I prayed to it, like a silver gilt idol, with *all* my might, and a little voice in the back of my head began to sing, "The Battle Hymn of the Republic"—repeating over and over again the verse that went: "As He died to make men holy, let us die to make men free"—*free* as I *ached,* body and soul, to be, to live by my *own* will and whims, not wholly at the mercy of Father's, or some other man's, sufferance!

Gripping the handle tight, holding on for dear life, I walked slowly back to the house, with the hatchet's glistening blade hidden in the folds of my skirt. When I glanced down and saw it nestled against the part that was stained with paint it occurred to me then that the reddish-brown color looked just like dried blood.

I went upstairs to my room. I laid the hatchet down reverently upon my bed. I stood and stared at it with heavy, drowsy suddenly very sleepy eyes, swaying like a woman mesmerized. As the sunlight pouring in through the open window played over the silver gilt like sunshine reflecting upon a river, I thought of water and baptism, of being cleansed of my sins, renewed, reborn. I began to take off my clothes. I just wanted to lie down and go to sleep and never wake up, and if God was truly merciful, I thought, that was what would happen. He would gather me to His bosom instead of foisting me into David Anthony's arms.

Through the thin wall I heard Abby singing in the guest room. David's visit had interrupted her before she had finished tidying it up for Uncle John. That was Abby's way; I knew she was trying to distract herself and put all the unpleasantness out of her mind until Father came home.

I tossed my paint-stained housedress onto the bed—sky-blue diamonds merging with navy, like ripples of water, light and dark, in sunlight and in shadows. I pulled my chemise up over my head and peeled off my petticoat and stepped out of my slippers and drawers. I scowled in annoyance at the single pinprick-sized spot of blood on the back of my petticoat; it was the kind of stain the women of Fall River discreetly referred to as a flea bite. I think I meant to change the heavy, blood-sodden towel for a fresh one. I even pulled the pail out from under my bed. I heard . . . saw? . . . the slosh of bloody water and the soiled napkins swirling inside the pail. It sounded as far off as the sea, the vast blue waters that had once carried me away to another continent, another life, another world, and given me one sweet, sweet taste of freedom.

My head felt unbearably heavy. I thought my neck would surely break beneath its weight, like a pile of bricks balanced upon a toothpick. My sight was shrouded by a rolling red mist and exploding stars, bright bursts of light popping against the red, making me fear that one of them would extinguish my sight forever and leave me stone-black blind. I wanted to lie down, I felt so sleepy and faint, heavy and light-headed all at the same time, but my feet were already moving with a mind and determination of their own and the hatchet was in my hands, hell-bent on securing my freedom. Now was not the time to waver or succumb to weakness like some swooning heroine in a romance novel waiting for the hero to save her. There was no "hero born of woman" to "crush the serpent with his heel" (the little voice in my head was *still* singing random snatches of "The Battle Hymn": only it wasn't one voice anymore. It was a whole chorus all singing different verses and snippets at the same discordant time so I could hardly think, only intuitively understand what they were telling me I *had* to do). There was only me ... that song, and the hatchet, "the Great Emancipator." "His truth is marching on. ..."

Wearing only the bright red-flowered pink calico belt that held the cumbersome towel in place between my raw, red thighs, with the silver gilt of the hatchet's head cold as ice against my hot, sweaty breasts, I approached the guest room door. I laid the hatchet down on my desk while I lifted and shifted the end that partially blocked the door just enough for me to open it. I vaguely remember my nipples puckering as I paused on the threshold and stared down at my feet as though I had never seen them before. I wiggled my toes, sweaty and pink, against the faded flowers of the ancient carpet.

I hefted the hatchet in my hand and shivered as it grazed my breasts. I closed my eyes and let myself dream I was the true-hearted heroine whose hope sprang evergreen being caressed by her long-lost love, one of over a hundred souls presumed perished on an ill-fated Arctic expedition. I felt so weak, and then, as I stood upon the threshold of the guest room, I tingled with a surge of sudden strength, like a jolt of electricity, that made my spine snap erect.

Abby was still singing. "From this valley they say you are going/ Do not hasten to bid me adieu/Just remember..." She had her back to the door; she was bending over the bed, plumping a pillow she had just put in a fresh white slip and adjusting the coverlet. She never sensed that anything was wrong. The hairs never tingled warningly on the nape of her neck. No guardian angel tapped her shoulder to alert her that Death was sneaking up behind her.

"He has loosed the fateful lightning of His terrible, swift

sword. . . ." I raised the hatchet high, I felt its heaviness in my shoulders, and I brought it down *HARD*. It pulled and hurt me too as the blade bit deep with a terrible crunch into the back of her head. *This hurts me just as much as it hurts you*. . . . I wanted to tell Abby, and maybe I did; I just don't know if the whisper was only inside my own aching, pulsing, pounding head. *I wish it didn't have to be like this*. . . . Then I did it again. And again. Again and again and again and again . . .

The popular singsong rope-skipping rhyme that came afterward says I did it forty times, but the coroner counted nineteen blows. But I wasn't counting; I only know I did it several times. After the first blow, or maybe two, she fell facedown, jarring the whole house. I half-feared she would fall crashing through the floor. I almost wish she had; maybe they would have thought her death was just a terrible accident? But she didn't; she just lay there twitching and bleeding on the floor, her blood reviving the faded flowers on the carpet. I'd never seen them look so bright before.

I planted my feet wide, standing firmly astride her, and raised the hatchet high. One blow cut through her switch of false hair and it flew up onto the bed like a wild black bird that raised goose bumps all over me and nearly startled me out of my skin. I felt her blood splash my face, salty and hot. I *tasted* it on my lips. *The blood is the life*—I *tasted* her life as I was taking it away! I never felt such power, or such horror, or such a terrible sadness. I hated myself; I hated Abby; I hated David Anthony; I hated that I had been driven to this murderous madness. But what choice did they give me? *They drove me to it!* It wasn't *my* fault! So I just kept hitting her. *I couldn't stop!* I don't think I wanted to, but in a little part deep in my heart I did, but I couldn't. I just kept hacking away at the back of her head.

Blood and gristle and bone kept flying while the muscles in my arms, shoulders, and back felt like they were fraying, screaming and straining with every blow. My breasts ached and felt painfully heavy as they swung free. *Free!*—the way I had always wanted to be! *Free!* But there was *always* something or someone that wanted to enslave me, to keep me chained and bound like a dog or a slave or a criminal to an owner or some outmoded or unjust social convention! There was a large flap of skin on the back of Abby's scalp that kept opening and closing, like a bloody mouth, mutely crying out for me to *Stop!* Finally I listened; I really did stop.

As suddenly as it began, all the rage and resentment left me. Like a great wave of icy water had just struck me and knocked me off balance, I slumped, shivering mightily, onto the floor. It was the hottest summer in human memory, yet I'd never been so cold in my life. My knees simply buckled and I dropped down onto the floor beside Abby. "And then she saw what she had done . . ." So goes the rhyme. They got that part *exactly* right.

Breathless and quivering, I sat there, naked as a babe in a diaper, in Abby's blood, feeling it soaking through the towel and mingling with my monthly blood. For the second time in my life I was sitting in my mother's blood; only this time it was my *step* mother's blood and *I* had been the one to spill it. *I* had *killed* her. *I* had made the blood *pour* out of her.

"*Mother!*" I whispered, and reached out a tentative hand to touch her shoulder; it was still twitching. My hand was still there when it finally stopped, when the last little bit of life left her, and then I began to cry.

In my mind I saw Abby, her moon-round open and friendly face and sweet, shy smile, her crinoline billowing wide, like a big plum-colored cloud, as she crouched down to shake my hand for the very first time. I remembered mincemeat pies sprinkled with rosewater and love like a dash of fairy dust, a pretty pink dress and the unexpectedly becoming sunny yellow sash she tied around my waist, the painstaking care she had taken to curl my hair into perfect gleaming red ringlets garnished with ribbons, "just like a little French doll." She beamed with proud delight as she stepped back to admire me; anyone who saw her face then would have truly believed she was my mother—I could *still* hear her! She *had* loved me; she had *liked* me then. In those days she really was my friend! I could have been the daughter, and she could have been the mother, whom we both wanted and needed so badly, but . . . I chose to let Emma step into our dead mother's shoes and take my hand and lead me away from Abby. I thought it was my duty. I was a good little soldier; Emma said so.

Abby . . . She had *never* stopped trying to win back my love, but every time I felt my heart start to soften . . . Emma was right there like an evil black crow cawing in my ear to remind me and stiffen my resolve, like a good little soldier serving Mother's memory like a queen. And then David Anthony had come along and changed love to hate forever; he had made certain that there was no going back, I could never change my mind. Even if I decided to let Abby into my heart again, hers would be closed to me, locked and barred forever because of what I had done in the hayloft with David Anthony. I was not the kind of daughter any respectable God-fearing woman would ever want to call her own. Did those women who walked the streets in their gaudy gowns and painted faces, selling their bodies, even have mothers or had they all disowned their daughters, cast them out of their hearts the way Abby had me? Even being a mere stepmother to one such as me would shame Abby. I was an object of disgust, riddled with sin, more loathsome than any toad, snake, or slug! I suddenly wanted very much to be invisible, so no one could look upon my shame.

But there was another reason I chose to hate Abby, one that no one else ever guessed. When I looked at her I sometimes thought I was looking into a magic mirror that foretold the future—*my* future. I saw too much of myself in her. It frightened me so much that I shrank and ran from her and pushed her away every chance I could even as I secretly despised myself for my cruelty, simply because I didn't want to wake up one morning and discover that I had become her.

Abby knew what it was like to live without love. She had married Father for security and to acquire a ready-made family. It was a match of convenience, not love. For thirty-seven years she had stood by and watched her friends and female relations marry and give birth while she sat home alone, a dutiful and obedient daughter, an old maid without prospects seeking consolation in sweets, watching her hips and belly broaden with fat instead of a baby. I pitied her, and I also understood her, we were two of a kind beneath the skin, and then the likeness truly began to *show*.

I knew how it felt to hear the dressmaker cluck her tongue when my dresses had to be let out an extra inch or she measured me for new ones and paused to make a note of my broadening girth. I had seen a photograph of Abby as a young woman when her figure could still be called pleasingly voluptuous, but as the years passed, her waist disappeared, all pretense at fashion faded, and her dresses became more like sacks and then tents. Whenever I ate cookies for comfort, I thought of Abby. I thought of the future and saw myself becoming her and it terrified me.

And I knew in my heart, no matter what hopes and dreams I harbored, that if I ever made a match of my own it would be because my husband saw a great big dollar sign whenever he looked at me and not the love of his life. Father *was* right, no matter how much I denied and despised that hard and brutal fact—and *he* would *never* let me forget it—and whenever I looked at the mirror of Abby and saw myself in her, *she* wouldn't, and *I* wouldn't, let me forget either. The truth *is ugly* and *viciously unkind!*

I don't know how much time passed before Bridget found me, sitting there in the blood, stroking Abby's back. Bridget just suddenly seemed to materialize like a spirit out of the ether there beside me.

"Oh, Miss Lizzie, *what have you done?*" she wailed.

I looked up at her with a quivering chin and eyes wide and dumb as a cow's.

Bridget had always liked Abby and her eyes were filled with tears as she crossed herself and muttered a quick prayer for Abby's departed soul to rest in peace.

I began to sob and shake; I felt the emotions building within me like a volcano that was about to erupt with a vengeance and destroy *everything*. I had killed Abby, I hadn't made things better, I had made them worse, and now I would surely hang or spend the rest of my life in prison. I would *never* be free!

"Hush now, *macushla*." Bridget started to reach for me, to take me in her arms, but then stopped herself at the last moment and drew back quickly, as I was covered in Abby's blood. "Shhh . . . you just sit quiet now, Miss Lizzie, an' stay *right* here, don't you move a hair now, an' I'll be right back, I will. . . ."

I heard her footsteps hurrying briskly down the stairs. Then up again. I heard a rustle of paper behind me. As she came back in I realized that Bridget was laying a trail of old newspapers from my bedroom to where I now sat beside the guest-room bed in a sticky fast-cooling pool of Abby's blood.

"Come on now, *macushla*. Up you get. Keep to the paper now. There, that's it, good. Follow it now, just like a trail; there you go, good girl, good girl!" she said, walking backward, beckoning encouragingly with her hands, urging me to follow her back into my bedroom.

Once I was inside she bade me stand on a square of old newspapers, then she rolled up her sleeves, poured lukewarm water from the pitcher into the basin and took a fresh menstrual towel from the bottom drawer of the bureau where I kept them and went to work bathing me, scrubbing me clean with swift efficiency. From time to time she would pause for a fresh towel, tossing the soiled one into the pail from beneath my bed. I think she used three, or maybe four. Then she fastened a fresh one between my legs. I remember her clucking sympathetically and daubing some thick, greasy yellow ointment onto my raw red thighs, tending me as though I really were a helpless tiny naked newborn babe incapable of doing anything for myself.

Hands on hips, she stepped back and looked me over carefully. My hair was damp where she had wet it to wash the blood out, but in the sweltering summer heat it would soon dry, and if need be I could always claim I had lain down to nurse my headache with a cold compress over my brow. She dressed me as though I were a child, kneeling at my feet to roll the black stockings up my legs and lace my numb, clumsy feet into my boots. At her urging I stepped dumbly into my drawers and petticoat. I seemed to suddenly awaken from a trance at the hard tug of corset strings cinching my waist in, followed by the heavy, stultifying folds of my best blue bengaline town dress sliding stiflingly over my head. For a moment

I thought I might faint. I turned blank faced to Bridget and pointed down at the stained and crumpled blue housedress lying on my bed. I didn't understand why she was dressing me up as though I were about to go to town. My housedress had been lying there innocently on my bed all along while I went naked to kill, so why couldn't I put that back on?

"You're to town now, *macushla*," she gently explained as she nimbly did up the back of the bengaline with swift, sure fingers that didn't shake a bit, "to the dress goods sale at Sargent's, you know, an' I'm to follow just as soon as I finish those blasted windows—Devil take them! You told me about the dress goods sale they're havin', at eight cents a yard, remember that when they ask, an' sure they will, you know. Here's your hat now, an' your gloves. Be quick now! It won't do for us to linger hereabouts. They'll all be wantin' to know where we were an' what we were doin' when they find her lyin' dead up here; sure they'll be wanting to know where we were an' what we were doin' when it happened. There now, *macushla*." She hugged me quickly and kissed my cheek. "It's all right; your Bridget's taken care of ev'rything. Come along, step lively now."

She nudged the pail of bloody napkins, with her foot, back under the bed to tend to later.

"They'll *never* go pokin' their fingers an' noses in there! Thank the Lord policemen are all men, an' they're a finicky bunch an' want to hide their eyes an' stop their ears at the mention o' a woman's monthly!" She paused and looked at me again. "Step lively now, Miss Lizzie; time's a-wastin'!" she said, jerking her head, beckoning me to follow her, as she went out the door.

As I followed dumbly, numbly, my feet feeling like they were shod in lead and my hem dragging like a deadweight, moving just like Trilby in a trance following her Svengali, Bridget passed me on the stairs with a thick wad of soiled newspapers held at arm's length out in front of her. By the time my sluggish feet carried me into the kitchen the newspapers were already in the stove, burning. And on the table, now clean and sparkling, lay "the Great Emancipator," the hatchet that would either be my avenging angel and set me free or be the demon that would damn me to Hell for all eternity. I started to reach out and touch it, then snatched my hand away as though the hatchet had reared up and snarled and threatened to bite me.

"My purse, I forgot my purse," I said with a stupid, slurry tongue. How curious, I was standing close enough to reach out and touch her, but my eyes . . . it was as though Bridget were standing miles away at the end of a long, dark tunnel.

"I'll fetch it," Bridget said, but I stopped her.

"No, I'll go," I said, and started for the stairs before she could stop me. My eyes still weren't right and I had to grope like a blind woman for the banister. It took a great effort to pull myself up; my feet were still as heavy as stones and every step seemed as high as a mountain.

I was on the landing when there was an exasperated rattling followed by a loud, sharp knock at the front door. Bridget and I both froze. Our eyes met. All the color drained from our faces. Bridget silently crossed herself. I watched the motion of her hand; moving from brow to breast, shoulder to shoulder, it seemed to take forever. In those moments—I know they were mere moments—Time seemed as sluggish as my feet and hardly to move at all. But the odd, slow sensation only lasted an instant; then life was speeding by as though I were watching it all from the window of a moving train.

Thinking so quickly I surprised even myself, I took off my hat and yanked off my gloves and tossed them down to Bridget.

"I've just come in!" I whispered.

She nodded and set them down, then braced herself, squared her shoulders, and at a nod from me went to open the door.

It was Father. While she was tending me and cleaning up the mess I had made, Bridget had had the good sense to lock the front door from the inside, rendering Father's key useless.

I forced a smile and went down to greet him.

"I'm sorry, Father." I hugged him and kissed his cheek. "How thoughtless of me. I've only just come in. I wasn't thinking and must have locked the door."

"How typically careless of you, Lizzie," Father said as he shrugged out of his old musty black Prince Albert coat and swatted away the hands I raised to help him. "I would only be disappointed if I dared let myself expect more from you these days. But I know you all too well, my girl—*you never* take the time to do *anything* right!"

"Father!" I cried, leaping back as though he had just struck me. "That's hardly fair! Anyone can make a mistake—"

"Here!" He thrust his coat at me. "Hang this up! And make sure you take the time to do it *right* so it doesn't wrinkle or fall on the floor."

"Yes, Father." I sighed dutifully, clutching the coat against my chest as though it could hide my heart's frantic pounding. I didn't feel like arguing; trying to defend and justify myself was just a waste of words and never yielded the hoped-for results. I should have given up a long, long time ago. Why bother? He had made up his mind and Father was *always* right about everyone and everything.

"Where is your stepmother?" he asked.

"She's gone out." I had to think of something—and *quickly!* "There was a note. . . . Someone was sick!"

"Who?" Father asked.

"I don't know. I was still feeling under the weather when I came downstairs—really, Father, if we make one more meal of that mutton I'm sure it will be the death of us all!—and I saw her with the note, but I wasn't really paying attention. . . ." I smiled and shrugged apologetically as I trailed after him into the sitting room with his coat still draped over my arms.

"If someone else is sick it can hardly be the mutton," Father said. "Something must be going around."

"You look a trifle peaked, Father," I ventured. "Wouldn't you like to lie down on the sofa for a bit? A nap might make you feel better. I promise I will call you the moment Abby comes in."

"Yes." Father nodded. "I think I will." He lay down, or rather half-reclined, on our hard, unyielding black monstrosity of a sofa. It was too short for him to stretch out properly upon, but it had come with the house.

"Hang that coat up properly, Lizzie," Father called after me, "before it gets wrinkled or you lay it down God only knows where and forget all about it."

"Yes, Father." I just nodded and smiled, like the good dutiful daughter he expected me to be.

As I went to hang it up, wrinkling my nose at the rank odor that rose from it—it really needed a good washing, but Father *would* wear the same suit *every* day—a stiff roll of papers bound with twine fell from the pocket. I picked it up. With a glance back toward the sitting room, to make sure Father wasn't standing in the doorway watching me to make sure I treated his coat properly, I called back cheerily, "I'll be in the kitchen if you want me, Father; I have some handkerchiefs to iron."

If he answered, I didn't hear him. I had already torn off the twine and unrolled the document and discovered that it was his will and that he had already damned me before David Anthony even had a chance. Though it had not yet been signed and witnessed, it was only a matter of time. "I can read His righteous sentence by the dim and flaring lamps. . . ."

He had set it *all* down in black and white, for a lawyer to read aloud, for *everyone* to know, after he died, telling the world that Emma and I were a pair of frivolous and foolish, naïve, and gullible old maids who didn't know the value of a dollar and could not be trusted to govern and guard ourselves wisely, or the fortune he had spent a lifetime accumulating, against the ravages of fortune hunters and our own imprudent impulses. Thus the bulk of his estate would go to his loyal and obedient widow, the ever dutiful Abby Durfee Gray Borden, to administer as he herein decreed. "He is sifting out the hearts of men before His judgment seat . . .

"Oh, be swift, my soul to answer Him . . ."

As for Emma and me, his flesh and blood daughters, he was leaving us a measly $25,000 each *in trust* to be administered by Abby, to be doled out as *she* saw fit, *at her discretion,* and upon her death a suitable administrator of *her* choosing was to carry on the task as long as we lived, making us beg and account for every cent.

From beyond the grave, Father would continue to control us; we would *never* be free of him. I had wasted my youth, miserably and helplessly watched it pass by, for *NOTHING*, $25,000—not even $1,000 for every squandered stolen year of my life! Thirty-two years *wasted,* sitting wretchedly at his feet, like an odalisque in a tyrannical sultan's harem, suffering and secretly seething, *Die, just die, before it's too late for me to live!* And the cage wasn't even gilded, the shackles weren't silver, only the cheapest and basest of base metals that raised an angry maddeningly painful red rash upon my very soul. And now...now Emma and I were, by this document, bound forever by Father's will, denied all hope, and even the dream, of the freedom that only money can buy. We would be slaves in one form or fashion until our dying day, like chattels, imbeciles, and little children on a penny per week allowance, denied the right to *choose,* to *live* our lives as we saw fit; we must *always* answer to another.

Even if Abby didn't long survive Father, with the reins of power so firmly in her grasp she was certain to remember every petty slight and pain we had caused her and pass them on to her precious piglet, Sarah, and *she* would not hesitate to make us suffer for every tear we had caused Abby to shed! Even if Abby didn't, Sarah would be sure to humble us; she'd have us barefoot and in burlap sacks if she could! And, by Father's will, she *could!* Abby would cede that power on to her! I was so outraged, I completely forgot that Abby was dead!

He might as well entomb us with him, like the pharaohs used to do to ensure their slaves would be there to serve them in the afterlife! I thought as I crumpled Father's will furiously in my fist. I felt *rage,* rabid, red-hot rage, like a feral cat trapped inside me, *yowling, scratching, biting, clawing, desperate* to get out! Without even stopping to consider the consequences, I shoved Father's will into the stove and slammed the lid. *Burn, burn, burn!* I silently screamed. *Devil take your will! Burn in Hell, Father! I will be your slave no longer!*

And then a glint of silver caught my eye. Tempting me, enticing me, a second time. "I have read a fiery gospel writ in burnish'd rows of steels, as ye deal with my condemners so with you My grace shall deal..." There was "the Great Emancipator" lying on the table where Bridget had left it, ready to free me from bondage once and for all if I only dared use it. And I *did* dare! *I DID! Oh by God and the Devil I DID, Heaven help me!*

"As He died to make men holy, let us die to make men free. . . ."
Father would die to make *me* free.
It was the *only* way. . . .

The next thing I knew the red mist was receding and I was lying huddled on the blood-speckled faded flowers of the sitting room carpet sobbing at Father's feet, naked except for the blood-soaked towel between my thighs and Father's Prince Albert coat—I *couldn't* let him see me naked; he might have laughed! He would have certainly told me that I was fat. He *always* told me that; I was his "piggy in a blue gown."

"The Great Emancipator's" silver blade was buried deep in Father's mangled red and now unrecognizable face, cleaving his left eyeball in half. It was dangling by its bloody roots down against the bare bones of his cheek.

A red bubble burst inside my brain and I saw my fat, blotchy breast pop out of Father's black coat as I hefted the hatchet high above my head. Father's eyes snapped open wide. He was *LOOK-ING* at me! He was about to say something. . . . I *knew* it would be mean!

"*DON'T LOOK AT ME!*" I screamed, and brought the blade down.

A thick spurt of hot blood hit my face, just like a fist. I staggered back, but I didn't stop. I *couldn't!* I thought of the will—his will telling the world that I was a fool and a spendthrift, too stupid to govern myself, to know what my own best interests were, that a stupid cow had more common sense than me. *How could he do this to me?*

I raised the hatchet high and brought it crashing down on Father's face again. "He is trampling out the vintage where the grapes of wrath are stored. He has loosed the fateful lightning of His terrible swift sword. . . ." It wasn't a sword, it was a hatchet, but it was sharp, angry steel just the same! Up and down, up and down, up and down, up and down, over and over and over again! Ten or eleven times the coroner afterward said, but to me it felt like a hundred.

How *dare* he look at me, at my ugly naked flesh *and* even uglier angry naked soul? How *dare* he make me his *slave* for *thirty-two years*—wasting *MY* life away when I was on *FIRE* to *LIVE, LIVE, LIVE!*—and then try to keep me chained and bound to him even beyond the grave? To give my deed to Abby, to let *her own* and *control* me the way he dictated! Negroes were free, but women were still slaves, their father's property until he deeded them over to a husband he deemed worthy, but if no worthy husband ever appeared . . . slaves to the parental hearth and home until death set them free one way or another, but *my* father had found a legally binding way to circumvent that and keep me imprisoned eternally until . . . "The Great Emancipator" struck blow after mighty, bloody blow to set Lizzie Borden free! "In the beauty of the lilies Christ was born across the sea, with a glory in His bosom that transfigures you and me. As He died to make men holy, let us die to make men free." I won my freedom and baptized it in blood, with Death acting as midwife at the bloody birth that spawned my new life! In one blood-bathed day *I* was *transfigured!* I was set *FREE!* Free, rich, and orphaned all in the same bloody day!

Then Bridget was there, just like before, crouching down beside me, comforting me. "Glory, glory hallelujah!" It was over! I was free! She took care of me, just like she had before. She carefully shucked Father's coat from my shoulders and wadded it up and thrust it beneath his head, since it was covered in blood and too bulky to burn in the kitchen stove.

Bridget carefully pried the blade from Father's face and reverently carried "the Great Emancipator" away. *God bless you, President Lincoln!* I thought as I caught a last fleeting glimpse of his profile imprinted in the wood of my savior's hickory handle. *You set me free, just like you did the slaves!*

More newspapers, more bloody towels. I was having a painful and heavy period. Then I was clean again and back in my comfy old soiled and faded blue diamond housedress, my town clothes had been put away, and Bridget and I were sitting at the kitchen table, heads together, hands tightly clasped, as we hurriedly pieced together our story. A note had come for Mrs. Borden, from someone who was sick, we didn't know who, we were both still feeling poorly from the night before and barely paying attention, and Abby had rushed out without even changing into a proper town dress. Bridget had been washing the windows all morning but had been taken ill and after vomiting in the yard had come in to have a little lie down, perhaps ten or fifteen minutes or so. Then, feeling better, she returned to her work; she wasn't a one to leave a task undone. And I had been lounging about not doing much of anything all day. I had trifled over my breakfast of cookies and coffee and taken a few bites of a banana while leafing through an old magazine and waiting for the iron to heat so I could iron some handkerchiefs. When Father came in I was there at the door to welcome him, just like I always did, and see him settled comfortably on the sofa for his nap. Then someone had come in and killed him. Bridget and I heard nothing, saw nothing. I just walked into the sitting room and there he was, dead on the sofa, his face a bloody mangled mess with one eyeball dangling against the bare bones of his cheek. It was a sight I would never forget no matter how hard I prayed to.

I tried to take it all in, really I did, but I was feeling sluggish and heavy headed, like I was walking underwater again in leaden shoes and hems, Bridget's urgent words reaching me as though from far, far away. I could tell she was badly shaken as well, though she was trying hard not to show it. No wonder there were so many inconsistencies when the time came for us to tell our stories under scrutiny. Neither of us realized that the alleged note would become so vital, that it would be endlessly sought for and debated; rewards would even be offered if the author would only come forward, but no one ever did, because there was never any note at all; it was entirely our own invention.

"I'm goin' for Dr. Bowen now," Bridget said as she let go of my hands and got up from the table.

But I snatched them back and clutched them to my breast. "Bridget!" I cried fervently. "Promise you'll never leave me!"

"I promise." She bent swiftly and kissed my cheek, but she lied. She lied! She never really came back, not to me. *No one stays; everyone goes. No one loves me; everyone knows.*

I trailed after her to the back door and leaned there, slumping against the screen, watching her round the corner, heading across the street to Dr. Bowen's house. Nosey old Mrs. Churchill, our next-door neighbor, was peeping through her curtains.

"Is something wrong, Lizzie?" Her voice floated out to me.

I heard myself answer, "Oh, Mrs. Churchill, do come over! Someone has killed Father!"

The next thing I knew I was swooning in a rocking chair and she was leaning over me, laying a cold compress across my brow and rubbing my hands vigorously.

"I shall have to send for the undertaker," I think I said. I was so deep underwater and my words were up there bobbing on the surface with the waves crashing around them. Then Mrs. Churchill was leaning over me again, speaking comforting words and rubbing my hands, I saw her mouth moving, but the waves were crashing and roaring *so* loudly I couldn't hear a word she said; I only knew that her mouth was moving. And the stars came to dance before my eyes. I knew they weren't fireworks. It was past the Fourth of July.

A parade of brass-buttoned blue-uniformed policemen passed before my eyes. They all had different names and faces, but I couldn't tell them apart. They all looked the same. Blue coats, brass buttons. I don't think I ever saw so many handlebar mustaches in my life! And questions! *So many questions!* "Where is Mrs. Borden?" *Note. Sick friend.* "I think I heard her come in. Oh, do go and look, Mrs. Churchill!" A scream from upstairs. A syringe in Dr. Bowen's kind, capable hands, a needle pricked my arm, and I think my head floated away and got lost in the clouds and then they *burst* into powder and Lulie Stillwell was there, stark naked and smiling at me.

Concerned women from the neighborhood hovered over me uttering comforting words and condolences as I lay upon my bed, wandering half-lost in a lovely world of hazy morphine dreams. I smiled and said, "Thank you, you are very kind," every time anyone spoke to me, and turned my flushed, hot pink face into my pillow and let them think I was stifling tears instead of laughter, because they would have *died* if they had known I was thinking about Lulie all the time they were being so very kind to me.

Someone, Alice Russell I think, helped me change my dress. An excuse to search my body for wounds and bloodstains no doubt, but the only blood was oozing out between my legs, and that explained the one tiny dot on the back of my petticoat. I left the soiled towel to soak in the pail beneath my bed with the rest, I would attend to them later, and obediently donned the fresh one Alice handed me. Then I let her help me into clean undergarments, meekly stepping into the drawers she held open for me and raising my arms so she could slide a chemise and then a petticoat over my head. Glassy-eyed and docile, I stood still and let her help guide my arms into the sleeves of my candy-pink-and-white-striped housedress. As she fastened the gay red belt around my waist, I regarded the stripes on my sleeves and smiled. That delicious bright pink had me thinking of Lulie again. But I didn't care! I just wanted to lie down and lose myself in a world of dreams, to turn back time ... to unmake the mistakes I'd made. Lulie should never have married Johnny Hiram; she should have been *mine!*

Late that afternoon Emma arrived, gnawing at her lips and wringing a tear-drenched handkerchief in her hands, summoned back from Fairhaven by an urgent telegram from Dr. Bowen. I remember her leaning over my bed, her dark eyes boring into mine.

"Lizzie, did you ..." she began tremulously, the words hovering, trembling like tears, upon her raw, bitten lips.

"Ask me no questions and I will tell you no lies," I whispered back dreamily.

And she never did. *Never!*

Of course Emma *knew* the moment she looked into my eyes, but she would spend the rest of her life pretending not to and in public she became my staunchest defender, especially after I told her about Father's will. But in private, a wall of impenetrable ice grew up between us.

I always thought Emma was the strongest one, the one with all the backbone despite her brittle, fragile appearance. But Emma had been content only to grumble like a sour stomach, to damn Abby with every glance and thwart her plans whenever she had the chance. Cordially detesting our stepmother had been Emma's way of dealing with the situation. Her fury was meek and mostly obedient. But *I . . . I* had taken up the hatchet and actually *done* something about it! *I* had hacked away the chains and set us *both* free. Emma's public support was her way of thanking me. But when we were alone and no other eyes were watching us, we were sisters bound by blood and secrets only; otherwise we were cold and chilly strangers.

Emma, embracing ignorance like the lover she would never know, asked no questions, but everyone else . . .

Questions, so many, many questions! Why wouldn't they shut up and leave me alone? I just wanted to roll over and go to sleep, but they wouldn't let me no matter what Dr. Bowen said. Policemen are very tenacious and very mean! Why couldn't they let me rest? I felt like I was back in school being put to the test and made to stand up there in front of the blackboard and the whole class! Everyone was staring at me! I just wanted them to stop!

"*Must* I see *all* these people *now?*" I wailed. "It seems as if I cannot think a moment longer, my head pains me so!"

A policeman—maybe more than one, I'm not quite sure; why did they all have to dress alike and confuse people?—asked me what I had been doing before I walked in and found Father dead upon the sofa.

I said I had been out in the barn, up in the loft, eating pears— three pears or maybe four—and after that I was ironing handkerchiefs in the kitchen, reading a magazine while I waited for the iron to heat and gossiping to Bridget about a dress sale at Sargent's— only *eight cents a yard!*—*you see, Bridget, I* did *remember!* Later they would say that I said I had been out in the barn, up in the loft, rummaging about in a box of odds and ends, amongst bent and rusty nails and old doorknobs and broken locks, looking for some pieces of iron suitable to fashion sinkers for a fishing trip I was planning to Buzzards Bay. Maybe I did say that? The details sounded right. But I honestly don't remember. Or maybe I wanted the iron to repair a screen? Someone said I said that too. I really cannot remember! Every time I look back upon that day it feels like being caught, trapped, and at the same time lost, in a bad dream that just drags on forever.

The hatchet was "the Great Emancipator" who set the slave Lizzie Borden free, but Morphine was "The Great Muddler" of Lizzie's memory. I shall be forever grateful. That's all I have to say about that awful, awful day.

Chapter 7

〜

E ven though I knew I was guilty, I believed implicitly in my innocence. That is what saved me and saw me through the dark days that followed when I languished, for ten months, my fate uncertain, in a prison cell and the shadow of the hangman's noose hung always over my head like the sword of Damocles. That and the gallantry and gullibility of men.

Chivalry, I discovered, had not died; it wasn't just the stuff of legends and fairy tales, and it went *much* further than doffing hats, offering chairs, and opening doors for ladies. Not a man upon my jury could believe that a prim New England spinster, a virtuous old maid who taught Sunday school, and was a member of the Women's Christian Temperance Union and the Fruit and Flower Mission, could ever be guilty of such a bloody and violent crime. They could not imagine my ladylike hands wielding any sharp, steel object more threatening than an embroidery needle.

It also helped that Fall River at large abhorred the possibility of posterity remembering the city as the home of a murderess. They wanted this over and done with just as much as I did. We were all ready to sweep it under the rug. Every time an enterprising hack driver met an arriving train at the station and bellowed out an invitation to see the notorious Lizzie Borden house, we all cringed and looked ill.

And my gallant jury, my twelve New England knights in black broadcloth suits instead of shining armor, were far too fastidious to consider that menstruation might have helped mask murder. That very night, when Emma and I were left alone, though under guard, at the house on 92 Second Street, I had descended the cellar stairs, lamp in hand in my dressing gown, with Alice Russell, who had volunteered to stay with us, hovering anxiously at my side, walking right past a policeman, with the pail of bloody towels in my hand. He had politely looked away and pretended not to see us. I left the pail shoved out of sight underneath the sink to await laundering in time for next month's need and thought nor heard no more about it. Since Bridget had broken her promise and left us—left *me!*—to divert suspicion away from herself, she had made a fine show of panic and refused to sleep another night under our roof, I have no idea who eventually did the laundry; I suppose Emma hired someone, or sent it off to the Celestials.

Later, during the course of my trial, that one tiny speck of blood, the size of a pinprick on the back of my petticoat, that "flea bite" as they politely called it in lowered, ill-at-ease voices, had caused the men no end of embarrassment, so they gave it the shortest possible shrift. When it was brought up in court, ladies and gentlemen alike blushed and averted their eyes as the lawyers steered me past the issue as quickly and discreetly as possible. It was obvious to all that it could have nothing to do with the murders, and why the prosecution felt the need to mention it at all was something no one could fathom, unless they thought the humiliation of having my intimate female functions discussed in open court would cause my composure to crumble entirely and lead me to confess just to have done with it.

The morphine Dr. Bowen gave me and the paint-stained housedress that I had burned a few days after the murders further muddied the waters, making it impossible for anyone to clearly divine my innocence or guilt.

Everyone argued and took sides, but it was just too cloudy to ever be settled for certain. I fancied myself living out the rest of my life as a mystery wrapped in an enigma. There were days when I would sit in court, my chin pillowed on my palm, and imagine myself in an embroidered silk dress of shifting shades of blue covered all over with countless question marks and an ermine opera cape with the little black tails dangling down like even more question marks, an ensemble evocative of the eternal question of my guilt, the one that would never die; it would outlive me, and everyone I knew.

In truth, I recall little of my trial, it passed in a muddled and perplexing litany of drab dresses, blue dresses, Bedford cords, and bengalines, corded cottons, and heavy silks, a light-blue ground with a dark-blue figure, or a dark-blue ground with a light-blue figure, diamond patterns, nondescript, or unmemorable patterns, stylish town dresses, and ordinary, common, not particularly attractive housedresses, unsullied by any stains detectable to the naked eye or ruined by unsightly smears of reddish-brown paint suspiciously similar to the shade of dried blood, a stylish town dress presented in court, and one conspicuously absent paint-spattered old cotton housedress that refused to rise before their eyes like a phoenix from the ashes of our kitchen stove. Everyone who had seen me on August 4 was called to the stand to describe what I had been wearing at the time, and none of them, it seemed, had a particularly good memory or eye for fashion, with the notable exception of a handsome young policeman who made quite an impression upon the ladies when he described in meticulous detail the candy-pink-and-white-striped housedress with the red belt I had changed into after the murders even though it wasn't particularly relevant. When called to account for these precise remembrances, he sheepishly explained that he liked to paint in his free time and had always had a keen and appreciative eye for colors and patterns. Many thought it downright lamentable that he had never seen me in the blue; his sharp memory could have cut through the confusion like a knife.

Alice Russell forfeited our friendship by testifying in great detail about the day I burned that faded, filthy old housedress in broad daylight, shoving it into the kitchen stove, right in front of her astonished eyes.

On and on, day after day, the confusing litany continued—my lingering so leisurely and long in the baking oven of the barn on a blistering hot day, the pears I claimed to have eaten, one, two, or three, maybe four, iron scraps and sinkers for a proposed fishing trip to Buzzards Bay versus a torn window screen, whether or not the dust on the floor of the loft had been disturbed by my footsteps or the sweeping hem of my skirt, handkerchiefs and heating flatirons, dirty windows, locked doors, the dress goods sale at Sargent's, and whether Bridget and I were upstairs or downstairs, indoors or out at any given time; *every* second must be accounted for.

My imprisonment made a far greater impression upon me than my trial ever did. I spent the better part of ten months in the Bristol County Jail in Taunton, as the one in Fall River lacked accommodations suitable for the long-term housing of female prisoners, they apparently being somewhat of a rarity in wholesome, hardworking Fall River. It shook and scared me as nothing else ever has. It gave a whole new meaning to the word *trapped*. Whereas before I had felt stifled and trapped, like a prisoner in the grim, outmoded confines of my father's house, now I was confined to a single cell, allowed out only for an hour's exercise each day and when my presence was required in court. And the stark iron bedstead, washstand, and single chair made my room at the house on 92 Second Street seem luxurious as a grand hotel suite in comparison.

The worst part was being left all alone in the darkness at night, unable to sleep; even the drugs, all the sleeping syrups and calming injections I tried, failed to usher in a few blessed hours of quiet, restful oblivion. Some thought it symptomatic of a guilty conscience; others said fear. The course Justice would take could never be predicted with absolute certainty; murderers had gone free before and truly innocent souls had languished decades behind prison bars or lost their lives upon the scaffold, so I had every reason to be afraid.

Although the matron, Mrs. Hannah Regan, was kind and quite lax about enforcing many of the rules, like letting me wear my own clothes instead of prison garb and having my meals brought in from fashionable restaurants in lieu of the usual prison rations of fish hash, bread, and water, and my cell was constantly filled with flowers and boxes of candy from well-wishers, and lots of books to read, including my Bible and a complete set of Dickens, no matter how I begged and cajoled she would not permit me a light when I needed it most—at night. My lamp *must* go out at the same hour as all the other prisoners' did. I think it was a punishment, that we all must sit, or lie, restless in the darkness, alone with our thoughts and fears, and any guilt, remorse, or regret our hearts might be harboring.

I passed a lonely Christmas behind bars. Emma knitted me a big black wool shawl trimmed with thirty-two tassels, one for each year of my life. It shrouded my shoulders like a silent and perpetual reminder that I was supposed to be in mourning and reminded me that I might not live to see thirty-three if the tide of the trial turned against me. At least it helped keep me warm on those cold, cold nights when only lustful thoughts about Lulie Stillwell or Bridget Sullivan reminded me that my blood was still hot even when my limbs felt like they were turning to ice.

Unable to sleep, I sat up on my cot, wide awake and alert to every noise, hugging my knees in the dark, watching the sky through the iron bars, waiting for it to lighten, and longing for a glimpse of the moon, praying for a flash of lightning, as over and over in my mind I relived the days after the one rash, mad one that had changed my life forever, for worse or better.

The doctors the police sent had no sense of decency. They stripped Father and Abby stark naked and laid their bodies out on the dining room table and autopsied them there. Emma and I glimpsed them as we fled, sickened, upstairs. We would *never* eat at that table again; we both agreed we would have it taken out and burned as soon as it was seemly. The doctors' assistant *threw* the bloodied clothes carelessly down the cellar steps so that I tripped over one of Father's boots and entangled my slippered feet in Abby's bloody mint-sprigged housedress and would have fallen had Alice not been there to catch me when we descended to the privy. Red water sloshed out of my pail and the soiled napkins floating inside it swirled like angry white fish, churning sickeningly in the bloody water. I felt so sick that I set the pail down and lurched unsteadily to the privy, braced my hands against the wooden box seat, and vomited until I thought my eyeballs would pop out. Then I saw Father's eye, dangling, bloody, and broken, against the exposed ivory bone of his cheek, that *I* had laid open with the hatchet, and I vomited again, even though I hadn't eaten anything since the few nibbled bites that had been my breakfast and brought up only bile, I didn't think I would ever stop until I disgorged my very heart and stomach.

Then the undertaker, Mr. Winward, had come. He dressed Father and Abby in their Sunday best, and laid them out in the sitting room where Father had died. Abby looked so serene it was as though she were only sleeping; the lace-bordered white satin pillow she laid her head upon and the undertaker's finesse with reattaching her switch of long, thick black hair hid all the damage my rage had inflicted on the back of her skull. Had one not known otherwise, she might have died peacefully in her sleep. Father's head was swathed in layers of cotton bandages, wound round and round, creating a perfect plump white ball. He looked curiously like a featureless, blank-faced snowman whose jolly round body had melted into gauntness and been dressed in a severe black suit and tie worthy of the undertaker he had been in his ambitious youth.

I couldn't bear to look at them for more than a moment. As Emma bent, dutifully, to kiss Father's bandage-swaddled brow, I squeezed my eyelids shut tight as hot tears seeped out and clamped a hand over my mouth and fled as the burning bile rose like a geyser in my throat. When I came back, the caskets were mercifully closed.

I didn't have a black dress and even with the tightest lacing I was still too fat to fit into any of Emma's. I felt like a hippopotamus when I stood beside her before the mirror in my petticoat and stays and glumly regarded my bulging arms, broad shoulders, and bounteous hips. Rather than brave the crowd of curiosity seekers still gathered outside the house, or send Alice out shopping on my behalf, I wore my darkest blue, one that might easily be mistaken for black. But the August sun showed me no mercy; like an accusing beacon, it shone down upon me and everyone knew I wore blue to my parents' funeral. "*Blue!*" they whispered in damning disapproval. "She wore *blue* to her own parents' funeral!" As though my disrespect would kill them all over again! Every time they looked at me they damned me with their eyes.

What kind of girl didn't own a black dress suitable for funerals or move Heaven and earth to procure one in time for her own parents' funeral? all Fall River, it seemed, was asking. A *guilty* girl who didn't care what anyone thought. To them it was plain as day; that blue dress was my way of flaunting it. I was not a good daughter; I was not a dutiful daughter like sorrowful black-clad Emma in her plain, somber, and sweltering high-collared, long-sleeved heavy silk, bereft of ornamentation, even lace, proper black gloves, stockings, and sturdy, practical black leather shoes, black-bordered mourning handkerchief, and trailing crepe veils. She looked just like a bride who had fallen into a vat of ink, weeping sorrowful tears when she led the procession to Oak Grove Cemetery; all that was missing was a groom for her to lean upon. They said I was cold, indifferent, and devoid of emotion, that I just didn't care. I didn't even cry. I didn't even pretend, or leave people to wonder by shrouding my face in a veil. I left it bare, stark naked in my brazen lack of feeling, for *everyone* to see that my eyes were dry. They thought I had no tears, but the truth is I had no tears left; I had spent thirty-two years crying them in secret.

While the preacher's sonorous voice spoke words I don't remember, I stood between the pair of stark black caskets and laid a sheaf of golden wheat on Father's and an olive branch atop Abby's. It was my way of thanking Father for his bounty there was now no barrier to our inheriting and my sad, silent way of making peace with Abby. I was sorry, and yet I wasn't. I had done the right thing, even though it was wrong. If only things, if only we—all of us—had been different it might never have come to this. If only, if only, if only . . .

The funeral procession was like a parade, only without the cheers, costumes, and flag waving. People lined the streets thousands strong all the way to Oak Grove Cemetery. I think the whole population of Fall River except infants and bed-bound invalids at death's door must have turned out. People confined in wheelchairs had even had their nurses or spinster daughters wheel them out to gawk as the pair of glass-enclosed hearses bearing the coffins of Father and Abby, and our carriage, rolled past. Did I only imagine it, or did I *really* see Lulie in a royal-blue satin and black lace gown, her perfect porcelain-white complexion shaded by a big black leghorn straw hat trimmed with blue satin roses and a black lace half veil, standing on the sidewalk idly twirling a black lace parasol trimmed with royal-blue satin bows amongst the throng of fashionably dressed women who had assembled on the sidewalk to watch us pass? They weren't in mourning, so they didn't have to wear black; they could trick themselves out like tropical birds and no one would criticize them. As we rode past, my hand *ached* to reach out and rip her veil off just so I could see her face again. But there was too much distance between us. I imagined she was as beautiful as ever; everyone knew Lulie was Mother Nature and Father Time's favorite child.

At Oak Grove Cemetery, as the coffins sat beside the open graves, a hysterical old Irishwoman with rosary beads wrapped around her gnarled fingers broke from the crowd and threw herself down on top of Abby's casket. She claimed to have been the Grays' Maggie before "Miss Abby married Mr. Borden." Maybe she was? Or she might have been exactly what she seemed—a crazy old woman avid for attention. The undertaker's men had to forcibly tear her away; she was clinging so tight to the lid I was afraid she would take it with her.

But to the crowd surrounding us, this was barely a ripple upon a pond; they could hardly bear to tear their eyes away from *me*. That poor madwoman could have torn her clothes off and danced a lascivious Can-Can right on top of Father's casket and *I* would have still been the star, center stage in their attention. They just kept *staring* at *me,* watching intently, scrutinizing my every move, my every gesture, if I blinked my eyes or twitched my nose, brushed back a stray wisp of hair, rubbed my ear, tugged at my glittering jet earbobs, or adjusted my collar or a fold of my skirt. I heard the word *fidgety* whispered several times behind my back. They were waiting for me to crack and break down. They wanted to see *me* weep, tear out my hair, and fling myself into Father's grave no doubt, throwing myself instead of a clod of earth down onto his coffin.

Outwardly, it was all very proper, of course. One could expect nothing less from Fall River. No one said a word aloud, but the whispers were *deafening*. "She didn't shed a tear!" "Not *one* tear!" "She wore *blue!*" "Unnatural!" "Unfeeling!" "Unseemly!" "Heartless!" "Cold!" "Improper!"

They were about to lower the coffins into the ground when a pair of policemen came hurrying up and spoke in hushed, hurried words to the minister. They had come for the heads. We could do what we liked with the bodies, but they *must* have the heads. To boil the flesh from the skulls, to bare the broken and naked white bones, to better see if any of the blades of the various hatchets they had found fit into the wounds.

I thought all hatchets were more or less the same size, but what would an old maid know about such matters? It made me feel as though I would vomit my heart out, right into Father's empty grave. I had no idea what had become of "the Great Emancipator." I *didn't* want to know; now that I didn't need it anymore, I only wanted it to be gone, to forever disappear. I just wanted to forget and not think about any of it anymore!

My ignorance upon the subject of the hatchet was never feigned. I heard the police had found the head of a hatchet in a box in the cellar, the handle broken off, and the blade coated in ashes as though *someone* hoped to fool the police into believing it was dust, but the glimmer of gilt betrayed it was not as old as *someone* might like to pretend. If this was indeed Bridget's handiwork I thought it quite clever of her; it was just like something out of a detective story. I, for one, would never have thought of it. When they said they found a second hatchet, rusty and red, caked with blood and hair, it gave me such a fright, I almost died. I felt my heart jolt like Frankenstein's monster coming to life, but some clever scientific gentlemen at the college at Harvard did some tests that proved it was very old and the blood and hair belonged to a long-dead cow.

While Emma protested this desecration of the dead and wept on the Reverend Buck's shoulder, I stood a little apart from them all, lost in my own little reverie, watching dispassionately—everyone said—as the police, assisted by the undertaker's men, carried the coffins into a nearby vault and a pair of doctors, toting black leather bags, followed grimly in their wake. We didn't wait to see them come out again.

That night the mayor himself came to the house at 92 Second Street with Marshal Hilliard, the chief of police. They gathered us—Emma, Uncle John, Alice Russell, and me—in the sitting room and delicately informed us that it would be better for all concerned if we did not leave the house for the next few days.

They were worried about the crowds; the curious continued to congregate outside from dawn's first light to well after dark. Word had spread far and wide thanks to the newspapers, and enterprising cabdrivers met every incoming train, crying out, "Come and see the Borden Murder House! Only twenty-five cents a head!" They would park outside and regale their spellbound audience of out-of-towners with vivid accounts of the murders, and should they spy anyone peeping out from between the curtains or any female coming in or out of the house they would point and cry out, *"THERE SHE IS NOW, FOLKS! THE MURDERESS—LIZZIE BORDEN HERSELF!"*

Alice Russell nearly died of shame when one of the hackney cabdrivers brandished his whip at her when she was returning from an errand for us. She spent the rest of the day sitting, shaking her head, while her whole body trembled, feeling *"mortified,* simply *mortified,* to think that people would think that *I . . ."*

Doubtlessly if any of their passengers recalled from the news accounts that I was a redhead, not a blonde, the clever cabbies would retort that it was a wig on the lady's dome and the cunning killer was in disguise to avoid being lynched by the outraged populace for daring to venture out amongst decent God-fearing people.

The denizens of Fall River were angry and afraid, news was spreading across the nation, and even the ocean, and they didn't like being the center of this macabre spectacle, or worrying that if I was indeed innocent then that meant that the real killer was still at large and they might be murdered in their beds at night or some ax-wielding maniac might suddenly burst in on them in broad daylight while they were sipping their morning coffee or buttering their toast.

Someone might be hurt, the Mayor said. Someone might hurt us, the Marshal said. So it was best that we stay inside.

Emma nodded mutely, and Uncle John worriedly posed a question about how we would get our mail. But I boldly met the Marshal's and the Mayor's eyes and asked, "Why? Is someone in this house suspected?"

Of course, gallantry having been ingrained in them since birth, they were reluctant to tell me. There really weren't any suspects at all beyond our threshold. It was true Dr. Handy claimed that he had seen a person he described as a "wild-eyed young man," dark haired and mustachioed and of approximately twenty-four years, loitering about on our street the day of the murders, but the police didn't think much of his story. Fall River was *full* of dark-haired young men and mustaches were the fashion, so the police were hardly going to go chasing every one down and asking him to account for his whereabouts the day old Mr. and Mrs. Borden died.

To my mind, Dr. Handy's description sounded suspiciously like David Anthony, and I wouldn't put it past him to be lurking about, waiting to claim me as his own, like the Devil hankering after another lost soul, but his was a name I'd rather cut my tongue out than speak aloud. The murders seemed to have also killed his "love" for me, and I was heartily glad of it and hoped it would never be resurrected and that David Anthony would stay away from me *forever*.

"I want to know the truth," I insisted, staring the Mayor straight in the eye, then favoring the Marshal with the same unwavering gaze. I already knew, but I wanted to hear them say it. I wanted to know that it wasn't just fear and guilt or my imagination getting the better of me; I *needed* to *hear* them *say* my name and that I was suspected. Uncertainty is always worse than certainty. The unknown is a devil that gnaws and niggles at the mind and soul and only knowledge can stop him even if it also wounds.

"Very well, Miss Borden," Mayor Coughlin said quietly, "if you *must* know, then yes, *you* are suspected."

I nodded crisply and, calling up every drop of courage I possessed, I stood and faced them. "I am ready to go now." I held my hands out, bracing to feel the cold steel embrace of the handcuffs closing around my wrists. But both the Mayor and the Marshal demurred; it was not necessary to subject a lady to such an indignity, they insisted, and I should just continue to bide quietly at home for the time being.

Emma wept, Uncle John shook his head and stared speechlessly at the carpet and heaved a heavy sigh, and I wondered how it would all end. Would I ever know the sweet taste of freedom again or would the last time I ever danced be the Gallows Jig when my feet kicked and dangled in the empty air to the music of my own neck snapping?

All we could do was wait, carry on this pretense of mournful seclusion, of politely acceding to an official request to remain indoors to avoid unduly exciting the populace. But we all knew it was only a matter of time before I would be taken away, to await my fate sitting in a jail cell.

We offered a reward, Emma and I, $10,000 to bring the killer to justice, but no one ever claimed it. How could they? It made my stomach ache with fear; I was afraid the lure of an easy fortune would tempt Bridget to turn on me. But Emma said we must, it would look odd if we did not, form must be seen to be observed. "It's all for the best," she said. We would discreetly send Bridget back to Ireland in grand style, in the ruched and ruffled green gown with gaudy bows all down the bodice and on the big bouncy bustle she had always "hankered after," and the golden slippers she was always singing about, with a jaunty red feather waving good-bye to America and us on her hat.

Emma took care of it all. She said it would be best if Bridget and I didn't see each other again apart from the imminent legalities, since there was no avoiding that of course. When I resisted, Emma said I was acting silly mooning over a servant girl, and the tone of her voice, so scornful, venomous, and biting, and the piercing dark eyes that seemed to stab right into my soul made me give in. Bridget would land on her feet, just like a cat, Emma said, and catch herself a fine husband, and I knew in my heart she was right. But the heart is not an organ of reason, nor does common sense repose between our thighs. I dreamed of Bridget every night and prayed that when it was all over and done she would, of her own free will, come back to me.

But Bridget didn't love me any more than Lulie Stillwell had. It really was all just a dream. We had no future, only a past that was best forgotten, one that owed more to my forbidden fantasies than any actual truth or tender feelings. *Romance* was just a word to describe the kind of literature that fed the flames of an old maid's dreams; it had nothing to do with real life, at least not for the likes of me. Love was a beautiful gift given only to beautiful people who deserved a gift from Cupid.

While I might, if my last rendezvous wasn't with the hangman, be a lady presiding over a grand house someday, Bridget would never come live with me and be my love. My poor Cinderella masquerading as a maidservant by day with slippers of gold, not glass or the sturdy black leather boots of a typical Irish Maggie, hiding beneath her plain hems, and lying naked in silken sheets in the golden glow of lamplight beside me every night, pampered like a princess, the queen of my heart. She would wear silks, velvets, and laces for me in private, for my eyes alone, so no one else could ever fall under the spell of her black Irish beauty and sparkling green eyes and steal her away from me. I would give her diamonds; I would give her pearls, emeralds evocative of the wistful green dream of Ireland, and rubies red as blood to show her how precious she was to me, she who always called me "*macushla,*" the Gaelic endearment braiding heart's blood with true and sacrosanct lasting love. Every time I fastened a necklace of the sparkling bloodred stones around her lily-white throat I would tell her that she was worth more than all the rubies in the world to me. I would reign, as society and appearances dictated, but she would rule my heart entirely.

But it was just a dream! Our fairy-tale castle was only in the clouds; it could never exist in brick and mortar in the world we knew. Reality blew it away, scattering it like ashes upon the wind, leaving me in the end with nothing but forbidden dreams and an aching yearning, an undying thirst, and a gnawing hunger I feared could never be sated.

Then came the morning when I had walked nonchalantly into the kitchen with the soiled and dingy blue diamond housedress wadded up in my hands. Emma had been pressing me to dispose of it and now, I knew, was the time to do it.

"I think I will burn this old thing up," I announced as I headed for the stove, and had shoved it in before anyone had time to approve, or disapprove, of my intentions.

I tried to be blasé about it, treating it like any other old, useless rag I was disposing of. It bothered me how closely the reddish-brown paint mimicked the color of dried blood; I was worried that the resemblance might occur to the police and in some way damn me. I knew just how Lady Macbeth felt with blood that only she could see staining her hands, impervious to soap and water and vigorous scrubbing. I just couldn't stop thinking about it! I kept seeing the glistening gilt head of the hatchet nestled in those paint-streaked blue folds, *feeling* it nudging against my leg like a living animal's head as though a bloodthirsty silver demon possessed it, giving life to the inanimate. Faded diamonds of warring blues, the glimmer of silver, and the ugly brown-red smears all down the left side. They looked *so much* like blood, I was afraid if people sat and scrutinized those stains they would come to believe it actually was blood. Father had been unexpectedly generous and allowed me to choose the color of paint, and I, feeling grateful, had tried to choose a conservative color that he would like, hence the bloody brown. One thinks the oddest things at times and now I simply *loathed* that color and wished with all my heart that I had been true to myself and chosen something more charming and cheerful, like apple green, lemon yellow, dusky mauve, or apricot.

"Yes, why don't you," Emma said without glancing up from

where she sat stirring her coffee at the kitchen table. "That's a *very* good idea, Lizzie." She *hated* that dress and never understood why I bothered to keep it, much less wear it, after my mishap with the wet paint. She thought it most slovenly and lackadaisical of me, and now that she knew there *might* be blood on it she didn't even want it in the house. When she saw it hanging in my closet the night before she had told me it made her sick just to look at it, and that if she were me she would "burn it up."

Alice Russell had stood right beside me at the kitchen stove and watched as the flames devoured it. Then, as though butter wouldn't melt in her mouth, that prim goody-good had looked me right in the eye and said, "If *I* were *you*, Lizzie, *I* wouldn't have let *anyone* see me doing *that*. I'm afraid that burning that dress is the *worst* thing you could have done!" *Besides killing your parents of course!* her chilly blue eyes silently finished the sentence.

With wide, innocuous eyes, after it was already too late to snatch the dress back from the grasping flames, I turned to Alice, dug my fingers into her arms, and cried, "Oh, Alice, *why* did you let me do it? *Why* didn't you tell me? I *never* thought . . . *Oh, Alice! What have I done?*" Whereupon I burst into tears and fled the kitchen.

I knew then that she would turn on me. A friend had become an enemy. And I was right. Alice went and tattled straightaway to the Pinkerton man hired to assist the investigation. Then, two-faced as the head of Janus, she came in tears and told us what she had done. Emma squeezed my hand tight and squared her shoulders and told our former friend, "You must do what you think right." We would never speak to Alice Russell again.

To make matters worse, that ignorant, imbecilic ass of a druggist Eli Bence had gone scurrying, like the scurvy rat he was, straight to the newspapers to tell his story. **LIZZIE BORDEN VISITS A DRUGSTORE TO INQUIRE ABOUT POISONS!** the headlines screamed.

I chose to be dignified and deny it. "It's a *LIE!*" I hotly insisted. "I was never in that store in my life! I wouldn't be caught dead there; it's on the *wrong* side of town!"

And when a rumor implying that my father's discovery of a damning secret, that I was with child, provided fodder for more headlines, I demanded a retraction or else I would sue. I received an apology in print two days later, but the damage was done. I always wondered if David Anthony hadn't been behind it and whispered his "theory" in the right ear. But in the end it didn't matter. I never saw him alone again. He eventually married and had a family. I would occasionally catch glimpses of them from a distance riding out together, for a picnic I imagined, in first an open black carriage and later a shiny red motorcar. His wife always wore very large hats and kept her veil down—to protect her eyes from the dust or to hide the black eyes he gave her? I suppose both could be possible.

My inquest was like an open-invitation talent show, so many people turned up and took to the stage, seizing on anything they could to have a few minutes of public attention and see their names in the newspapers. And the ears of the reporters and the doors of the newspaper offices were equally open and inviting. I soon ceased to marvel at anything I might hear or read about myself. My hometown papers always used the most unflattering likeness of me they could muster, showing me scowling with protruding eyes and jowls like a bulldog, but the out-of-town papers offered their readers an idealized image, stylishly dressed with a flawless hourglass figure and curves in all the right places. There was one picture of me swooning in court while wearing a hat covered with petunias that I particularly admired, I looked so lovely, fresh, and enchanting. No wonder all the marriage proposals I received came from hundreds of miles away. It really is surprising how many gentlemen are gallant enough to want to offer the protection of their good name and holy matrimony to an accused murderess.

My cousin Anna Borden, who had been with me on the Grand Tour but whom I had hardly seen since, turned up looking more beautiful, buxom, and voluptuous than ever, with her silver-gilt hair and violet eyes, complemented by a violet linen suit and a hat heaped high with a colorful array of silken pansies and green silk fern fronds, to tell the Attorney General how upon the return voyage I had often bewailed my misfortune at having to return to such an unhappy home. She looked *so* beautiful when she lifted her net veil to swear to tell the truth and nothing but, with her lace-gloved hand resting light as a feather upon the Bible; the sight of her made me dizzy.

My mind in a fog of fear and morphine, for three whole days I muddled and blundered my way through the inquest testimony, vexing everyone with my jumbled recollections of the story Bridget and I had hastily concocted at the kitchen table.

When the District Attorney, Hosea Knowlton, questioned me, like a tenacious bulldog, about Abby, referring to her as my mother, I blurted out rudely, raising my voice in a manner I admit was most ill becoming to a lady, "*She is not my mother; she is my* step *mother!*"

That caused quite a stir in court. Soon everyone who claimed to know me was running to the newspapers with a mean-spirited tale to tell or to quote rude comments I had supposedly made about Abby, like the dressmaker who said I had called her "a mean old thing." Maybe I did; maybe I didn't. I didn't keep a journal of every word I uttered.

And when Mr. Knowlton asked if my relations with my *step* mother had always been cordial, I coldly retorted, "That depends entirely on one's idea of cordiality!"

Cold, cold, cold! Everyone said I was, icy and unfeeling, a human icicle. But I didn't care. Despite the sweltering August heat, I felt like an ice queen swathed in crystals and ermine sitting on a throne carved out of ice despite the blood-boiling heat of that courtroom. I knew that was how they must all imagine me. *Cold, cold, cold!* "That girl has a heart of ice!" I heard a lady seated behind me hiss to her neighbor, who was emphatic in her agreement. *Cold, cold, cold!*

Everyone kept waiting for the incessant and probing questions to wear me down, for my icy cold composure to crack, and finally it did.

"I don't know what I have said. I have answered so many questions, I don't know one thing from another!" I practically shouted in Mr. Knowlton's face as I wiped the exhausted and angry tears from my eyes.

I saw triumph in his expression; he *knew* he had gotten the best of me, God blast him! He'd made me crack, and I wanted to slap him *so hard* his eyes would stay *permanently* crossed. How *dare* he smile at me in that condescending gloating fashion? *That* was no way to treat a *lady!*

Yet in spite of their *private* suspicions, *publicly* no one wanted to believe that I, a respectable New England spinster lady who taught Sunday school, had done it; that would have been unthinkable and shattered too many dearly cherished illusions. *The New York Sun* summed it up best: *She is either the most injured of innocents or the blackest of monsters. She either hacked her father and stepmother to pieces with the fierce brutality of the ogre in Poe's story of the Rue Morgue or some other person did it and she suffers the double torture of losing her parents and being wrongfully accused of their murders.*

Of course, the public wanted to believe the latter, that poor innocent Lizzie was the living victim of this tragedy, but it was admittedly very difficult to do, even the most charitable souls were sorely tested. No one liked to think of a *lady* simmering day in, day out for *years* with such a potent stew of pent-up rage, grievances, frustration, self-denial, secrets, and maybe even—gasp!—repressed carnal passion, all bottled up for *years* just waiting to *explode!*

Yet what fool or madman would be so bold as to stride, hatchet in hand, into a house in the broad bright light of a summer morning, with the maid outside washing windows, and the womenfolk most likely still at home at that hour, and go right upstairs and kill Abby while she was bending over making the bed in the guest room, then linger about, hiding somewhere on the premises, for well over an hour hoping he would not be discovered while he awaited a fortuitous opportunity to kill Father, and me downstairs in the kitchen desultorily ironing handkerchiefs or lazily leafing through a magazine or loitering outside under the pear tree or out in the barn rummaging for bits of iron for one reason or another? It was just too mad, too brazen to believe; not even the most crazed killer would take such risks. Only Bridget and I were in the right place at the proper time, and Bridget, pardon the pun, "had no ax to grind." She had always spoken highly of Abby, and had been seen by several passersby that morning outside washing the windows just as she always said she was and hanging over the fence having a gossip with Mary Dooley, the neighbor's Maggie. So it *had* to be *me*. Practical, New England common sense could point the finger at no other culprit than Lizzie Borden. No one else had so much hate in their heart for the miserly millionaire and his fat cow of a wife.

I knew things were going badly. I barely made it back into the matron's room before I vomited twice and my face broke out in mottled purple blotches and I could not draw a deep breath. When they came to arrest me I was lying slumped over on a sofa with my stays unlaced after receiving another injection from Dr. Bowen, with Emma and the police matron appointed to watch me hovering anxiously over me, one armed with smelling salts, the other vigorously rubbing my hands.

Since Fall River's jail did not have suitable accommodations, they informed me I would be transported to Taunton in the morning, to the Bristol County Jail, there to await trial for my life.

I remember standing up. Then everything went black. The next thing I remember is the train station, walking sandwiched between Reverend Buck and a police matron, with uniformed officers trailing behind and all the people, curious and crowding close, hemming me in, pointing and hissing, "There *she* is! *Lizzie Borden! The murderess!*" while I stood there stoically with my veil down—the police had insisted on it, but no one was fooled—and not moving a muscle. Many took my air of detachment as proof of my guilt. I suppose they expected tears and terror or even for me to swoon. I remember the Reverend Buck holding tight to my arm and loudly insisting to all, "Her calmness is the calmness of innocence!"

Shellshock I think now would be a better word for it. Years later when I saw the walking wounded come back from the Great War stunned and scared, with that glazed, vacant look in their eyes, starting at every sound, I saw myself in them the day I was taken to jail.

Our family attorney, Father's boyhood friend, Mr. Andrew Jennings, was most solicitous; he promised to care for me, and my interests, as though I were his very own daughter. A gentle, portly man with a horseshoe of white hair encircling his shiny bald pink pate and brows like snowy fat caterpillars, he held my hand in a fatherly manner and spoke softly, as though he were endeavoring to gentle a wild, frightened horse. "It's going to be all right, little girl," he told me over and over again until I almost believed him. He seemed so confident and sure, and so very kind, consoling, and warm. . . . If only my father had been like that! It might all have been a different story—one of the nice ones with a happily ever after ending.

Mr. Jennings urged me to have a greater care for my image and valiantly set to work trying to undo the damage I had done in the court of public opinion. *Black* dresses and nothing but until the verdict, he emphatically insisted; not even my darkest blue would do. And to redress the persistent reports of my icy indifference, he had me give an interview from my cell, filled to near bursting with flowers from well-wishers, and cards inscribed with such uplifting and inspiring sentiments as "God is with the poor storm-tossed girl. He will vindicate and glorify her."

"The thing that hurts me most," I dutifully confided in an exclusive interview with Mr. Edwin H. Porter, the reporter from *The Fall River Globe* Mr. Jennings arranged to have visit me, "is to hear people say that I don't show any grief. Of course I don't in public, I was not brought up that way, and I cannot change my nature now, the habit of containing my emotions is too deeply ingrained. They say I don't cry," I continued, pausing to blink back the tears from my eyes. "Well . . . they should see me when I am alone. I see nothing but the deepest shadows. I see no ray of light amid the gloom. I try to fill up the waiting time as best I can, with my Bible and volumes of Dickens, but every day feels longer than the last. I cannot sleep nights, and nothing the doctor gives me will produce sleep. The hardest thing for me to endure here is the night, when there is no light. They will not allow me even a candle to read by, and to sit sleepless in the dark all night is very hard. I know my life can never be the same again if I am ever allowed to leave this place and go home. But I know that I am innocent, and I have made up my mind that, no matter what happens, I will try to bear it bravely and make the best of it."

When Mr. Porter took his leave I thought I saw tears in his eyes. Almost like a suitor, he bowed gallantly over my hand and brushed his lips fleetingly against my quivering flesh. His mustache tickled and I almost swooned.

"God be with you, Lizzie Borden," he said.

I dreamed of him that night, that I was acquitted and when I left the courtroom he knelt down at my feet and asked for my hand in marriage. The very next day he sent me a box of bonbons tied with a big blue satin bow and a bouquet of lilacs to thank me for my graciousness in granting him such a personal and emotional interview. I hoped he would come to visit me again, to bring a breath of spring and maybe even romance into my grim, tiny cell, and he began to vie with Bridget and Lulie for a place in my dreams, but I never saw him again except as a face in the crowd. I was just another story to him, as time, a book about what he called "The Fall River Tragedy," and further headlines would tell. He never really was my friend. He had a wife named Winifred; I alternately imagined her as sour as pickles or a honey-blond temptress. "Any way the wind blows, that is the way *you* go, Mr. Porter!" I used to shake my head and say with bittersweet tartness in years to come whenever I spied his byline.

On the legal front, things were looking brighter for me as the brilliant Mr. Jennings craftily scored several pivotal victories. He succeeded in having my inquest testimony stricken from the record, and since no trace of poison had been found in either Father's or Abby's stomach, he managed to bar any mention of that tattletale Eli Bence's story from the trial. I thought it was an indecent invasion of privacy for a druggist to go about gossiping about what people bought, or *tried* to buy, in his shop, and I sincerely hope he lost numerous customers from the fear that he would be similarly indiscreet with their own personal business! It also helped that

Hyman Lubinsky, an ice-cream man who had been driving slowly down our street August 4, hoping his cold treats would prove tempting on such a hot day, had unexpectedly come forward and claimed to have caught a glimpse in passing of a redheaded woman in a blue dress in our backyard walking in the direction of our barn. Who else could it have been but me? Mr. Jennings was also able to persuade our three-times former governor, George Robinson, to help represent me.

Despite his blue blood, old money, and Harvard education, Governor Robinson had a charming, folksy, backwoodsman style akin to Davy Crockett that juries just loved; they just ate him up "like deer eatin' corn out o' my hand," he boasted proudly. And during his term of office, he had raised Judge Dewey, who would be presiding over my trial, to the bench, and Governor Robinson had an inkling that my trial might be the perfect occasion for Judge Dewey to again say "thank you."

These legal triumphs made my hopes soar. I knew I had made a poor show at the inquest, and the story of my visit to Smith's Drugstore kept coming back to haunt me. Everyone kept hounding me, insisting they *must* know if there was *any* truth in it, the better to safeguard my interests.

Finally, to shut them all up, I drew Emma down to sit beside me on my prison cot, and confided that I had been feeling *so* melancholy and miserable, stuck and stagnant, watching my life and all my hopes and chances pass me by, that I had decided to kill myself and I had gone to that drugstore on the wrong side of town where no one knew me, to buy poison to put an end to my wretched life. But I had changed my mind and didn't want anyone to know I had been so foolish and weak or to think I might be a danger to myself and need to be locked away in some sanitarium somewhere for my own protection. I *swore* to her that my desperate thoughts had truly been just a fleeting fancy and had *never* darkened the threshold of my mind again. But if the public knew of my misery they might misunderstand and think it a just motive for murder, that I had not been in my right mind at the time, and the legal men might all put their heads together and decide to save themselves a lot of bother and just have me committed to an asylum instead of letting me hang or leaving me to rot in prison, and I just could not bear that.

"I just don't want anyone to know," I told Emma.

Of course she ran straightaway and told Mr. Jennings. I *knew* she would! But it gave me an excuse to sulk and avoid her tedious and tearful visits, at least for a few days.

"Emma, you have given me away!" I stormed the next time she came to see me, and turned my back on her even as she wept and swore on her heart, "*Never! I swear,* Lizzie, I did no such thing!"

As the fickle sprite of luck would have it, the matron, Mrs. Regan, overheard, and had to tell her little tale to the newspapers. But all she truly knew was that Emma and I had quarreled and fallen out about something. But when the journalists came clamoring, Emma loyally denied everything and kept her mouth shut. It really was just a tempest in a teapot, and soon my sister and I were weeping in each other's arms and forgiving each other everything, including murder, though it remained unspoken of course, politely ignored like a bloodstained elephant in the parlor, and we went on offering a reward no one could possibly ever claim and pretending that some unknown audacious madman had snuck in and killed Abby and Father.

"It's all for the best," became Emma's mantra. Whenever the need arose, and the specter of my murderous deeds loomed over us and cast too giant a shadow, my sister would hug me tight, pat my back, and whisper, like a devout Catholic saying the Rosary, "It's all for the best; it's all for the best. . . ." That was Emma's way of dealing with it. In this life, appearances and reputations must be maintained, form and formality come first, but everything after that she would leave to God, for Him to dispense divine and final justice. She simply washed her hands of it. Of course, it helped that hers weren't stained with blood. Lucky Emma! She may have looked brittle and bird boned, but her spine was solid steel; she never bent or broke.

But the luckiest strike of all, the golden mother lode of legal triumphs, came mere days before my trial began when Bertha Manchester, a rawboned redheaded dairy farmer's daughter, was hacked to bloody bits with a hatchet in broad daylight in her own kitchen at nine o'clock in the morning by an unknown assailant who just walked in through the back door, then vanished like a phantom. In a demise eerily like Abby's, Bertha took twenty-three blows, one for each year of her life, to her head and back while she was bending over putting breakfast on the table.

Clearly *I* could not have done it; I didn't even know Bertha Manchester, and I was locked safely away in jail at the time. The culprit turned out to be a Portuguese farmhand who thought himself short-changed and ill-treated by Bertha's father, and Bertha herself because she wouldn't lift her skirts for him, but no matter, everyone knew that I hadn't done it, and it cast a lovely cloud of reasonable doubt over my supposed guilt. I could not have been more grateful. Months later it came out that the Portuguese couldn't possibly have killed Father and Abby, as he had not yet emigrated from his native country when they were slain, but my trial was all over by then, so it didn't matter.

Despite all this, I was still afraid. I knew I had come off badly with all my contradictions and that worried me incessantly, even when both Mr. Jennings and Governor Robinson held my hand and promised me that everything would be all right. To help allay my fears, Dr. Bowen was called to the stand and queried about the effects of morphine upon an anguished mind. "Might it not affect the memory and change and alter one's view of things and possibly even cause hallucinations?" Mr. Jennings asked craftily.

"Yes, sir," Dr. Bowen answered emphatically. "Most certainly!"

Across the crowded courtroom our eyes met and I knew that was his gift to me—a clouded mind and the perfect excuse to cover it. But *why* did he do it? Was it because he knew what my life was like in the house at 92 Second Street and felt sorry for me? Or was it one single frayed and lingering shred of affection he still held in his heart for me? I like to think it was the latter—a much-belated Valentine.

My trial, also known as "That Carnival in New Bedford," began on June 5, 1893, at the courthouse in New Bedford. It lasted fourteen days. I sat beside Emma, my jaw pillowed on my fist, and wore the same heavy, boring, and distinctly unflattering black silk dress Emma had bought off the rack for me every single day. Sometimes

I played with my fan. Fluttering it did nothing to alleviate the heat. But I *must* do *something* or go mad!

Even though it was mostly about me, the testimony was *dull, dull, dull,* and I sat there glassy-eyed and almost catatonic. There were times when it made my cramped little jail cell seem almost like a paradise I *longed* to return to; at least Mr. Dickens's novels were there waiting for me. I did not take the stand; I let Mr. Jennings speak for me, and he did it quite well. He was *almost* worth the $25,000 bill he sent. *Almost.* The worst moment, by far—besides waiting for the jury to come back with their verdict—was when the skulls were brought in and the blade of the handle-less hatchet that had been found smeared with ashes in a dusty old box in the cellar was shown to fit the wounds. I leapt to my feet in a fit of panic, wanting to flee, only to turn green and teeter precariously. I almost fainted. Fortunately, Mr. Jennings, Governor Robinson, and Emma all rushed to catch me in time. Only later did I learn these skulls were made of plaster and the real skulls had been returned to Oak Grove Cemetery and interred above Father's and Abby's coffins. It was a *cruel, dirty trick* for Mr. Knowlton to play upon a lady! I *never* forgave him for it!

The time the jury was out was the longest hour and six minutes of my life; each instant seemed to *creep* by like an eternity. The tension was unbearable. I gnawed my lips raw and shredded my handkerchief into my lap. My head began to throb with the searing red pain of a migraine and my vision wavered and rippled like heat waves with flashes of starry red Fourth of July fireworks. I had never been more afraid. *Innocent, innocent, you are innocent!* I kept chanting in my head, *willing* the jury to see it *my* way, to do the *right* thing for *me and* for Fall River. Later, when I learned that they had voted to acquit me in less than two minutes but had sat and bided their time merely as a formality, so no one would think they had reached a verdict in unseemly haste, I wanted to slap each one of them *hard* across the face for torturing me so needlessly. To my mind, if they had come immediately back it would have been a *greater* victory; it would have shown the world my innocence was so obvious they didn't even need two minutes to debate it.

I was *so* relieved to hear the word *not* before *guilty* that I fainted dead away. I just dropped like a stone, right where I was standing. I fell so heavily I'm constantly surprised that no impertinent jokester in that hell-hot and overcrowded courtroom stood up and cupped his hands around his mouth and shouted, *Timber!* like a lumberjack. When Emma, Governor Robinson, and Mr. Jennings helped me up, they had to repeatedly assure me that it wasn't all a dream. When they had me in my chair again I covered my face with my hands and burst into tears. "Thank God! Thank God!" I exclaimed over and over again as relief and joy flooded me until I thought I would surely drown. And then I began to laugh. I was *so* happy and *relieved* I was afraid I wouldn't be able to stop.

"God has given me the greatest gift of all!" I exclaimed to everyone and no one. I was so happy, so very happy! *Glory, glory hallelujah!* It was *all* over now and I was *truly* free at last!

When I appeared at the top of the courthouse steps surrounded by Emma, Uncle John, Mr. Jennings, Governor Robinson, and the Reverends Buck and Jubb, everyone cheered and a band began to play "Auld Lang Syne," and with tears in my eyes I declared, "*I'm the happiest woman alive!*" I just stood there dumbly with tears in my eyes and kept repeating it until the words lost all meaning.

Uncle John, his deplorable behavior disguised by the crush of the crowd, patted my bottom, then leaned even closer and whispered in my ear, "Lizzie, my girl, the afternoon before I arrived to see Andrew, God rest him, I visited a fortune-teller. She took one look at my palm and went white as death and shoved my hand away. She said she would not tell me what she saw even if I offered her fifty dollars, so I offered her one hundred dollars, waved it right in her face like a flag, but not even that would loosen her tongue and persuade her to tell me what evil calamity she saw in my palm. Curious, isn't it?" Then he pinched my bottom so hard it brought fresh tears—tears of *pain!*—to my eyes, and tipped his hat to me. I never saw him again. As he strode down the steps, away from me, hands in his pockets, whistling a jaunty tune, I wanted to kick him, in the seat of his cheap, threadbare old pants, but I couldn't very well risk it with everyone watching and thinking so well of me. It would not have been ladylike or at all becoming to a Fall Riverite descended from one of the first families.

As I descended the courthouse steps, with Emma's arm clasped in supportive, sisterly fashion, around my waist, a church choir in white robes with bloodred hymnbooks appeared and began to sing, of all things, of all the songs in the world they could have sung, "The Battle Hymn of the Republic."

"Mine eyes have seen the glory
Of the coming of the Lord
He is trampling out the vintage
Where the grapes of wrath are stored
He has loosed the fateful lightning
Of His terrible swift sword
His truth is marching on

"Glory, glory, hallelujah
Glory, glory, hallelujah
Glory, glory, hallelujah
His truth is marching on

"I have seen Him in the watch fires
Of a hundred circling camps
They have builded Him an altar
In the evening dews and damps
I can read His righteous sentence
By the dim and flaring lamps
His day is marching on

"Glory, glory, hallelujah
Glory, glory, hallelujah
Glory, glory, hallelujah
His day is marching on

"I have read a fiery gospel
Writ in burnish'd rows of steel
'As ye deal with my condemners
So with you My grace shall deal'

Let the hero, born of woman,
Crush the serpent with his heel
Since God is marching on

"Glory, glory, hallelujah
Glory, glory, hallelujah
Glory, glory, hallelujah
Since God is marching on

"He has sounded forth the trumpet
That shall never call retreat
He is sifting out the hearts of men
Before His judgment seat
Oh, be swift, my soul
To answer Him,
Be jubilant, my feet,
Our God is marching on

"Glory, glory, hallelujah
Glory, glory, hallelujah
Glory, glory, hallelujah
Our God is marching on

"In the beauty of the lilies"

At that moment a little girl, all dressed in angel white, with long red curls—was it mere coincidence that she reminded me of me?—stepped forward, curtsied, and presented me with a bouquet of beautiful white lilies.

"Christ was born across the sea
With a glory in his bosom
That transfigures you and me
As He died to make men holy,
Let us die to make men free
While God is marching on

"Glory, glory, hallelujah
Glory, glory, hallelujah
Glory, glory, hallelujah
While God is marching on

"Glory, glory, hallelujah
Glory, glory, hallelujah
Glory, glory, hallelujah
Our God is marching on"

Hearing that song at that moment felt like a punch in the stomach. I wasn't sure if it was being sung in celebration of my victory or to remind me that I still had to face *God's* judgment. The tenor who soloed was *delectable*—even if he was damning me to perdition with his glorious voice—Irish, I thought, with jade-green eyes and the waviest dark hair I had ever seen. One *really* does think the most peculiar things at the most peculiar times!

Since I didn't know what was intended by the choir's singing of that particular song, I forced myself to just keep nodding and smiling and hoped no one could smell how badly I was sweating. Tears and sweat burned my eyes, my armpits were soaking, and my mouth ached from smiling. I just wanted to go where no one could see me so I could abandon all pretense. And, above all else, I wanted a cold bath!

"I'm the happiest woman in the world!" I said again, and again, to no one in particular, the smile straining painfully at my mouth, as tears streamed down my face to join the sweat soaking my black collar.

Then the whole enormity of everything I had been through seemed to strike me like a gigantic fist and I sagged weakly against Emma and laid my head upon her shoulder. "Take me home," I whispered.

I clung to Emma and hysterically laughed and wept, as though I couldn't make up my mind what I truly felt and must bounce like a rubber ball between one and the other, all the way to the carriage that was waiting to take us to the train station where a train would whisk us back to Fall River and, for the first time in almost a year, back to the house at 92 Second Street. But everyone seemed to understand. I was deluged with flowers, hugs and handshakes, and pats on the back, all the way to the carriage, and babies were held up for me to kiss and caress. People ran after us waving and flinging yet more flowers into the carriage. They aggravated Emma's hay fever and she sneezed all the way to the train station. By the time we arrived, her eyes were almost swollen shut. I should have been more sympathetic. But I couldn't help myself. I rocked back and forth on the leather seat beside her, hysterically spouting tears and spurts of wild laughter and crying out like some mad fool, "Thank God! Hallelujah! Glory, glory Hallelujah!"

If life were a theater play or a novel this is where my story would end—happily, in a spirit of jubilation, with me vindicated and set free.

But life is not like that.

Setting foot in the house on 92 Second Street for the first time in over a year, I felt like a stranger in a strange land. Everything seemed so foreign, yet painfully familiar. There was a conspicuous bare spot in the sitting room where the sofa where Father had taken his fatal nap had been, the wallpaper bore a pale outline of its back, and pieces of the carpet had been cut out, presumably to remove bloodstains as evidence or because they defied all attempts at cleaning. It made me shudder to be back in that room. I kept seeing myself standing over Father with the hatchet raised, so I quickly made my excuses and retreated upstairs.

In my room, I stood and stared at the prints and pictures, souvenirs of my Grand Tour, on the walls as though they belonged to a stranger. I ran my fingers over the spines of the books on my shelf. I had been away so long, I felt like I didn't belong here, but then I remembered I had never belonged here, but now . . . I was a bird with wings and free to use them to fly away from this wretched, miserable place where I had known nothing but unhappiness! A merry giggle escaped me. I clapped my hands over my mouth and darted my eyes left and right, fearful that someone might have heard, and then I remembered—I was *FREE!* Free as the air! Free as a bird! *Acquitted! NOT* guilty! I was no longer a prisoner! I could laugh if I wanted to! At *anything* and *everything!* And I could snap my fingers in the face of anyone who didn't like it! I could even *dance* if I pleased! I threw back my head and began to laugh and spin around in dizzy, delighted circles. "I'm not only the happiest woman in the world; I'm also the *luckiest!*" I cried as I collapsed on the bed and gave my pillow a fierce hug.

When I changed my dress that evening to attend the party the Holmes family on Pine Street were hosting to celebrate my victory I vowed I would never wear black again. *I was done with mourning and regrets!* I made my grand entrance in a royal-purple satin dress, with its full skirt draped back to reveal an underskirt of crimson satin, and gracefully arcing sleek purple and red feathers in my hair and framing my bare shoulders.

My appearance in such brazen attire stunned everyone speechless; even the orchestra fell silent for a long, awkward instant before hastily resuming their rudely interrupted melody. I knew Emma, trailing behind me looking like a tired old black crow, didn't approve; she couldn't understand how I could be so brazen as to appear in public in such a dress when I was supposed to be in mourning, but I didn't care what anyone thought, and that included Emma. I was sick and tired of being told what to do! Of course, she made excuses for me, about the joy of freedom going like wine to my head, trying to justify my "peculiar conduct" and "brazen choice of apparel." She was quite right, freedom *had* intoxicated me, I was giddy and drunk upon it and hoped to be so for the rest of my life, but I nonetheless resented her need to try to justify me. Justice had set me free, and what better way to celebrate it than by doing *exactly* as I pleased?

Dr. Bowen smilingly swept me away to lead the first waltz.

"The world is yours now, Lizzie," he whispered in my ear at the end of the dance.

"Indeed it is," I answered coyly as he bowed over my trembling hand. He *still* had the power to make my knees weak!

"And I wonder just what you will do with it." He smiled back at me.

But I just shrugged and stood there smiling like a fool. Then Phoebe Bowen was there, all elegant but boring simplicity, in her ivory satin gown—not that it wasn't a monumental improvement over the bridesmaids' dresses at her wedding—with a forced and frigidly polite smile straining at her lips as though being nice to me was the hardest thing she had ever had to do in her life. The diamonds tipping the pins in the dark pompadour of her hair were as hard and cold as her eyes. Her gloved hand reached out to rest possessively upon her husband's arm, fingertips digging in deep as she led him determinedly away for the dance he had promised her. She never did like me, and a part of me, in the secret heart of me, always wished I were her. She was *so* beautiful and poised, slender and superior—no wonder Dr. Bowen loved her so much!

As the orchestra began another waltz, I strolled out into the garden. Humming and swaying my crimson and purple feather fan in time to the music, I followed the white gravel path out into the warm summer night, to stand and stare up at the stars, blissfully unencumbered by high stone walls, iron bars, and the alert and vigilant eyes of authority. *Free!* No more prison matrons and guards! I sighed and breathed deeply, inhaling the heady, fragrant scent of the summer roses. *Free! I am free as the air, free as the stars!* The full moon above was like a milky crystal ball in which I could see my future, or ... better yet ... a blank page on which I could *write* my future! I trailed my fingers through the fountain and caressed the statue of Cupid. "Free to find love!" I whispered with delicious anticipation into his delicate little marble ear.

The very next morning I put on a smart navy-blue suit with bright cherry red lapels and piping and a gay pillbox hat trimmed with a clacking cluster of red-lacquered cherries and, with a smile on my face as cheerful as my attire, and Emma trailing disapprovingly behind me in yards of weighty black silk and crepe mourning veils, went out in search of my dream house on The Hill.

I was so happy and intent upon my purpose that it didn't quite sink in that every time I nodded pleasantly and said "good morning" to passersby they turned away and completely ignored me. I simply smiled and shrugged aside their rudeness. I thought them, like me, preoccupied with their own business. I didn't know it then, but for the second time in my life my world had changed completely overnight. Yesterday I had been Fall River's vindicated darling; today I was their grudgingly tolerated pariah, their resident leper. I just didn't realize it yet; happiness blinded me. I thought all my dreams were *finally* coming true. Freedom, riches, unbridled luxury, limitless decadence, and, God willing, at long last—*love!*

Chapter 8

The moment I saw the big white house on French Street nestled amongst the maple trees I *knew* it had been waiting for me all my life; that was why it was vacant at such an opportune time. *This* was *my* house! *My home!* The one I had always dreamed of! *This* was where I belonged! *Welcome home, Lizzie!* the maple trees whispered like a bevy of ardent beaus as a caressing breeze gently stirred their leaves. *Maplecroft*—the name sprang unbidden to my lips the moment I set my foot upon the first gray granite step. I knew then that as soon as it was mine I would send a stonemason to chisel that name into the top riser, facing boldly out onto French Street in big capital letters: *MAPLECROFT!* When the moment came, I didn't even haggle over the cost; I paid it without comment: $11,000; I would have paid *ten* times that if they had asked me to.

We put the house at 92 Second Street up for sale, determined never to set foot in it again, and had a hired girl come in to box up everything that had belonged to Abby and send it on to "that slattern Sarah," as a remembrance of her sister.

The ink was barely dry upon the deed before I set to work decorating the palace of my dreams. There was nothing cramped or dark about my Maplecroft; it was all spaciousness and light, four-teen big rooms, with high ceilings and an abundance of windows to welcome in the light. I ordered stained glass for some of them and the light poured in, blissfully clothing me in all the jewel-vibrant colors I had longed for all my life.

I swore that this would *never* be a house of dark, ugly secrets, shameful, sinister shadows, and lies; beneath this roof I would *never* be anything but my true, honest self. *This above all: to thine own self be true,* I ordered carved above the fireplace in the room I chose for my winter bedroom—yes, it was the height of ostenta-tiousness, I know, but I had *two* bedrooms: one for summer, and one for winter, on opposite sides of the house.

It was luxury every inch, floor to ceiling, wall to wall, in Maple-croft, even in the servants' quarters, kitchen, pantry, and laundry the floors were golden oak with dark-walnut wainscoting for con-trast.

Throughout the house there were parquet floors, crown mold-ings, and high white linen ceilings, either painted, embossed, or creamy clean; some I even had adorned with gold maple leaves. The woodwork, golden oak, maple, mahogany, rosewood, and rich deep-red cherry wood, was beautiful, smooth as satin or ornately carved, and the walls were all papered in silk. What fun I had choosing the patterns! I chose ice-blue silk with an elegant gold lat-tice pattern framing bountiful clusters of purple and green grapes and bouquets of white roses for my winter bedroom, and rich chocolate silk with bold gold stripes alternating with rows of bright pink flowers for my summer bedroom.

There was a grand piano in the parlor although I didn't play, heavy rose silk drapes lined in ice-blue silk, rose and gold brocade upholstered sofas and chairs, matching cushions on the window seats, and, eventually, a large, gilt-framed portrait of me, gowned in ice-blue satin, sapphires, and pearls, with a white lace shawl draped loosely about my shoulders and a deep-pink rose in one hand as I leaned pensively against the pedestal of a Grecian statue of lovers embracing.

The artist had flattered me and minimized my shoulders, waist, hips, and heavy jaw, making me more beautiful than I ever had been or ever would be in real life. But I was grateful that he, with his artist's eye, could also see the Lizzie of my dreams, or Lizbeth as I had secretly called myself ever since my architect had so christened me. And, for one brief moment, it made me feel a little less alone. Long after I knew it was a dream that could never come true, I used to stand before that portrait and imagine myself making a grand entrance down the sweeping, elegant cherry wood staircase embellished with carved and gilded maple leaves to greet a parlor full of guests, all eager and happy to see me, the men vying to kiss my hand and the women to embrace me.

But Maplecroft, at least, was no longer a dream—it was solid and *real*, the embodiment of all my dreams. There were Italianate arches, pillars, and Turkish and Aubusson carpets, and a billiard room even though I didn't play, but I fancied it the epitome of elegance to have such a room and imagined it filled with handsome gentlemen enjoying fine cigars and sipping brandy from fine etched-crystal glasses as they stood around the green felt–topped table.

My library, one of the largest rooms in the house, and yet also the coziest, had every wall lined with floor-to-ceiling shelves that it gave me immense delight to fill with leather-bound volumes. I had never owned so many books in my life—Father thought it a waste of money since one generally read each volume only one time—and spent many happy *hours* pasting my specially designed monogrammed bookplate inside the cover of each one.

There were *four* bathrooms with toilets like thrones, Queen Victoria herself I'm sure never sat upon a finer, and the sides of the gleaming pearl-white porcelain claw-footed bathtubs were painted with exquisite floral motifs to match the rugs, curtains, and wallpaper. And there were colorful cakes of perfumed soap in floral-painted and gilt-edged white porcelain dishes in each one. The soaps in my summer bathroom were pink and molded in the shape of roses in memory of that lovely, long-ago day I had shared with Lulie. The soaps in my winter bathroom were white or ice blue.

There were six large fireplaces each with an elaborate mahogany mantel carved with fruit, flowers, foliage, or animals, and a bit of posy I had chosen because of its personal significance to me. A pair of iron bulldogs sat faithfully flanking each hearth, and painted metal peacocks fanned out tails inlaid with glass mosaics as fire screens.

For the mantel in my library, which opened directly into my summer bedroom, so my beloved books would always be close at hand on the many nights when sleep eluded me, I chose a verse particularly dear to my heart, one my Englishman, the architect who had built such sweet, wonderful dreams in my heart that fate, Father, and my own timidity and doubt had demolished, had recited to me that magical day at Glastonbury:

> *The green leaf of loyalty's beginning to fall.*
> *The bonnie White Rose it is withering an' all.*
> *But I'll water it with the blood of usurping tyrannie,*
> *An' green it will grow in my ain countrie.*

It spoke to me in a secret way none but my own lonely and tormented heart could ever understand. Father's will and soft Abby's sudden hardness as a result of David Anthony's damning revelations had destroyed whatever loyalty and sense of duty I had left for my family. *I* was the white rose withering in the house at 92 Second Street, but their blood that I had spilled had *saved* and *revived* me and allowed me to go on and flourish in my own little kingdom—Maplecroft!—*My Ain Countrie!*

I had thistle blossoms and leaves carved in a border slightly suggestive of a heart embracing the words.

And in my bedroom, within sight of my bed, where I could lie warm as toast beneath my eiderdown quilt and drowsily watch the dance of the flames, I had carved a verse embodying the wistful, hopeful dream I still believed in those blissfully, blind days might still come true, and, God willing, soon:

> *And old time friends, and twilight plays*
> *And starry nights, and sunny days,*

Come trooping up the misty ways,
When my fire burns low.

Emma had the room across the hall. As stark as a nun's cell, it was the bleakest room in the house, just plain white walls and a bare wooden floor, a bed with a small table beside it, her Bible and a lamp reposing on top, a chest of drawers, a washstand, and a chair by the fire, all of the plainest design, like something a Quaker would have ordered; there was not even a fern or a china shepherdess or even a bright rug to add a touch of warmth and cheer. The pitcher and basin on the washstand didn't even have flowers painted on them; they were *plain white!* Though in the years to come Emma would develop a mania for religious pictures, books, and bric-a-brac, mostly of distinctly Catholic taste, eventually crowding her room with a whole host of saints, angels, Madonnas, and baby Jesuses, with a splendid gilt-framed reproduction of da Vinci's *Last Supper* hanging right over her bed, until it bore more than a passing resemblance to a dusty and disorderly gift shop I had seen in Rome nestled right in the shadow of the Vatican. There came to be so many little tables covered with china figures and framed pictures, postcards, and prayer cards that the maid could hardly turn around when she came in to clean and hardly dared breathe lest she inadvertently break something with an accidental brush of her elbow or hip or the gentle whisk of her feather duster. It was worse than the Quaker-plain furniture and white walls had been and I hated to even glance inside the room if the door happened to be open when I was walking down the hall. More often than not, whenever I did Emma would glance up from where she was kneeling in prayer at the foot of her bed or sitting with her head bowed over her Bible or some other religious text and give me a long look that implied this was exactly what *I* should be doing. I couldn't stand it! It never failed to make me shudder! I felt like ordering a placard carved with the words *Abandon hope, all ye who enter here!* to hang above the doorway as a warning to any potential visitors, though the Reverend Jubb and his sister were the only ones who ever came to visit Emma; all her former friends proved to be fair-weather and drifted away the moment I was acquitted.

I knew we would never agree—Emma was intent on turning her lone room in our great, grand house into a convent cell, while I had sold my soul for the gay life and luxuries galore. Now that we could afford all of life's finer things my sister perversely wanted no part of them. It was a perfect example of the old adage: *after you get what you want, you don't want it.* It was most exasperating! In truth, it made me *sick.* I felt betrayed by my own sister.

"You're behaving just like Father," I stamped my foot and shouted at her more than once. "You're rich enough to have *anything* and you want *nothing!*"

But we both knew the sad truth. Emma only continued to live with me so people wouldn't talk. I suppose I should have been grateful for that, only . . . people *did* talk, and *plenty!* But Emma said if we went our separate ways everyone would take her leaving me as a silent admission of my guilt, they would say that my very own sister believed I had gotten away with murder, so it was better that we stay together. Together . . . yet apart. Though we lived under the same roof, sometimes a whole string of *days* would pass without our even seeing each other. We kept to ourselves and only presented a united front before witnesses; then we stepped into our roles like consummate actresses. Our devotion was truly remarkable; no acquitted murderess could ever have wished for a more loyal and ardent champion than I had in my sister, Emma.

But it was all for show, those all-important, sacrosanct appearances we must always, at all costs, keep up. It was as though the death of Abby, her sworn enemy, had freed Emma from the promise she had, at only thirteen years old, made to our dead mother to "always look after Baby Lizzie." The moment I was acquitted, Emma ceased mothering me, and left me to fend for myself, except for those all-important appearances and those, thankfully few, awkward moments when she felt beholden to try to be my conscience. She just suddenly seemed to lose interest and let the cloak of duty fall from her shoulders. Only when it was gone did I begin to miss what I had for all those years resented. Now there was no one to hold me back and try to fetter me with prattle about morals and etiquette, I was truly free to do exactly as I pleased. And yet somehow the joy was somewhat dimmed, though I would spend the rest of my life lying to myself and pretending that it wasn't.

I was so full of hope back then, when I set out to furnish Maplecroft, it was like I had been reborn, filthy rich and free! No one could stop me or say to me nay! I was determined to deluge myself with all the luxury and decadence and creature comforts I had ever craved but been denied by my father's penny-pinching tyranny. Now I would have nothing but the finest frivolities, not just humdrum boring necessities. I ordered crystal chandeliers, quality reproductions of paintings and statues I had admired on my Grand Tour, I splurged on Tiffany lamps, and mother-of-pearl sconces shaped like scallop shells with pearl and crystal prisms dangling beneath, fine crystal, china, monogrammed silverware, and linens for my table, and not one but *two* of the heaviest and fanciest silver tea services money could buy from Tiffany's, with my monogram prominently worked into the design of course.

And I developed a sudden, inexplicable mania for collecting souvenir spoons made to commemorate special occasions and historical events, like the World's Columbian Exposition, the Midnight Ride of Paul Revere, and the Salem Witch Trials, whimsical figures like Mother Goose, or famous folk like George and Martha Washington and William Shakespeare, and I had at least one for every state and every country. I really can't explain it; I just woke up one morning and impulsively started collecting them and never stopped.

I ordered every room to be *always* filled with vases of flowers that were to be replenished with new ones the *moment* any of the blooms started to wilt.

And upon my walls, each in a gilded frame, chaste, benevolent, and serenely smiling Madonnas hung beside plump nude courtesans lolling wantonly on rumpled beds, French ballet girls, Turkish harem girls, and geishas from Japan, mermaids, nymphs and goddesses of ancient myths naked but for their long, flowing hair and diaphanous draperies, royal mistresses and queens, including Nell Gwyn, Madame Pompadour, the scandalous du Barry, Marie Antoinette, and Empress Josephine, heroines of history and legend, including a proud and mighty bare-breasted Boudicca in a metal corselet and helmet hefting a sword high, Lady Godiva wearing only her long auburn hair, and Cleopatra with a poisonous asp sinking its fatal fangs into her bare, perfect breast.

My neighbors said I had more naked women on my walls than a bordello, but it was art and perfectly respectable. Each piece was purchased pedigreed, and at great expense, from a well-known and prestigious gallery in Boston, New York, Chicago, Washington, or San Francisco; some even came from London. If I hadn't been Lizzie Borden, no one would have said a word. They also deemed the numerous small tabletop reproductions of classical statues scattered throughout the house unseemly because they were all nudes, some even depicting lovers passionately entwined. One girl I hired for the day to hem the drapes in my summer bedroom spread it all over town that I had a little pert-breasted pink marble slave girl, stark naked and in shackles, on the table beside my bed standing on the gilded pedestal of a rose-silk-shaded lamp and that she looked "shiny from rubbing." But I didn't care; people were *always* gossiping about *something!*

And I had a telephone and electricity, the best plumbing money could buy, hot and cold running water, and every modern, newfangled convenience I could find to buy. All the salesmen had to say was "new" and "modern" and I was sold! I would *never* go back to the primitive way of life I had known at the house on 92 Second Street!

I gave my wardrobe a complete overhaul too. I ignored the mirror and my dressmaker's and Emma's advice and bought to suit my tastes, *not* my figure, and clothed myself in a veritable rainbow, a whole wonderful spectrum of pinks, purples, oranges, greens, blues, yellows, and reds; solids, stripes, plaids, paisleys, prints, and polka dots. I indulged my love of lace and fancy trimmings like silk fringe, frogs, and braid, tinsel and beads, buttons both bold and dainty, silver or gold, shiny and new or antiqued, some even set with precious stones, and, of course, long rows of dainty pearls snaking from the nape of my neck to the base of my spine. I bought great behemoth hats heaped high with wax fruit or vegetables, feathers, or even entire stuffed birds, some sitting on nests replete with speckled eggs, and silk and velvet flowers, ruffles, and ribbons, many with brims wide as serving platters with lace or net veils to draw like a curtain over my face so I could enjoy some occasional sweet moments of anonymity in public, especially when I visited cities where I was known only because my picture had been in the newspapers—thank Heaven some of the artists, seeking to sell more papers, had flattered me and depicted me as a willowy wasp-waisted damsel in distress utterly unlike my actual short, stout, jowly-jawed self. I bought elegant high-heeled shoes and exquisite high-buttoned boots, gloves, shawls, and parasols, fur coats, wraps, muffs, and velvet coats with embroidered lapels and silk frogs and tassels.

When I woke up one morning and decided that my jewelry box was as bare as Mother Hubbard's cupboard I impulsively marched into Gifford's and proceeded to fill it with sapphire, ruby, emerald, and diamond rings, set in gold and in platinum, simple band styles and ornate clusters, a lady's gold watch, a set of tortoiseshell and gold combs for my hair, four cameo brooches, and a heart-shaped pendant paved with ruby and diamond chips that I liked so well I ordered a second one made with diamonds and sapphires, and then, as soon as I got home, I phoned back and commissioned a third one with emeralds. And I went back the next day having suddenly conceived a passion for opals. It felt *so good* just to be able to buy whatever I wanted, heedless of need, motivated only by desire and, yes, greed, without having to answer to anyone for my frivolous and selfish impulses.

I tried to pretend I didn't care how broad and mannish my shoulders looked beneath all the ruffles and frills, and great big bows and flounces, or how my jowls dripped like puddles of melting pink wax over the lace edges of the high collars that were meant to make a lady's throat look like a white marble pillar. I looked dumpy and lumpy, but I stood far back from the mirror and scrunched up my eyes and squinted until I thought I truly saw Lizbeth of Maplecroft, elegant, gracious, and lithe in her new finery.

And beneath the lavish fabric confections of my dresses, in joyful defiance of Father now moldering in his grave, I indulged my every frivolous and extravagant whim upon the garments that no one but a maid, laundress, and perhaps a husband or lover would ever see. Good-bye, plain, prim white cottons, cheap calico, and flannel! Henceforth, even in the coldest winter, I would cover my bosom and nether regions only with silk—white, champagne, baby-blush pink, ice blue, the most delicate lilac, mint green, butter yellow, and pale peach, and, upon occasion, when I was feeling especially daring, black silk trimmed with French lace threaded with red satin ribbons! Cotton and wool, I vowed, would *never* sheathe my limbs again, only the finest silk stockings—black, white, pink, and flesh colored. Every undergarment was trimmed with lace and ribbons; some even had exquisite little rosettes and seed pearls or meticulously stitched pleats and tucks. I ordered corsets in apricot, apple green, blush, and ice-blue satin, and ruffled taffeta petticoats that rustled every time I moved, and later, when narrow skirts came into fashion, sleek silk ones inset with lace.

Every night when I went, alas alone, to bed, I was clad in a nightgown, matching robe, and high-heeled chamber slippers fit for a French courtesan or a lavishly embroidered silk kimono worthy of the most desirable geisha. I didn't care what the servants, or anyone else, thought, though in my heart of hearts it made me terribly sad to know I was going to bed dressed like a woman ready to receive her lover and yet I had none. *Someday,* I hoped and prayed, though for a lover more than a husband, I admit. After Father, I feared giving any man the power to dominate, rule, and control me ever again. My freedom had been so hard, and violently, won, I was loath to ever again put it in jeopardy. Better to love immorally, I thought, than to be enslaved. And I already had even worse sins that I must someday answer to God for, so what was one more? Just another cherry on the cake. So I might as well enjoy myself and live life to the fullest while I was alive, since after I was dead I would surely be damned. I know that sounds blasé, but I had to live with myself and what I had done, and it was better to keep on dancing as long as possible than pay the fiddler and send him on his way and let fear-filled silence reign.

Quiet moments were always the worst. I kept hearing Father's voice in my head calling me a "spendthrift" and saying, as he always had in life, that I could not have a penny without it burning a hole in my pocket. It was most distressing and I tried to drown him out with the rustle of greenbacks and the clink of coins. *Oh, shut up, Father!* I wanted to scream. *Money is made for spending, not hoarding!* I was having fun and even from beyond the grave he was trying to spoil it! He *really* was a mean old man! Sometimes I had to take the sleeping syrup Dr. Bowen prescribed just to quiet Father enough so I could sleep.

Now that the dream of Bridget had died, I disdained the idea of hiring another Irish Maggie to take her place and opted for a kindly and sensible Swedish housekeeper named Hannah instead, and two more Swedish girls, Elsa and Greta, to serve as maids, one for upstairs the other for down. They were all pleasant, moon-faced girls with stout, sturdy figures, none of whom tempted me to lascivious thoughts in the least. And to tend the grounds, I engaged a plainspoken but polite Yankee gardener—though with some degree of imagination, thank goodness, since I considered that essential. And, though it raised a great many eyebrows, I acquired a devilishly handsome French chauffeur, Monsieur Tetrault, liveried, of course, in gray broadcloth, gilt buttons, and black shiny boots and cap, with my monogram worked in dark blue upon his sleeves and chest so everyone would know he belonged to me. Admittedly he did stir my blood a bit, but alas, he was married. His wife was my cook, and a most excellent one too, so I was loath to risk offending her. Madame Tetrault was a *marvel* in the kitchen; she could do all the traditional, comforting American dishes as well as the most decadent gourmet delights from France and Italy, and desserts were her specialty—just thinking about her marvelous jelly roll makes my mouth water!

And for Monsieur to drive me about in I had two carriages. Black-lacquered with a gold maple leaf and my initials monogrammed in gilt upon each door, one was upholstered in ice-blue velvet and the other in midnight, drawn by an elegant high-stepping quartet of snow-white or coal-black horses. Later, when motorcars became all the fashion, a gleaming black Buick sedan and a sleek silver Packard replaced them. I had the only private gas pump in town, set prominently alongside the white-graveled driveway outside my glaze-windowed garage, which was heated and even equipped with hot and cold running water so Monsieur Tetrault could wash the grease off his hands after working on the cars. Of course everyone stuck their noses in the air and denounced it all as *ostentatious* and *vulgar*. But I didn't care!

My neighbors on The Hill were, of course, quick to criticize *everything* I did. They were always declaring themselves *scandalized* and endlessly cataloging my social faux pas. One would have thought they had all gone senile the way they went over my excesses and perceived failings every time they met; no one's memory is *that* short.

It seemed I could do *nothing* right. They disapproved of my ordering glazed glass and putting iron bars—"Like in a prison!" they gasped—on all the downstairs windows after one too many times I caught curious faces peeping in at me if I didn't keep the curtains shut tight or found suspicious scuffs and scratches upon the outside sills suggesting someone had tried to jimmy the locks. It *never* occurred to them that I was only trying to protect myself and safeguard my privacy. They thought it meant I had something to hide, that I was doing things I didn't want anyone to see. I suppose they thought I should live in a glass house and leave myself entirely open, vulnerable, and naked to their scrutiny, just to prove to everyone in Fall River that I had nothing to hide. But if I had done that I would have been branded a vulgar exhibitionist. I just couldn't win.

When I grew weary of being stared at like an animal in a zoo, I had the veranda enclosed with ivy-covered lattices and climbing pink roses, so I could sit and enjoy myself in peace, sip my tea and eat cake at the little round wicker table, or sit on the porch swing and lose myself in a book or daydreams. I also had the back porch glassed in so I could sit there and watch the cardinals, orioles, woodpeckers, catbirds, and black-capped chickadees that were such a delight to me. I accounted each one of them a blessing, God's little winged wonders, angels in animal form. Watching the squirrels frolic in the trees always lifted my spirits and made me smile, and I always kept a goodly supply of nuts on hand to scatter on the ground as a treat for them. I had pretty little painted wooden houses built for them and placed about the yard and in the trees, and I provided a big marble bath and ordered the gardener to keep it full and refresh the water every day, and I always made sure the dear creatures had plenty to eat. I even ordered a statue of Saint Francis of Assisi, like one I had glimpsed in a beautiful garden in Italy, in his monk's robe and tonsure, holding out a great basin before him that I kept filled with bread and seeds, leading some of my neighbors to arch their brows and scathingly remark that they were afraid I had "gone Catholic" like the "good-for-nothing" Maggies and Paddies they employed as servants.

The name I had given my house, and dared to have chiseled on the top step facing out onto the street—"like a tradesman's storefront!"—sorely incensed my neighbors. They deemed such a vulgarity most unwelcome up on The Hill. *No one* named their house in Fall River, not even the castles they had imported piecemeal from Europe; if they had a name there they were shorn of it once they reached our shores. It was "not the done thing" and I was accused of "putting on airs." And perhaps I was. I had lived by my father's penurious dictates for thirty-two years and it felt *so good* to step out of his shadow and come into my own at long last and make up for lost time and chances in bold, magnificent ways and gaudy gestures. I never felt so free!

And when I decided, mirrors and the truths they showed be damned, it was time for Lizbeth to step out of my dreams and into real life and changed my own name accordingly, my calling cards, engraved with my new name, Lizbeth A. Borden of Maplecroft, wreathed with hand-painted violets, became at once collector's items and objects of curiosity, ridicule, and disdain. Ladies—*real* ladies—did *not* change their given names, only their surnames when they married. No one could understand why I did it, and I didn't even try to explain. I wanted to come out of the dark cocoon I had inhabited for so long. I was tired of being a plain, drab little moth;

I wanted to spread my wings and soar sky high and be a bold, splendid, beautiful butterfly. I wanted to be elegant, refined, cultured Lizbeth, who I had always been in my secret soul, the woman my architect had seen lurking inside me, not dull, boring, inept, inelegant Lizzie, whose very name sounded like a coarse, common, clumsy, ignorant slut of a barmaid. He had called me "Lizbeth," and that was who I wanted, more than anything else, to be, and I knew that it was now or never. And, to be honest, after the notoriety of the murders and the trial, I just wanted to be someone else, to be reborn fresh and new, to have a fresh coat of paint and new decorations just like I gave my Maplecroft.

I waited in vain for the invitations to dinner parties, balls, sewing circles, book club meetings, card parties, Sunday concerts in the park, the theater, picnics, clambakes, oyster suppers, and weekend house parties to come pouring in. And I hadn't heard a word from the Women's Christian Temperance Union, the Fruit and Flower Mission, or the Christian Endeavor Society since they had sent cards and flowers to me in jail, nor had I been asked to resume my duties as a Sunday school teacher.

Maybe they thought I was still in mourning and not ready to socialize yet? So after the decorators had finished their work, I took the reins into my own hands and sent invitations with beautiful gold script embossed upon creamy parchment cards with gilt maple leaf borders to all my female neighbors and friends and acquaintances in Fall River, including every member of the clubs and societies I had belonged to. I invited all the Sunday school teachers and every woman who sung in the choir at Central Congregational Church and even the ladies of the book club to which Emma had belonged but which I had left because their selections habitually lacked excitement and imagination. They had all sent me flowers and cards expressing their good wishes when I was in prison, so it *never* crossed my mind that they would forsake me now. I thought I was about to pick up the thread of my old life even as I spread my wings and soared on to bigger and better things. After all my nest, my home, my haven, was in Fall River and, in spite of all my lofty ambitions, I never wanted to change that.

To welcome them to Maplecroft, I had Madame Tetrault bake a big five-layer maple cake with waves of creamy frosting decorated with pretty little candies shaped like maple leaves that melted deliciously in the mouth to let the tongue savor the sweet maple flavor. And I instructed Elsa, the downstairs maid, in her black dress and starched snow-white frilled cap and matching ruffled white apron, to pass around amongst my guests with a silver tray, shaped like a maple leaf, with yet more of these special candies arranged elegantly upon it. Then I would make my grand entrance and graciously receive their kind words and embraces.

I had a new dress made just for this occasion, maple-colored silk, trimmed with beautiful frothy cocoa-colored heirloom lace and dark-chocolate satin ribbon edged in gold. I even commissioned little gold maple leaf earrings and a maple leaf brooch set with champagne-colored diamonds to wear with it and bought a rope of pearls in a lovely, soft golden color and a fringed silk shawl worked with a pattern of vines and leaves in various shades of browns, amber, orange, and gold to complete the ensemble.

I couldn't bear to sit upstairs fidgeting and watching the clock, so I went downstairs. I could always rush back up before Elsa opened the front door, so I could still make my grand entrance. But the change of scenery didn't calm me a jot. I anxiously watched the clock, my fear mounting as every second ticked by, gone forever. I couldn't sit still more than two minutes; I kept darting up from my chair and running to the window and back again, and then I found myself walking the floor, pacing back and forth until I feared I would wear out that stretch of carpet. But I never saw a soul coming through the front gate.

I wondered if the clock could be wrong. I waited an hour. And then two. But no one ever came. No one even sent a servant to my door with a polite excuse about illness. Even Emma was conspicuously absent, keeping to her room; she found my wanting to socialize when I should have still been in deep mourning "morally reprehensible" and "almost criminal."

Almost, I answered her in tart, angry silence. *I suppose the only thing that could possibly be more criminal is the double murder I was acquitted of!*

I finally sat down upon the sofa in front of the tea table and ate each one of those little maple candies myself; even when I felt full and sick, I kept on eating, trying to fill up the emptiness inside me even though I *knew* it had nothing at all to do with my stomach. And then I started on the cake. That *beautiful* cake and all my elegant plans, the care I had taken and lavished upon each and every last little detail—it had all been such a waste! I sat there, alone in my splendid parlor, and ate *every* morsel of that beautiful cake and was sick all night, a miserable green-faced and bloated-bellied queen sitting on her gleaming white porcelain throne. It served me right for being such a wretched glutton; I should have sent it back to the kitchen for the servants to enjoy, but that never occurred to me.

When I sat there glumly staring at the last crumbs on my gilt-bordered yellow rose–patterned plate letting the tears run down my face, Emma appeared like a menacing black crow in the doorway.

"More tears are shed over answered prayers, *Liz-zie,*" she said, drawing out each syllable of the name I had shed like a snake's skin—Emma would *never* call me "Lizbeth"—"than unanswered ones. God sometimes punishes those He only *seems* to favor by giving them *exactly* what they want."

And then she turned on her heel and in a loud, sickening swish of black silk skirts and crepe mourning veils left me alone to contemplate a blessing that suddenly seemed like a curse, like some cruel masquerader who had *ripped* the mask off to reveal a strange unknown and unexpected face sneering and jeering at me.

As if that were not bad enough, at that *very* moment one of those infernal hack drivers drove up with a near-bursting load of out-of-towners he had met at the train station and brandished his whip at Maplecroft and bellowed: *"THERE IT IS, FOLKS—THE HOME OF THE NOTORIOUS LIZZIE BORDEN, WHERE SHE LIVES NOW!"*

*   *   *

That Sunday I nervously put on a fussy pink and peach gown covered collar to hem with appliquéd flowers and a matching hat and pinned a pink cameo onto my high white lace collar and picked up a lacy, beribboned parasol and bravely strode down the aisle of the Central Congregational Church to my pew.

It was the first time I had been to church since my acquittal. I had wanted to let things quiet down and return to normal. As soon as my flower-covered rump touched the polished walnut *every single person* sitting near me, before, behind, and alongside me stood up and moved away to find themselves another seat. And the Reverend Buck, who had been *so* kind to me, sitting and praying with me for hours in my jail cell, sending me edifying books to read, and loudly proclaiming my calmness as "the calmness of innocence" every time I was publicly accused of coldness and indifference, wouldn't even look at me. I tried time and again to catch his eye, but he was blind to me.

At last, I stood up and, head held high, retreated back up the aisle. I never set foot in that church again or any other in Fall River. I knew I would not be welcome. From that day forward I would spend my Sundays reading my Bible and singing hymns alone at Maplecroft. Madame Tetrault was kind enough to teach me to play the piano in the parlor well enough so that I could accompany myself, and, later, I would have a fine phonograph and a collection of records so I could hear beautiful voices raised to the glory of God.

I knew then, without a doubt, that Fall River society had slammed its doors on me. This stinging rebuff made in the house of the Lord where all were supposed to be merciful, kind, and charitable was the final proof. No one wanted to know "the self- or hatchet-made heiress," as they called me. I was an oddity, an aberration, an embarrassment, and no doubt many wished I would pack my bags and leave Fall River forever.

Perhaps that's why, mulish and stubborn, just like Father in his most hard-fisted penny-pinching moments, I dug in my heels and *swore* I would make my home in Fall River until the day I died. When a reporter from *The New York Sun* stopped me on the street

and asked me about it I held my head high and, with cordial frank-
ness, replied, "A great many persons have talked to me as if they
thought I would go and live somewhere else when my trial was
over. I don't know what possesses them. This is my home and I am
going to stay here. I never thought of doing anything else."

Though I had often hungered for a bigger, richer, more exciting
slice of the world's pie, I was too proud and stubborn to let them
drive me out and chase me away like a whipped and whimpering
dog with its tail tucked between its legs. Even though in truth I
might have been able to reinvent myself and lead a far happier life
elsewhere I was too proud to make the attempt. I had my pride—
my stubborn, arrogant, hurt, and angry pride! And I would *never*
let them see me cry or know just how much they had hurt me!

Every day, I would sit behind my glazed and barred windows,
or on my ivy-shrouded veranda, and try to lose myself in a book or
hug Laddie, my Boston terrier pup, or with Daisy, my white Per-
sian cat, purring softly on my lap while I stroked her silky fur, and
try to pretend I didn't care as I listened to the hack drivers regale
their passengers with the blood-soaked saga of Lizzie Borden,
never sparing them a single gory detail about the murders. Sometimes the hackneys even drove them out to see the house at 92 Second Street and the graves in Oak Grove Cemetery where Father
and Abby reposed without their heads.

They never went away. I'm afraid that when the day dawns that
finds me lying on my deathbed the last thing I will hear is a cab-
driver crying out my name like some annoying carnival barker who
never shuts up for long. Whenever a cabby caught a glimpse of me,
sitting peacefully on my own front porch not bothering a soul, or
going in or out of the house, minding my own business, he would
stab his whip in my direction and shout, *"THERE SHE IS!"* His
passengers would always ooh and ahh or slump back in a swoon
against the leather seats as though they had just had the thrill or the
scare of their lives. And there was *always* someone who would attempt to boldly stare me down as they declared, "She *LOOKS* as if
she *DID IT!*"

Some even brought cameras and posed in front of the house; for a time there was even a photographer who made a good income carting his camera out to cater to the tourists' desire for such a ghoulish souvenir. "There we are in front of the Lizzie Borden house!" I could just hear them exclaiming over the picture once it was pasted in their album. As much as I embraced modernity, I more than anyone regretted it when cameras became more portable and commonplace, so that any fool with enough money to squander or spare could afford one.

I grew *so weary* of it all! I think the last time I really laughed about my notoriety was right after the trial when someone started a rumor that every unmarried man on my jury had proposed to me and I was delightedly dallying over deciding which one I would marry. I remember I was having breakfast in bed one morning, my shoulders surrounded by billowing layers of lavender chiffon ruffles and my hair up in curl rags, when I saw the headline screaming **LIZZIE BORDEN TO WED ONE OF THE JURY THAT ACQUITTED HER!** above a portrait of the twelve men looking so solemn and serious and an article discussing the personalities and prospects of the unattached gentlemen and speculating on which one I would choose to be my husband. I laughed myself silly. Tears rolled down my face and I almost wet the bed.

But my amusement didn't last long. Too many outlandish and intrusive headlines soon curdled my sense of humor and left me with a sick headache and sour stomach and I no longer had the heart to laugh at *any* of it. It grew so I couldn't *abide* to even look at a newspaper for fear that I would find my picture or name in it.

To the children of Fall River, I became a source of fearful curiosity, like a witch in a storybook, the butt of countless childhood pranks and dares to knock upon my door or climb my garden fence. They pelted my windows and walls with raw eggs and gravel. More than once some brave little soul made it all the way up to the front door to insert a pin into the doorbell so that it rang shrilly until the pin was extracted. It quickly became the headache-inducing custom for children walking along the sidewalk to break into a run while screaming at the top of their lungs and flailing their arms wildly whenever they passed Maplecroft. But some, instead of screaming as they rushed past, would march by brave as little soldiers, or even stop to skip rope on the sidewalk, while chanting loudly the popular singsong rhyme:

> *"Lizzie Borden took an ax*
> *And gave her mother forty whacks.*
> *When she saw what she had done,*
> *She gave her father forty-one."*

Sometimes they added a second verse:

> *"Andrew Borden now is dead,*
> *Lizzie hit him on the head,*
> *Up in Heaven he will sing,*
> *On the gallows she will swing."*

The bravest ones, the ones who ventured onto my property and didn't run away shrieking before I could speak to them, I rewarded; I gave them candy and cookies and cups of hot cocoa and slices of cake or Madame Tetrault's marvelous jelly roll, that scrumptious, sumptuous miracle of moist golden cake filled with rich cream and raspberry jelly.

And some of the poorer ones, who showed promise and a love of learning, I gave gifts of books and paid for them to have a college education just as I would have done for my own sons and daughters if I had been so blessed.

I loved children; the older I got the more I regretted that circumstances, and my too deeply entrenched private fears, never permitted me to marry and have a family, and it hurt my heart to know that so many of them feared me, even though I understood and never blamed them for it. But understanding isn't a balm for pain. Those who dared approach me I always befriended. I bought them birthday and Christmas presents and never failed to send them amusing cards to let them know that I was thinking of them. And there was one dear, sweet slow-witted boy, the son of poor

Irish Catholic mill workers, whose parents only sent him to school to have someone watch him during the day because they both had to work. I bought him picture books and colored pencils and drawing paper to keep him entertained while his classmates were at their lessons, and I always made sure he was decently dressed and had shoes on his feet so the other boys and girls wouldn't make fun of him for being dirt poor. He always came to stay an hour or two after school with me, we had tea together on the veranda, or in the parlor when the weather was cold, and on the days when there was no school I found little chores for him to do around Maplecroft that I always paid him for. He was the sweetest of them all, a pure soul who never saw any evil in me; he hugged me until I thought my back would break and called me his "auntie Lizbeth." It broke my heart when he drowned one summer trying to keep up with the other boys. I paid for his funeral.

When the constant curiosity, the shunning and hostile silence, the knowing that I could not even visit a shop with my veil down without being gaped and gawked at and gossiped about and reading all about it in the newspapers the next day with all manner of embellishments, became so unbearable I thought I couldn't stand it a moment longer, I would order my trunks packed and leave for a while. I loved to lose myself in the bustle of a big city and become just another face in the crowd, to be able to sit in a public square or park and feed the pigeons in peace with my veil up and no one pointing or staring at me.

I would go to Boston or New York, Chicago, Washington, or even San Francisco, or New Orleans, book myself a suite in the city's most prestigious hotel, and spend my days shopping and visiting museums and strolling idly in public gardens, and every evening at the theater, opera, or dining in fine restaurants and my nights basking in silk-sheeted luxury. And not always alone. That lovely illusion was one more thing money could buy.

In Washington one spring, in a pink silken suite at the Cochran Hotel, while the cherry blossoms fell outside, a beautiful young woman who bore a striking resemblance to Lulie Stillwell at seven-

teen made all my secret, forbidden fantasies come true, for a fee of
course. I gave her a gold and diamond pendant shaped like a heart
and a sable wrap for her snow-white shoulders as a token of my
gratitude in addition to her hourly wage and a week's worth of private steak and lobster suppers. Every year after that I *longed* to be
in Washington, back in the pink suite at the Cochran Hotel, when
the cherry blossoms were falling, and sometimes I was; after all,
price was no object. The only thing missing was my one true love to
share it with. Even in ecstasy, I could never forget that this compan-
ionship came at a price that *I* paid; it was *never* a gift given freely to
me out of love, respect, kindness, or even pity.

Sometimes I thought I had made a friend. But their interest was
always motivated by macabre curiosity, every last one of them
wanted to be *the one* who would pry the truth out of Lizzie Borden, and when I refused to oblige them they dropped me. After all,
they didn't really *need* me anymore. They had what they wanted;
they could continue to dine out on the story of how they had once
known the notorious Lizzie Borden for the rest of their lives. I had
been reduced to a dinner table anecdote and newspaper item instead of a human being with a beating heart and feelings that could
be hurt. If I was in the news again, because I had been seen about
somewhere or the anniversary of the murders was near, their remi-
niscences were enough to get their names in the paper, columns of
print they could clip and paste into their scrapbooks.

Sometimes they wanted money. Sometimes I obliged, if I liked
them and thought their need was genuine, but most of the time I refused; I really wasn't the spendthrift fool Father always took me for.

My life was not entirely a selfish one, I gave much to charity,
though always in secret; I didn't want people to think I was trying
to buy their good opinion. I loved animals; I firmly believed that
they alone amongst God's creatures were the only ones capable of
unconditional love, in that way these dumb animals were so much
smarter than humans, so I gave thousands of dollars away every
year to various societies for the protection and prevention of cruelty to dogs, cats, and horses.

Sometimes those I encountered baited their hooks with the

promise of love. Sometimes I succumbed even though I saw through their tricks. I was lonely, longing for a human touch, a warm body next to mine in bed, the feel of naked limbs entwined and lips covering mine. There was *always* the hope that they might, during the time they spent with me in luxurious hotel suites where discretion was included in the price *truly* come to care for me as something more than just a carnal conquest or a story to tell, a name to drop, to thrill and impress their friends. Sometimes I refused and turned a cold shoulder to their hot advances; just the thought of the disappointment to come left me feeling sad and so unbearably weary. Knowing it was all pretense didn't ease the hurt any. I tried *so hard* to harden my heart, to turn it to stone, and just be a body enjoying another body, like a wild animal in heat, a purely carnal creature, but I could never quiet the longing *screaming* out, *LOVE ME!* from the depths of my soul. I wanted to be loved, by a man or a woman. By that point it didn't really matter which; it was love, *real love,* the kind that is true and lasts forever like in songs and storybooks that I was after.

Most of the time I kept to myself; I went about alone with my veil down, bothering no one and hoping no one would bother me. I had my pets, my books, the freedom and funds to travel and shop, to buy whatever I pleased, Maplecroft, my beautiful house waiting for me to come home to, my sparkling jewels, my ravishing gowns and the exquisite lace-and-ribbon-trimmed lingerie I wore beneath, banquets for the stomach and soul: evenings of gourmet feasts, grand opera, and the theater; I tried *so hard* to convince myself that it was enough, that luxury could fill, and fulfill, my lonely heart. I spent a lifetime lying to myself, trying to convince myself to believe the lies *I* told myself.

I loved to lose myself in the make-believe world of the theater, the magic the actors and actresses spun with words, gestures, and costumes. I liked the tragedies best, tales of love doomed and thwarted—*Romeo and Juliet, Antony and Cleopatra, Mary, Queen of Scots,* and *Elizabeth of England,* the Virgin Queen who never married or bore a child. I thrilled to Trilby and Svengali, and, my favorite, Marguerite Gautier, *La Dame aux Camélias,* the consumptive courtesan, and her noble, self-sacrificing love for young Armand Duval, whose love she selflessly and nobly renounced for his greater good, so that the sins of her past would not shame him and tarnish his bright future. I watched them all countless times.

I spent a few weeks every summer at one of the fashionable resort hotels. Palatial white hotels like wedding cakes, with tiers and balconies, rising several stories, and emerald lawns spreading out as far as the eye could see, whitewashed summer palaces where I could wear ruffled white dresses and big shady hats and sit out on the veranda every day, sipping lemonade or iced tea, idly plying a palmetto fan, and dreaming while I watched the other guests play croquette and lawn tennis or return singing from clambakes and boating parties that I never dared join in. I wanted to belong, but I couldn't—not as anything more than a novelty of gruesome notoriety. I was too proud and stubborn to register under a false name. I knew I would look a fool when the truth came out, as it *always* did; someone *always* recognized me. I wanted to be loved for myself, and I knew with complete and utter certainty that any love that began with a lie, no matter how well-meaning, was doomed. I could never emerge from underneath the dark cloud that always hovered over me. Whenever I walked into a room it stilled all the people, long enough for a tingling shiver to run the length of their spines and for the hair on the back of their necks to stand on end, and then the whispering started. There was no escaping it.

Inevitably, I returned to Maplecroft, my magnificent empty-halled mausoleum-palace devoid of fawning and adoring courtiers, where my eyes, and those of servants who cleaned and dusted, were the only ones that gazed upon its manifold comforts and luxuries. I would sit alone dressed like a queen feasting on silver trays of petit fours, chocolate éclairs, and slices of Madame Tetrault's marvelous jelly roll making promises I knew I would never keep to start dieting the very next day, or the day afterward at most, but my dressmaker's measurements proved that I was never capable of keeping that promise.

Little did I know when I bought it that Maplecroft would become a prison, a sanitarium, and a living tomb for me as well as the palace of all my desires and dreams. That here, behind glazed and barred windows, triple-locked doors, iron fences, and locked gates, I would hide from the world whenever the curious pressed too close, the newspapers pried too deep, and those I dared let get close to me hurt, disillusioned, and disappointed me as they were always destined to do.

The year after my trial Mr. Edwin H. Porter, the charming reporter *The Fall River Globe* had sent to interview me in my jail cell, published a book called *The Fall River Tragedy: A History of the Borden Murders*. I felt dismayed and so betrayed. I ordered my business agent, Mr. Charles Cook, who dealt with all those tedious, mundane day-to-day matters attached to all the real estate, rental properties, and investments Emma and I had inherited from Father, to buy up every copy he could find. I didn't care what it cost, I told him. "Pretend you are the Grand Inquisitor, sir, and hunt them down like witches! I *want them burned!*"

Late one night, after the servants and Emma were all asleep, so no one could see me cry, I burned every last one of them in the library fireplace. I never even cracked the spine to read one word. I didn't care what Mr. Porter had written, whether he had been scrupulously honest and fair to me or wildly embellished the whole sorry, sordid saga. I only cared that he had written it. It smarted like a slap. My heart felt like he had taken a whip to it even though it had no cause; he was a hardened newspaperman just doing his job. I was just another story, albeit the biggest of his career. If he hadn't written a book someone else would, it was to be expected, but that didn't mean I had to accept or like it. Whoever the author was, I would have done the exact same thing—made a bonfire of the books.

All I wanted to do was forget. And I wanted everyone else to forget too and just leave me in peace to live my life the way I saw fit. I didn't go prying into their business and private lives! Why couldn't they accord me the same respect? But I had traded the prison of my father's house for actual prison bars, only to find when I was vindicated and freed from those that I had become a prisoner of my own notoriety and a higher judge had decreed that it should be a life sentence with no possibility of parole. Ostensibly, I was free to come and go and do as I pleased, but I would never be *truly* free.

Then, like a mournful black ghost who could read my mind, Emma appeared in the doorway, her dark hair streaked with broad bands of gray and a black shawl draped over her prim and proper white nightgown.

"The Lord giveth and the Lord taketh away, Lizzie," she said as she stood behind me, resting a comfortless claw-like hand on my shoulder, and together, in silence, we watched Mr. Porter's books burn.

Chapter 9

Time is a curious thing. Sometimes it seems to fly by on the swiftest wings; others it seems to have lead in its heels and just *drag* by oh, so slowly, like weak and weary prisoners on a chain-gang. One sultry morning in 1896 I had just sat down at the elegant little rosewood writing desk in my summer bedroom to write a letter to Mr. Cook when I looked at the calendar to inscribe the date and noticed that it was the fourth of August. Four years—*four whole years!*—since the deeds that had made me infamous. *Four years* and I had not felt *anything* at all. My soul, my mind, had not seen fit to mark that macabre anniversary in *any* way; only a chance glance at the calendar had reminded me. Otherwise it would have just slipped by like any other ordinary day. Of course, I had not forgotten, I never could forget, but Time has a way of dulling the razor-sharp edge of emotions and memories.

I decided on a whim that I would like to see the farm at Swansea again. The happiest days of my childhood had been spent there, frolicking and fishing, at that farm, and suddenly my heart was filled with nostalgic yearning for those simple, peaceful, rustic pleasures.

I could not stay at the farmhouse of course. There were tenants

in residence, a big family of pleasant-faced Swedes who often sent
me gifts of eggs, butter, and cheese, a grateful gesture they would
no doubt have made to any landlord, but I would never force my
company on them. Instead, I made arrangements to stay with our
former neighbors and cousins, the Gardners. I knew they would
not shrink from the thought of having me in their home and would
welcome me with open arms. Caroline Mason Gardner was one of
the kindest women in the world; she had sent me many kind and
supportive letters and cards while I was in prison. "There but for
the Grace of God," she was fond of saying; she always lived by
those words and had raised her children to always heed that guid-
ing phrase. "It is the candle that will *always* show you the way," she
told them.

As soon as the train pulled into the station her redheaded son
Orrin was there waiting to meet me, smiling and waving in a crisp
white linen suit with a red carnation in his lapel and a straw boater
with a band to match his blue-and-white-striped necktie. Indeed
he was right there at the steps before the train had barely stopped,
close enough to touch the skirt of my biscuit-colored linen suit, so
close I literally tripped over him and fell into his arms.

When I looked into his blue eyes I felt such a jolt, like a bolt of
blue lightning coursing through my soul. It was *electricity!* It was
ecstasy! In this man of thirty with the round freckled face and unruly fire-colored cowlick of a perpetual child I recognized the little
boy who used to follow me around like a kitten's tail all those sweet
long-ago summers. We had played hide-and-seek and made mud
pies together and dug for worms to bait our fishing hooks and sat
side by side, shyly bumping our bare feet together, waiting for the
fish to bite.

He was the first, and only, baby I had ever held. When I was a
little girl of seven Caroline had trustingly placed him in my arms. I
had spent that whole summer wheeling his pram around, crooning
to him, rocking him in his cradle, feeding him from a bottle, changing his diapers, and pretending he was mine. And when he was old
enough to walk, at first clinging to the strings of my pinafore and
later on his own two feet, he became "my dear pest" and followed

me everywhere I went. No matter how old we were, heedless of the seven years between us, he was *always* there and ready to oblige me. We used to cut the brides and grooms from the fashion plates in *Godey's Lady's Book* and play Wedding Day or couples in evening clothes going to a ball or opening night at the opera. Later, when we were a little older, we gave up paper dolls and played bride and groom ourselves, with an old tattered lace curtain to serve as a veil thrown over my hair and a crown of daisies to hold it in place. We were "married" in the pasture with the milk cows as witnesses mooing their good wishes. And on other days, we played Lancelot and Guinevere, or Robin Hood and Maid Marian, or he was a knight in shining armor out to rescue me, his lady fair. The other little boys laughed and teased him for it, but he could never say *no* to me or stray far from my side, and I loved "my dear pest"; he always held a special place in my heart.

I hadn't seen Orrin in years. There was no tiff or rift, no estrangement due to the trial or anything else. We lost touch long before that, except for the obligatory yearly Christmas cards we exchanged; we just grew up and apart. I suppose it was simply the nature of things: Boys and girls lead very different lives—girls, for the most part, stay home, and boys go out into the world to make their mark upon it; sometimes they come back, and sometimes they outgrow their hometowns and head off for larger, and greener, pastures. Orrin went away to school, to college in Rhode Island, to study to become a teacher.

Absence doesn't always make the heart grow fonder the way it does in romance novels; sometimes it makes us forget and chills even the hottest emotions. With the passing of years the memory of the devotion that used to glow like an eternal blue flame in Orrin's eyes every time he looked at me melted away; it just got lost and crowded out by other things. We were just little children only playing at love and marriage; it would have been the pinnacle of absurdity for me to take our youthful games and childish affection as a sign of things to come.

But that flame was *still* there. When I looked into Orrin's eyes I saw it *flare* and spring ardently back to life again after being suppressed for so many years, like a dead heart suddenly starting to beat. And something in me answered in turn. I felt my soul *sing,* its voice soaring like a soprano's straight up to Heaven.

In the years since my acquittal, I had tried to guard my heart like a miser, to make it grow hard and small. Not out of meanness, but for my own good, so it would not hurt so much when people let me down. But now, when I looked into Orrin's eyes, I felt it change; I felt it grow and expand. Like a tight, new-formed red rosebud it suddenly unfurled, to burst into full, magnificent bloom. I felt *alive* again! He *resurrected* me!

It was almost like what I had felt all those years ago in England. I felt my knees grow weak and tremble beneath my skirts. Orrin's hand was instantly at my waist, steadying me. It was almost like being hurtled back through time to that magical day at Glastonbury when my wonderful handsome blond architect had kissed me under the thorn tree.

And then, standing in the station, in broad daylight amongst the bustling crowd of travelers and porters, as we stared deep into each other's eyes, lost in our own little world, blind and deaf to all around us, I let my carpet bag fall like a stone as Orrin Gardner took me in his arms and *kissed* me. I entwined my arms around his neck and returned his kiss wholeheartedly. *I'M ALIVE! I'M ALIVE!* my heart sang.

I had only meant to stay a week, but I kept postponing my departure; I kept making excuses, saying I would stay for just one more day, and then another, and another, until another week had whirled giddily past like a drunken dervish leaving me breathless and dizzy in its wake. And all the time my happy heart kept on singing.

Caroline just nodded and smiled knowingly. "Stay as long as you like, my dear."

Orrin and I used to sit out on the porch at night and gaze up at the stars. Out in the country without city lights and tall buildings to obscure the view it was like an infinite midnight-colored carpet onto which God had spilled a million flawless diamonds.

One such night, Orrin saw me shiver and went back inside to

fetch my shawl. He draped it about me, tenderly arranging its crimson and gold paisley folds, and then he dipped his head and kissed me.

"We met again because we were meant to be together," he said, and then he knelt, took my hand in his, and asked me to be his wife.

I didn't even have to *think!* In that instant *all* my fears fell from me and when I looked into his eyes I didn't see myself reflected back as a dollar sign; I only saw his love shining bright and true for me—*ME!* When we were children Orrin could never say *no* to me; now I had forgotten that there was even such a word as *no.* I said *yes,* with all my heart and soul. I said *YES!*

There was a streak of vivid light in the sky above us and we both looked up to watch the silvery tail of a shooting star arc its way across the sky. And I could not help but think, *God is smiling down on us—this is a sign!*

Orrin's eyes met mine and I knew he was thinking the same thing: *This* was meant to be! *We* were meant to be!

"Did you make a wish?" he asked.

I shook my head. "No; everything I want is right here," I said, and drew his face down to mine. And this time *I* kissed *him.*

When school started I used to walk out every day to the little red schoolhouse where Orrin taught with a picnic lunch for us to share while the children scampered off with their lunch pails to play outside in the sun. The weather was still warm and Orrin left the doors and windows open so the heat would not be trapped inside and stifle the children and, like me, he was always prone to headaches. I used to love to stand outside, out of sight, and watch him teach.

Orrin *loved* children, and he loved teaching, and he was *so good* at it! And the children loved him; they responded to his warmth and kindness. He used to say that to make a child smile was his greatest reward; if he could lay his head down on his pillow at night knowing he had done that then he knew beyond a doubt that the day had been worthwhile. He strove to make learning fun, to leave an indelible impression, not just to drill facts they learned by rote into his pupils' minds. "They're not parrots," he said to me, "so why should they learn like them?"

He told stories from history, interesting and amusing anecdotes not to be found in textbooks; he wanted the people, the kings and queens, the presidents and warriors, explorers and inventors, he taught the children about to be *real* to them, personalities that came to life in their imaginations, not just names printed on the pages of dull, dusty old books. Sometimes he even devised little plays, "history pageants," for his pupils to act in, "to make history come alive."

Sometimes he would tell them to put away their slates and books and they would go outside to make kites with paper and string and fly them, or just go fishing, or catch frogs and race them. He taught the children about nature amidst nature as bees flitted from flower to flower and butterflies lighted on their little fingers and birds sang in the trees.

And when it came to mathematics, Orrin was a man of *infinite* patience even with the slowest learners. He devised games and contests and, as an incentive, and to reward effort, gave candies and little toys and trinkets as prizes. Every Friday they had a spelling bee with a special prize for the winner and when the day was done Orrin stood by the door as his pupils filed out, placing a candy in each grateful little hand and wishing them all a good weekend. Knowing they had chores waiting for them at home, he never overloaded his pupils with a superabundance of homework, and he never blistered palms or rapped knuckles with a ruler or left stinging red stripes on a bottom with a birch rod. And in Orrin's classroom no child *ever* sat in the corner wearing a dunce's cap.

When we met again Orrin had just begun building a home of his own. He was a grown man of thirty and felt it was time he left his parents' house. The timing was *perfect,* he said; the construction was not so far along that changes weren't possible or practical. He took me to see it and then we sat down with the builder and his plans; it was to be *our* home, not his alone, Orrin said; he wanted to be able to look at it as he came up the road from the schoolhouse at the end of the day and say to himself "she chose that door" and "that rooster weathervane on the roof was my idea." He wanted us to merge our souls in brick, mortar, glass, and wood; even the flowers and vegetables in the garden would be born of the mingling of our desires.

We went up to Boston on the weekends and chose decorations and furnishings. We found a lamp set with midnight-colored glass with a pattern of shooting stars worked into the silver metal between the panes and bought it for our sitting room to remind us of the shooting star we had no need to wish upon—we had each other; we were the *luckiest* people in all the world. We tried to be discreet, I kept my veil down and never gave my name, but I suppose it was inevitable, someone recognized Lizzie Borden, and it was obvious that Orrin and I were in love. The truth shone in our eyes whenever we looked at each other; no one could have looked at us and doubted it for even a moment. But we were too caught up in each other and our mutual dream to care or take heed.

We planned to be married at Christmas in a quiet, private ceremony with just a few family and friends as witnesses and to honeymoon afterward for six months in Europe. I had always wanted to go back and had often thought about it, but somehow I could never bring myself to actually *do* it. Something always held me back; I am still at a loss to explain why I never went. It was certainly not the money or time; I had an abundance of both.

I ordered my wedding gown and a lavish trousseau from my favorite dressmaker, Mrs. Cummings on Elm Street, all to be rushed and ready in time for Christmas. I even paid extra for her to take on two more girls to help her. She promised me that she would be discreet and neither she nor those in her employ would spread any gossip about me. If anyone inquired she said she would tell them that the clothes were for a European excursion.

In early December, as the home Orrin and I would make together was nearing completion and the furnishings were being put in place as they arrived, he took me there one afternoon after school. It was already getting dark, and we both knew it was not, by society's standards, an entirely proper thing for us to do, but I had already begun to notice that as each year passed such things mattered less and less to me, if they had ever truly mattered at all. He built a fire in the new fireplace crafted of great river stones and brought blankets and cushions for us to rest upon.

We never discussed it, and there was really no need to; we both knew what was about to happen. There was no need for words of any sort, passionate or practical. The silence between us was a comfortable one, a quiet, mutual contentment, that needed no conversation or nervous, awkward chatter to fill it; the love and trust between us was more than enough.

He lifted the hat from my head and laid it aside, and then he took my hands, first the right and then the left, and slowly, starting at the tips, eased the gloves from my hands. Then his fingers were at my throat, carefully unfastening the row of black silk braid frogs fastening my dusky mauve velvet coat.

I shut my eyes and shivered as his knuckles and wrists brushed against my breasts as he patiently worked his way down the front of my coat, then, after pausing first to kiss me, pushed it from my shoulders and freed my arms from the wide pagoda sleeves. I turned my back to him, presenting the row of tiny pearl buttons his mother's maid had painstakingly fastened for me that morning. His fingers moved diligently downward, and as the pearls parted from the buttonholes I felt the cold kiss of the air upon my skin followed by the warmth of Orrin's lips.

I shifted my position and rose up onto my knees so he could gather up the velvet skirt, cumbersome layered flounces fading from deepest plum to the most delicate pink, and lift it over my head. I kept my back to him, bowing my head and blushing a little, shivering with cold, and nervous eagerness, as I felt his hot blue gaze burn my bare shoulders, followed swiftly by his ravenous lips. I had never felt the sun on my naked skin, but this was what I imagined it must be like. Then his hands were on my shoulders, kneading and caressing, and his lips were at the nape of my neck, then the sides, roaming over my shoulders, covering me with a hundred hungry kisses that made me so dizzy and weak I had to shut my eyes and pray that I would not faint.

His fingers fumbled with my corset until I was blessedly free of my restrictive whalebone cage and could breathe deeply and easily and feel my breasts rise and fall naturally. My nipples hardened and glowed like rosy embers through the thin wedding-veil-white silk of my camisole. I gasped in delighted surprise as his hands crept round to gently cup my breasts. I sighed and arched my neck and leaned back against his chest as his lips once against found the sensitive curve of my neck while, through the thin silk of my camisole, his hands massaged my skin where my stays had plowed angry red furrows before he lifted it over my head.

I can't remember every detail, the distraction of pleasure began to deliciously muddle my mind, but I was soon shed of my petticoats and lay back. I felt the warmth of the fire on my skin as he unlaced my boots, then peeled off my pink satin garters and rolled my black silk stockings down, kissing my knees, ankles, and toes as he bared them. Then I felt his hands at my waist, gently easing my drawers down over my ample hips. My legs lifted of their own accord to help him, and I felt the lace and pink silk ribbons that trimmed them tickle my naked ankles.

I sat up and wrapped my arms around Orrin's neck, and our lips met in a soul-stirring kiss, passionate, devouring, and deep. I pushed his brown broadcloth coat from his shoulders and left him to deal with the sleeves while I tugged and struggled with his green silk tie. I had never undressed a man before, and my fingers fumbled nervously over the row of buttons down the front of his white linen shirt. My fingers were even clumsier when it came to undoing the row of little black buttons on the front of his trousers. I found myself flushing bright as a boiled lobster when I felt his manhood straining against them, eager to come out and play. But this time I wasn't frightened or repelled in the slightest—Orrin was *nothing* like David Anthony!

I had to pause for a moment to bow my head as I blushed and smiled sheepishly, nearly laughing out loud at myself, at the shock and surprise of my unexpected carefree, brazen wantonness. Here I was, a confirmed spinster, an old maid of thirty-seven, sitting on a plaid blanket before a stone fireplace, orange flames crackling and dancing, casting their shadows over our skin, stark naked, with my legs spread wide in indecent abandon, all modesty forgotten and forsaken—and good riddance to it! To see the most intimate part of my body all Orrin had to do was look down, but I didn't care if he did; I *wanted* him to. I know I should have felt at least some degree of unease and embarrassment, but I didn't, not at all, not the least little bit, it all felt *so* natural and right. This beautiful, blissful experience with Orrin was God's gift, the one I had been waiting for all my life, blundering and rushing out and searching the world for when I should have known better; all I really had to do was be patient and wait for it to come to me, all in God's good time. Orrin's love renewed my faith and I felt myself reborn in his arms.

Orrin said he loved every part of me and then proceeded to prove it. My body was like a virgin island and there was not a part of me this bold conquistador did not explore with his eyes, mouth, and hands. And I . . . I was equally bold with him; I didn't give a fig for all society's teachings about womanly modesty. I could not let any shyness, real or instilled or affected, inhibit and deny me this joy. I *gloried* in the feel of his skin against mine, with no barriers of cloth between us, not even the sheerest, most delicate silk, and the delicious warmth and weight of his body atop mine.

As he entered me, Orrin looked deep into my eyes. I held his gaze, and I felt our souls merge and become one just as our bodies did. Then I was lost in a heady, dizzying maelstrom of pleasure and sensations that defy my ability to accurately describe them. Some things are not meant to be put into words, and this, I think, is one of them.

When I felt him start to withdraw from me in precaution, to prevent his seed from taking root, I wouldn't let him. I wrapped my legs tight around him and pulled him closer, drawing him deeper into me.

"You were the first baby I ever held, Orrin," I said to him, "and I want the second to be the one we made together."

And it was not too late, though I was closer to forty than thirty and the perils of childbirth increase as a woman ages. I still bled every month, and I was not afraid. When I thought of having a child—*our* child, Orrin's and mine, born of our love—the danger seemed so very far removed I couldn't even see it as a speck upon the horizon. And even if it had stood looking right over my shoulder, breathing the fetid breath of Death right onto the back of my neck, I still would have chanced it; it was a risk well worth taking.

Every night in the casinos of the world people risk their money for more money, or just for the thrill of it, or to stave off boredom; I thought surely the miracle of a new life was worth greater stakes. An old life for a new life, and if one trumps the Reaper the rewards are infinite beyond measure. I had gambled with my life before. I had risked death via the hangman's noose or a living death walled up behind the bricks and bars of a prison, and I was not afraid to try my luck again. Before, I had done something wrong to try to make my world right. I had taken lives to give myself a life, the life I had always longed for. My motives had been material and selfish, but this . . . this was noble and pure, and right in *every* way; this time I would risk my life to bring a new life into the world, to create something wonderful and good. And if I lost my own . . . it would still be worth it. But I hoped that once again—*please,* God, just *one* more time!—my luck would prevail, and I would win and live to hold our child in my arms and nurture and watch him, or her, grow and thrive, and be there to tie our son's silk cravat on his wedding day or adjust the fall of our daughter's heirloom lace veil and coronet of pearls and silken orange blossoms on hers.

Afterward, Orrin fell asleep with his head upon my breast. And for the first time in my life I felt as if my bosom had a purpose—to provide a pillow for my beloved's head. I stroked his wild red hair and caressed his freckle-spotted shoulders, my fingertips, light as a feather, tracing the length of his spine as the fever sweat of love cooled against his naked skin. And though there was a fine new ceiling blocking my view, I was *still* looking at the stars. But I still felt no need to wish upon them; I would give my wish to someone who needed it more. My dreams were already coming true. I felt like my life had for so long been a great big jigsaw puzzle, with all the pieces scattered about willy-nilly with no rhyme or reason, some here, some there, some near, some far, some missing altogether, but now, since the day I stepped off the train in Swansea and straight into Orrin Gardner's arms, the pieces were all falling into place, and *nothing* was missing after all. For the first time in my life, I truly felt complete. I was in love. I truly was the happiest and luckiest woman alive!

* * *

"We met again because we were meant to be together," those words were to come back to haunt me, as the worst and cruelest mockery of all. And they are *still* there, like a ghost in my dreams, they *still* haunt me in an endless echo, but *now* they only bring pain; they have completely lost their beauty; there is no miracle or marvel, or hope, only mockery—stinging, bitter, mean mockery!

There is nothing crueler, I think, than a miracle that is snatched away like a cup of cool sweet water from the parched lips of a man who has just crawled out of the desert sunburned and dying of thirst. God works in mysterious ways; sometimes the answer is *yes;* sometimes the answer is *not yet;* and sometimes the answer is *no;* but, regardless of the answer, and the tears and joy, the ecstasy and despair, the frustration and fulfillment, it may bring, God is under no obligation to explain Himself, He does not deign to tell us why, and we are left to ponder the mystery and grope blindly for the solution ourselves, though we may never find it.

I sometimes wonder if those who do not believe in God are happier since they have no faith to lose or become disillusioned in, no higher power to prostrate themselves before, to pray and beg and cry out the eternal despairing *Why* to with no real hope of receiving an answer. They accept such things as the way of the world, the luck of the draw, as a gambler does the roll of the dice or the fall of the cards. Perhaps the more romantically inclined chalk them down to chance, or fate, if they believe in that either, if they believe in anything at all.

"Everything happens for a reason," some say in sage and lofty tones as if they have some wisdom that the rest of us are lacking. But, if this is true, and the reasons really are there, perhaps we are, for the most part, doomed to blindness where our own lives are concerned. Perhaps it is all a matter of distance and perspective? I've tried and tried, but the reasons still elude me. And even if I knew why, it would not change anything. Why does not come bearing the gift of Peace of Mind. The heart is often stone blind and deaf to Reason. It is stubborn and recalcitrant; it wants what it wants.

WEDDING BELLS FOR LIZZE BORDEN!
LIZZIE BORDEN TO WED SCHOOLTEACHER!

. . . the headlines *screamed* in boldly inked inch-high black letters.

> Friends of Lizzie Borden, who was once accused of the murder of her father and stepmother, and whose trial was one of the most famous the nation has ever known, are congratulating her upon the approach of her marriage. The husband-to-be is one Orrin Augustus Gardner, a schoolteacher of the village of Swansea, which lies a few miles across the bay to the west of the city. He has been a friend of Miss Borden since childhood days, when they spent summers together upon adjoining farms. The engagement has been rumored about for weeks, but it lacked confirmation until a few days ago, when it was learned that Miss Borden has given to a well-known dressmaker an order for an elaborate trousseau. It has been given out that the garments are for a European trip, but as one of the dresses is known to be a beautiful white satin creation, the knowing ones simply smile when asked about the matter. Mr. Gardner has had erected a fine new house. It is said that the wedding will take place about Christmas, with a European honeymoon to follow.

There it all was spelled out in black and white for the whole world to read. *DAMN YOU, Mr. Edwin H. Porter!* I wanted to spit on his byline and gouge out his eyes with one of my silver spoons! I threw the paper on the floor and stamped on it, then ground it to pieces with my French heels. Did he pay the Judas who betrayed me thirty silver dollars for the story? *Damn him! How dare he spoil it? How dare he deny me* my *greatest desire? He* had a happy home, a wife and children, so who was *he* to decide that *I* didn't *deserve* the same? That I hadn't been punished enough, that since I had gotten away with murder, I should be deprived of a true and lasting love and made to grow old and die alone? He was just a newspaperman, *not God,* but he set the dogs on me. *GOD DAMN HIM, he,* Edwin H. Porter, led the pack of filthy newshounds straight to my door and ruined *EVERYTHING!*

Reporters laid siege to Maplecroft, shouting impertinent questions about the seven years' difference in our ages, making it sound more like seventy, like I was a dirty old woman snatching a baby boy from his innocent blue-blanketed cradle. To make matters worse, Emma looked at me as if she agreed, pursing her lips and dolefully shaking her head. *For shame, he's just a child, Lizzie!* her damning dark eyes seemed to say every time she looked at me. But the only thing she ever actually said to me upon the subject was even worse: "Of course you lost him; you didn't deserve him, Lizzie. You would have only brought him sorrow, and Orrin deserves better." I *hated* her for saying it, and I hated her even more for being right. I tried to avoid her as much as possible. Fortunately that wasn't at all difficult; the sisterly bond was well and truly broken, and when no one was looking we didn't bother to keep up the pretense of liking, let alone loving, each other. We were just a pair of strangers sharing a roof, old maids bound by blood in more ways than one, nothing less, nothing more.

Locked gates didn't deter the bloodhounds of the press; they simply climbed the fence, ruining the roses with their boots. Forgetting, for the moment, that they were rivals employed by competing papers, they affably gave one another boosts; they trampled the flowers, pressing their noses right up against the windows trying to see in through the lace curtains, iron bars, and glazed glass. Their constant ringing finally broke the doorbell; then they rapped their knuckles raw knocking on the door. Calling the police did *nothing* to deter the reporters! The officers they sent out only proffered a nominal good-natured chiding: "Come on, boys, leave the old girl in peace"—*old girl, indeed, I was only thirty-seven, blast their eyes!*—while they hung about outside the gate for a while smoking and catching up on their gossip. One of the reporters actually put on women's clothes and tried to gain entry by impersonating a cleaning woman replete with pail and mop and another pretended to be a messenger bringing "Miss Borden flowers from her fiancé"! *Oh, how wickedly low they were!* All that just to sell newspapers!

I locked myself in my winter bedroom and took the phone off the hook until after midnight, when Orrin would call, and refused to let the servants answer the door unless they recognized the person on the other side and knew with complete and utter certainty that it was not a reporter in disguise. When Emma invited her friends the Reverend Jubb and his sister into the parlor I flatly refused to come down; I just *knew* they were talking about me—what else could they possibly have been talking about?—but I was too proud, and stubborn, to show my face. Since I was not welcome in his church anymore, I had no use for the Reverend Jubb or his sister! I didn't want to see or talk to anyone except Orrin. Late at night, after everyone was asleep, he would telephone, and I held on to that receiver like a lifeline, clinging *desperately* to the sound of his dear voice and the soft, comforting words he whispered into my ear.

The so-called "*gentlemen* of the press" were relentless! They flocked to Swansea, to lay siege to Orrin's parents' home, to see the new house, to interview the workmen, and every time he set foot out of doors they chased poor Orrin like a lynch mob. He ran so much he lost eight pounds!

Poor Caroline couldn't even do her marketing in peace without reporters trailing after her writing down everything she purchased, asking what was for supper and if she was going to share the recipe with me and just how she felt about me marrying her "baby boy." That roast, and the carrots and onions that accompanied it, provided fodder for a whole newspaper column! And at the barbershop the reporters crowding around the chair actually made the barber so nervous that he nicked Orrin's father on the throat. It bled quite badly!

The reporters even went to the school to pester the poor innocent children! They offered them candy and coins, cat's eye marbles, dollies, and tin soldiers to answer their questions and tell what they thought of their teacher and what they had seen and heard of me. One little girl even got a new doll with long golden curls for confiding that she had seen me leafing through a fashion magazine with a wedding dress on the cover! The parents of Orrin's pupils were naturally *very* upset. They *hounded* him as if *he* had done something wrong, as if he were himself a criminal, not just the betrothed of a murderess whose wily lawyers had helped her to elude worldly justice. And wherever children played, they chanted that never-dying ditty that has dogged my every step since 1892 and will doubtlessly live on long after me:

> *"Lizzie Borden took an ax*
> *And gave her mother forty whacks.*
> *When she saw what she had done,*
> *She gave her father forty-one."*

It was "that carnival in New Bedford" all over again! Only this time I wasn't on trial for my life; I was fighting for my happiness, my dearest dream! *Why was everyone so nasty and mean?*

A week before what would have been our wedding day, Orrin and I met in Boston, in a little out-of-the-way tearoom. We sat in the shadows. Both of us were pale and gaunt with sunken eyes, red from weeping and lack of sleeping. I kept my veil down. I wore black as if I were in mourning even though I had vowed to never wear that woeful color again. But, for the first time in my life, I *truly* was *in* mourning; no one will *ever* know how much I grieved for what I had lost, the love, the rosy golden glowing future that now could never be mine. It was the last time we were ever to sit across from each other with our hands touching on the tabletop, fingers fondly clasping and entwining. We could barely bear to look in each other's eyes! The reporters had turned our love into something ugly and awful and made it the butt of jokes. *Everyone* was laughing at us!

He just could not do it, and I could not do it to him. He did not deserve to be tarred and feathered by my notoriety, to become Mr. Lizzie Borden and live the rest of his life like a specimen under a microscope, his every deed open to scrutiny and published in the newspapers, even his simplest actions exaggerated and embellished just to sell more newspapers. He would lose his identity. He would no longer be Orrin Gardner, schoolteacher; he would be "Lizzie Borden's husband," "Mr. Lizzie Borden," just as the world would never let me retire from the public stage into a quiet private life as Mrs. Gardner. No matter what name I took, whether I changed it myself like when I became the self-styled Lizbeth of Maplecroft or I married and took my husband's name, I would *never* be free of Lizzie Borden, I could never be anyone else; the world simply would not let me. And I could not bear it that they might take teaching away from him; several parents had already threatened to keep their children away from his classroom if he married me. Teaching was Orrin's life, and there are more ways than just murder that you can kill someone. I did not want to see the light go out of his eyes; it would make the gold of my wedding ring glow ostentatiously bright, a gloating golden emblem of shame.

And so we said good-bye. I never saw Orrin Gardner again. He abandoned our dream house, sold it to a pair of newlyweds, and moved away to Tennessee, to a small, primitive backwoods town called Sewanee, and a rough-hewn one-room schoolhouse with a leaky, sagging roof on the verge of falling down, filled with barefoot children in clothes made out of burlap sacks. His mother, Caroline, told me the only thing he took from the house was the lamp with shooting stars on it. Maybe we should have wished on that star after all? We should not have taken it for granted!

As the headlines screamed **LIZZIE BORDEN JILTED BY SCHOOLTEACHER!** I wrote letters to acquaintances and so-called "friends" who, avid for gossip, wrote in feigned solicitousness, denying the whole thing, denouncing the whole engagement as just a silly rumor, a ludicrous tale, concocted by the press to sell papers, explaining that Orrin was my cousin, and childhood playmate, nothing more, and that I had volunteered to help him choose furnishings for his new house. I *lied,* I *denied* our love, I *sacrificed* my heart's fondest dream, to give Orrin back his life; the sooner the story was forgotten, the sooner he could go on. It was the *only* thing I could do that would not destroy him!

I gave him back his ring, that precious platinum band set with a sapphire heart with dainty white diamonds trimming it like lace, and went home to Maplecroft and withdrew from the world again, to wait until some new sensation came along and caught the fickle public's fancy and made them forget, at least momentarily, all about me. I sat beside the fireplace in my bedroom and hugged my wedding gown over my broken heart as the tears poured down my face.

It was pale-blue satin with the faintest hint of gray, *not white*—the newspapermen had gotten *that* part wrong. I had chosen it because the color reminded me of the eyes of someone I had known long ago, someone who had given me a moment of magic underneath the thorn tree at Glastonbury that I had never ceased to cherish. And when I saw his eyes in that bolt of blue-gray satin it just seemed right, like he was reaching out to me from across the distant sea and giving me his blessing.

It was a gaudy, magnificent thing festooned with bows and swags of ribbon, seed pearls, and silk roses over row upon exquisite row of silver-veined white lace.

Slowly, I tore the roses off, one by one, and then the bows. As I cast each one into the fire a door slammed shut in my mind, with a harsh, brutal, adamant finality, but not before I had caught a tantalizing glimpse of what might have been. Scenes of domestic tranquility, the life I longed for more than anything, and the future that could never be.

A door slammed shut upon our wedding day, Orrin and I staring deep into each other's eyes as we solemnly spoke our vows, promising a lifetime of devotion, and shared our first kiss as husband and wife.

Another door slammed shut on the tender scene of our wedding night, as Orrin carried me to our marriage bed and ever so gently laid me down upon it and undressed me, slowly, almost reverently, shedding each lacy layer of feminine frills until I was naked as a newborn babe. Oh, the *exquisite* torment as he took his own sweet time over the long row of tiny pearl buttons marching down the back of my gown! And oh, the passion that followed! It was just as well that the door slammed shut. I didn't want to see it; I didn't want to remember that night by the fireplace in the home that should have been ours, our little nest of domestic bliss.

Then through another closing door I saw Orrin embrace me from behind, and kiss my neck, as his hands reached round to enfold and caress my stomach, swollen great with our child, as the door cruelly slammed shut like a gunshot, right in my wretched, tearstained face.

Then another door closed, just as I caught a glimpse of myself sitting up in bed, wearied and disheveled, worn out by the travail, but smiling, in triumph, the greatest victory of my life, as I held the blue-blanket-swaddled bundle of our newborn son in my arms, and Orrin sat on the bed beside me and embraced us both. How bittersweet that banished joy! It broke my heart all over again!

When all the roses and ribbons were gone, I ripped away the pearls and lace; then I buried my face in the folds of my would have been, should have been, wedding gown and let the smooth cool blue satin caress my hot, swollen, raw, red face and soak up some of my tears before I consigned it too to the greedy, always hungry flames. I sat and wept as I watched it burn. I cried until I had no tears left, then I got up and went to my cold and lonely bed, but I didn't sleep; instead I lay awake in the darkness and said farewell to all my hopes and dreams, and tried to find some semblance of peace in the solitary future I knew lay before me.

"We met again because we were meant to be together," Orrin had said. But I knew now with complete and utter certainty that I would spend the rest of my life alone. Was *this* my punishment, my penance, justice delayed catching up with me when I least expected it and condemning me to a lonely and loveless existence before I died and God banished me to Hell to burn for all eternity?

Although I said farewell to my dreams that night, *they* have *not* said farewell to me; they still come unbidden to torture me. It has been thirty years since I last saw Orrin Gardner, but there are nights when I still start awake from the dream of him lying atop me, naked and warm, gazing deep and longingly into my eyes as he enters me.

Upon waking I feel such emptiness; it is unbearable and almost indescribable, because I once knew what it was like to be filled, to be complete. My arms *ache* to enfold him, my legs to twine around him, and there is such a keen, sharp yearning in the intimate place between, such an unbearable, aching emptiness to have him back and hold him deep inside me, to feel again that sacred moment of completeness. And to know that I never will again... I do not think the Spanish Inquisition could have devised any torture equal to or greater than the feeling that accompanies that knowledge.

In Orrin's arms I felt complete, as if I had been wandering lost all my life and had *finally* found my home, my home sweet home, not gaudy, magnificent Maplecroft as I always thought, but my *true* home, the place where I belonged that I had been searching for my whole life long. *They say home is where the heart is,* and my heart was—and still is—with the man I love, but I am a wanderer once again, damned like the Wandering Jew, destined to walk alone for the rest of my life, and perhaps for all eternity as well. Emma was right! God sometimes punishes those He only seems to favor by giving them *exactly* what they want—but I would amend that and add "and then He snatches it away again."

And *that* is even worse.

Chapter 10

After I lost Orrin, and the frenzy of public interest had subsided somewhat, I ran away from Fall River. I wanted to mourn, to shed my tears, in solitude, without everyone in town staring, straining to see through my veil, avid to catch a gloating glimpse of my red-rimmed, swollen eyes when I finally did come out of hiding. I couldn't hide from the world forever, and the longer I put it off I knew the worse it would be. Finally, when I couldn't stand the dread gnawing at my stomach a moment longer, I decided to just get it over with so I could put it behind me. I couldn't go back in time, and I had lingered in limbo long enough, so the only choice left to me was to go forward.

I put on a fancy fringed dress of chartreuse and emerald satin diamonds all sewn together like patchwork with bold gold thread and a hat like a gilt-sprigged chartreuse chiffon nest cradling a dark-green bird and hung my throat and ears with pearls and emeralds and ordered Monsieur Tetrault to get the carriage ready and drive me to Gifford's. I held myself erect and regal as an empress carved out of ice as I bought a set of fruit forks with mother-of-pearl handles, and a second set of monogrammed silver pickle forks, and a faux eighteenth-century music box with a white-wigged couple dressed fit for a ball at Versailles dancing to Mozart's *Eine Kleine Nachtmusik*. Then I went home, packed a single carpet bag, and away I went with the dawn on the first train out of Fall River.

I took a cottage on Cape Cod. It was the off-season, so most of them were empty, leaving me blessedly free to walk the sands in peace and blame my red eyes and nose on the wind without being subjected to false smiles, smirks, and knowing nods. And there were no lovers or happy families on the beach to torment me with reminders of all that I had lost. Every day I stood for hours, hugging myself and shivering beneath my shawl, staring out at the choppy gray sea that seemed to mirror the turmoil within my soul, watching the waves crash and roll, and the gulls soar and dive, always seeking, sometimes finding.

One day the wind snatched my shawl away. I let it go. It was just one shawl, a common knitted one, and I had many more much finer. I watched it fly away, like my love, beyond my grasp, its maroon folds momentarily taking the shape of a heart—a *bleeding, wounded heart!*—as it rose high in the grim gray sky.

To my surprise, sometime later—mere minutes or hours I cannot tell you; I had by then, in all those aimless hours spent walking the shore, lost all sense of time—I felt it settle comfortingly around my shoulders again. It came back to me, the way I wished Orrin would. I spun around to find myself staring into the kindest pair of brown eyes I had ever seen. They warmed me like a cup of hot cocoa.

She looked as weary as I did, there were fine crinkled lines and dark shadows around her eyes, and even when she smiled sorrow tried to pull her pink lips down. Though she couldn't have been much older than me—ten years, just like Emma, Time would soon reveal—the golden hair coiled high atop her head was threaded thickly with silver. I would soon learn that arthritis was her own private devil that had tormented her joints unceasingly since early childhood and she was in almost constant pain. She had traveled several times to Europe searching for, if not a cure, at least some relief, in the baths or in liniments, but *never* drugs; she could not *bear* to have anything dull her mind.

Her name was Sarah Orne Jewett. She was a lady novelist who had come to Cape Cod to finish a book unencumbered by the distractions of daily life. Lately there had been too many of them; seemingly every time she turned around another tempest was brewing in the teapot or someone was making demands upon her time, wanting her to do this or that and making it impossible for her to say *no*. Finally, she just had to throw up her hands and say *Enough!*, pack her bags, and run away. Quite renowned, famous even, she knew a little something about notoriety and insatiable public curiosity. That was the common ground we met upon. In her case, love at first sight with her publisher's wife had led to a cordial, if not legal, severance of the marital bond and the two ladies setting up house together in Boston. It was *almost* as shocking as murder. The number of books the scandal sold almost made up to Mr. Fields for the loss of his wife.

Sarah gave her hand to me. I took it. She was easy to talk to. She seemed to understand as no one else did. That night I found myself sitting before a fireplace again, nestled in a cozy cocoon of cushions and blankets, orange flames dancing, crackling, casting a magical golden glow to warm both my body and my cold, ailing soul. Staring into a cup of hot spiced tea, I saw myself before another fireplace, with Orrin on the night that made me think that Heaven could very well be a place on earth. Tears rolled down my face, drip-dropping into my tea, as I remembered, and relived, every excruciatingly sweet caress and tender kiss, and the way he had filled and fulfilled me.

Sarah took the cup away and put her arms around me and I leaned into her gratefully.

"God never closes a door without opening a window, Lizbeth," she said, her lips so soft and warm against my face as her kisses gently followed the trail of my tears. I shivered, arched my back, and sighed as her lips strayed down to the hollow of my throat. "There is always something more for us, Lizbeth," she continued, "waiting out there; we have only to go out and seek . . . and find . . . or invite it in to us. . . ."

I turned to her. I needed someone *so* badly; I was in *so much* pain and *throbbing* with need! Our lips met and our bodies followed suit, merging and melting together until I felt I was alone no longer.

For two weeks, history repeated itself every night. Every day I walked the sands while Sarah wrote, and we made love every night in front of that fireplace, and in bed one last time before putting out the light, and every morning before we rose to breakfast. Sarah firmly believed "love feeds the soul like nourishing food feeds the body, Lizbeth, and a wise person always starts the day with a good breakfast."

God had been kind after all; when He slammed the door on Orrin He opened a window and showed me Sarah. I had *finally* found someone who *really* could understand me, someone who had also drunk from the vinegary cup of fame and wouldn't be frightened away by its foul taste. Or so I thought, and then I found the notebook.

One night when I couldn't sleep and didn't want my tossing and turning to wake Sarah, I picked it up in idle curiosity from the desk and went to sit by the fire with it. I'm both glad I did and wish that I didn't. It was like opening Pandora's box. It was *all* about me, page after page, a rush of words written in frantically flowing black ink, as though she had been desperate to get it *all* down before she could forget a single thing, the script cramped and crooked because of her painful hands, ideas for a novel based upon my life, with all the names and places changed of course, but still completely recognizable so that any half-wit would know her inspiration, her muse, was Lizzie Borden. There was my heart laid bare and bleeding upon those ivory pages just as though Sarah had *ripped* it right out of my breast and offered it up as a cannibal sacrifice for the greedy public to devour! My every confidence betrayed! *Everything* I had told her and ideas about how to weave it into the plot. Descriptions of people and places, snippets of dialogue, and whole scenarios!

I had been a *fool* to trust her! So desperate and needy that I was blind! The only thing to be thankful for was that I hadn't told her the truth about the murders or mentioned David Anthony; I clung tenaciously to the truth of my innocence. I had told her that I only stayed in Fall River in the hope that someday the *real* killer might be discovered and I would truly be vindicated and acquitted in the court of public opinion, which seemed in the end to matter more than any legal one.

As I closed the covers I thought I heard God laughing. He seemed to take a fiendish delight in slamming doors upon my heart. Would it *ever* hurt and bleed enough to satisfy Him?

I flung the notebook from me in disgust, straight into the fire, without stopping to think that it wasn't mine to destroy. But I didn't care! To me that was just a trivial point. It was *my* life filling that notebook; thus, to my mind, I had the right. I sat and watched it burn. Then I silently gathered up my clothes and went back to my own cottage. I packed my carpet bag and caught the first train I could. I didn't care where it took me, as long as it was far away from Sarah and the place where I thought I had found happiness when I was least expecting it.

I left no word for Sarah. The cold and dead ashes she would find in the fireplace would convey everything I had to say more succinctly than any actual words spoken by me ever could.

She never wrote to me to apologize or explain. I suppose she was too ashamed. No phoenix ever rose from those ashes. For years to come I would always feel afraid whenever a new book by her appeared on the store shelves, but she never wrote a character or situation that seemed even remotely inspired by me, and for that I was most grateful. God extended me *one small* mercy at least.

That summer I found myself aimless and adrift and not quite sure what to do with myself in Providence, Rhode Island. I shopped to alleviate the boredom and bring more beautiful things into my life. One of my favorite stores was the city's oldest and finest, Tilden & Thurber, a combination art gallery, gift shop, and jewelry store that had been in business since 1790. As I idly browsed their shop on Westminster Street I was smitten by two little oval paintings on porcelain in frames like golden lace.

I was rather surprised to see them in Tilden & Thurber; their amorous motif seemed a trifle risqué for such a formal and reserved establishment. The first, *Love's Dream,* depicted a beautiful young woman sleeping as Cupid, with his arrow poised, like an erect phallus, hovered above her. She was naked and her black hair tumbled over the pillows; one arm was flung out as though her slumber was a restless one, troubled by dreams. As further proof of her restlessness, she had kicked the sheets off, and one knee was bent and her legs slightly parted, suggesting perhaps that her dream was an amorous one. Roses, their pink petals suggestive of a woman's intimate parts, wreathed the entire scene. The second painting, *Love's Awakening,* showed a lover in powdered wig and knee breeches, stealthily approaching, and the sleeping beauty rousing, aroused, and opening her arms and legs to him as she drew him down into her welcoming embrace.

What struck me most was the young woman's resemblance to Lulie Stillwell at the height of her ebony-haired, ruby-red-lipped, snow-white-skinned fairy-tale princess beauty. The titles that had been given to the paintings seemed to fit *so* perfectly our, or rather my, peculiar circumstances. Lulie had been my ideal, my dream of love, for so many years, and the passage of years and her marriage to Johnny Hiram had never diminished that; she was still the ghost who haunted my dreams, the figure in my favorite fantasies, the one whose reincarnation I was always hoping to find in the women I took to my bed. She had been the one who had truly awakened my desires.

Then I did a foolish thing, a *very* foolish thing. I was sick of seeing my name in the newspapers, of *everything* I did being gossiped about, so I asked the clerk if I might see a vase that was locked in a glass display case. While she had her back to me, I swiftly slipped the two little paintings into my handbag.

On impulse, as soon as I returned to Maplecroft I packed them up carefully in blue tissue paper and sent them to Lulie. *I dreamed of you last night,* I wrote with a tremulous hand, *but I don't dare put my dreams down on paper.* I let the paintings speak for me instead, and be my declaration of desire, the words I could not say.

Lulie's response was to wait until she was next in Providence to do some Christmas shopping and take the paintings back to Tilden & Thurber. The labels I had left in place, pasted on the back of each painting so she would know that my gift came from one of the finest shops in all New England, made it quite easy for her to do this. She explained to the clerk that she had received them as a gift—*an unwanted gift!*—from Miss Borden, but they were really not to her taste and she would like, if possible, to exchange them for a toiletry case or perhaps a lap desk as a gift for her husband to take with him, as a constant reminder of her love, as he traveled often on business.

The clerk at Tilden & Thurber knew quite well that the paintings had never been purchased by me, or anyone else for that matter; on the contrary, they had simply disappeared one late-summer day. She remembered me visiting the shop, and records soon confirmed that I had bought a vase the same day that the paintings had first been missed and had it shipped back to Maplecroft.

Lulie left the paintings at Tilden & Thurber and emphatically declined their polite offer of an exchange; they were after all the rightful owner of the items and she didn't want anything further to do with the matter, or Lizzie Borden. "That woman makes my skin crawl every time I think of her!"—Lulie actually said *that* to the clerk! Lulie asked that her name be kept out of it entirely, as she didn't want the police or reporters showing up at her door. She had been brought up to believe that a woman's name should appear in the newspapers only when she was born, engaged, married, or buried. Before she left, Lulie bought a handsome ebony wood toiletry case inlaid with mother-of-pearl and filigreed silverwork complete with mother-of-pearl-and-silver-handled accessories inside, everything the immaculate and refined gentleman would need for grooming, as a gift for her husband. It was her way of making a point, I suppose.

A warrant was sworn out for my arrest, but it was never served and, when the episode found its way into the papers, as it inevitably did, with headlines shouting **LIZZIE BORDEN AGAIN! A WARRANT FOR HER ARREST! TWO PAINTINGS MISSING FROM TILDEN & THURBER STORE!** a fictional female name was substituted in place of Lulie's.

I threatened to sue and set Mr. Jennings on it. I explained that the paintings had been inside the package with the vase that I had bought and had shipped to me. I thought they were included as a small gift to show how much Tilden & Thurber appreciated my business, and it never occurred to me that there was anything amiss when I sent them to an old school friend in token of fond memories I still cherished.

Everything was settled out of court eventually for a few hundred dollars, after which Mr. Jennings and I parted ways, with him heatedly declaring, "I will have nothing more to do with that woman!" by which he of course meant me, the client whose murder trial had made him famous and earned him the stupendous sum of $25,000. As Father would have said, some people just don't know the meaning of gratitude.

Chapter 11

I spent the next several years living quietly, mostly at Maplecroft, and occasionally at grand hotels whenever the wanderlust seized me and I couldn't abide sitting still in the same old place a moment longer. But I was increasingly a solitary creature, ill inclined to let anyone get too close to me; I shied away even from paid companions and more often than not chose fantasy over reality. I just didn't want any more disappointments or complications. As lonely as I was, my head kept telling my heart it was better to be alone. It seemed the world just kept on kicking me when I was already down. Orrin, Sarah, the humiliating and idiotic incident at Tilden & Thurber, my bold yet veiled baring of my feelings to Lulie, and her rejection, it was all just *too* much, too soon, coming all in a row like that. I needed time to heal, to lick my wounds and get back up on my feet again.

In those days, I preferred to find my romance in books and plays instead, and I still had my dreams. I would always have those. It was safer and less painful that way, though it made the loneliness that consumed my soul throb like a toothache sometimes. Many sleepless nights I lay awake wondering if it was love itself that I was in love with more than I could ever be with any real-life man or woman. Did love ever really last a lifetime? Was "happily ever after" just an idyllic ending for storybooks as I suspected? Did all those novels and plays only foster false and impossible hopes in the hearts of the lovelorn? Nevertheless, I thrived on them, I devoured books, and wherever I was I arranged to have a bookshop send me a new batch of novels every fortnight.

I read so much I wore my eyes out. I began to sport an elegant pince-nez, silver or gold depending on my whim and what I was wearing, but always accented with diamonds, and I had some lovely lorgnettes, silver and gold, with enameled and jeweled accents that I wore on long glittering chains around my neck when I went out in the evenings to restaurants and the theater. I felt so chic, elegant as Lillian Russell herself, scanning the menu at Delmonico's with a gold lorgnette flashing radiant red rubies to match my red velvet gown or a silver one sparkling with amethysts to complement my lavish embroidered and appliquéd silver and lilac. It was just an illusion, I know, but, for a moment, at least, it made me feel good . . . until I caught a glimpse of myself in a mirror. Lillian Russell I was not.

My fortieth birthday found me back in Fall River. I stood before the gilt-framed mirror in my summer bedroom after my bath and opened my robe and took a long hard look at myself. For most of my life, I had promised myself that I would start dieting, but it was *always* tomorrow, just *one more* slice of pie or piece of cake, another bonbon or cookie . . . but all those one mores added up and as a result, I had the stout, dumpy, lumpy figure to show for my lack of fortitude. But I knew better than to think I had the willpower to do anything about it. I would never have the perfect hourglass figure as curvy and breathtaking as the roller coaster at Coney Island in real life, only in my dreams, where I was always young and beautiful as a Gibson Girl, coveted and courted by gallants galore.

I was dismayed to see how much white was encroaching upon the red of my hair. In some places the color had actually faded to a soft peach or was entirely white. I thought it a most unattractive combination to grace the human head, this parti-colored streaky mass of dark rusty red, peach, and white. I would have to do something about it. I just was not ready to be a white-haired old woman yet. I had lost so much of my youth as a prisoner in my father's house, I just wanted to go on pretending and prolong that pretense as long as I possibly could. Was that so wrong of me?

There was something else I noticed, though Lord knows I wish I hadn't—I had my father's face. Maybe the white hair brought out the resemblance or I had been too blind to see it was there all along, but from that day forth whenever I looked into a mirror I didn't see only me; I saw him too, like a ghost haunting me, possessing my own skin and bones so I could never be free of him. The courts might have acquitted me in 1893, but that July morning in 1900 I *knew* that the mirror would condemn me every day and night for the rest of my life. Abby was in my body, Father was in my face, murder was in my soul and on my conscience, and I *was* guilty no matter how much I pretended and proclaimed my innocence. Our deeds travel with us from afar; they make of us what we are. No matter what I did, or where I went, I would *never* be free, of him, or me, or my murderous deeds.

"This is what it is like to be damned," I said to my face, and Father's.

Rather than calling in a hairdresser to attend me and having her go gossiping all over town that "*Lizzie Borden is a dyed-haired woman!*" I asked Monsieur Tetrault if he would be so kind as to help me. He had trained as a hairdresser in his youth in Paris, before immigrating to America, and had worked at that trade for several years before going into private service with his wife as an inseparable coachman and cook combination. He was a kind man and readily agreed. By then he had been in my employ a number of years and I felt I could trust him.

The next morning right after breakfast, he arrived with an armful of jars, bowls, and brushes and sat me down at my dressing table with a combing cape draped over my pink dressing gown and gave my hair a good brushing. One hundred strokes—he counted each one, in French. Then he wet it and snipped off the dead ends. He sang in a loud, and slightly discordant, tenor voice as he happily mixed his ingredients with all the enthusiasm of a housewife baking a birthday cake. I was a little alarmed to see that the concoction he ladled on top of my head, then used a brush to spread in long, even strokes from roots to tips looked just like bright green cake batter, but he assured me the results would be *ravissante!*

"You mustn't worry about a thing, Mademoiselle Lizbeth," he said as he wrapped a thick towel around my head like a Turk's turban and sent me to sit as near as I could bear beside a blazing fire, instructing me not to stir for two hours. So I obediently sat there, sweating like a racehorse that had just won the Kentucky Derby, and tried to lose myself in a book and not worry about what was happening to my hair beneath the towel.

When the two hours had passed, Monsieur Tetrault promptly came back and guided me into my bathroom and instructed me to kneel by the tub and hang my head over it. I groaned miserably and nearly burst into tears when I saw the stream of brown liquid as ugly as mud running toward the drain as he rinsed my hair.

"Do not despair, Mademoiselle Lizbeth; when you look in the mirror you shall fall in love with yourself," Monsieur Tetrault promised as he helped me up and guided me gently back to my dressing table.

When I saw myself I was stunned speechless. I gasped, burst into tears, and then I began to laugh and flung my arms around his neck. I must have kissed his face two dozen times in sheer delight. My hair was as bright as a blazing fireball. I'd never seen a redder head of hair in my life! I was *ecstatic!* I looked, and felt, *striking!*

Unfortunately, it was at the precise moment that I was clinging to Monsieur Tetrault and kissing him that Emma walked in. She took one long sour look at us, then turned around and walked right back out. I don't think it could have been any worse than the expression she would have worn if she had walked in on me while I was wielding the hatchet over Father's face as he lay napping on the sofa. But, at that moment, I was too happy to give a fig what Emma thought; I knew better than to expect her to approve of anything I did.

As soon as my hair was dry and Monsieur Tetrault had styled it in a high curling pompadour just like a Gibson Girl, I put on a gay dress of emerald green, ruby red, and white stripes and a turquoise extravaganza of a hat dripping green wax grapes over the broad brim and went right out to Gifford's and, to express my gratitude, bought him the biggest and most ornate gold watch they had and ordered it engraved with his initials. Impulsively, I also selected a large gold fob set with an onyx intaglio carved with a horse's head to go with it; since he had been my driver all these years, first horses, followed by automobiles, I thought it a most fitting gift.

Of course, the clerk at Gifford's talked. What other man could I possibly know in Fall River with the initials *J.H.T.* but Joseph Henri Tetrault? The design on the fob confirmed the recipient's identity. Speculation was so rife that it quite eclipsed the townsfolk's wonderment at how red my head had suddenly become. *And why should Lizzie Borden be giving her coachman such an expensive and extravagant gift? And what does his wife have to say about it?* Everyone wanted to know, arching their brows and suspecting the worst as they *always* did where I was concerned. And when Monsieur Tetrault was seen about town wearing my gift, it confirmed all their dire and dirty-minded suspicions. Obviously he was being paid to do more than just drive me. He was French after all, they said with knowing nods, and no woman employs a chauffeur that handsome unless she has something more than driving in mind. Soon they were all putting their heads together and tallying up all the times they had seen him trailing after me in his elegant uniform carrying a pile of parcels, my fur coat, or one or the other of my pair of Pomeranians, Cinnamon and Sugar, and saying that my hand had lingered overlong in his whenever he was handing me into or down from the carriage or car, and that his fingers had lingeringly brushed my thighs in a caressing manner when he draped a fur lap rug over my knees for my wintertime rides. Of course, it was all nonsense. There had *never* been any impropriety between Monsieur Tetrault and me.

Emma was so mortified by all these lascivious insinuations that right after church one Sunday she burst into my room, her face red as a tomato, her whole body quaking like a volcano about to erupt, and *demanded* that I discharge the Tetraults *at once.* Before I could say a word she *dragged* in a tall, gangly-limbed man named Clayton Fogg to replace him as my coachman, then shoved him right back out the door again before he could say so much as *how d'you do* so we could talk privately. I *hated* him on sight and said so.

"He looks just like a frog!" I told Emma. "I will not have such an ugly man as my chauffeur!"

But Emma said that was all well and good: "No one will ever suspect *him* of hopping into your bed, Lizzie!"

I was so angry I almost slapped her. Heaven knows, I had to sit on my hands not to I was so *furious*. She was *my sister;* how *dare* she say such *awful* things to me? It was almost as though she actually *believed* the lies! I was so hurt, I couldn't help but weep.

Emma was adamant, "Cry all you like, Lizzie, but the Tetraults *must* go and *now*."

There was no discussing the matter with her; Emma was impervious to my tears and wouldn't hear a word I had to say in my defense or theirs.

"Either the Tetraults go or *I* go," she declared, "and think how bad it will look if *I* go, Lizzie. Everyone will think you have chosen your French *lover* over your own sister—the one who stood by you through thick and thin and would defend you to her last breath!"

Oh, how scornfully and witheringly she spoke that word— *lover!* She made me feel filthy inside and out, even though I had done nothing wrong. I felt so dirty I had to take the hottest bath I could stand as soon as Emma left me alone.

It wasn't fair! My relations with Monsieur Tetrault had always been perfectly proper; no amorous thoughts about him had ever entered my head. And Madame Tetrault had *never* suffered a moment's disquiet because of me! Both of them had told me they were as sorry as could be that my innocent and generous gift had led to such gossip; I was a good woman, they said, and didn't deserve to have everything I did distorted and twisted all out of proportion. It was such a shame; I couldn't even reward a faithful servant who had been in my service for years without everyone seeing evil and immorality in it. But Emma was *not* as understanding as Monsieur and Madame Tetrault. And she was also right, as much as it pains me to admit; it would look *very* bad for me indeed if she left and the Tetraults stayed. In the end, I gave in. I paid for the Tetraults to move to Canada, to start a new life there, even though I wept to see them go.

As I stood on the porch, with Emma glowering beside me, and watched them drive away with all their belongings tears rolled down my face.

"Everyone leaves me," I whispered tremulously.

"I never will." Emma laid a hand on my shoulder that I'm sure was meant to be reassuring but felt more like a steel-toothed bear trap springing shut upon my soul. "*Someone* must have a care for your soul, and reputation, Lizzie, since *you* won't."

I started and spun around to face her. My heart was pounding so, I pressed a hand against it as though that would keep it from bursting out of my breast. "Emma! You sound just like Father!"

"He wasn't wrong about *everything*, Lizzie," she said over her shoulder as she went inside and upstairs, back to her religious bric-a-brac, leaving me alone, the way everyone always did in the end.

Chapter 12

I can hardly bear to write the next chapter. Some wounds go so deep not even twenty years can heal or even cauterize them.

The first time I saw Nance O'Neil was on Valentine's Day 1904 at the Colonial Theatre. I had arrived late in Boston and, to my supreme annoyance, missed half the play. As the usher escorted me to my box, I was so spellbound by the sight of her that I quite forgot to sit down until the lights went up and the applause broke my trance. I simply could not take my eyes off her! I could hardly bear to blink for the moment it might deprive me of the sight of her. I almost forgot to breathe!

There she was—a slim gilt figure, like a beacon of softly glowing golden flame, living, breathing, sparkling champagne that went straight to my head! So tall for a woman, almost six feet, yet thoroughly feminine, she was at once sensual and vulnerable in a flowing midnight-blue velvet dressing gown, the collar furred with ermine that at times drooped to reveal the curve of a bare shoulder and breast, with a girdle woven of gold and jewels snugly hugging the hourglass of her waist, hair like waving fields of golden wheat flowing down to her waist in the most beguiling disarray, as though she had indeed just risen—naked, as a thrilling flash of white thigh revealed through the folds of her robe when she moved—from the rumpled bed that stood at the far corner of the stage in the shadowy background. She was like no one I had ever seen before—virgin and harlot, siren and sweetheart, vampire and angel all in one body I would give ten years of my life to hold and caress.

Entranced, as if she were a mesmerist's gold watch swinging to and fro before my eyes, I followed her as she moved sightlessly across the stage as the sleepwalking Lady Macbeth. Center stage, seeing without seeing, she turned to face the audience and sank slowly to her knees—there was that lightning-fast flash of white thigh and trim, slim limbs again; surely no other actress who ever portrayed Lady Macbeth had ever been so sensual and bold!— scrubbing frantically at her lily-white hands with soap and water that only she, in her slumbering madness, could see. The great ruby on the ring finger of her left hand shimmered like a teardrop of fresh-spilt blood and drew my eyes like a firefly.

"*Out, damned spot! Out, I say! One; two; why, then 'tis time to do't: Hell is murky! Fie, my lord, fie! A soldier, and afeared? What need we fear who knows it, when none can call our power to account? Yet who would have thought the old man to have had so much blood in him?*"

Her luscious lips trembled in a way that portended tears and the desperation in her voice rose with every angst-sodden syllable, chilling and scalding my soul at the same time and raising every hair on the nape of my neck. I felt the gooseflesh rise and prickle all over me and my nipples spring painfully erect, hard and adamant as accusing, pointing pink fingertips straining against the gold-and-champagne-beaded bodice of my apricot satin evening gown. I wanted my fur to warm me, but it had slipped from my shoulders and fallen, unnoticed, to the floor, and I couldn't bear to tear my eyes from the stage long enough to retrieve it.

"*Yet who would have thought the old man to have had so much blood in him?*" Those words almost felled me like a blow from a hatchet. In my memory's eye, vivid and clear as if it were only yesterday, I saw Father napping on the sofa as I brought the blade down, for the first time, and then again and again and again. Even after a dozen years I could still *feel* his blood upon my skin, warm and red as rubies, soaking in, *scorching* my soul, staining it forever with my rash and impetuous sin. I could still *taste* it, salty and metallic upon my tongue, and the smell still filled my nostrils. I felt nauseous and a red starry mist drifted across my eyes, momentarily obscuring the dazzling blue and gold vision upon the stage.

Like a modern-day Lady Macbeth, my hands could never be washed clean; in my own sight or society's, my soul was caked and sticky with blood, I was marked with guilt like Cain, and there were moments when I feared that madness was close enough to reach out and touch me. Whenever people saw or spoke of me blood filled their minds. It had become a part of me. *Blood is the life,* both the Good Book and Mr. Stoker's fiendish count Dracula said, and I more than any other saw the truth in it. Blood was *my* life; it *defined* who I was—the self- or hatchet-made heiress. To buy my freedom, my *worldly* freedom, I had bathed my soul in blood that could *never* be washed away.

"What, will these hands never be clean? Here's the smell of the blood still: all the perfumes of Arabia will not sweeten this little hand. Oh, oh, oh!"

With every word she spoke to my soul, she reached across the footlights and darkened void where the audience sat enraptured to my box and *touched* me, reaching right through skin and bone, as no one else ever had, not even Orrin. Though Shakespeare, not Nance O'Neil, had written the words that came out of her mouth, like a spirit speaking through a medium it was the *way* she spoke them, the *anguish* and *torment* and *pain* with which she imbued them, that told me that *she knew, she understood.* My body was made of glass and she was looking through it clear to my soul! There would be no keeping any secrets from her. I would *always* be naked with Nance no matter how many layers of clothes I wore or locked doors I hid behind. It both *thrilled* and *terrified* me to be so helpless and bare.

I was back the next night to see her in *Judith of Bethulia,* as the beautiful but chaste widow who, to save her people, under siege by the Assyrians and nearing starvation and surrender, dons her finest raiment and goes to the enemy camp and offers herself as a sensual sacrifice to the lust of General Holofernes. But the cunning beauty outwits him, and as he lies deep in a drunken slumber she cuts off the tyrant's head. The Assyrians, left without a leader, scatter to the winds and Bethulia is saved and Judith celebrated as their savior.

Even though she could not know it, through the parts she played Nance O'Neil spoke to me. In every role she played I seemed to find something of myself. Like Judith, I also had spilled a tyrant's blood for the greater good.

I was there every night as the woman the papers hailed as "the most emotional actress of our age" worked through her repertoire. I saw her in *Camille, Trilby, Sappho, Leah the Forsaken, Hedda Gabler, The Passion Flower, Lysistrata, The Magdalene,* and *Elizabeth, Queen of England.* I applauded so hard I split my gloves every time and went back to the Bellevue Hotel with sore and smarting palms, yet feeling there was one alone out there in the world who could understand me better than any other even though we had never exchanged a single word or even a polite nod in passing and were in truth strangers.

After that first night, I was never late again. I was early, the very first in line; I was so anxious all day that some mishap might occur to make me late and I couldn't bear to take that chance. I must have loitered about for an hour or more outside the theater before each performance, gazing at her pictures, trying to decide if her eyes were truly mint green with a smattering of little chocolate kisses, ice blue with drifts of hazel, or the delicate gray of a dove's feathers lightly brushed with copper, and if the hue of her hair was more like honey or wheat. I anonymously sent her two dozen long-stemmed red roses and every night as she made her final bow I saw them handed to her, cradled in her arms, adoringly against her beautiful breasts, like blood on snow.

My eyes *adored* her! And so apparently did every other pair of functioning eyes in Boston. The headlines proclaimed **BOSTON IS NANCE O'NEIL MAD!** Photographs and exquisite hand-tinted postcards of her in costume for her most famous roles or elegant gowns from her own wardrobe were sold in shops and I became an avid collector, giddy each time I discovered a new image not already pasted in my album.

Her beautiful face graced candy boxes, and in magazines she

was seen advertising *Lady Elegant Bridal Pink Powder* and *Egyptian Dreams Perfume;* these I tore out too and even bought the products just to feel closer to her, that the powder and perfume that touched my skin were the same as graced hers.

Copies of her hats and dresses appeared in shop windows and I was amongst the many who, in our enthusiasm and adoration, forgot the fact that we lacked Miss O'Neil's tall, willowy-slim physique and such fashions would not flatter us in the least, and flocked undeterred to buy them. It was not an uncommon sight in those days to see two, four, or even five, or maybe more, women of various ages and shapes promenading in the park or sitting in church on Sunday with the same hat on their heads or dress on their backs, forming a discordant chorus of would-be Nance O'Neils. Some were not content just to have her hats and coveted what was under them and the city's wigmakers did a thriving trade in Nance O'Neil wigs; many a poor lass in need of money I'm sure had her head shorn down to stubble to supply the demand for those golden waves. When a necklace Nance wore in *Elizabeth, Queen of England* was auctioned at a charity benefit I was ready to beggar myself to win it. Even if the stones were paste and the metal was base that turned my skin green I was *wild* to possess it because it was a *true* relic of *her*—the one I worshiped from afar with all my body, soul, and heart!—not just an imitation of something she had worn.

It was only when it was almost too late that I found the courage to approach her. When she bid farewell to Boston with an encore performance of *Elizabeth, Queen of England,* I boldly bribed my way backstage, into her dressing room, after the show to present my roses in person. I knew it was now or never and I would forever despise myself as a coward if I didn't.

Her maid was just finishing fastening the back of a shimmering olive-green dress overlaid with sparkling black net and lace adorned with teal, purple, and orange beaded lotus flower appliqués while Miss O'Neil stood before a full-length mirror fussing with the emerald and diamond tiara—a gift from the Khedive of Cairo, it had been in all the newspapers—perched atop the high-piled gleaming masses of her golden hair.

The moment our eyes met ... it was electricity and ecstasy, a quivering, rapturous *frisson* rippling through our bodies head to toe.

Blushing berry ripe, I clumsily blurted out a compliment about the women she brought to life upon the stage. Nance came to me and took both of my trembling hands in hers and stared deep into my eyes before she led me to sink down upon a red velvet sofa beside her.

"I know who you are," she leaned in close and whispered in a soft, husky voice, breathy and sensual.

I started to draw back in alarm, but she would not let me.

"No, no." She held tight to my hands. "Don't be alarmed! I wish only to say that your story has touched me. And with the words you have just spoken to me. . . ." Her eyes lit up like stars! "You have divined my secret! I find the character of unloved, shunned, and misunderstood women—women like you if I may so presume, my dear Miss Borden, who have been *crucified* by conventional traditions—*fascinating;* it strikes a chord deep within the soul of me and provokes and stirs me more than any happily ever after storybook heroine ever could! Give me a role like that over a musical or a comedy no matter how sparkling or witty any day, for *there,* in a forsaken and mistreated woman's life, is *true* tragedy and drama! Far too often, I find, women live out their destinies in the small places to which they have been *driven* and *thrust, forced,* into, and there is a storm that broods inside them that far too often hardly ever bursts because womankind is constrained to corset her soul, and her emotions, like her waist, and keep her emotions in check because the powers that be—men and society!—think it undignified to express them. *Tradition has made women cowardly!* But when, on rare occasion, that storm *does* break . . ." She squeezed my hands and her eyes were like mysterious, exotic opals, dancing, playing a coy, flirtatious game, and shifting shades with the wooing light. "*Better to be an outlaw than not to be free! We* are *rebels* because those who govern or claim to love us, to be acting for our own good, all too often *betray* us! The unloved and misunderstood woman is usually thus, the victim of someone, some man, too stupid to know the difference between Heaven and earth!"

She was the most passionate person I had ever met!

"How right you are!" I breathed, and squeezed her hands right back. She might have been painting a portrait of me with her words! No one had ever gleaned the tragedy of my life so completely and precisely! She had indeed seen straight into my soul!

From then on there was no more Miss O'Neil or Miss Borden. We would be only Nance and Lizbeth, close as a pair of those tragic twins one sees in freak shows and dime museums, joined perpetually at the hip.

She was everything I ever wanted and ever wanted to be; I spent my whole youth dreaming of being just like her—beautiful, celebrated, and adored! Worshipfully I knelt at her feet and fastened the emerald and diamond bracelets around her slender wrists, feeling the pulse throb against my fingertips. When she stood to leave, I draped a white fur cape about her shoulders, then, carrying the bouquet of roses—*My* roses! She said she would have no others!—reverently in my arms, like the Christ child, I trailed after her, following blindly even if she would lead me to the very ends of the earth.

Smiling and waving, vague and vacantly, haughty as the great queen she had just portrayed onstage, to the left and to the right, she sailed majestically past all the stage-door johnnies offering her diamond bracelets, lobster dinners, and proposals of marriage, bypassing all the gleaming chauffeured cars and carriages, including one where a group of college boys in their fraternity colors had taken the place of the horses, just to have the honor of pulling "the marvelous Miss O'Neil" back to her hotel.

"I'm all yours tonight, Lizbeth," Nance whispered sensually into my ear, making me shiver and my whole body quiver; then she asked me to lead the way to my carriage.

"This is the *happiest* night of my life!" I breathed.

"I aim to make it so, dear Lizbeth," Nance answered.

And she did! She took a beautiful silver flask with her initials flashing in diamonds from her garter, raised it to her lips, and drained it, then with a carefree laugh and a cry of "Catch!" tossed it out the carriage window, into the white-gloved hands of one of her tuxedoed and top-hatted admirers, laughing delightedly and blowing him a kiss when he called back that he would treasure it all the days of his life and that it would be buried with him, right over his heart when he died. And then she turned and reached for me—*me!* It was *me* she wanted! Not any of them!

"*'That which hath made them drunk hath made me bold,'*" she whispered huskily against my quivering, shivering flesh, quoting Lady Macbeth just for me as her hand cupped my breast. "*'What hath quench'd them hath given me fire!'*" And then she kissed me and I tasted the burn of whiskey on her lips.

As Nance would say, "Leave the audience wanting more and then don't give it to them," so I let the curtain fall, Dear Reader, upon that blissful night of wonder when I held a star in my arms.

As there is often dust lurking beneath a carpet, all too frequently—and quickly!—tinsel turns to ashes. The audience sees only the splendor, the costumes, smiles, and gaiety; they never smell the sweat in the actor's armpits or see the ugly bunions and painful, seeping blisters disfiguring the dancer's feet that look so lovely in their satin slippers as they glide, and prance, and leap across the stage. All too soon, the stardust cleared from my eyes, and Truth pulled my golden goddess down from her pillar but never quite succeeded in completely destroying my fascination with her, only tarnishing it somewhat. She was such a beautiful dream, I held on as long as I could. I simply could not bear to let her go, and vanish, upon my awakening to reality's jarring slap. And Nance had her own reasons for entwining her arms and clinging tight to me. So we sustained the beautiful, mutually agreeable illusion as long as we could.

She was born plain Gertrude Lamson, a strict Baptist minister's tall, gangly corn-fed daughter. At sixteen, when she declared her intention of going on the stage, her father, determined to publicly shame this intent to sin out of her and see her settled down and married to a respectable dairy farmer, denounced her from the pulpit before his entire congregation. As they all sank to their knees, praying fervently for her wayward Satan-tempted soul, Gertrude Lamson shed her name and life as she knew it like a snake does its skin and became Nance O'Neil as she walked, tall and proud, down the aisle and out of her father's church, never deigning to turn an eye left or right or backward, looking only forward, determinedly, to her own future. She was like a pioneer woman setting out to forge a new life for herself out of the wilderness, and all the dangers she might encounter be damned!

She made her way to San Francisco, hitching rides in wagons laden with hay, pigs, or watermelons, and with traveling peddlers in flashy checkered suits who could not wait to get their hands inside her bodice and drawers. As soon as she arrived in this great big city that would have made most little country girls quail and quake with fear, Nance inquired of a newsboy which was the best and biggest paper. Soon she had wiled and beguiled her way into the affections, and the bed, of a famous drama critic. He was only too happy to write her a letter of introduction to talent agent McKee Rankin, a man with a shrewd instinct for discovering and developing new talent.

Here is a young friend of mine who wants to go on the stage, his note read. *Kindly discourage her.*

But the moment Mr. Rankin laid eyes on Nance he *knew* he was looking at a diamond in the rough. A star! Relentlessly, like a slave driver cracking the whip, day and night he honed and polished her. Heartless as Simon Legree when, exhausted, she fell down at his feet and cried that she was too tired to go on a moment longer, he simply jerked her back up and put her through her paces again and again until he was satisfied; he would accept nothing short of perfection from her. "Mark my word," he always said to Nance, even when she lay at his feet and cried and cried, "you'll thank me for this someday!"

She made her debut at the Alcazar Theatre in a bit part as a nun, standing out only because she was the tallest one, but when she took the lead in du Maurier's *Trilby,* playing the artist's model who falls under the spell of Svengali, daringly displaying her bare feet, and the rest of her body wrapped in the scantiest and sheerest draperies the law would allow on the "respectable" stage, a star was born. Everyone fell in love with Nance O'Neil.

From that point there was no stopping Nance. Soon she was touring all over the United States, practically living on a train, saying good night in one city and waking up in another. Then across the sea she went, to play before the crowned heads of Europe, touring like a whirlwind through England, Scotland, Ireland, Wales, Australia, New Zealand, Turkey, India, Africa, and Egypt, and being wooed with jewels by princes, dukes, khedives, maharajahs, and sultans. One even pried the priceless blue diamond eye out of a sacred golden idol as a gift for her. The newspapers published pictures of Nance wearing it on her forehead or in her hair when they reported her dusky regal swain was devoured by wild dogs while out hunting as a divine punishment no doubt for the act of sacrilege he had committed out of his profane love for her.

Critics and crowds alike adored her, universally praising the passion, subtlety, naturalism, raw, naked emotion, and earthy sensuality she brought to each part she played. Lillian Russell, Lillie Langtry, Sarah Bernhardt, Eleonora Duse, Mrs. Leslie Carter, Mrs. Patrick Campbell, Constance Collier, and Ellen Terry were all compared to her and found wanting. And I daresay if Nance had applied herself to musicals and comedies with the same determination as she did to dramatic roles, she would have left Lotta Crabtree and Eva Tanguay coughing and gasping in her dust too, like crippled invalids in comparison, but tragedy was Nance's métier, or her meat and potatoes, as she liked to say.

Offstage, she was earthy, not ethereal; flawed; and far from perfect. Her life was complete chaos, motion and mayhem, and she lived it like a whirling dervish with never a dull or still moment. But that was how Nance liked it. She never thought of the future, of hard times and old age, and lived only for the instant. She was a notorious spendthrift; it was as though money burned her like red-hot coals and she must fling it from her as fast as possible. She ran up debts she could never hope to repay and was always trying to keep one step ahead of the process servers and debt collectors. Anyone who would extend her credit or loan her money was her new best friend. In spite of her habit of not paying, jewelers, furriers, couturiers, milliners, glovers, shoemakers, and perfumers continued to court and oblige her; just to have her photograph in popular periodicals and picture postcards wearing their creations meant money in the bank to them. And Nance was always glad to give them a signed photograph of herself wearing their wares to display in their shop windows.

Morally she was equally bankrupt. Nance was deep in the thrall of a lovely green liqueur she called "the green fairy" and simply could not do without it, nor did she want to, and she constantly smoked strange, exotic cigarettes that made her alternately languid and giddy. She was vain and self-centered and had no concept of fidelity. "People are people; we love who we love!" she would declare grandly before tumbling into bed with whoever took her fancy, was readily available when she was in an amorous disposition, could do something for her career, gave her money, or, like a magician, could make her financial and legal woes vanish for the time being. Male or female, it didn't matter, Nance was far too broad minded for "a little thing like that" to matter. And after her passion was spent, she always proved that the meaning of loyalty was equally elusive to her; once Nance was sated, the need past, the bankroll depleted, or the requisite favor granted, the moment she didn't need her paramour anymore, the affair was over. Her lovers learned all too quickly it did no good to cling; it only annoyed her and turned her sweet memories of them to bitter, as Nance was all too ready to warn them.

Whenever anyone tried to take her to task for her heartless heedlessness, Nance would simply shrug her lovely shoulders and quote Shakespeare: *The fault, dear Brutus, is not in our stars, but in our selves.* Though that hardly excused her conduct and only confirmed that she knew *exactly* what she was doing and didn't care if she rode roughshod over the whole world's hearts. She would happily have trampled every heart in Christendom if it suited her, just to get her way. It was *all* about Nance. *She* was the only one who mattered.

Cataloging her flaws like this, so clear eyed and dispassionate in my old age and hindsight, I cannot help but wonder how I could have loved her so much, but I cannot deny that I did with a passion that still burns like a fever.

As her star rose, Nance also acquired a menagerie, including a baby alligator; an African honking gander; a pink pig she had saved from slaughter because its color exquisitely matched the chiffon gown she was wearing the day she passed it squealing in its pen "as though the poor thing was pleading with the executioner for its life!"; two Great Danes; a matching pair of Russian wolfhounds; a dozen assorted pug dogs, each named after the state in which she had acquired it, and several Pekingese and Pomeranians; a quartet of constantly squawking and talking parrots, including a particularly salty-tongued gray called "Jolly Jack" after the sailor who had been Nance's lover for a night and given him to her at their dawn parting; an exotic toucan with a vibrant striped beak; a pink cockatoo, as well as a white one with a golden crest; five Angora cats; a tiger cub from a smitten maharajah; an ever-increasing family of floppy-eared rabbits; a raccoon; an orange baboon; a chimpanzee; a pair of capuchin monkeys that mated incessantly and an equally amorous set of marmosets; a performing seal that liked to "sing" in the bathtub; an armadillo from an ardent admirer down in Texas who had also named one of his oil wells after Nance; a tortoise whose shell had been encrusted with precious gems by a love-struck millionaire; a snake Nance delighted to wear in lieu of a feather boa; and a large, lazy green lizard that looked rather like a dinosaur and delighted in eating strawberries by the score; all of them sporting diamond collars and gold tags with her initials set in diamonds. A buck-toothed Japanese in silken robes, whom I was never quite sure was male or female, took care of them all.

Nance also added a husband who doubled as her press agent to her entourage, even though his dalliances with stage-smitten young girls got him into no end of trouble. A former carnival barker and medicine show man whose English accent was as false as the noble pedigree he proclaimed to all who would listen, Alfred Hickham had a hungry wolf's eye for nubile beauty, the naïve possessors of which he lured into his den to play Little Red Riding Hood. He promised that through the private acting lessons he was offering them, for only a nominal fee, in the privacy of his hotel room because their talent deserved *special, personal* attention they could not get in a classroom full of dull and mediocre pupils, and under his superior and experienced tutelage, he could transform them into "a glittering star to rival my own wife's dazzling luminosity." It was both sad and surprising how many gullible girls believed him.

Nance always paid off the authorities and angry parents to keep Alfred out of jail or from being tarred and feathered and run out of town by a lynch mob, shrugging her shoulders and saying good-naturedly that Alfie would have done the same for her. And everyone knew she had her own peccadilloes—she liked girls as much as he did. It was not at all an uncommon event for her to usurp one of his prettiest and most promising pupils to serve as her understudy, personal maid, or traveling companion, until boredom set in, of course; then Nance threw the poor girl back to Alfie if he would have her.

By the time I met Nance, the novelty of marriage to a faux English aristocrat had faded and she didn't care what Alfred did or who he did it with, only that a husband was a useful thing to have around at times, like a baby alligator in a diamond collar, and he was overall an amusing fellow and, even more important, an excellent press agent, and a capable but bland, lackluster leading man who knew his place onstage and kept to it and never presumed upon her spotlight.

Unfortunately, Alfred was as fiscally irresponsible as Nance; neither of them was capable of managing the company's, or their private, finances, and money flowed through their fingers like water. Several times the costumes and props of her company had been attached in lawsuits. Once she even showed up in court wearing the very fur coat she was being sued over nonpayment for. But Nance didn't care; she was wild, irresponsible, and thoughtless, the freest of the free spirits. She took the Bard's immortal line *all the world's a stage and the men and women merely players* quite literally. She lived by it and was *always* on. There was *never* a moment of quiet with Nance unless she was unconscious. And yet, despite her flamboyance and her reputation for releasing raw, unbridled emotions upon the stage that breathed new life back into all the old but perennially popular roles, in real life there was a curious almost soulless quality about her, as though she were merely an empty vessel for others to fill, a medium that the spirits spoke through. You never really knew if it was the *real* Nance O'Neil speaking or if someone else, a playwright or press agent, had written the lines.

I think a reporter from *The Boston Herald* described her best. The morning after our first night together, while I still lay cocooned in Nance's champagne-colored satin sheets, tensely enduring the orange baboon's insistence on searching my head for fleas, Nance donned a demure dress of flowing white chiffon, loosely did up her hair, sent for the Angora kittens, kissed me *"adieu* for now," and went out into the sitting room to assume her carefully calculated pose for the man *The Boston Herald* was sending to write a feature.

At once pensive and playful, maternal and virginal, she arranged herself upon the floor, playing with the kittens, with the sunbeams pouring in through the windows, catching her just right, and shining a spotlight, like a halo, onto her golden hair. When the reporter walked in and saw her thus, he was completely enchanted.

In her sun-flooded apartments, he wrote, *her masses of glorious golden hair were caught loosely up on the top of her shapely head, and held in place by a huge Spanish comb. Nance O'Neil is not always tragic, nor even serious minded. She impresses one from the start as a girl, a very young girl. She is as unaffected by her great success as a child. It may be truthfully said that she is even more interesting personally than she is as an actress—and that is saying a great deal. She is subject to melancholy and decidedly moody in temperament. There is a constant intermingling of sunshine and shadow in her nature. And it is this that makes her so entirely fascinating.*

When she came back to me, she laughed about it as she nestled on the bed beside me, snuggling deep into my arms.

"Don't *ever* believe *anything* an actress ever says, darling; we never open our mouths to speak or even to kiss except to further our careers. All the kisses and pretty speeches are to that end and no other. The stage is the only lover we can ever be true to."

I laughed with her at what I thought was a clever quip, a featherlight flippancy of her profession. I should have seen the warning in those words. I should have heeded it. In all the time I knew her, it was the most honest thing she ever said.

She was a rare charmer and very skillful at manipulating her image, as well as other people. But none of that mattered at the time, though in hindsight it should have. But I was head over heels in love and willing to overlook any and all of Nance's foibles and flaws; she was only human after all. I chose to be blind and believe our souls had been wandering in the wilderness all these years, crying out for each other, until, at long last, fate brought us together and that she would never discard me as coldly and cavalierly as she did all her other conquests. *I* was different; *I* was her soul mate.

Before the next leg of her tour, we detoured, for a much needed respite. I took Nance to Maplecroft. It was Heaven having her there with me despite Emma's sour-faced frowns and private protests that Nance was using me and making a fool of me and I was too blind to see it. Emma's small Fall River mind equated all actresses, even a star like Nance O'Neil, the greatest tragedienne of the modern stage, with common whores. She considered Nance's presence in our household not only a scandal we could never hope to live down but also a personal insult against all decent, God-fearing women. Father, Emma said, would turn in his grave, like a chicken roasting on a spit, if he knew we were hosting a troupe of actors in our house. We quarreled every time Emma could get me alone. She said I was dazzled by the footlights and glamour and bewitched by the world of make-believe and happy endings. She was right, she summed everything up so precisely, if not at all nicely, but I didn't care. I was in love.

"If I am dreaming let me dream some more!" I said dismissively, and blocked my ears to the outraged torrent spewing from my sister's mouth.

I remember the first morning when Nance floated downstairs straight into my arms, just like a dream, in a flowing gown of soft pink mousseline with wisps of her flaxen hair, caught up in a loose topknot, caressing her cameo-perfect porcelain-pale face, idly swinging a straw bonnet, trimmed with silk flowers, by its broad pink satin streamers. She looked like she belonged at Maplecroft. I have a picture of her in that dress, holding that bonnet behind her back, staring coyly out at the camera, at once angelic and fey. It stands in a silver frame beside my bed and, even now, I lay flowers, as an offering, a tribute, before it each and every day. Sometimes I even light a candle. The heart wants what it wants; I still love her. But I was just a new sensation, a novelty, the latest in a long line of diversions, to Nance. I am too wise a fool to pretend it was ever anything more no matter how much I like to imagine otherwise. Like Mr. Carroll's muse Alice, Nance took me to Wonderland: *Still she haunts me, phantomwise, . . . moving under skies / Never seen by waking eyes.*

I spared no expense to entertain her and her troupe. Every night the house blazed with golden light, and glorious music, played by a full orchestra, wafted out into the darkness. There were hothouse palms in gilded pots and silver trays of sweet and savory delights. Lobster tails and oysters, steaks, and cakes galore. Tiered silver trays towered over the tables displaying the most tempting array of pastries. Champagne and Nance's magical elixir of the green fairy flowed like water, and if any of my fair-weather friends from the Women's Christian Temperance Union had dared say one word about it I would have snapped my fingers in their face.

Nance wore a clinging mint-green silk gown embroidered in silver and gold with a wreath of blue-green satin roses around her naked shoulders, and she sparkled with emeralds, sapphires, and diamonds everywhere she could think to put them.

And I wore the most *fantastic* creation of chartreuse and amber, cut daringly low and baring my shoulders in a fashion that was far too young for me. But that was how Nance made me feel—young and alive! When I was with her I was in the springtime of my life and not the autumn. My freshly hennaed hair was piled perilously high in a root-straining pompadour garnished with gold tinsel fringe and amber and chartreuse satin roses and I was weighed down with jewels.

I was a woman of forty-five making a fool and a spectacle of myself, but I was so in love I didn't even care if the whole world was laughing at me. I was so *gloriously* happy I could even laugh at myself.

We danced in each other's arms; none of the theatrical folk thought there was anything unusual about it, and even Nance's husband smiled indulgently and saluted me as we waltzed past. I took puffs from her strange cigarettes and heady, intoxicating sips from her glass that made my head spin beautifully. The green fairy seemed to make the whole world shine; everything and everyone was beautiful and brilliant that night, and I couldn't stop smiling and bestowing a thousand compliments left and right. I just had to stop everyone and tell them how wonderful they were and to thank them for coming to grace my home with their glorious presence.

As the evening wore on, Nance and I stole away to my summer bedroom. I was wild to be alone with her. Every time I looked at her I wanted to tear off her clothes and mine. On the pink-and-chocolate-striped sofa, Nance sat back, lost in ecstasy, the liqueur in her crystal glass glowing like the most perfect peridot or that subtle hint of green at the heart of a white rose, as I knelt reverently at her feet, lifted her skirts, and licked her sex, lapping it up like a cunning, greedy cat left alone in the kitchen where a bowl of rich cream had been left sitting out on the counter. I couldn't get enough of her! She felt like liquid silk and I was *starved* for her!

That was when Emma walked in like a black storm cloud to rain on our picnic.

That was the end. That one wild, rash, uninhibited "lewd and unnatural and unforgivable" act cost me my sister. Emma hurriedly packed her clothes—every garment she owned fit into a single carpet bag—and walked out without a backward glance. She left all her religious ephemera behind for me, saying tartly that I had greater need of the Lord's grace and forgiveness than she.

I ran down the stairs after her, weeping and shouting at her— "Emma, *PLEASE!*"—heedless of what my guests might think, trying desperately to make her understand, but she wouldn't stop walking or even turn around and look at me.

"*I fear for your soul, Lizzie!*" Those were the last words my sister ever spoke to me, shouted back over her shoulder, as she slammed the front door.

I never saw her again. We never exchanged another word, not even by letter; those I wrote to her were returned unopened. She went to live briefly with the Reverend Jubb and his sister, and then with Orrin's mother, Caroline Mason Gardner, in Swansea.

Caroline doted on Emma, they were not that far apart in age, and the two of them became best friends. She even insisted that my sister accompany her on a holiday trip to sunny Catalina Island one year. Orrin, back from Tennessee to visit his mother, was with them. I heard he also became "quite fond" of Emma. Caroline sent me many postcards, enthusing about the fragrant fruit trees, bright, sunny beaches, Sugar Loaf Bay, and the fascinating fishes spied through glass-bottomed boats while sailing over the sunlit blue waters, but not one word from, or about, Orrin or Emma. Did that silence, I have often since wondered, say more than words? They had such a good time in Catalina that the following year the three of them went to New Orleans, and there were more postcards about Mardi Gras and alligator parks.

I've often wondered, despite the seventeen-year age difference, did Orrin, unable to have me, transfer his affections to Emma? I knew my sister was far too timid to defy social convention and marry a man almost two decades her junior, but that doesn't answer the question: *Did they fall in love?*

Over the years that followed, I heard many bedeviling rumors that kept me awake at night. But I never discovered the truth, if there ever was any truth behind those rumors. I never delved into the matter or asked any questions of Caroline or any mutual acquaintances who would have been in a position to know. I was too afraid of what might be the answers. The truth is, I didn't want to know.

Three years later, Emma abruptly left Caroline's home and moved to Newmarket, New Hampshire, where, calling herself "Miss Gardner," she led a reclusive existence in a cheap rented room on a farmstead belonging to a pair of spinsters, the Connor sisters, leaving only at dusk to take a long, solitary walk in the gloaming. She attended church services every Sunday with her veil down and rebuffed all attempts at friendship. Sugar cubes, which she had long been addicted to sucking on—they were cheaper than candy—and a rocking chair were the only luxuries she permitted herself. She kept her money in the bank and wore her plain black dresses and sturdy leather shoes until they fell apart and were past mending before she would deign to purchase new. Word later came back to me—as any unpleasant news had a way of doing—that whenever people asked about her family, Emma said she had had a sister once, but that she was dead.

I suppose it *had* to end sometime, but I wish it had not been like *that*.

But at the time of our parting, I was too enraptured with Nance to try to win Emma back, and later . . . after Nance . . . I was too embarrassed. Emma would have only said, *I told you so,* and even if she only actually spoke those words once, she would say them again every time she looked at the disgusting, unnatural thing I had become in her eyes. And by then there were also those rumors about Orrin and Emma standing between us. So I just let it go. For better or worse, I let things be.

"Never mind," Nance purred huskily into my ear as she led me back to my bedroom, soothing me with sips from her glass, urging me to let the green fairy take all the shameful, painful feelings and inhibitions away and leave only the body behind and all its wild naked animal urges. Her hand was at my breast, and then between my legs, making me forget . . . at least for a time. "Never mind, Lizbeth; you still have me. . . ." she purred.

But in the end, I lost Nance too. Nothing worked out the way I thought it would!

Our idyll continued. There was still time before Nance must resume her tour and she *begged* me to come with her to Tyngsboro; she *longed* to show me her farm. After Emma's abrupt departure, I just wanted to run away, to forget and escape, from all the gossip in Fall River about our abrupt parting after so many years and lose myself in the world of waking dreams I dwelled in whenever I was with Nance. So I went most willingly to her farm. I would have followed her anywhere, I think.

She was so proud of that quaint brown and white—or "chocolate and ivory," as Nance picturesquely described it—Tudor-style gingerbread house sitting ensconced in the heart of a lovely garden. She called it "Brindley Farm." She was always buying cows, donkeys, goats, pigs, and sheep whose sweet, docile dispositions or attractive appearances caught her eye and having them shipped back to the farm. She chose the chickens for their plumage too, declaring that the speckled hens' eggs tasted the best and she absolutely abhorred the plain, boring white ones.

Every morning, sitting up in bed, with diamonds sparkling like stars on her ears and around her wrists, she would blissfully breakfast on scrambled eggs and champagne and sigh about how many times she had to absolutely "*stifle,* like a murderer pressing a pillow over a victim's face, with all my might, the urge to abandon the stage for the simple life, domesticity, sweet tranquility, the homely virtues, the fireside, and little children calling me Mother."

She played this scene several times to great effect for the so-called "gentlemen of the press" who applauded her selfless self-sacrifice, nobly devoting her life to bringing pleasure to thousands of theatergoers while steadfastly denying herself the dearest, sweetest, most natural instincts of a woman's homebound heart.

"It is one of the vain regrets of my life!" she would heartrendingly sigh. "But I have schooled myself to say to all who talk to me of a home life, though that is ever a sore and tender spot with me, that I have no thoughts of settling down at all—the stage is my life, and I have ground my very soul under heel to succeed there!"

I remember a magazine feature, "A Day at Nance O'Neil's Farm," in which she posed for a series of photographs gathering eggs; herding the sheep; sitting by the pond playing with fluffy yellow ducklings; milking a cow; bathing a billy goat in her own bathtub with her lily-of-the-valley-scented soap; standing proudly, like a domestic goddess, beside the kitchen stove holding a large potato speared awkwardly upon a fork and smilingly declaring in the caption below that she was about to *bake* it for her husband's supper before plunging it into a pot of boiling water; gingerly holding a broom as though she hadn't the faintest clue what to do with it; sitting with a lapful of knitting needles and a mound of hopelessly tangled wool; and relaxing by the fire at day's end dozing dreamily with her head resting on Alfred's knee as he, per their nightly custom, read to her from one of the great classics of literature—actually a sporting magazine concealed inside a copy of *David Copperfield*. Life for Nance was indeed a stage, and she was *always* on it, playing a part; I sometimes wondered if she had *any* idea who she truly was.

It all reminded me of Marie Antoinette's pretend farm I had read about where servants bathed and perfumed the animals before they were led into the royal presence. Nance even had two cows named Blanche and Brunette that she liked to take for walks as though they were dogs while she smiled and waved hello to the locals, or "quaint peasants," as she called her neighbors. And she liked to dress up like Little Bo Peep, replete with sunbonnet and ringlets and ruffled pantalets, in a Mother Goose pantomime to herd the sheep, all of them curiously clean for farm animals and wearing blue or pink satin bows to denote their sex.

Like carefree young girls in bare feet and dresses of cheerful calico—Nance in green and yellow and me in blue and red—with our hair down in pigtails, the ends tied with ribbons to match our dresses, we wandered hand in hand all over the farm. One wonderful drowsy afternoon we made the most passionate love in a haystack. Afterward, Nance told me that the farm was haunted, that on nights when the moon was bright a pair of lovers from a bygone century roamed about and relived their own forbidden passion.

Back in the days when the Puritans still held sway, the farm had been an inn. The innkeeper had had a beautiful daughter, with long golden hair and a sweet, docile disposition. One day, while gathering mushrooms in the forest nearby, she had met a gypsy girl, part of a roving band that camped on the outskirts of town. The two had fallen instantly in love. And though the innkeeper's daughter struggled with what she perceived as a great and terrible sin and fears for the fate of her immortal soul, she could not renounce her love. They continued to meet, whenever they could, in the woods, but as the weather grew colder they grew bolder and moved their secret trysts inside the barn. One night they were discovered in a naked embrace in the hayloft. The gypsy girl was accused of using witchcraft to seduce the innkeeper's daughter and taken out and hanged from a tree on the grounds. Her beloved died shortly afterward, of a broken heart, the legend said. Some versions of the story claimed she had hanged herself from the same tree or drowned herself in the pond.

"And to think I shall lose this place," Nance sighed as she lay in my arms, her head on my shoulder, drowsy with love, "if I cannot raise seventy-five hundred dollars."

"We shall have to see what we can do to prevent that," I answered, thoroughly under her spell, so caught up in her web I would have promised her the moon on a velvet pillow or the stars for a necklace if she had hinted that such was her desire.

One late Sunday afternoon, our last at the farm before the tour resumed, Nance and I were lazing away the day in the library. She was restless and got up from beside me and went and plucked a book from a shelf and carried it to the desk. I thought nothing of it and went on reading my own volume until she leaned over the back of the sofa and kissed my cheek and presented the book to me with a flourish.

It was a beautiful book with a deep-mustard-yellow cloth cover embellished with wreaths of golden flowers and a sky-blue satin marker sewn into the binding. It was a collection of poems by her friend, and sometime lover, Thomas Bailey Aldrich, who had turned his epic poem about Judith of Bethulia into a play to create a worthy showcase for Nance's "immense and awe inspiring talent."

She had taken the trouble to copy one of the poems out onto the flyleaf just for me. It was called "Flower and Thorn."

> *Take them and keep them,*
> *Silvery thorn and flower,*
> *Plucked just at random*
> *In the rosy weather—*
>
> *Snowdrops and pansies,*
> *Sprigs of wayside heather,*
> *And five-leafed wild rose*
> *Dead within the hour.*

Take them and keep them:
Who can tell? Some day, dear,
(Though they be withered,
Flower and thorn and blossom,)
Held for an instant
Up against thy bosom,
They might make December
Seem to thee like May, dear!

For My Lizbeth
With Love from
Your Daphne

Daphne—that was my secret name for her. I alone called her
that. The idea had come to me one day when I saw her swimming
naked in the pond, her body white, her hair like liquid gold floating
out about her bare shoulders, among the pink and white water
lilies. Daphne, for the chaste and beautiful water nymph of ancient
lore, upon whom the gods took pity and transformed into a laurel
tree the moment the lascivious Apollo's eager arms closed around
her—thereby preserving her chastity and saving her from rape. There
she would stand by the river, stiff, proud, stately, and unyielding
forever as a warning to presumptuous lovers who would force their
lust, and their will, upon another.

Why couldn't I see beyond the sentiment, that this pretty gift of
poetry contained an implicit warning? My Daphne was telling me
that if I tried to hold on to her I would be left with nothing. But I
couldn't think then; she was in my arms again, nuzzling and nest-
ling, and telling me how happy she was that I had decided to go to
Chicago with her.

In hindsight I suppose Nance was very happy to have me there.
A lawsuit was looming and costumes and scenery she needed had
been seized by an irate theater manager after Nance defaulted on a
loan. Nance insisted it was all "mean-spirited meanness" and she
couldn't remember any such loan; the money was a gift, she in-

sisted. She was *determined* to challenge the charges in court, and I followed her bravely into the arena, despite the clamor of photographers and newspapermen. I put on a dress of pearl-gray and pale-mauve satin trimmed with dotted black net, ropes of pearls, my silver fox fur, with a mammoth corsage of orchids, and an enormous veiled hat the size of a serving platter erupting with a riot of silk orchids and sleek pink, purple, and magenta feathers, and sat beside Nance, holding her hand and nodding encouragingly throughout the ordeal. And when she lost the case and burst into tears because she had spent the last $25 she had in the world on the orchid corsage she was wearing and her own lawyer was going to sue her because she couldn't pay his fee, I consoled her by writing a check, to discharge her legal obligations and secure the release of her costumes and props. The smile she gave me in return was like the sunlight breaking through the rain and vivid blue skies chasing away the grim black thunderclouds.

After Chicago a train whisked us away to New York. We dined every night at Delmonico's. I remember sitting there simmering with jealously over a lobster dinner while Nance danced, flirted, and laughed with her admirers. I clenched my fists so tight my white kid gloves split. My face, captured in the mirrors lining the silk-papered walls, was as red as the velvet gown Nance had chosen for me. I sat there and watched her waltz obliviously right past me in the arms of a handsome, silver-haired financier, anxiously fingering the gold scorpion brooch, Nance's own, that she had herself pinned on to my bodice as we dressed for the evening as a gift to thank me for chasing her financial woes away and to remember her by forever. As if I could *ever* forget *her!*

She reveled in the attention of her admirers, male and female; she simply could not get enough of their adoration, gifts, and flattery. Though she kissed me every chance she got and called me her "angel" and her "lady bountiful," I was no longer enough. She had even started to plead exhaustion and headaches to keep me from her bed.

At first, I believed her, until, restless, and unable to sleep without her beside me, I rose and peeped out into the corridor and saw Nance's door open and a black-haired girl with caramel skin in a beaded topaz satin gown softly slipping out with the dawn, satin high heels twinkling with faux diamonds in her hand as she tiptoed in her silk stockings down the rose-carpeted corridor to her own room. I recognized her as Alfred's latest protégé and the newest member of the troupe, a Brazilian beauty named Ricca who was obviously taking her role as Nance's understudy quite literally into bed and directly under the great star herself.

Yet I couldn't leave Nance or even openly reproach her. I feigned blind ignorance and never said a word about Ricca and just went on smiling, showering Nance with affection, gifts, and money and playing the charade of love, hoping she would eventually tire of her new dalliance and come back to me. More fool I not to realize that there would *always* be a *new* diversion to delight Nance. If she didn't find them, they would find her. Variety was the spice of Nance's life; she lived for novelty and could not abide stagnation and boredom.

But the curtain always has to fall. The night *finally* came when it was no longer possible for me to pretend anymore and she turned all my gold and silver tinsel dreams to cold gray, dead ashes. I was dancing in her arms, in my bloodred velvet gown, cheek to cheek, heart to heart, gold scorpion at my breast, when Nance coyly alluded to the *greatest* gift of all, one that only *I* could give her. Then, when the hint eluded me, she came brazenly out with it and asked the impossible of me.

"Give me your life, dearest Lizbeth," she begged, her voice sultry and hot against my ear, her tongue flicking out, to tease the lobe, just like a snake's forked tongue.

She was asking me to give her the once in a lifetime role all actresses dream of, the one she would be forever identified with; no matter how many other actresses attempted it in the decades that followed, it would always be *her* role. She wanted to portray me in a play. I would be given *full* credit as authoress even if I didn't write a single word and left it all to an anonymous phantom pen Nance would hire, and we would appear together before the press and I would publicly declare that Nance was the *only* one I trusted to do full justice to the story of my life, that no other actress could breathe such life and heart into my personal tragedy.

I felt stung, used, and betrayed. For the first, and only, time I said *No* to Nance. And so she said *good-bye* to me, but not in actual words, at least not then. And I was still too much in love with her to see the truth behind her sad little smile as she laid her head upon my shoulder and let her tears soak through my lace collar as we finished what was to be our last dance.

"It was just an idea, that's all; let's forget the whole thing," she whispered. Of course, she didn't mean a word of it. Forget and forgive was a concept completely foreign to Nance.

But I was only too happy to agree and go on pretending.

When the music ended and we sat down, as a conciliatory gesture I drew my checkbook out of my purse.

"Now you need never worry about losing your farm," I whispered as I handed her a check for $10,000.

I thought it was enough. But Nance didn't even say thank you. She just folded the check in half and stuffed it down the front of her marigold velvet bodice for safekeeping, then sat forward and moodily pillowed her chin against her fist and wearily began reciting:

> "Tomorrow, and tomorrow, and tomorrow,
> creeps in this petty pace from day to day,
> To the last syllable of recorded time;
> And all our yesterdays have lighted fools
> The way to dusty death. Out, out brief candle!
> Life's but a walking shadow; a poor player,
> That struts and frets his hour upon the stage,
> And then is heard no more: it is a tale
> Told by an idiot, full of sound and fury,
> Signifying nothing."

Then she yawned right in my face and languidly lit another cigarette.

I knew then, with my sinking heart, terrified by the plunge it was so suddenly and abruptly taking, back into darkness and lonely oblivion, that she really was bored with me, and tired of me, and that Ricca and all the other casual dalliances were not just passing fancies, merely the continuation of a long-established pattern. And, even worse, Nance was disappointed in me, because I had finally said *no,* where before I had *always* said *yes.* That *no* was the death knell of our love, if it ever really was love, and about that I had my doubts even if I didn't want to acknowledge them. I only knew I felt let down, like *I* had failed *her,* even though I knew I hadn't done anything wrong; I just didn't want my life story paraded before the footlights. I didn't want to be a playwright or provide the fodder for any more headlines. It wasn't a slight against Nance herself, or her talent. I just wanted the scandal to die and to be allowed to live out my life in peace, blessedly free of the macabre notoriety that had for so long surrounded me.

And if I had failed her, well . . . *she* had also failed *me.* She was the one acting like a fickle, petulant child casting aside a once-favored toy just because it was no longer new. The only thing I didn't know was how to fix it without crumbling and caving in, saying *Yes* in spite of every screaming instinct I possessed, and forever hating myself for it.

If I gave in and gave her what she asked, I would only be buying more time with Nance, but history was bound to repeat itself eventually, boredom would again set in, and I would silently simmer with repressed resentment, I would get tired of saying *Yes,* and the death knell would sound again, and then it really would be final; there would be no last-minute reprieve for the condemned.

It really is better, a little voice in the back of my mind that I didn't want to hear whispered, *to just get it over with.*

Sometimes it really is hard not to hate the truth. But I was *desperate* to hold on even though I knew it was like trying to pull a tiger back by its tail when it wants nothing more to do with you; it is bound to turn around and bite you. I just didn't want to let go of the dream.

I knew something was different the moment my foot crossed the threshold into her splendid suite at the Bellevue Hotel. I *knew* she was leaving; I think I even knew that she was leaving me, not just New York, but I didn't want to face the truth. I kept hoping the check that would allow her to keep her precious farm was recompense enough for denying her my life. I kept praying, *PLEASE let everything be all right!*

A flush of shame suffused my cheeks as I remembered the last time I had been in this suite. Pictures I would rather forget flashed like lightning through my mind. The drink of the green fairy. The bedroom. Naked skin. The sweaty tangle of satin sheets soon kicked to the floor.

I was willing to do *anything* to please Nance, to hold on to Nance, except the *one* thing she wanted most—to take my life and make it her own, to flash and flaunt my tragedy before the footlights, to make my ghostwritten play my all too public confession, brazenly delivered to all and any who could afford the price of a theater ticket.

Shame flooded me as the memories came rushing back like a series of rude slaps. Nance's husband, Alfred, in his plush purple velvet dressing gown and matching slippers, a tassel bobbing on one toe as he swung his foot to the rhythm of the record playing on the phonograph, something whimsical and merry by Gilbert and Sullivan. *The Mikado:* "Three Little Maids from School Are We" played over and over endlessly. And was there, at some point, at least for a time, another body between Nance's and mine in that big bed, one with smooth golden-caramel skin? My mind is all a cloudy muddle and in truth I do not *want* to remember.

I can only blame the green fairy. No, that is a lie! I can only blame myself! Maybe it wasn't *The Mikado* after all; maybe it was *The Pirates of Penzance?* I hope so! Somehow that is easier to live with than "Three Little Maids." Am I making any sense at all? My mind is so muddy not even a catfish could see in the sluggish, murky water that fills my head whenever I recall that night, my last night, with Nance.

Yes, I am nearly certain now that it was *The Pirates of Penzance!* I see myself clinging tight to Nance, bathing her bare skin with my tears, *begging* her not to leave me to pine, alone and desolate. And I hear her laughing, boldly declaring it better by far to live and die a pirate king, just like she always said that it was better to be an outlaw than to not be free. And Alfred, sitting with all the sangfroid of a modern major general, with a snifter of brandy in one hand and a cigar in the other, in a wing chair at the foot of the bed, swaying his foot to the music, the golden tassel on his slipper jouncing, jiggling like a worm on a fisherman's hook, *watching* as Nance and I... Nance and I... the green fairy's magical elixir... the giggling wanton naked loss of inhibition, wiggling and writhing, skin upon skin, hot flesh upon cool satin, the taste of her... the feel of her... like melted silk!

I shut my eyes against the shameful flood of images, like lurid photographs flickering past in a pornographer's hands, just a quick peek, to titillate and entice a purchase, then opened them again on the sun-flooded scene of chaos that lay spread out before me like the debris a hurricane had left behind.

There were trunks, boxes, and valises strewn everywhere, their contents spilling out or stuffed haphazardly in. Dresses, undergarments, jewels, hairbrushes, shoes, stockings, hats, gloves, shawls, and parasols and all sorts of things were scattered everywhere, across the floor, draped over tables and chairs. A monkey and an angora cat were climbing the curtains; they had already succeeded in pulling down one and it lay pooled upon the floor providing a sumptuous feast for the baby goat that was the latest addition to Nance's menagerie. The baboon was swinging from the crystal chandelier, the parrots were squawking and talking, Jolly Jack was alternately swearing and asking for a cracker, and all the dogs dashed about in circles barking. What the management would say when they beheld the damage Nance's pets had wreaked upon their finest suite I could only imagine. I supposed I would have to write another check.

Talking ceaselessly of everything and nothing, Nance flitted about like a hummingbird from flower to flower, never lighting anywhere for more than a moment, issuing a volley of instructions to her black maid, Jemimah, and her new secretary, the effete Patrick in his skintight lemon-and-chocolate-checkered trousers and lavender waistcoat, with a green carnation in the buttonhole of his forest-green velvet coat marking him as a lingering devotee of the dead and disgraced Oscar Wilde. Her golden hair was caught up loosely in a disorderly topknot, and she was still in her petticoats. Jemimah dogged her steps, diligently trying to lace up her sea-green satin corset and imploring Miss Nance to be still, "just for a moment, honey!" But Nance must always be in motion; stillness was for corpses, she always used to say.

"Nance!" Alfred bellowed as he strode into the room, trailing a cloud of cigar smoke behind him, fluttering a paper angrily in his hand. "Have a look at this, Nance!"

She paused only for an instant, so that I marveled that she could take in even the barest gist of what was written there.

"Violet gloves accented with gilt embroidery and garnets—what a frivolous expense!" she declared, tossing her head as she moved off again, causing a long hank of golden hair to tumble down her back and her maid to roll her eyes and heave an exasperated sigh as she fumbled about inside an open trunk for more hairpins. "If I were you, Albert, I would refuse to pay it!"

That was Nance's way. And when Alfred bellowed back, "I intend to!" she nodded her approval.

When she saw me reflected in the mirror above the mantel where her raccoon was trying to fish the poor goldfish out of their bowl for breakfast she spun round to greet me. It was then that I saw a certain disturbing vacancy in her eyes. There was a twitch at her lips, causing them to hover momentarily somewhere between a frown and a smile, before the switch was thrown and she became *The* Nance O'Neil, the flamboyant and famous actress whose whole life was a stage.

"*Lizbeth!*" she extravagantly exclaimed, and theatrically flung wide her arms and came to embrace me as if she were crossing a stage and there was an audience watching and applauding her entrance. There was something distinctly artificial in the way she kissed me once upon each cheek, her lips, and her hands at my waist, barely touching the skin she had once so fervently caressed.

I had been right. Something *was* different. I knew it. I felt it. I could not deny it. I wanted to cry, I wanted to scream, I wanted to fall down on my knees and beg and plead and do whatever I had to do to fix what was wrong, but I didn't know how except by giving up, giving in, and giving her the story of my life, and *that* I could *never* do. I felt confusion and hurt flood every part of me. Words deserted me; if I ever had any gift for them it abandoned me, leaving me feeling stupid and small, as if my tongue were of no more use than a fat and lazy garden slug.

I didn't hear her—I was too lost in my frantic, fearful emotions—but Nance sent the others out.

And there we stood, face-to-face, amidst the chaos of Nance's belongings, for what we both now knew would be the final time.

"It's over." I felt the words being torn out of me, but I *had* to say them.

For one mad moment I thought that perhaps if I said them first they would not hurt so much. But they did; oh, they did! Tears overflowed my eyes and I felt them on my cheeks and I *hated* myself because I could not keep them back. I didn't want Nance to see me weep. I wanted to be sophisticated and regal at the end of our affair, blasé and nonchalant in my defeat; I didn't want anyone to see my humiliation and know how much it hurt me.

I thought of the things I had done with this woman only last night, and before an audience, and shame flooded in and drowned any desire I might have still felt. I felt dirty and vulgar. In the deep, dark recesses of my heart, locked away to try to keep me from feeling the pain again and again every day, I *still* loved Orrin Gardner and longed for his touch. I still awoke some nights after dreaming of him easing into me and our bodies becoming one. But then Nance had come, like a whirlwind, into my life, and now I had to reap the storm.

Nance, forgetting that her corset was only haphazardly tied, turned away to carelessly pull a dark-green afternoon dress embroidered with coral and gold roses over her head. She didn't bother with the back; her maid and the others would return in a little while, after I was gone, and someone would attend to it—*someone always did*. Someone *always* took care of Nance O'Neil and cleaned up the chaos and disarray that were as natural to her as breathing.

"Long ago when I was just a silly green girl my first lover taught me an invaluable lesson, Lizbeth. As a parting gift I shall pass it on to you so that you may profit from it on future occasions." Now she was speaking to me like a stranger despite the deep intimacy of the subject.

Always the actress, she spoke as if she were onstage; her car-

riage, her tone, her gestures, the way she held herself, suddenly became different, as if she were positioning herself, subtly shifting
angles, considering the lighting and the audience's view of her,
calculating how to show herself to best advantage. She was playing
a beautiful, sophisticated woman of the world who was about to
confide, to a more drab and naïve old-maid acquaintance, a perti-
nent secret as the audience sat forward in their seats breathless with
anticipation.

She put her hands lightly upon my shoulders and asked a question: "If you are afraid someone you love is going to leave you, what
do you do?"

"Find a way to make them stay?" I whispered in a tear-choked,
tremulous little voice, *hating* myself all the time for it, and her too,
for making me play out this ludicrous and demeaning finale. I
glanced down at my purse, dangling from my wrist, and thought of
money and everything it could, and could not, buy.

Nance tilted her head and sagely posed another question: "And
if you cannot?"

I shook my head as my detested tears rolled down my face.

Nance tilted my chin up and made me look at her.

"You leave first so you do not have to watch them walking away
from you." She smiled sadly. "You should have left me first, Lizbeth, instead of waiting for me to leave you. It was inevitable, you
know, my dear. It is *always* better to be the one who walks away
rather than the one who is walked away from. It's all a question of
timing." She patted my hand and smiled at me. "And over the
years, I've gotten rather good at it. My timing is *impeccable—everyone* says so!"

She looked at me expectantly, as if she were waiting for a round
of applause. But I would not give it to her, I would be damned first!
Instead, I pulled my veil down over my hat brim to hide my red and
blotchy wet face. I suddenly felt as if my reddened eyes and nose
and the tracks of my tears were victories to add to her lengthy list of
accolades, trophies she would prize forever.

"You've been pretending for so long you have forgotten what is
real!" I said bitterly. "I was never real to you, not as a person. I was
just a diversion, a novelty, a bottomless purse and a story you

wanted me to give you so you could make it that once in a lifetime role every actress longs for! Tell me, Nance, was it *thrilling* to bed a supposed murderess? That's one more thing you can boast about! Another story you can dine out on!" As my tears overwhelmed me, I rushed out the door, thankful only that I did not crash into the wall beside it; I was crying so hard I could hardly see.

I never looked back, so I don't know how she received my words, or if they even made a dent, the faintest little pinprick in the hard, high-polished, glossy veneer of the actress Nance O'Neil. I only knew that she would go on. She never *really* loved me; I was never *real* to her, only a character, a role, one of those shunned and unloved women she excelled at portraying, that she hoped to add to her repertoire, to cement her everlasting fame as the actress who had brought the *true* story of her intimate friend Lizzie Borden to the stage. Nance might regret losing the part, but she would never regret losing me, no more or less than she did any other lover at the end of the affair.

Headlines—the bane of my existence, the hammer striking the killing blow to my heart, shattering it like scarlet glass—*screamed* at me from the breakfast tray I had forgotten to phone downstairs and cancel.

LIZZIE BORDEN TO BE A PLAYWRIGHT!

DECLARES NANCE O'NEIL

THE ONLY ACTRESS

WHO CAN DO JUSTICE TO

THE STORY OF HER LIFE!

It would surely be the role of a lifetime, more memorable even than Miss O'Neil's passionate and intense portrayal of Lady Macbeth my nemesis, Mr. Edwin H. Porter, opined.

She had been *so* sure of me, that I would do *anything* she asked, she had given an exclusive story to Mr. Porter!

I picked up the phone on the table beside the bed in my own opulent suite at the Bellevue Hotel and asked to be connected with my bank. I canceled the check that I had given Nance. Then I packed my bags, summoned a porter, and ordered a carriage to take me to the station and went back to Fall River, and my maple-shrouded haven, to lick my wounds in splendid solitude. I knew then, I would be alone for the rest of my life.

I was done with love.

Chapter 13

After Nance, I wanted to wrap my heart in barbed wire so no one could ever touch it again. It was always the same: every time I let someone in . . . they raised my hopes only to dash them, and when I lost them, when they left me, as they *always* did, the pain was *so* great, I wanted to die.

Then the telegram came. It arrived on August 4, 1905, the thirteenth anniversary of that fateful day. It was signed only *B,* but I *knew* who it was who was asking to be remembered to me from a little town I had never heard of called Anaconda, somewhere in the wilds and wide rugged open spaces of Montana.

I traveled discreetly by train, with my veil down, under an assumed name, in a private compartment. My heart felt like a hummingbird fluttering inside my chest, its feathery wingtips tickling my rib cage all the way. I shivered and shook. I was happy and afraid. What did she want? What did this mean after all this time? There were long, breath-stealing moments when I feared it was more than nervous excitement that assailed my heart but the sort of palpitations and shortness of breath that might require a doctor's attention instead.

But I held on. I sat at my window and watched the miles of countryside roll by, the trees giving way to barren spaces, the brown earth to bloodred, and I saw buffalos and wild horses running free and unfettered beneath the most beautiful blue sky I had ever seen.

The hot Montana sun made me regret my choice of a plain, serviceable navy blue broadcloth traveling suit and black hat with net veiling; the velvet violets that adorned it soon looked as wilted as if they were real. My hair frizzed wildly and my face was a sweaty, florid, mottled mess, and perspiration plastered my white shirtwaist and undergarments to my skin, making large unsightly stains blossom beneath the armpits that would leave permanent yellow stains. I was most uncomfortable and the dust made me cough and sneeze and my eyes red, watery, and itchy despite the protection of my veil. I was constantly employing my handkerchief to try to get a piece of bothersome grit out.

At the depot, I hired a carriage to take me to her.

I found Bridget on a tumbledown farm, with a roof that no doubt let in more rain than it kept out, with an equally dilapidated lean-to attached to serve as a barn for the family's cow, and a parched and pathetic vegetable garden where only straggly sunburned weeds seemed to flourish. Barefoot and smiling, radiant despite the squalor, surrounded by several small ragged, barefoot children, with chickens pecking in the dirt around her feet, Bridget sang as she wielded a rusty, weather-worn hatchet to chop logs from the woodpile into kindling.

I recognized the song at once.

> "Oh, dem golden slippers,
> Oh, dem golden slippers
> Golden slippers I'se going to wear
> Because they look so neat.

> "Oh, dem golden slippers,
> Oh, dem golden slippers,
> Golden slippers I'se going to wear
> To walk the golden street.

> *"Oh my golden slippers am laid away*
> *'Cause I don't expect to wear 'em*
> *'Til my wedding day...."*

But the lively and curvaceous green-eyed, raven-haired Gaelic enchantress of my youth was gone, and a broad-hipped, ample matron of thirty-eight with cheeks plump and rosy as apples and swollen ankles, wearing a loose, tent-like dress of dirty and faded flowered mauve-colored calico, stood in her place. Her condition was such that she looked as if she might at any moment have to halt her chores and send for the doctor or midwife.

"Glory be, 'tis Miss Lizzie!" She laid down the hatchet, brushed a stray wisp of dark hair back from her brow, and came to greet me with twinkling eyes and a smile that sparked so many bittersweet memories.

"I didn't know you had returned to America," I said. "I thought you meant to stay in Ireland."

"Aye, so I did, but things don't always go as we plan." She laid her hand, sun browned and calloused, over my smooth pale-white one. "Don't be afeared, Miss Lizzie," she said kindly, with a smile that put me instantly at ease. "Sure, I'm no blackmailer, ya know. It's just all these years, you've been in my thoughts, an' I've seen your name so many times in the papers, though news travels slow out here. There was times when it seemed you was standing on the brink o' happiness, only to have it snatched away from you at the last instant, like your engagement to that Mr. Gardner, he seemed a nice man he did, an' I just . . ." She smiled sheepishly, shrugged her shoulders, and shook her head as though she could not find the right words to explain. "I just wanted to . . . send my regards . . . I guess . . . I'm sorry I can't think of any better way to put it; you've just been in my thoughts, so . . ."

The tension inside me evaporated and for the first time in days I drew a deep, easy breath. I had been so afraid. . . . *Blackmail*, the word had been constantly in my thoughts, hovering over me like a dark storm cloud ever since I first read that telegram.

Emma and I had given Bridget money before; we had paid her well, a small fortune for her silence, to disappear, to forsake notoriety and return to Ireland and never set foot in America again. But here she was. . . . Did she truly *not* want *something?*

We sat on the bench by the well, sipping cool water from the dented tin dipper, and watching the swarm of barefoot children run and play, while the eldest boy took over for his mother at the woodpile, and Bridget told me of her life since she had left Fall River.

She had indeed returned to Ireland just as she had promised and had intended full well to bide the rest of her lifetime there.

"I bought a fine farm for me da an' mam an' stocked it with horses, an' cows, an' a little flock o' sheep, some lovely fat pigs, an' chickens o' course, good layin' hens fit for the table too there was. Aye, I did well by my folks, Miss Lizzie, I did, so never you think your money was frittered away an' no' put to good use. It made a lot o' folks happy, saints bless an' keep you for it!"

She had also found the love of her life in Ireland. John Sullivan. "The name's the same but no relation," she explained, "or if he is, 'tis a long way down the road an' not worth frettin' about." He was a big, burly, red-haired Irishman, a smelter in the coal mines and a fine singer and storyteller, though he liked to drink a drop more than was good for him sometimes, but, thank the Lord, not too often.

In 1897 they had decided to immigrate to America and "go west," as far away from society as they could, to seek their fortune. They had heard many grand, exciting tales about "The Wild West" that seemed to promise riches galore to all who dared venture forth, "stuff an' nonsense don'tcha know about gold nuggets litter-in' the ground, just lyin' there a-waitin' for you to just pluck 'em up like daisies as easy as you please!" She chuckled at the memory.

"An' you see where it has brought us!" She jerked her head back toward the ramshackle farmhouse.

"But I'm not complainin'. 'Tis a good life, Miss Lizzie, not an easy one, I'll be the first to admit, but, Lord knows, nothin' worth-while ever is."

Since her marriage, she had borne a child every year, without respite, twice even twins. "My mam bore twelve children, Miss Lizzie," she said proudly. "Now I am mam to a dozen o' me own with another on the way!" She proudly patted her big, round belly. "My John, he threw away my stays. 'No need tryin' to get your figure back, me fine lady,' he said to me. 'Once you're empty I'll fill you up again, an' I'll not be stoppin' till you're past breedin'!' An' he's been true to his word, he has." Bridget patted her stomach again, and her radiant smile, the joyous laughter on her lips and in her eyes that still sparkled like emeralds, told me that this was a woman who had found happiness in its truest, purest form. "After this one's born, as soon as I'm able, we'll be goin' at it again like bunnies until my belly's big again! Aye, 'tis a *grand* life, Miss Lizzie! I wouldn't trade places with the Emperor o' China if he got down on his knees an' askt me!"

I lifted my skirt and turned back the dusty hem to reach the secret pocket I had sewn there and took out a thick envelope and pressed it into Bridget's hand. "For the children," I said, "and for you."

"Oh no, Miss Lizzie. . . ." Bridget tried to push it away, but I shook my head and stood up and started to walk back to the hired carriage that had brought me out to the farm, where the driver dozed with his straw hat pulled down over his eyes.

"Wait!" Bridget called after me. "Jack!" she called to her eldest boy, and beckoned him over. "No—bring that here!" she said when he started to lay the hatchet down. She took it from him and ruffled his tawny hair and smiled down at him. "Off you go." She nodded brightly, smacked his bottom, and shooed him away to join his brothers and sisters.

Holding it in two hands, like an offering, Bridget brought the hatchet to me. I recognized it at once, though when I had last seen it, it had been shiny and almost new. There was that funny, peculiar mark in the wood that looked like a man's bewhiskered profile. "Aye, 'tis President Lincoln hisself, the Great Emancipator!" Bridget had quipped when I first pointed it out to her. But there was no shine left on it anymore; though still trusty, it had been dulled and dirtied by the years, use, and exposure to the elements, the gilt was long gone, the hickory handle was stained and well weathered, and, like all the rest of us, it showed its age.

"I kept it all these years," Bridget explained. "I never told anyone who I was, Miss Lizzie, except my John; a husband an' wife can't have secrets like that between 'em, ya know, but not another soul, I swear." She crossed herself. "I'll take the truth with me to my grave, I will, Miss Lizzie."

"Thank you, Bridget," I said gratefully, "for more than you know—you have restored my faith in humanity." But it was too little too late. I let my hand linger on her arm and leaned in to kiss her cheek before I took the trusty old hatchet and walked away.

I never saw or heard from Bridget Sullivan again. I buried the hatchet in the garden at Maplecroft on the servants' Sunday afternoon off, when they and all the neighbors were at church and there were no prying eyes about to spy on me.

On the train, as the wheels turned, taking me home to Fall River, I sat on the floor in my private compartment with my back against the wall, feeling the floor sway beneath me, and hugged my knees to my chest, and wept. I was almost forty-six. I now needed to wear my spectacles all the time, not just for reading, unless I wanted to blunder about in my vanity like a blind bat. Time had dulled the fire of my hair and streaked it with snow and I had just let it go. I hadn't hennaed it since I lost Nance; it was time to grow up and act my age. I was no longer young, and there is something to be said for aging gracefully. Or maybe I was just tired of fighting the inevitable? I had not had my monthly bleeding in over a year, and I knew that my womb was now dry and barren as the desert sands and would never bring forth life a new and precious love that was uniquely, and unconditionally, mine.

"Nothing has turned out as I thought it would!" I sobbed.

I should have known reality never lives up to the fantasy, the dream glimpsed through rose-colored glasses or gleaned from the pages of romances and plays on the stage; songs and stories only present an ideal that we all aspire to but rarely attain. I had bought my freedom with the life's blood of my father and stepmother, and I had acquired many of the wonderful things, the creature comforts, I had always dreamed of, but not the one that was dearest to my heart, the zenith of all my dreams—true and lasting love, *real* love, not fleeting, opportunistic, or casually carnal, but the kind that stands the test of time, in sickness and in health, till death us do part.

My life is a life of hard and sad compromises, cruel and brutal facts, and the splendid isolation of a millionaire leper, fated to live out my days like an aging, withering white-haired Rapunzel perched high up in her ivory tower resigning herself to the truth that her prince is never going to come and repenting her one attempt to rescue herself because it also ruined all her hopes and chances. Even as I set myself free with that impetuously wielded, fury-fueled hatchet, I made myself a perpetual prisoner, for life, and ever after, destined to walk alone under the dark cloud of suspicion.

Was it worth it? Another scandal-ridden and society-shunned scoundrel, Oscar Wilde, said it best I think: "The pure and simple truth is rarely pure and never simple." For me, *Yes* and *No* are twins conjoined, most inconveniently, but perpetually; one cannot exist without the other. I can only tell you this, for whatever it is worth to you, all those old adages about money embroidered on so many samplers are absolutely true; it *cannot* buy happiness and it *is* the root of all evil.

Perhaps my destiny was written in the stars the day I was born? Had I not interfered, had I not taken Fate, in the form of that hatchet, into my own hands, had Father and Abby been allowed to live out the span allotted to them according to God's plan, I would have still died a lonely and unloved old maid, with no husband or children; the only thing their blood bought me was a life of *lonely* luxury. Magnificence and money, I have long since discovered, are cold comforts—gold and silver are hard and cold; satin and silk are cold and slick—they cannot hold you close like a lover or kiss you good night. There is a reason money is often referred to as "cold, hard cash"; it can buy many things, but not the warmth and loving softness, the comfort, of the welcoming arms and beloved body of a devoted husband or lover. A paid paramour, hired, transitory pleasure, yes, it *can* buy that, for an hour or a night or maybe even longer, but that is *not* love; it is only a lovely and diverting illusion, a semblance, a night of wonder and enchantment, like when you pay to watch a magic show—*voilà!* a moment's delight, then *puff!* it is gone, the beautiful, fleeting ephemeral fancy vanished into the ether, and you are left all alone again, with memories you would rather forget because they only remind you that there is no such thing as *happily ever after. That* is the price I paid for wealth and independence and the right to do exactly as I pleased. I did not become the creature of my dreams, a woman of the world, sophisticated and fashionable, feted and adored; I became a shunned and friendless woman alone *against* the world.

Nothing turned out the way I thought it would.

$\mathcal{C}hapter\,14$

When I returned to Maplecroft I emptied both my summer and winter closets and spread all my dresses and hats out upon the bed in each room. There were so many they spilled onto the floor and covered every table, sofa, and chair. I stood and stared for a very long time at this once-enticing array of candy pinks, sky blues, sunny yellows, the whole gamut of greens, bloody crimsons, vivid oranges, and regal purples. Whole rainbows of stripes, polka dots, plaids, and paisley. I listlessly fingered a gown of cocoa lace trimmed with silk braid and champagne-colored seed pearls, and another of cool lime chiffon floating over a white silk skirt and sleeves garnished with pearl and crystal bead dangles. They all left me cold now. Even the sky-blue hat covered with stuffed blue birds posed as though poised to take flight from the high turned-back brim.

"My life is over; nothing exciting will ever happen to me again," I said, both sorry and glad.

I ordered the maids to pack them all up and take them away, *give* them away, I didn't want to see them anymore. It was time to go into mourning, for myself and the life and love that had passed me by. But I couldn't abide black and I had sworn after my acquittal to never wear it again. That was *one* vow at least I definitely could keep. I remembered reading in a book that white was the color the royal family of France wore when they were in mourning. Henceforth, like Mr. Dickens's tragically eccentric Miss Havisham, I would dress only in white, cascading ruffles, lace, and pearls, like the bride I never would be, entombing myself in the splendid solitude of Maplecroft, mourning the great expectations I had for my life that never came to fruition.

The years passed. They *always* do, whether they drag or fly by. Time waits for no one; it keeps on flowing like a river out to the sea.

I spent my days longing for night so I could lose myself in the world of dreams, the only place I could be happy, where I could rewrite history, make everything right, and blissfully be with Orrin, Nance, or even Lulie. Sometimes Bridget or my handsome young blond architect even came back to me. Or someone else born entirely of fantasy came to pass a night or fortnight with me.

Yet when I wakened, restless, with an odd melancholy feeling sitting like a rock upon my chest, I found myself impatiently longing for day, to chase the lingering trace of the dreams away because the distance between them and my sad reality only made me feel worse. They were dreams, and that was all they ever could be, never anything, or anyone, tangible I could actually hold in my arms.

I filled my life with pets. A more commonplace menagerie than Nance's—songbirds in gilded cages, dogs and cats, and the occasional bowl of goldfish, though they never seemed to last long. And I spent hours sitting on my discreetly screened porch watching the birds and squirrels feast upon the bread and seeds I left for them each day.

And I had a phonograph. I had a fine collection of classical works like Mozart and Beethoven, popular songs and soul-stirring hymns, the clever whimsy of Gilbert and Sullivan, and sparkling operettas like *Naughty Marietta* and *The Merry Widow,* and several operatic recordings. I could sit and listen to the great Caruso's magnificent voice for endless hours, losing myself in the music, the passion and feeling, remembering the time I had seen him as Rodolfo in *La Bohème* at the Metropolitan Opera House and heard his majestic voice soaring as though up to Heaven when he sang "Che Gelida Manina [Thy tiny hand is froze]." I'd never heard anything so powerful and beautiful; his voice truly seemed to touch the divine.

But there was another song that struck a deeper chord in me. Whenever he sang "Vesti la Giubba [On with the motley]" tears poured down my face like rain.

I felt a special kinship with Canio, the tragic clown of *Pagliacci,* who after discovering his wife's adultery must nonetheless go out and give a performance, only, overwhelmed by heartache and madness, to kill the treacherous pair onstage, in full view of the audience. He rips the mask off with an anguished cry, "I am a clown no longer!," and plunges the knife in, and then he does it again. And then the broken man sobs out, "*La commedia è finita!* [The comedy is finished!]"

> *Recitar! Mentre preso dal delirio,*
> *Non so piú quel che dico,*
> *E quel che faccio!*
> *Eppur è d'uopo, sforzati!*
> *Bah! Sei tu forse un uom?*
> *Tu se' Pagliaccio!*
>
> *Vesti la giubba e la faccia infarina.*
> *La gente paga, e rider vuole qua.*
> *E se Arlecchin t'invola Colombina,*
> *Ridi, Pagliaccio, e ognun applaudirà!*
> *Tramuta in lazzi lo spasmo ed il pianto*
> *In una smorfia il singhiozzo e 'l dolor, Ah!*
>
> *Ridi, Pagliaccio,*
> *Sul tuo amore infranto!*
> *Ridi del duol, che t'avvelena il cor!*

Recite! While in delirium,
I no longer know what I say,
And what I do!
And yet it's necessary. . . . Make an effort!
Bah! Are you a man?
You are a clown!

Put on your costume and powder your face.
The gentlemen pay, and they want to laugh.
And if Harlequin shall steal your Columbina,
Laugh, Clown, and all will applaud!
Turn your distress and tears into jest,
Your pain and sobbing into a funny face—Ah!

Laugh, Clown
At your broken love!
Laugh at the grief that poisons your heart!

It took me back to a time when, my mind befuddled and dulled by morphine and panic, I didn't know what I was saying. And the life I had led afterward, bravely putting on my paint and powder and fine dresses, my own particular fool's motley, hennaing my hair a clown-bright red, plastering a smile on my face, and going out into the world, trying to live my life, as though the past were dead and didn't matter. It always made me wonder when the comic tragedy of my own life would be finished.

And there were books, always books. Romances, adventure stories, and collections of poetry. I began to keep a scrapbook of sorts, a blank book, like a diary, into which, on dragging, dreary afternoons, or long sleepless nights, I wrote or pasted snippets of prose or verse that struck a chord within me, words of wisdom I wished I could live by, a path of letters I hoped might someday lead me to peace of mind and contentment. Things like:

Driftings, anchorings,
All in God's keeping,
This is life!

And these lines by Alexander Pope:

> *Honor and shame from no condition rise.*
> *Act well your part: there all the honor lies.*

And a touching snippet of a Christmas poem by Edith Matilda Thomas:

> *Deep in the heart*
> *As each heart doth know—*
> *Is a buried village*
> *Called Long Ago.*

Once, just once, I dared attempt to reach out to Nance. I sent her a poem I copied out of a book, *The Wings of Icarus* by Susan Marr Spaulding:

> *Two shall be born the whole world wide apart,*
> *And speak in different tongues, and have no thought*
> *Each for the other's being, and no heed.*
> *And these o'er unknown seas to unknown lands*
> *Shall cross, escaping wreck, defying death;*
> *And, all unconsciously shape every act*
> *And bend each wandering step to its very end—*
> *That, one day, out of darkness they shall meet*
> *And read Life's meaning in each other's eyes.*
> *And two shall walk some narrow way of life,*
> *So nearly side by side that should one turn*
> *Even so little space to left or right,*
> *They need must stand acknowledged face to face,*
> *And yet, with wistful eyes that never meet,*
> *With groping hands that never clasp, and lips*
> *Calling in vain to ears that never hear,*
> *They seek each other all their weary days,*
> *And died unsatisfied, and this is Fate.*

I enclosed it in a pebbled-leather folder with a gilded clasp shaped like a heart that I found at a stationer's shop on one of my increasingly rare trips to Boston. The deep-red color was called "Heart's Blood." It seemed like a good omen. At the height of our passion, I had given Nance a heavy golden ring set with a large heart-shaped pigeon's blood ruby. She said she would wear it forever. So I sent the poem and waited, but she never replied. By then she was the darling of Broadway under the personal management of impresario David Belasco. Faithless as ever, with not even a shred of loyalty clinging to her heel, the moment Belasco beckoned Nance had abandoned her mentor, McKee Rankin, the man who had made her a star. It was all about who could do the most for her career. Sentiment, Nance firmly believed, had no place in the life, or the heart, of a star. Rankin promptly sued her of course, but there was a whole muddy tangle about contracts and borrowing money on her jewelry and in advance against her salary, and a lot of ugly bickering back and forth in the newspapers, but it was all sorted out eventually and Nance stayed with Belasco. But she would leave him eventually, the moment a brighter prospect appeared upon the horizon.

I kept my promise to myself and never let love into my life again. I kept everyone at a distance, even those who looked my way and smiled and made overtures. I couldn't trust their intentions or believe in anyone's sincerity anymore. I didn't want to be an anecdote, a footnote, in someone's life, or the dollar sign in men's eyes. And it was already too late for me to be a mother, and the passage of the years and the reflection in my mirror told me the only alluring thing left about me was my fortune. No, I was done with love, and lust, forever. Fantasies were better; I made a diligent effort to convince myself I was content with those and to live vicariously and idealistically through novels and songs.

As the decades rolled past, my body began to wear out, just as Fall River itself went into a decline. The mills began to fail in the 1920s; the once grand and prosperous "Spindle City" simply could not compete with the cheaper cotton-producing facilities down south. Every day it seemed like more and more mills were closing.

Jobs were lost, and the wages of those still fortunate enough to have employment plummeted, until the antiquated machinery finally ground to a halt and the massive brick buildings stood empty, and the immigrants who once worked in their humming, thrumming interiors began a mass exodus to the South to find work in the mills down there.

It seemed like my fate and Fall River's were indelibly entwined; we had, in a sense, grown up together, and now we were both falling apart at the same time. I no longer bothered to fight the ravages of time or worried about my weight. I grew quite stout. In my white dresses I looked just like a big marshmallow that had sprouted a snowy head waddling about with stubby, stout little arms and legs. But I didn't care anymore. I ate what I liked. And if one more piece of cake made my lonesome plight more bearable, so be it.

In 1926, I had to go into the hospital for a gallbladder operation. It simply could not be postponed any longer. I chose the prestigious Truesdale Hospital in Providence, Rhode Island, and had myself admitted as Mary Smith. But of course everyone *knew* who I was. As I felt myself groggily emerging from the fog of the anesthetic I heard one nurse whispering to another, "Do you know whose abdomen you just had your hand inside? *LIZZIE BORDEN'S!*" She shuddered and spoke my name in a delighted whisper-squeal.

I proved a difficult patient. As soon as my wits had fully returned I demanded that my gallbladder be brought to me in a glass jar. I was afraid that if I didn't it would soon be touring the country, the star exhibit of many a county fair, sitting on a table in a tent, under a spotlight, while a man in a straw boater and striped jacket stood outside shouting, *See Lizzie Borden's gallbladder—only five cents a gander!*

I flatly refused to eat the dreadful bland hospital food. They actually expected me to breakfast on a single raw egg floating in a dish of milk, and for luncheon there was some indescribable mush I shuddered just to look at. I insisted that my chauffeur bring me meals three times a day from the finest restaurants in town, with orange sherbet for dessert. I also disdained the bedpan. I didn't care one whit if using it would make things easier on the nurses; when Nature called, my dignity demanded to be supported and escorted to the bathroom. Soon all the doctors and nurses had had enough of me and I was allowed to go home to Maplecroft to convalesce, though Dr. Truesdale insisted I must have round-the-clock care from experienced nurses. By that point, I was so eager to go home, or anywhere, to get away from there that I would have agreed to anything.

Blissfully back in my private sanctum, I continued to relish the role of difficult patient. I doubt even my thorny rose Nance could have played it half so well as me. The nurses came and the nurses went. I couldn't keep the same one a fortnight. An *enfant terrible* verging on seventy, "the devil with white hair and granny glasses," they called me.

But at least they came, my money ensured that, and dying ensconced like a queen in my own bed at Maplecroft is far better than dying in a stark, sterile, white hospital. Here I can breathe my last safely, comfortingly, cocooned by my dearly bought velvets, satins and silks, heirloom laces and quality leathers, polished oak, parquet, maple, cherry wood, and marble, fine china and crystal, stained glass, silver, and gilt, all purchased upon the credit of my eternal soul, in this magnificent mausoleum of a mansion, my os-tentatious Maplecroft, this palace devoid of fawning courtiers, the house on The Hill I spent my whole life dreaming about.

Oh, how I vex them! I keep them on their toes and constantly running to complain on the telephone to Dr. Truesdale like tattle-tale children. But I don't care! I *refuse* to live my life such as it is now by their clock. I won't take naps, send my pets out, or lay my book aside when they say it's time, or even attempt to carry on a conversation with anyone who insists on addressing me in a conde-scending singsong voice as though I were a small child, or submit to enemas and sponge baths—one really *must* draw the line some-where!—and I shove away the bland invalid foods they lay on a tray before me; if I *must* have my meals in bed on a tray they must equal or surpass the fare at Delmonico's.

I imperiously demand my daily bowl of peach ice cream crowned with crumbled golden cake and a warm, decadent, rich topping of brandied peaches, a dessert fit for a queen, as I sit propped up in bed against a mountain of lace-trimmed, gold-embroidered pastel sherbet-colored satin pillows, wearing a ludicrous, flirtatious lacy beribboned ivory silk negligee that looks laughable on a fat, florid-faced, pendulous-bosomed bespectacled woman of sixty-six with only a few lingering streaks of fading peach left in her snowy hair to remind everyone of the angry red it used to be.

My dogs and cats curl loyally up beside me so that I am not quite alone in the vast and lonely barren wasteland of this gilded monstrosity of a bed, four postered, gilt tasseled and fringed, cano-pied, curtained, and king-sized, fit for a French courtesan, like a valentine from Louis XV to Madame Pompadour. But the comfort of my dear pets' presence and their unconditional love cannot quite erase the sorrow of all the lovers I longed for who never came or only lingered for a while, arousing my hopes as well as my body, yet never staying.

Even my collection of souvenir spoons evokes only sadness and longing for that which is lost and, despite a lifetime of looking, never found; the way they nest together never fails to remind me that there is no one to curl up behind me and wrap their arms around me.

No matter how many spoonfuls of peach ice cream I shovel into my mouth, it cannot mask the bitter taste of regret. Or the fear that when I face Father again in whatever life of bliss or unrelenting tor-ment comes after this mortal span he will frown, nod knowingly (*always* right, even in death!) and say, *You see, Lizzie, I was right all along. . . . No one ever did love you for yourself, only my money, and even then . . . not for long. I built a fortune that outlasted any* love—I hear the scorn drip like poison from his lips as he pronounces that word, turning it into something sinful, ugly, vulgar and wrong—*you were ever given.*

Though my frail body must humbly submit, my still-proud spirit shuns and despises the nurses' ministrations. I don't want their eyes or their hands upon me, their humiliating help with my private functions, or the medicines they administer that might loosen my tongue. I learned long ago to be wary of morphine. "Did she confess?" they always whisper, thinking I can't hear them, whenever they meet to change shifts. One night I came fearfully close.

Tossing on waves of red-hot, molten-lava pain, I was given morphine. A nurse named Ruby—red, red, red, how it does run like a river of blood through my life!—was in attendance at my bedside. I was dreaming about David Anthony. He came unbidden to my mind even though I had not seen him in years except in passing, riding in fine cars with his family, his weary, wary-eyed wife with large shady hats and powder hiding her bruises, and their brood of children. I heard that he had died two years ago, that he had broken his skull riding his motorcycle out by Durfee Farm.

In my hazy, muddled morphine dream, I told Ruby that David and I had been very much in love, that we were lovers, keeping secret, passionate trysts in the barn, and that he wanted desperately to marry me. But my father did not approve because David was a butcher's son and socially beneath me, and quite bluntly informed me that I would make a laughingstock of myself if I married him, because he was ten years younger.

"He killed for me, to set me free"—I don't know why I did it, but I spun a tragic tale of star-crossed lovers for Ruby, and perhaps for myself as well, because I wanted to rewrite history and if it *had* to be, that's how it *should* have been—"because he thought my parents were the only obstacle. He was so much younger than me and didn't really understand that I also had misgivings. When I walked into the sitting room and saw him standing over Father with the hatchet . . . it was too late to stop him! I was *horrified!* Even as I bathed all the blood off him and dried his tears, I knew I would not have him. I broke off all contact with him. At first, I let him believe that we still might have a future, that the distance I insisted on putting between us was for his own good, to keep him safe from suspicion. But that was a lie; I wanted nothing more to do with him and was just too cowardly to say so. But I would never tell what he had done, because in my heart I blamed myself; if I had taken greater pains to make him understand maybe it would never have happened. I didn't want to ruin his life, to see him hang, so I took the blame. I never mentioned his name or saw him alone ever again. And in the end, he shunned me too, like all the rest. He went on with his life and married someone else and had a family and, as far as I know, a happy life. I suppose he just couldn't bear the blood between us, and maybe Time taught him that I *was* to blame, at least in part. He died a few years ago. . . . He sleeps now in the cemetery only a few feet from Father."

It made a good story. Nance would have loved it. But not a word of it was true except that David Anthony had been my lover and right before the murders had wanted me for a wife even though I didn't want him. But the hatchet, my hickory-handled Great Emancipator, killed that too and set me free forever from David Anthony.

It has been thirty-five years since the bloody deeds that made me infamous. My body may be falling apart, but my mind is as sound and solid as the granite memorial standing in the midst of our family plot at Oak Grove Cemetery where I know they shall very soon lay me at my father's feet. A position I once scorned and rebelled against but now see as just and emblematic of a wayward daughter's humble plea for a forgiveness she doesn't deserve.

Thirty-five years spent watching people I once called "friends" cross to the other side of the street in order to avoid me, and listening to schoolchildren chant in innocent cruel singsong:

> *"Lizzie Borden took an ax*
> *And gave her mother forty whacks.*
> *When she saw what she had done,*
> *She gave her father forty-one."*

Will it *never* end? God help me, I am tired of living, but even more afraid of dying. Like Canio, I long to rip the mask away and see the comic tragedy of my life come to an end, to be free of every care, pain, and woe, freed from suspicion, guilt, and ostracism. But I also know that Justice is a thing not only of this world. There is *always* a price to pay . . . for *everything,* and there is a debt of blood I still owe. *God help me!*

Postscript

⟬~~~⟭

Lizzie Borden died on June 1, 1927, of complications resulting from her gallbladder operation. She slipped away quietly in her sleep; her heart simply stopped beating. She was sixty-six years old. Though she had spent lavishly, she still left a sizable fortune, the bulk of which was bequeathed to various animal charities, "because their need is great and so few care for them." The Animal Rescue League of Fall River was the largest beneficiary. She left nothing to Emma "as she had her share of our father's estate and is supposed to have enough to make her comfortable."

Per Lizzie's instructions, there was no funeral. Dressed in a white lace gown with a bouquet of pink verbena, Lizzie Borden lay in state in her black coffin alone in the parlor at Maplecroft.

As the sun set, Vida Pearson Turner, the soloist from the Central Congregationalist Church, came in and sang "My Ain Countrie" in her rich contralto voice to the empty room, then quietly collected her fee from the undertaker and was told to go home and tell no one about the service she had just rendered for the deceased.

After nightfall, six Negro pallbearers in black suits carried Lizzie Borden to her final rest. She was laid at her father's feet in Oak Grove Cemetery.

After reading about Lizzie's death in a newspaper, Emma suffered a dizzy spell and fell down the basement steps of the Connor sisters' farm and shattered her hip. She never recovered and died nine days later on June 10, 1927. Orrin Gardner was at her bedside, holding her hand when she died.

Emma had been frugal with her inheritance and lived simply and reclusively, in a manner that would have made her father proud. Through thrift alone, rather than shrewd management and investments, she had nearly doubled her fortune by the time of her death. She left funds for a business scholarship to be established in her father's name, with Orrin Gardner to act as administrator; the rest was divided amongst various charities, including numerous old-age homes, hospitals, orphanages, the Society for the Prevention of Cruelty to Children, the Boy Scouts, the Girl Scouts, and the YMCA. The lone personal bequest was $10,000 to Orrin Gardner. Her body was taken by train back to Fall River and she was buried beside Lizzie in Oak Grove Cemetery.

Orrin Gardner never married. He continued teaching and eventually became a high school principal. He died in a convalescent home in 1944.

Nance O'Neil capriciously abandoned the stage, determined to replicate her success on the screen. But her vibrant stage presence failed to translate to the new medium; on film her gestures seemed too broad and histrionic. Exciting new stars, like exotic vamp Theda Bara and Mary Pickford, with her plucky personality and long golden curls, had captured the public's imagination, and Nance O'Neil was soon forgotten. Her roles diminished in both quality and quantity until the former great lady of the stage was reduced to playing bit parts, often glimpsed fleetingly as a face in the crowd, for $5 a day and a boxed lunch. She died forgotten, penniless, and alone in an old-age home in 1965 surrounded by souvenirs of her former glory. To her chagrin, whenever the occasional reporter came to interview her they were always more interested in her relationship with Lizzie Borden than hearing Nance reminisce about her life upon the stage.

In 1943 when she thought she was dying, Bridget Sullivan summoned a trusted friend, Minnie Green, to her bedside to hear a secret she longed to be unburdened of. Before Minnie arrived, Bridget recovered, and reconsidered. She died on March 26, 1948, at her Montana home surrounded by her children and grandchildren. She was eighty-two years old. Whatever her secret was, this time there was no attempt at a deathbed confession; Bridget took it with her to the grave.

The house at 92 Second Street still stands. Restored to appear as it did at the time of the Borden murders and rumored to be haunted by unquiet spirits that figured in the tragedy, today it is a popular bed-and-breakfast.

A note regarding Edwin H. Porter: Mr. Porter was a journalist for *The Fall River Globe* and the author of the first full-length book about the Borden murders, which Lizzie Borden is rumored to have bought up and burned en masse, with only a few copies escaping the bonfire. In this novel he appears as a composite character to personalize Lizzie's enmity for the intrusive press coverage that dogged her from the time of the murders to the end of her life. This portrayal should not be taken as a true indication of his actions or character.

Further Reading

Brown, Arnold R. *Lizzie Borden: The Legend, the Truth, the Final Chapter.* Nashville, TN: Rutledge Hill Press, 1991.

Kent, David. *Forty Whacks: New Evidence in the Life and Legend of Lizzie Borden.* Emmaus, PA: Yankee Books, 1992.

Lincoln, Victoria. *A Private Disgrace: Lizzie Borden by Daylight.* New York: G. P. Putnam's Sons, 1967.

Martins, Michael, and Dennis A. Binette. *Parallel Lives: A Social History of Lizzie A. Borden and Her Fall River.* Fall River, MA: Fall River Historical Society, 2011.

Radin, Edward D. *Lizzie Borden: The Untold Story.* New York: Simon & Schuster, 1961.

Rehak, David. *Did Lizzie Borden Axe for It?* CreateSpace Independent Publishing Platform, 2010.

Spiering, Frank. *Lizzie: The Story of Lizzie Borden.* New York: Random House, 1984.

THE SECRETS OF LIZZIE BORDEN

Brandy Purdy

About This Guide

The suggested questions are included
to enhance your group's
reading of Brandy Purdy's
The Secrets of Lizzie Borden.

DISCUSSION QUESTIONS

1. Despite his great wealth, Andrew Borden denies his daughters even commonplace luxuries like modern plumbing and lighting; he uses the threat of disinheritance to control them and keeps them from leaving home and marrying by denouncing all men as fortune hunters. Why do you think he does this? Is it fear of the poverty he experienced as a child returning, is it really about domination and power, or is he scared of being alone in his old age?

2. Lizzie secretly admits that she sees much of Abby in herself. Under different circumstances could they have been friends? How did their relationship change as Lizzie grew up and how did Emma's hostility influence it?

3. Discuss Lizzie's Grand Tour. Was the trip a wise decision or did it leave her hopelessly dissatisfied with her life in Fall River? Would Lizzie's life have played out differently if she hadn't gone to Europe and experienced an unattainable lifestyle? What do you think of the handsome young Englishman she met? Was the romance real or all in Lizzie's mind? What do you think of her father's reaction to the romance and her subsequent behavior regarding the letters?

4. Discuss Lizzie's sexuality and various romances. Which ones were real mutual attractions and which ones were only wishful thinking on Lizzie's part? Could any of them have led to lasting happiness? Was Andrew Borden right to discourage his daughter by repeatedly warning her against fortune hunters or was there more than a grain of truth in his cruelly worded warnings? When it comes to men, caution and fear always temper Lizzie's desire, yet in her world passion between women is forbidden. Do you think Lizzie only wanted a real and lasting love regardless of gender?

5. Lizzie harbors an almost lifelong obsession with Lulie Stillwell. Why is Lizzie never able to forget her? What do you think of their schoolgirl friendship? What motivated it?

Was there truly a lesbian element? Look at it from Lulie's perspective. What did she feel for Lizzie?

6. Discuss the constant hostility simmering in the house on 92 Second Street—the anger, resentment, greed, control, petty crimes, and retaliations. Was there any way this family could ever have lived peacefully together? If you were a therapist and had the Bordens sitting in front of you what would you tell them?

7. Discuss the events leading up to the murders. What, if anything, could have prevented them? Was Lizzie unhinged by rage and panic and not responsible for her actions, was she driven to murder by others, or were her actions more calculated?

8. How do you feel about Andrew Borden's attempt to continue controlling his daughters' lives from beyond the grave through the terms of his will? Was this truly the ultimate betrayal Lizzie felt it was or just typical behavior of the man given his character?

9. Why do Bridget and Dr. Bowen each help Lizzie in their own way after the murders? What motivates them to take the risk?

10. When she is facing trial, Lizzie says, "Even though I knew I was guilty, I believed implicitly in my innocence." What does she mean by this? What do you think of her attempts to justify herself?

11. Discuss Lizzie's life after the trial. Does her inheritance bring her happiness? What do you think of the way she is treated by others? Do you feel sorry for her or did she get what she deserved?

12. Lizzie came very close to marrying her cousin Orrin Gardner. What do you think of their decision to end their relationship because of the public outcry over their engagement? Should they have stuck together and weathered the media circus or were they right to part?

13. Discuss the relationship between Lizzie and her sister, Emma, throughout their lives. How does it change after the trial? At one point Emma says to Lizzie, "More tears are shed over answered prayers than unanswered ones. God sometimes punishes those He only *seems* to favor by giving them *exactly* what they want." What do you make of this? Why does Emma eventually leave Lizzie? Was she right to do so? Was her life after leaving Lizzie better or worse?

14. Lizzie Borden's relationship with the flamboyant actress Nance O'Neil has always attracted a great deal of curiosity and controversy. What was the attraction? What did each hope to gain from the affair? Discuss the roles love, lust, fame, and greed played in the relationship.

15. Was Lizzie right to give up on love?